Praise for *Terms

'The perfect book to pop into you

'A delightful debut from an exci⸺⸺⸺⸺⸺⸺⸺ ⸺ustralian
fiction' – Rachael Johns

'Moving, funny and sharp, and with a plot that kept me
guessing, this is a gorgeous novel for all mothers and daughters,
told with real heart' – Kelli Hawkins

'Funny, warm and wise, and a delight from beginning to end.
Michelle Upton brings warmth and humour to even the darkest
corners of our lives. What a joy!' – Meredith Jaffé

'A darkly funny tale about the meaning of family and the
meaning of life. I loved how each of the four sisters had a
different perspective on both. *Terms of Inheritance* is a humorous,
heartfelt story of a family with all its imperfections. An absolute
delight to read!' – Petronella McGovern

'Witty, warm and wise … an uplifting story about family life
as our biggest challenge and our greatest comfort' – Sara Foster

'A touching family drama with deft moments of heartache,
humour and warmth' – Nicola Moriarty

'Told with bright, breezy wit and layers of love, *Terms of
Inheritance* is a sweet and sharp fable of family fortune and of
discovering who you really are. Upton brings us real women,
all their foibles and strengths sparkling with truth and warmth'
– Kim Kelly

'An entertaining debut about fraught family relationships, and the importance of being true to yourself' – Pamela Cook

'Laughter and loss, forgiveness, redemption – *Terms of Inheritance* explores what it means to be a family. A sparkling debut! With intelligence and humour, Michelle Upton explores contemporary family life in all its messy reality. Jacki Turner and her daughters – funny and daring, courageous and flawed – are unique yet entirely relatable' – Penelope Janu

'A warm-hearted story about the ups and downs of mother-daughter relationships, and learning to let go of the past to become the best version of yourself' – Rae Cairns

'Funny, relatable and warm-hearted, this story is a joyful rollercoaster ride about ambition, determination, honesty and the shifting dynamics of a family under stress' – Cass Moriarty

'Four sisters are challenged to become their best selves, embarking on a learning journey that is as funny as it is tender' – Sasha Wasley

Michelle Upton writes short stories and novels that examine our darkest fears and shine a light on hope and possibility. Born in Birmingham, England, Michelle emigrated to Australia in 2006 and is proud to call herself Australian. Michelle has a Bachelor (Hons) degree in Literature with Psychology, and before having children, she was a primary school teacher. Her debut novel, the much-loved *Terms of Inheritance*, was shortlisted for the HarperCollins Australia 2021 Banjo Prize. She lives in Brisbane with her family.

MICHELLE UPTON

terms of inheritance

HarperCollins*Publishers*

HarperCollins*Publishers*
Australia • Brazil • Canada • France • Germany • Holland • India
Italy • Japan • Mexico • New Zealand • Poland • Spain • Sweden
Switzerland • United Kingdom • United States of America

HarperCollins acknowledges the Traditional Custodians
of the land upon which we live and work,
and pays respect to Elders past and present.

First published on Gadigal Country in Australia in 2022
This edition published in 2024
by HarperCollins*Publishers* Australia Pty Limited
ABN 36 009 913 517
harpercollins.com.au

A catalogue record for this book is available from the National Library of Australia

ISBN 978 1 4607 6222 6 (paperback)
ISBN 978 1 4607 1500 0 (ebook)
ISBN 978 1 4607 4483 3 (audiobook)

Cover design and illustration by Christa Moffitt, Christabella Designs
Typeset in Bembo Std by Kirby Jones
Printed and bound in Australia by McPherson's Printing Group

For my mom

1

Rose

Rose pulled up to the grand iron gates of her childhood home in the exclusive Sovereign Islands on the Gold Coast, grabbed her phone off the passenger seat and re-read the text her mother had sent her and her sisters two days before.

EMERGENCY family meeting
Place – The Castle
Time – Sunday 5 pm
ROSE – That includes you too!

Sitting in her heat-blistered Kia Carnival, nausea swirled in her gut and she could feel sweat beginning to bead on her top lip. She desperately tried to recall what her therapist, who she'd stopped seeing over a year ago, had told her about the importance of boundaries and breathing.

She rolled down the window and gratefully inhaled the Queensland winter air as she reached for the buzzer on the intercom. It had been three years since she'd been to The Castle, which was what her mother, business tycoon

Jacki Turner, called her opulent seven-bedroom waterfront mansion.

Situated within an affluent gated community, The Castle sat alongside other multi-million dollar residences overlooking South Stradbroke Island. It wasn't called a millionaire's playground for nothing. These luxurious homes were reserved for the elite. When Rose was about eight years old, her mother had joked that she was the 'Queen of the Castle', and while Rose's sisters had giggled then fought over the dress-up costumes, each wanting to be the queen, Rose had fallen silent. Even back then, she knew her multi-millionaire mother's playful manner was a façade. Jacki Turner *was* the queen of her empire, and she expected everyone in her kingdom to play by her rules.

With a click and a buzz, the gates rolled open to reveal the white, sprawling, flat-roofed fortress. The black and white paved driveway led into a looming *porte-cochère* framed with tall white pillars and an oversized front door imported from Italy. It was the kind of opulent entrance you'd expect to see at an expensive hotel. The only thing missing was the porter waiting to park your car and whisk your luggage away.

Rose's sisters were already there. She pulled up in front of one of the three large garages, alongside Isla's brand-new BMW and Jess's Hyundai. She turned off the ignition of her well-loved, well-worn people carrier and waited while it spluttered into silence. Closing her eyes, she rested her head back and forced herself to breathe deeply. The quiet was a blessed slice of luxury, she had to admit. The one-hour drive south from Brisbane had felt like a mini-vacation, even if she was overwrought about being summoned by her mother. There'd been no one demanding anything of her. No one asking where their Taylor Swift T-shirt was or where their soccer boots were. No one needing feeding or burping or changing.

She'd been tempted to fly straight past the turn-off and keep going to Byron Bay. She could have stayed overnight at a B&B and got a full seven hours of blissful uninterrupted sleep. But the mere thought of missing overnight feeds for three-month-old Bethany had triggered a let-down that somehow managed to bypass both of her breast pads, leaving her with two wet patches on her pale-blue button-up blouse.

She gripped the steering wheel and bit down hard on her bottom lip. *Is it too late to change my mind? She can't force me to attend. And will anyone really notice if I don't show up?* It had been years since she'd seen her mother. She hadn't seen her sisters for a few weeks either, though they talked on the phone regularly.

As she contemplated this possibility, Rose's spirits lifted. She could be back on the M1 in no time. She was only ninety minutes from Byron.

Boundaries are healthy.

With a surge of confidence, she turned the key in the ignition. She'd just tell Mel, Isla and Jess she'd had her own family emergency and been called away.

'Boundaries are healthy.' Rose slipped the Kia into reverse and then laughed aloud, which even to her own ears sounded slightly hysterical. But just as she put her foot on the accelerator, her younger sister, thirty-eight-year-old Mel, dived in front of the Kia and slammed her palms on the bonnet.

'Jeepers!' Rose braked hard, and a breathless but grinning Mel made her way to Rose's window and squished her face up against the tinted glass.

For the last twelve years, Rose had tried her best to keep her curses G-rated. When Harrison was born, Rose had forced herself to tame her pre-parenting potty mouth, and in the last three years, ever since she'd cut her mother out of her life, she hadn't used a proper swear word at all. In fact, she could measure the equilibrium in her life by the amount of foul language she used – and by that measure, her life had been on a very even keel. But just like a gambling addict who longed for the fix of the slot machines, Rose *really* missed the thrill of those glorious dirty words.

'Rose! Rose!' Mel's breath fogged up the window. 'You're never going to believe it! Come quick, we're all round the back.' Mel's shoulder-length blonde hair was scraped into a scruffy ponytail, and her black leggings and Nirvana T-shirt clung to her stocky build. Her beaming face and bright eyes filled Rose with warmth, and she couldn't help but smile. Just the thought of seeing her mother again was making her feel unwell, but at least Rose wouldn't be alone at the family meeting: her sisters would be with her.

'Just give me five.' Rose rubbed her tired eyes and Mel gave her a thumbs-up before disappearing around the side of the mansion.

Rose put the car into park. She could only imagine the source of the excitement. As a kid, she'd come home from school over the years to find all kinds of bizarre things in their backyard. Farm animals, camels, horses. Circus entertainers, celebrities. And on one occasion, the prime minister. She'd even come home once to find a full-sized replica pirate ship tied to one of the pontoons at the end of the garden. It had cannons, giant red sails, and a skull and crossbones flag. Rose had been mortified. She found the extravagance embarrassing. These lavish expenses weren't even for birthday parties or special events ... These were just Jacki's average Tuesday afternoon splurges.

It was well known that wherever Jacki Turner went, drama and spectacle followed. And money was the fuel that kept the dragon well-fed. Jacki's never-ending pot of cash from her enormously successful chain of hotels and casinos meant she could have and do anything she wanted, whenever she liked. So she did.

Rose pulled down the visor and flipped open the mirror. She tucked her long, straight chestnut hair behind her ears and tried to flatten a rogue grey hair with the palm of her hand. Since turning forty a couple of months earlier, she'd found more and more short, wiry greys that had no intention of playing ball. The hair refused to be tamed, so she twisted it around her index finger and yanked.

Wincing, she rubbed her scalp hard, then ran her fingers over the sunspots on her cheeks and the dark bags under her eyes. Her usual rosy complexion had paled, a side effect of too little sleep, and she hadn't had time to put on any make-up. She'd just had time to pick up Harrison (twelve) and Taylor (ten) from their friend's house before she'd had to hit the highway.

As the kids had piled out of the car, she'd unclipped Bethany from the car seat and handed her to Tom, kissing the top of her head.

'There are two bottles of breast milk in the fridge. She'll need a feed in—'

'—in about an hour. I know. And Harrison needs to finish his science project tonight, and Taylor is only allowed an hour of screen time – *after* she finishes her homework,' Tom added with a gentle smile.

Rose was confident they'd be fine. Bethany was Tom's first child, but he was a natural. He'd taken to parenting with an ease she envied. He was the only one Bethany settled for, and he thrived when Rose's to-do list got out of control. Tom brought a reassuring calmness to their family. He made her feel as if everything was going to be okay.

She checked her phone. No missed calls. *I'm here,* she messaged Tom. *Wish me luck.*

She grabbed her keys and got out of the car, tucking her phone into the back pocket of her jeans. At the side gate, she lifted the safety latch and made her way to the back of the property. Her worn black ankle boots scuffed the marble paved pathway, which was lined on either side with carefully manicured cacti, and she could hear her mother's voice in her head telling her to pick up her feet. After weaving through the tall palms and lush ferns that sectioned off a sizeable undercover dining space, she quickly ducked into a small, secluded area surrounded by towering bamboo.

This hideout had once been part of the open dining area but was now a memorial to her dad, Peter. Partially screened by the tropical foliage, a white bench sat on pale grey Italian terrazzo pavers and faced a marble fountain. In front of it was a small white wooden cross. This had been the exact spot where he'd keeled over in the middle of Mel's sixth birthday party and died of a heart attack. Their beloved dad had been dressed as a clown at the time, having spent weeks learning how to make balloon animals specifically for the occasion. That day still haunted Rose, and poor Mel hadn't wanted a birthday party since.

'Hey, Dad.' Rose kissed her fingers and rested them on the cross. 'You gonna wish me luck? 'Cause I think I might need it.'

Steeling herself, she headed out towards the grand white pillars that framed the oversized swimming pool, spa and outdoor lounge area that overlooked the water and her mother's luxury yacht.

Rose's three sisters were standing under the tall palm trees in the middle of the manicured lawn, looking out over the sparkling aquamarine of the Broadwater. The tide was low and the air salty. Their mother was nowhere to be seen. As Rose made her way over, she looked towards the house, half expecting Jacki to jump out and accuse her of daughterly neglect.

Boundaries are healthy.

Isla, the eldest, stood with her shoulders back and her hands tucked into the pockets of her expensive-looking burgundy pantsuit. Her rich red locks sat twisted in a fashionable topknot and made her appear even taller than the 5 foot 8 inches she'd already been blessed with.

Isla caught sight of Rose, grimaced, then gave her an air-kiss on each cheek. 'You look like shit,' she said, tactful as ever.

'Rose!' Their sister Jess, who at thirty was the youngest of the four, beamed and threw her arms around her. Jess gave an extra squeeze and kissed her on the cheek. 'Did you bring the kids?'

'I left them at home with Tom.'

Rose had always been jealous of Jess's petite frame, warm golden-brown skin and rich deep brown eyes. Joy and contentment oozed from her, which Rose found soothing. Jess was like a burst of sunshine that warmed you after you'd spent all day standing in the rain. Wearing pale jeans and an off-the-shoulder turquoise jumper, which exposed her lacy black bra strap, Jess looked relaxed and breezy as always. Rose rolled her aching shoulders and tugged at the button of her own jeans. She couldn't wait to fit back into her pre-pregnancy clothes and longed to wear a dress that hadn't been chosen for its boob accessibility.

Mel nudged Rose playfully and shaded her eyes against the lowering sun as she looked out to the water. 'Glad you're here.'

'Did you come down last night?' Rose asked Mel. 'I told you I could have brought you today.'

'I had the day off, and Isla was in Brisbane for work yesterday, so she didn't mind picking me up. Plus, I wanted to see Helen and have her special stacked pancakes for breakfast.'

Helen was Jacki's general house manager. She'd been hired when the girls were little, initially to look after them while Jacki worked, which was all the time. In later years, Helen transitioned into an unofficial matriarch whose role was to prevent the Turner family from imploding.

'Is Helen inside?' Rose asked, suddenly eager to run in and find her.

'No, she's gone home,' said Jess. 'She left us with strict instructions to wait out here for Mum.'

'Why?'

'There she is!' said Mel, pulling out her phone. 'I've got to video this.'

'What are you talking about?' Rose's heart started racing and, once again, she considered bolting.

Rose made to leave, but Mel grabbed her arm. 'Where are you going?'

Clenching her hands into fists, Rose turned back and scoured the horizon. Her mother would probably arrive by speedboat, or on the back of a jet-ski ridden by some young ripped guy. 'Where the heck is she?'

'She's not out there,' said Mel, and she tilted Rose's chin up to the pink dusk sky. 'Up there.' Mel thrust out her arm and pointed to a tiny dot.

'What?!'

'Didn't you see the helipad?'

Sure enough, marked in the middle of an additional section of the floating pontoon was a giant painted H.

'You've got to be kidding!' Rose flicked her eyes back up to the sky and registered the distant purr of a helicopter. The sun began to sink further and, as the sky turned a deep rich purple, a white chopper came into clear view.

'Why does she always have to be so dramatic?' asked Rose.

'It's not dramatic,' shouted Isla over the growing noise. 'It's practical. She uses the helicopter to save time. For her, it's like … catching a bus.'

Rose sighed. Her mother hadn't been on public transport in forty years – she'd always had a driver. But a helicopter? In her own backyard? This new lavish expense was just another demonstration of her love of materialistic extremes. Where was she travelling from? Surely she could have come in a car like any normal human. This was *so* Jacki Turner!

The whirling air from the helicopter's spinning blades tugged at Rose's blouse and whipped up her loose hair, blasting long strands into her mouth.

'This is so cool,' said Jess, who had thrown her glossy hair into a low bun.

The helicopter's engine cut, the blades slowed, and a chiselled-looking pilot climbed out. In his early thirties, and dressed in sleek black pants, a starched white shirt and a thin black tie, he looked like he'd just walked off the set of *Men in Black*. He walked around to open the passenger door, took Jacki Turner's hand, and helped her out.

Wearing a black body-hugging dress, designer black trenchcoat, four-inch heels and sunglasses, Jacki stepped onto the floating helipad and gracefully made her way along the pontoon, holding onto the black silk scarf wrapped around her head. As she walked towards her daughters, she slid off her glasses and the scarf, somehow managing to leave her half-up backcombed hairdo perfect. Jacki stood before them like Audrey Hepburn in *Breakfast at Tiffany's*, and then, with one hand on her hip and the other holding her sunnies and scarf, she lifted her chin and paused as if she was posing for an artist.

Rose bit her lip. *Does she expect us to start clapping?*

'That was awesome, Mum!' Jess rushed over and hugged her. 'Can you take me up in it?'

'Of course, baby girl, but not tonight,' Jacki purred. 'I've just come from a meeting, and I need to leave for another one in an hour.'

'How much did that set you back?' Rose nodded at the helicopter, then crossed her arms.

Jacki looked her up and down. 'Good to see you, too. *Rose*, isn't it?'

Rose pursed her lips.

'Where's Eddie?' Isla kissed Jacki's cheek. Eddie was the Chief Operating Officer of Jacki's empire.

'He's gone ahead to the next meeting. Did you get the store in Perth?'

'It'll be open for business in August.'

'That's my girl. Nice jumpsuit.'

'Manning Cartell.'

Jacki surveyed her four daughters and, for a moment, Rose thought she seemed pleased they were all together again. But then Jacki frowned and strode towards the house. 'Let's go inside. I need a drink.'

* * *

They filed into the expansive living room, and Rose was struck anew by how *grand* everything was. A three-tiered crystal chandelier hung from the high ceiling, and tucked in the far corner sat the shiny grand piano that no one had learned how to play. The enormous white leather chaise sofa, which ran the length of the room, reminded Rose of the fun she and her sisters used to have on it when they were kids. It was the most ridiculously oversized piece of furniture she'd ever seen.

Rose took a seat at one end of the sofa and peered down at her blouse. 'Shoot!' Two buttons had come undone, exposing her white stained nursing bra for all to see. 'Blasted helicopters,' she muttered. As she hastily buttoned her blouse, she noticed a large patch of dried baby spew on her shoulder. *Great.*

'Did you bring my grandbabies?' Jacki asked Rose as she poured herself a generous measure of Bundaberg Rum from the ornate drinks trolley behind her. Bundaberg had always been Peter's drink of choice and had become her mother's after he died.

'You said this was an *emergency* family meeting, so I left them at home.' Rose crossed her legs and bounced her foot. She wasn't here to play happy families. She was only here because her sisters had thrown her own words back at her about the importance of showing up. When she'd stated how important boundaries were, they'd told her to stop being stubborn and suck it up. So she'd come, grudgingly, but after today she had no plans to see her mother again.

'How is that British boyfriend of yours?' asked Jacki. 'Is *he* looking after them?'

'His name's Tom, and it's not like he's just some random guy. He's Bethany's dad!'

'Of course. *Tom.*'

Rose clenched her fists. *I'm not going to swear. I'm not going to scream. I am in control.*

On the other side of the room, Jess stood at the piano and hit random keys, probably wishing, like Rose, that she'd taken the time to learn how to play.

Jacki wandered over to the end of the sofa closest to Jess and sat. After downing the drink she'd just poured herself, she placed the empty glass on the coffee table. 'There's something ... I need to ... I'm ...'

Jacki spoke so softly that Rose, Isla and Mel glanced at each other. None of them had caught what their mother had said.

Rose leaned forward. 'What did you say?'

Jacki's lips moved again, but again Rose didn't catch a word.

Jacki rarely spoke softly. It wasn't in her nature. *Typical*, Rose thought. *She's using it now to be even more dramatic, as if the helicopter entrance wasn't enough.* Jacki was just as egocentric as she'd always been. Her mother's goal in life was to always be the centre of attention – well, that and to make as much money as possible, no matter the cost.

Mel frowned at Rose, confused. 'What did she say?' she whispered. 'I missed it.'

Rose rolled her eyes and made her way over to her mother. 'We can't hear you. What did you say?'

Jacki sprang from her chair and threw her hands in the air. 'I'm dying!'

Rose stopped. 'What?'

'I'm. Dying!' said Jacki, even louder this time.

'*Dying?* Why?' Jess's voice broke. 'How?'

Jacki raised her chin. 'Colon cancer,' she said, clearing her throat. 'And apparently it's spread. They've given me less than two years, so I'm guessing eighteen months, which means I've probably got a year if I'm lucky.'

Rose froze. She couldn't think or move. Jacki didn't get sick. The only doctors she'd ever seen were plastic surgeons. Jacki Turner was far too *stubborn* to die.

Jess threw her arms around her mum, but Jacki didn't move, and eventually Jess released her and took a step back.

'I've known for a few weeks,' said Jacki. 'I wasn't going to say anything. I don't want *any* fuss.' Jacki grabbed the empty glass she'd just put down and shook it. 'One of you, grab me the bottle.'

Isla placed her hand on her chest. 'Is that … a good idea?'

'It's one of the best bloody ideas I've got.'

Mel scurried to the drinks trolley and handed Jacki the bottle, tears streaming down her cheeks.

'I've spent the last few weeks reflecting on my life.' Jacki poured herself another extra-large drink. 'And I got to thinking about how I raised you girls.'

'You mean, like how you threw us out as soon as we turned eighteen?'

Rose's sisters turned and looked at her in disbelief. The words had spilled from her mouth before she'd had time to filter her thoughts.

'That was for your own good,' said Jacki. 'My money gave you all a taste of what you could have had if you wanted it badly enough, but it was up to you to go and get it. And, as it turned out, only *one* of you was hungry enough to do that.'

Isla smiled.

'The rest of you went in other directions.' Jacki took a sip of rum.

A raging heat flushed across Rose's chest and neck.

'I know you think I was hard, Rose, but what kind of mother would I have been if I'd just handed all of this to you on a plate? You can only appreciate wealth if you've earned it yourself, otherwise you grow up thinking the world owes you something. Entitlement doesn't look good on anyone.'

'You can't die.' Jess covered her face with her hands and sobbed.

'I'm sorry, baby girl, but that's just the way it is.' Jacki sighed. 'I know I give some of you a hard time, but my actions only ever come from a good place. I want you all to know that before I tell you what I've decided.'

Rose's eyes narrowed. 'And what *have* you decided?'

Jacki walked towards the floor-to-ceiling windows that overlooked the swimming pool. Outside, the late afternoon sky had darkened, and the windows reflected the lavish diamond chandelier that sparkled overhead.

'We may not *all* be close,' said Jacki. 'But I do know each of you better than you think. I know your deepest desires and what you're capable of. And so, this is the gift I'm going to leave you. As I've said before, your inheritance will be large enough that none of you will have to work again. Still, as much as I want you to have financial security, I also want you to know what it feels like to chase your dreams, to succeed and fail, and to experience that over and over until you reach your goal.'

'That sounds *awful*,' said Mel.

'And so, in a last-ditch attempt to be the best mother I can be, there will be conditions on the inheritance of my fortune. You'll each have one year to complete the task I've set for you. Each task has been designed for you alone, to push you to be the best version of yourself. Should any of you fail, you will *all* fail, and my vast fortune will be left to Aussie Animal Rescue.'

'What the—' Mel twisted to face her sisters and stared crazily at them, then swivelled back to Jacki again. 'You can't do that!'

Jacki raised her eyebrows. 'Excuse me?'

'It's just ... You always said you'd split your fortune four ways ... I've got a mountain of debt I need to pay off. You can't change the rules on us now.'

Jacki laughed. 'Oh sweetie, it's my money. I can do whatever the hell I want.'

'Aussie Animal Rescue – they're the rehoming charity, is that right?' snapped Isla.

'That's right, they're wonderful. They have centres all over the country.' Jacki raised a brow. 'You girls should pay the local centre a visit.'

Jess wiped her wet cheeks with her sleeve. 'What do you want us to do?'

Jacki looked at Mel. 'Do you remember Amber Ryan?'

Mel's mouth fell open and the colour drained from her face.

'She was the girl who bullied you, the reason why you changed schools,' said Isla. 'The one who—'

'I *know* who she is, Isla!' Mel fumed. 'Oh my *God*, Mum! Why are you bringing Amber Ryan up now? It's been decades!'

'Amber tripped you up after you came last in the one-hundred-metre sprint at school, do you remember? You came home covered in mud because it had rained all day. When you got home that afternoon, you said to me—'

Mel gasped, 'No!'

'You said, and I quote, "One day, I'm gonna run circles around that bitch and run a marathon".'

'No, no, no—'

'So your task is to complete next year's Gold Coast Marathon.'

'Nooo!' Mel raised her hands protectively. 'Why are you doing this to me?'

Isla put her hands on her hips. 'You can *see* Mel, can't you, Mum? How is she gonna run a *marathon*?' Isla turned to her sister. 'What do you weigh? A hundred kilos?'

'Hey!' said Mel. 'Mind your own business. I'm perfect the way I am!'

'This has nothing to do with what the scales say,' said Jacki. 'We all know that bodies are beautiful at any size. No, this is about what it means to strive for something. You've been sitting in your comfort zone for the last two decades, Mel. You've got a degree you're too afraid to use, and you're stuck in a job that doesn't make full use of your skills. Well, I'm here to take away your security blanket. It's time to live a little, Mel. One year, one marathon, or all of my money goes to the animals.'

'Now, wait a minute—' said Rose.

'Rose, my tired little girl, you're always so' – Jacki reached over and lifted the ends of her tangled hair – 'weary looking.'

'I've got three kids, who I *look after*,' Rose fumed. 'I'm the one who cooks for them, cleans for them, takes them to swimming lessons, soccer, dance, baby-time at the library. I'm present in their lives because I *love* them, *Mother*, and you know what? They love me back.' Rose's lower lip trembled.

Jacki nodded blithely. 'Hmm, always exhausted, too tired to set yourself any real goals. Rose, you've spent so much time trying *not* to be like me that you've forgotten to chase your own dreams. I'm sure you don't really want to be an accountant for the rest of your life. Do you still write in that notebook of yours? You were always scribbling down your thoughts and ideas, but you never did anything with them. Once upon a time, it was your dream to write a children's book. Well, now's your chance. One year, one published children's picture book.'

'That's so easy,' whined Mel. 'Can't we swap?'

'No swapping,' said Jacki.

Rose's eyes welled. She'd managed to write for an hour in her journal that morning before the kids woke up, but she wasn't going to tell Jacki. Writing was a form of therapy and escape for Rose, it was where she could work through her thoughts and let her imagination run wild. Yet, here was her mother, supposedly sick and dying, using Rose's gift against her. This latest stunt proved that Jacki actually believed her children were puppets she could control, making them perform whenever she wanted.

Jacki swanned over to Jess and stroked her flushed face. 'My baby girl. Much loved. Gorgeously independent and a modest businesswoman. But you're thirty years old and haven't been in a relationship for longer than three months – no one's ever good enough.'

'I was married!' said Jess. 'It's not my fault it didn't work out.'

'I don't think a Vegas wedding that lasted a month counts as a marriage, does it?' Isla scolded.

Jess shot her a dirty look.

'Well, now is the time to commit,' said Jacki. 'I may not live to see you walk down the aisle, but knowing you're not completely alone will bring me comfort. Don't spend your good years waiting for Mr or Mrs Right.'

'She's straight, remember?' said Isla. 'She hooked up with the CEO of that health magazine, but she couldn't quite—'

'Stop!' shouted Jess.

'I'm just saying!'

'I don't care *who*.' Jacki cupped Jess's cheek with her hand. 'You've got one year to find a relationship you can commit to for longer than three months.'

Jess frowned. 'But—'

'*I'm* single,' said Mel. 'Why can't I have that task?'

'Because,' Isla cut in, 'you and Corey are a sure thing. You both just need to admit how you feel and f—'

'Isla!' Mel's face was beetroot red. She always got embarrassed when someone mentioned Corey. Rose thought they were sweet together, but Mel insisted they were just friends. Really good, best of the best, BFFs.

'It's gotta be the longest act of foreplay known to humankind,' ribbed Isla.

Mel looked like she was about to explode.

'You're relentless,' said Rose.

'Why thank you.' Isla smiled.

'My darling firstborn.' Jacki gazed at Isla with delight.

'Here we go,' Rose muttered. Isla and Jess, the eldest and youngest, had always held special places in their mother's heart. Rose was more of an afterthought. A kiss or a hug was extremely rare, and the phrase *I love you* never escaped her mother's lips. At least not around Rose.

Isla tilted her head to the side like a coy goody two-shoes.

'I've watched you rise, both in business and in your personal life,' said Jacki. 'Marrying Steve just after you left school, building a high-profile chain of distinguished jewellery stores from scratch. A-listers can't get enough of your collections. What you've achieved is truly remarkable.'

'Oh, Mum.' A smug grin crept across Isla's face.

Mel glanced at Rose and stuck her fingers in her mouth like she wanted to vomit.

'It's been fantastic to watch your business grow and thrive,' said Jacki. 'But *who* are you?'

Isla flinched slightly. 'What do you mean? I'm Isla. I'm *your* Isla.'

'Yes, you're *my* Isla and *Steve's* Isla, but who is the *real* Isla? You and Steve have been together so long I don't know where he stops, and you begin. You just kind of blur into—'

'StevLa,' said Mel, delighting in the opportunity to give as good as she got.

Isla scowled. 'Seriously? That needs work.'

Jess pressed her lips together and tried not to laugh. StevLa had been Mel's nickname for Steve and Isla for years.

'Mum's right,' said Mel. 'You finish each other's sentences. It's infuriating.'

'It's true,' nodded Jess.

'Well, at least I *have* a man.'

'Stop it,' said Rose. She hated it when her sisters bickered. 'This whole thing is ridiculous!'

Jacki raised an eyebrow but turned back to Isla. 'You have one year to find out *who* you are.'

Isla stepped back. 'What are you saying? You want me and Steve to break up?'

'I don't care what you do, but before I go in that oven, I want to meet the *real* you.'

'But how can you even measure something like that?' asked Isla.

'You can't.' Rose glowered at her mother in disgust. 'This whole thing is a farce. Why are you doing this? You're dying, and your response is to send us on a wild goose chase for your amusement. It's sick.'

'Nice choice of words.' Jess glared at Rose.

Jacki fixed Rose with a cold stare and refused to break eye contact. It was the most attention Rose had received from her in years.

'When you're standing at death's door, everything looks different. Everything!' Jacki took a deep breath, and Rose held hers. 'I feel like I've been swimming freestyle in the ocean for the last sixty-five years. I've been strong, I've paced myself, and I've overcome all the challenges that have crossed my path. But now, I've come up for air expecting the shore to be at least another twenty kilometres away, only to find that it's right in front of me. I'm at arm's length from my final destination.'

Rose exhaled, and her skin tingled as she and her sisters stared at their mother in quiet disbelief.

'Wow,' said Mel. 'That was beautiful, Mum. Maybe *you* should write a book.'

Rose winced. Mel's desperate need for their mother's approval made her sad.

'Weren't you listening?' Jess wailed. 'She means she's run out of time.'

Jacki raised her palms. 'I just want to die knowing I brought out the best in you girls,' she sniffed. 'If you don't like it, that's fine. Aussie Animal Rescue will happily take my money.'

2

Jess

Half an hour later, after changing her clothes and touching up her make-up, Jacki flew off to her business meeting, leaving Jess and her sisters in a state of shock.

Standing alone in the darkness of the backyard, Jess wrapped her arms around herself and shuddered as the wind picked up. *This can't be happening!* As the helicopter's lights faded, the ache in her heart intensified. Her mum was dying, and rather than letting her daughters shower her with love and affection, she'd left them, just like she always did.

Jacki was co-founder and majority shareholder of the prestigious five-star Turner Hotels and Casinos, located in five Australian cities. Her work meant she was seldom home. There was always someone, somewhere who needed Jacki Turner for one thing or another. Jess went light-headed, and widened her stance to steady herself. She felt strangely separate from her body. Was she in shock? Some people would argue this was a normal reaction after coming into contact with Jacki Turner. Her mum was like a cyclone: she didn't come through very often, but when she did, there was no telling the impact she would have, or the devastation she'd leave in her wake. Jacki managed both her business and her family with the same top-down approach. Although she was innovative when it came to staying ahead of the competition and often thought up creative ways to get more out of her colleagues and staff, Jess couldn't help but feel her leadership style was outdated. She pushed too hard, and often ended up pushing people away.

Over the last few years, Jess had become conscious of how her mum's presence had shaped her and her sisters. Isla had a purely business-focused relationship with Jacki, which didn't tolerate emotional vulnerability. This pretty much reflected Isla's default setting as a stone-cold bitch.

Rose was a different story altogether. She was *all* feelings and such a great mum to her kids. She'd based her approach to parenting on the rule that she wouldn't raise her kids anything like the way Jacki had raised them. It upset Jess that Rose and Jacki didn't get on. If only they'd listen to each other, or put themselves in each other's shoes for once, they'd realise they had more in common than they thought.

Mel was a sensitive soul who was sometimes reluctant to venture out of her comfort zone – Jacki was right about that. But Mel wasn't afraid to call her mum and sisters out in a jovial way if she thought they needed pulling into line. That said, Jess suspected her sister's gentle mockery was a way of keeping her deeper feelings hidden away.

Jess was the baby of the family. After her whirlwind marriage and subsequent divorce, she'd swapped her rose-tinted glasses for a pair with an unfiltered lens. Being eight years younger than Mel and having a different dad from her sisters, she'd always felt like an outsider in her own family. It was difficult when her sisters shared memories of their dad and recalled moments from before she was born, but she, too, had been blessed with a dad who loved her unconditionally. He lived in Cairns on his beloved banana farm and kept her grounded when the absurdity that surrounded her mum got too much.

Walking back into the house, Jess headed for the kitchen, where she found Isla sitting at the kitchen island and Rose trying to comfort Mel, who was pacing and wringing her hands. She almost collapsed with relief when she saw Helen there, pouring them all a glass of wine.

'You're here!' Jess whimpered.

'Jacki texted me to say I was needed.'

Helen was a short, full-figured woman who always wore her hair in a neat low bun. Sometimes, when Jess was growing up, Helen would untie her silver, waist-length hair and let Jess brush it for what felt like hours. It was one of many fond memories she had of her from when she was a kid.

At first sight, a stranger would think Helen was Jacki's personal chef or housekeeper, but although Helen did do some of the cooking, her contribution went far beyond the kitchen. Helen kept The Castle running, and tended to the wellbeing – both emotional and physical – of those who dwelt within it. She made sure the bills got paid, the work got done, hurts were soothed and troubles resolved.

Helen opened her arms and Jess fell into her embrace. 'Oh, Helen.' Jess didn't want to let her go. Helen's hugs always made her feel safe, and the world seem a little less scary. Jess pulled back and dried her eyes with the back of her hand. 'Is it really true?'

'Oh, sweetie. I'm so sorry,' said Helen.

'How long have you known?'

'Four months.' Helen clamped her thick white brows together. 'She made me promise not to say anything.'

'How could we not have realised? Why didn't she tell us?'

'You know what your mother's like. Once she makes a decision, there's no changing her mind. I told her she should tell you girls, but she wouldn't have it.' Helen rubbed the top of Jess's arms.

'I can't believe she's dying. It just doesn't make sense!' cried Mel, her voice breaking. 'Dad was too young when he died, and so is Mum. This isn't right.'

'Here,' said Isla, handing Mel a glass of wine, 'drink this.'

Mel stopped pacing and downed the contents of the glass.

'That should do the trick,' said Isla, leading Mel to one of the kitchen stools.

The large black and white kitchen would be the envy of any serious cook, with its imported La Cornue kitchen range, spacious butler's pantry, and oversized marble island. It overlooked the outdoor eating area, and the lush tropical plants and floor-to-ceiling windows blurred the lines between inside and out. Jess reckoned her mum's kitchen was about the same size as her entire one-bedroom apartment, just down the road in Southport.

'I can't believe she just left,' said Mel, glaring at the bowl of lemons in the centre of the island. 'Why is she going to a meeting at this time of day? Why isn't she here, with us? She's dying, for God's sake.'

'She may be dying,' said Isla, 'but someone still has to look after the business. Things don't just stop because your time's up.'

'Your mum's giving you some time to adjust, and to speak freely without her being here,' said Helen. 'It's kinder for both you and her, don't you think? Now, Jacki wanted me to speak to you on her behalf,' she went on, pulling some folders out of her tote bag and placing them on the kitchen counter.

'This is so typical.' Rose dragged her fingers through her dishevelled hair. 'She's so self-absorbed. She's given us our tasks, so now, as far as she's concerned, there's nothing left to discuss. I mean, who knows, she probably isn't sick at all. I wouldn't be surprised if this was just another ploy to get our attention. There's nothing I wouldn't put past that woman.'

Jess scowled at Rose. Her head throbbed. 'How can you say that? She's not a liar.'

'So why are we *just* finding out she's got cancer?' Rose looked at Helen. 'You never once mentioned she was sick.' Rose's cheeks burned a deep red, and Jess could tell that although she was trying to stay calm, a bitter rage was simmering beneath the surface.

'I'm sorry. It wasn't for me to say.'

'Well, if it turns out Mum really is sick,' said Isla, 'her medication is clearly making her irrational. I mean, what's with this "Who is the real Isla Turner?" business anyway?'

Helen picked up a dark green ring binder. 'Everything you want to know is in here.'

Jess opened the folder and flipped through an array of plastic pockets that showcased Jacki's medical results: colonoscopy and CT scans, referrals from various doctors and specialists; pages of instructions for cancer patient care. Her heart raced, and her hands shook as she leafed through letters detailing the diagnosis, prognosis and chemotherapy appointments plus information about what side effects to expect. 'So, it's true. She really is … *dying*.'

The fearless Jacki Turner, who always put a single x at the end of her texts to her, and who was ever patient when Jess couldn't cope with the attention that always came with Jacki's fame, was in the battle of her life, and apparently, she was going to lose.

'Jacki wouldn't lie about something as serious as this,' said Helen. 'She's not a monster. I know how harsh she can be in business, and with her family sometimes, but she doesn't want to hurt any of you. If anything, I think she's softened over the last few months. She's started seeing things differently.'

Rose folded her arms. 'How convenient.'

'Rose!' Jess hated how unforgiving Rose was when it came to their mum. It broke her heart. Jacki needed their love and support right now. Jess looked away from her sister, her throat aching.

'I understand why you feel that way, Rose,' said Helen. 'I really do, but this time it's different. She actually said to me, *I only want what's best for my girls.*'

'Except we're not *girls* anymore,' said Rose. 'She can't treat us like puppets, pulling our strings like she used to when we were kids. We're all grown up, and we can see her for who she really is. Tell me, how long did it take her to realise she'd missed it all? Was it before or after they told her she was going to die?'

Helen sighed. 'Oh, Rose.'

Jess noticed Rose was trembling, and wondered if it was with anger or heartbreak. Maybe both.

'She hasn't changed one bit,' said Rose. 'Because if she had, we'd be talking to *her* right now instead of you.'

Jess couldn't help it, she burst into tears again. Rose never had a kind word to say about Jacki, not even now that she was dying. The least she could do was keep her thoughts to herself.

Mel got up and wrapped her arm around Jess while Isla tapped a red-painted fingernail on the countertop. 'There must be a doctor *somewhere* who can help Mum.'

'Yes! I can't believe there's nothing else to be done,' said Mel. 'Surely she can buy the best treatment there is. *Please*, Helen. We have to do something.'

'We've seen absolutely everyone there is to see. Chemo will buy your mum a little more time, but that's all there is now.'

A heavy silence weighed over them, and lingered as the gravity of Helen's words sank in.

'Does this mean I've got to run a marathon?' Mel tried to smile, but her voice wobbled, then broke. The comment was typical of Mel. She often tried to hide her pain with a joke. Jess hugged her tightly.

'Mum *can't* be serious about those terms. Please tell us *that's* a joke,' said Isla.

'I'm afraid not,' said Helen.

'But I'm the very definition of success!' said Isla. 'I've achieved so much, built my own business. I know *exactly* who I am.'

Rose rolled her eyes.

'I'm not doing this ridiculous task when it's obvious I shouldn't have to,' continued Isla. 'And there's no way in hell I'm letting Mum's inheritance go to a load of animals, as much as they might need the help.'

'The only way to claim your inheritance is for all of you to complete the tasks you've been given.' Helen reached for the plastic folders she'd set out on the counter and handed one to each of them.

Jess took a breath, composing herself, and opened her folder. Typed in bold on the first page were the words: *Terms of Inheritance: Jessica Freeman-Turner.* 'What's this?'

'These are some materials I've put together to help each of you complete your task,' said Helen. 'In each folder, you'll find resources and ideas to help get you started.'

Jess flicked through her folder and came across an article entitled 'The Best Places in the Gold Coast to Meet Your Future Partner'. There was a page with a list of dating apps and, towards the back, a calendar of upcoming events.

'This is horrible,' said Jess. She may as well have been handed a folder that read, 'What to Do and Where to Go When You're

Desperate'. One of the reasons Jess hadn't been on a date in the last year was because the dating scene was so stressful. There were too many expectations and just too little in return for the effort. Raised hopes were constantly smashed, and it was far more comfortable to sit the whole rollercoaster out. But now she was being *forced* to put herself out there. She felt sick.

'I'm sorry, Jess,' said Helen. 'I have to admit your folder is a little … crass.'

'A *little*?'

'Although, there are one or two articles in there that make for an interesting read.'

'"Ten Questions to Ask on a First Date"? "How Not to Appear Needy"?'

'I know I'm no expert – it's been over four decades since I last dated – but I wanted to help you like I'm helping your sisters.'

'Well thanks, but I don't need help,' said Isla, closing her folder. 'I need to talk to Mum's lawyers.'

'If you turn to the last page of your folder, you'll see a copy of the terms that Jacki has had drawn up by her legal advisers. As you can see, it states that Jacki's assets, with the exception of her majority shares in Turner Hotels and Casinos, will be split equally among the four of you, on condition that you all meet the terms set out below. Evidence for passing the terms is to be submitted to Jacki's lawyer, Victoria Gilbert, no later than the evening of the Gold Coast Marathon next year, and she'll have the final say on whether the terms have been completed or not. In the event that you're unsuccessful, your mum's assets will be sold and the money given to her charity of choice, Aussie Animal Rescue.'

'So we're talking about a multi-million-dollar inheritance for each of us?' Jess chewed her bottom lip. She'd be able to expand her business just like she'd always planned. She'd have time to travel again. She shook her head. Thinking of her own good fortune at the expense of losing her mum made her nauseous, but how could she *not* think about it? Her inheritance was something she'd always thought about over the years. Hell, she'd even made some business decisions based on the fact that one day she would have no money worries.

'Can she do this?' asked Mel.

'Absolutely,' said Helen. 'It's her money, she can do whatever she likes.'

'And so can I,' said Rose. 'We don't have to do any of this.'

'Oh, *please*, Rose,' said Isla, scornfully. 'You've got three kids. You need this money more than any of us. Think about it. Your kids could go to private schools, you could buy a bigger house with a garden large enough for more than just a trampoline, and you could write full time – whatever you wanted, a novel perhaps.'

'That may be so, but—'

'But nothing. Money is money, Rose.' Isla sighed. 'Look at me, I don't *need* the cash, but of course I'll take my share. Mum spent a lifetime building her fortune and, as much as Aussie Animal Rescue might be doing a great job, it should be Turners who inherit Mum's wealth.'

'Let me remind you,' said Helen, 'that not only will this fortune set you all up for life, but these are your mum's last wishes. You may be angry and upset now – that's totally understandable – but once she's gone, how will you feel then?'

'Well, I'm in,' said Jess, fighting back tears. 'If Mum wants us to do this, then I will. I don't think it's too much to ask. She's only trying to help us.'

'She doesn't want to *help* us. She wants to *control* us. There's a difference!' said Rose.

'Plus, it's easy for you to say you'll do it, Jess,' said Mel. 'You've just got to go out and have a good time. You could date anyone for three months if you really had to. Whereas I've got to *run a marathon*! I don't know if that's even possible.'

'If you look in your folder, you'll see it's very possible,' said Helen. 'You should consider this opportunity, Mel. The money would certainly make things easier for you. You work so well with those kids, and it's such important work you do, but we all know neither you nor your colleagues get paid what you deserve.'

For the last fourteen years, Mel had cared for children with disabilities, and for the previous two she and a small team of co-workers had helped care for Lilly, a five-year-old with cerebral palsy.

'Plus, it would be an amazing achievement. Lilly would be so proud of you. Imagine how you'd feel telling her you'd finished. Imagine her face.'

'Oh, I'll do it. I *need* the money,' said Mel. 'I could pay off my debts once and for all. It would be such a relief. It's just … A marathon? Why couldn't she just give us the money?'

'It's absurd!' Isla stared into her wine glass. 'Mum has never shown any interest in Aussie Animal Rescue before, let alone animal welfare. She has allergies! After Dad died, Mum singlehandedly built the Turner empire. She didn't work this hard to have her fortune go to a bunch of cats and dogs.'

Helen raised her eyebrows. 'So, are you going to let that happen? Will you let strangers spend your mum's inheritance?'

'You *know* I won't.' Isla shut her eyes and took a deep breath. '*Damn it!*'

Jess and her sisters looked at Rose.

'Rose?' said Helen.

'We *all* have to do it, Rose.' Usually, Jess kept out of the feud between Rose and their mum. She'd tried to stay neutral over the years, even though she understood why Rose was so upset, but now Jess had no choice but to intervene. 'If you don't want to do it for Mum, will you consider doing it for us?' All Jess wanted was to make her mum happy in the last few months of her life. 'Please, Rose,' Jess whimpered. She didn't mean to cry again, but the thought of Rose denying her mum's last wishes broke her heart.

Rose turned away. 'I … I can't do it. Not for *her*, not after what she did.'

Jess's eyes blurred. 'Then *please*, Rose … for us?' she begged. A heavy silence filled the grand kitchen.

Rose sighed and pressed her fingers to her temples. 'I need time to think. This is all too much.'

'Right.' Helen went to the drinks cabinet and grabbed a bottle of whisky. 'I think we could all do with a real drink.'

'God, yes.' Isla gulped the last of her wine.

Helen fetched five shot glasses from the butler's pantry.

'Not for me,' said Rose, holding up a glass of water. 'I'm breastfeeding.'

Mel stared at her folder as Helen handed out the drinks. 'We should make a toast to Mum.'

'You're right,' said Isla, and she raised her glass. 'To Mum, and her bloody terms of inheritance.'

3

Isla

The next evening, Isla sat at Rose's kitchen table with her sisters. How Rose could live in such a cramped and cluttered space, she had no idea. In every room, there was some kind of baby equipment – play mats, change table, baby bouncer – and when Isla had first stepped into the house, she'd been hit with a sickly sweet aroma of dirty nappies, which seemed to linger everywhere. Isla had pressed her fist to her nose and asked whether Bethany needed changing. To her horror, Rose had literally *sniffed* Bethany's backside before strapping the three-month-old to her body and declaring she was 'all good'.

Rose's two-storey brick house in the bayside suburb of Cleveland, south of Brisbane, was about forty years old and in desperate need of redecorating. Isla doubted the walls had been repainted in the last two decades. Small patches of paint were missing where so-called 'non-stick' hooks had once hung, and she could see dirty, sticky marks on the walls at child height wherever she looked. The grouting between the floor tiles needed a good scrub, and there was a giant white stain on the beige living room carpet. Rose had asked Isla to leave her shoes by the front door to keep her floors clean, but Isla was more worried about keeping her feet clean. Who knew what lurked between those cheap polyester fibres?

Sitting at the Ikea kitchen table, Isla calculated that the entirety of Rose's furniture likely cost around the same as the two sofas in Isla's living room. Her stomach churned at the thought of ever having to live like that, but then she reminded herself that she would never be in that situation in the first place. She worked too hard and was too focused to let it all slip away.

Earlier that afternoon, Isla had picked up Jess from her Gold Coast apartment and driven them to Rose's house. Mel, who lived five minutes from Rose, was already there. For the second consecutive day, Isla found herself with all her sisters at the same time. She struggled to remember the last time they'd all been together, bar the day before at their mother's. It must have been years ago.

Rose opened the lid of one of the pizza boxes on the table in front of them, and Isla smiled thinly. She'd eat later, she decided.

'Dig in,' said Rose. 'I *was* going to whip up my famous spaghetti bolognese.'

'You were?' Isla would have much preferred one of Rose's home-cooked meals. Cooking was another of Rose's gifts, besides writing and motherhood. When Rose was younger she'd always helped Helen in the kitchen, and now whenever Isla got to eat one of her hearty meals she was filled with nostalgia.

'Tom insisted on treating us all to take-away,' said Rose. 'He's such a sweetheart. He said he wanted to give me a break, with all that's happened.' Rose handed each of her sisters a small plate, then tucked her scraggly hair behind her ears and served herself a slice. Jacki had been right about one thing yesterday: Rose *was* tired. She looked like she hadn't slept for seven years – unlike Bethany, who currently slept soundly in the sling Rose wore.

This Rose was a world away from the partying Rose from back in their clubbing days. That Rose would drink a row of vodka shots with no thought for the consequences. When she'd left home, Isla and Rose were as close as sisters could get. They were young, independent women who'd been freed from the clutches of The Castle and they'd spent their weekends drinking like there was no tomorrow and lapping up the attention that came with the Turner name. It was all sun, sea and shots. Of course, those days were never going to last.

For Rose, partying hard was an act of rebellion against what she said was their mother's foulest act: kicking them out of her home. Even though Jacki had explained her reasons time and again and insisted that they should see it as a challenge, Isla knew it had only fuelled Rose's abandonment issues. Sure, Jacki hadn't been around much when they were growing up, but she was building an empire! And for Isla, leaving home had been a magical time, the closest she'd ever felt to being truly free. She'd had no real responsibilities back then, other than to show up to her uni lectures and her part-time job at a local jeweller's. Her future was filled with every possibility and she was excited for it all. She was Isla Turner, and the world was her oyster.

Mel reached forward, grabbed a slice of pepperoni pizza, folded it in half and took a huge bite.

'Brilliant 360 no scope!' Tom's voice boomed from the adjoining living room.

'Who's he talking to?' asked Jess, taking a sip of red wine.

'Harrison,' said Rose. 'He's upstairs on the Xbox.'

Jess tilted her head. 'Why don't they just play in the same room?'

'It's a single-player game or something. I don't really understand any of it,' said Rose, shrugging.

Isla took a sip of her red wine and winced: merlot should not come out of a box. She scanned the table for anything edible. She was starving, but the thought of some pimply teenager preparing her food turned her stomach. 'Where's Taylor? I haven't seen her yet.'

'She's in her room watching Tom's YouTube channel on her iPad.'

'Tom's so *different* to Richard, don't you think?'

Everyone stopped eating, and an awkward silence fell.

Rose continued to chew her food and stared into the mountain of cheesy pizza on the table. 'Well, Rich is gone, and this is how it is now.'

Rose's husband, Richard, had died of cancer three years earlier. His diagnosis had been a shock, but Isla had been sure he'd make a full recovery. He'd been fit and healthy, had gone to the gym daily and was a strict vegetarian. At thirty-five, he'd been in his prime. That was why it was such a shock when he'd died. It had been heartbreaking. He had two kids and a wife who adored him. Whenever Isla thought about Richard, her chest tightened. He'd been such a good dad and a devoted husband, plus he was funny – laugh-till-you-cry funny. After his death, she'd made a conscious decision not to think about him anymore. It just hurt too much.

This time last year, Isla had been floored when Rose had called to tell her she'd had a one-night stand with Tom, a British YouTuber ten years her junior. Apparently, he made his living filming himself playing computer games and building Lego kits. Isla had nearly crashed her BMW when Rose announced she was pregnant two months later.

'I wasn't saying I don't like Tom,' said Isla. 'I was merely pointing out—'

'This isn't how I expected things to turn out either, but Tom's a good guy with a good heart.' Rose took a bite of her pizza and the silence returned, simmering around them.

'What are we going to do about Mum?' asked Jess, breaking the tension. 'Someone should be with her around the clock. She shouldn't be alone.'

'You know Mum, Jess – she's too proud for that,' said Mel. 'Anyway, Helen's there with her. I just can't believe she's dying. It's not in her nature. I was sure she'd live to be a hundred and five. She's stubborn like that.' She smiled thinly. 'I thought she'd be bossing people around until the end of time. I can't bear the thought of being an orphan.' Mel was getting teary now and Isla cleared her throat.

'Well, I don't know how you're going to run a marathon,' said Isla.

'Nor do I.'

Mel picked up another slice of pizza and Isla winced. 'But let's just start by assuming you have to stop eating crap and start running.' Isla wrestled the pizza out of Mel's hand and put it back in the box. A thin layer of grease coated her fingertips.

'Hey!' Mel picked the slice back up. 'If I'm gonna run forty-two point two kilometres, I'm gonna need my energy.'

'Who said we're even going through with this?' asked Rose.

Isla eyed the pizza on her plate. It took all her willpower not to gag. 'Mum wanting me to figure out who I am is clearly something she's just come up with so you girls don't feel bad about your own lives.'

Rose frowned and took a sip from a bottle of kombucha.

Isla ignored her. 'I'm already living a successful life. I've got my own business, a penthouse, I have three holidays abroad a year, a good husband—'

'That doesn't mean you know who you are,' said Mel.

'What?'

'Just because you're ticking all the boxes doesn't mean there's nothing missing. Mum gave us these conditions for a reason – maybe you should think about what that reason is.'

Isla sighed. Sometimes it felt as if her sisters lived in a completely different world. Honestly, it was hard to fathom that they'd all grown up in the same house.

Isla was saved from having to find a diplomatic response by Tom, who bounced into the kitchen. 'Brilliant, I'm starving!' He kissed the top of Rose's head and reached for a slice of pizza. 'You want me to take Beth?'

Isla scanned him with a critical eye. Tom's broad square shoulders and muscular arms tapered to a lean, masculine frame, but his Super Mario T-shirt and torn light-denim jeans screamed adolescence. It was hard to believe he was thirty years old.

'It's all good.' Rose smiled. 'She'll wake in a bit for a feed anyway.'

'I'll take her up to bed after. Can I get you ladies anything? Refill your glasses?'

'You can get me a boyfriend,' said Jess.

A deep, contagious laugh roared from Tom. 'Good one,' he said and disappeared into the living room with his pizza.

Jess sat back and pushed her plate away from her. 'I can't imagine a world without Mum.'

Isla's chest tightened. Her mum was her idol. Typically, she didn't care for other people's thoughts or ideas, but she hung onto every word Jacki said. Hers was the only opinion Isla cared about. Even her husband Steve's views didn't matter to her as much as her mum's. Making Jacki Turner proud was what fuelled Isla's ambition and drove her to succeed. Isla and her mum were a team. They saw things the same way, did things the same way. They understood each other. The idea of thriving in business without her mum to bounce ideas off felt hollow, lonely.

'I know this sounds crazy,' said Jess. 'But I think these tasks are Mum's way of showing us she loves us. This is the kind of thing she does. She's never played by the rule book; we all know that.'

'She could have just left us the money like any normal parent,' said Mel.

Their mum's fortune was vast. Jacki owned five – or was it six? – private residences, plus other real estate around the world. She had a super yacht in Italy, owned two restaurants in France and had an enormous collection of fine art, and that was in addition to her liquid assets.

'But she's never been a normal parent,' said Rose. 'She gave us a taste of the good life, then kicked us out when we were eighteen, abandoned us right when we needed her the most.'

'I've gotta say it came at the worst possible time for me,' said Mel. 'Everything changed when I left home. I thought I had it all under control, the living independently thing, but, as we know, I wasn't well equipped to deal with the cost of living. I just ... didn't have the skills.'

Isla was taken aback. She'd never heard Mel speak so openly about her debt before. Normally, when someone brought it up or offered to help her she vehemently denied having any financial difficulty. Isla had felt sorry for her. Mel had accumulated a lot of debt at uni – she'd had no idea how credit cards should or shouldn't be used, especially when you had an extremely low income, and she was still struggling, from what Isla could see. But Isla also knew Jacki's intentions had been well-meaning. Being financially independent was a skill everyone needed, and so she'd pushed them all out into the world and let them get on with it. It was just that Mel's confidence had been knocked one too many times already, and what she'd really needed was guidance. But rather than ask anyone for help, she'd hidden both her feelings and her failings.

'It was definitely a shock,' said Jess. 'I'm just glad you all warned me, and taught me a few things before I left home. I'm grateful for that.'

Isla straightened her back. 'Look, there's no doubt the money will help you all. Obviously, I'm okay … ' Isla glanced around at Rose's cream-painted walls and at the cheap office-issue vertical blinds that hung like rags over the grubby glass sliding door. 'But it really would be great to see you girls living the good life again.' It was true. Isla could see exactly how her sisters' lives would improve with the inheritance, but she was a self-made success who had worked damned hard to get where she was. She hadn't needed anyone's help. But of course the money would come in handy – it would mean she could escalate the growth of her own business much earlier than she'd anticipated.

'The money would mean I could pay off my credit card debts,' said Mel. 'I could finally buy a car, open some art therapy studios to help other kids like Lilly. I could buy a home at Raby Bay, and maybe a boat. And there was a stunning Jimmy Choo bag I saw online … Oh, and some gorgeous Gucci ankle boots.'

Rose and Jess glanced at each other with a look of concern, but Isla leant back and smiled. '*There's* the Mel I used to know. If you'd used your degree all those years ago rather than—'

'Hey, I love my job.' Mel scowled and ripped off another piece of garlic bread. 'Don't talk about my work like it's some kind of failing or disappointment, Isla. I do what I do because I love it. Lilly is inspiring and funny and clever. I'm not there for the money.'

Jess wiped her hands on some kitchen roll. 'Let's face it, Mum's tasks are a little … extreme, but none of us want to give up our inheritance, right? The way I see it, we have one year to give Mum what she wants, and then that's it.' Jess paused, composing herself, and Isla tried not to roll her eyes. Jess was always so emotional. 'After that she'll never ask anything of us again. Let's just do this to make Mum happy in her last few months, and then you can all go back to your normal lives.'

'Well, I'm sorry,' said Rose, 'but I'm not going to play her game. I've learned to live with having a mother who doesn't give a shit about me or my family. I'm not about to play happy families just to make her feel better. I want nothing to do with this.'

'And what about the rest of us?' said Jess. 'Don't you care about what we want?'

'Of course I do, but my therapist told me I have to control the toxicity in my life, and that woman will trigger a nuclear disaster if I let her back in.'

'This is so typical of you, Rose,' said Isla. Rose's relationship with Jacki had always been strained, but after Richard's diagnosis, Jacki had gone AWOL and Rose had vowed she'd never see her again. 'Not everything is about you and your feelings. You need to accept what's happened and move on.'

'I'm happy now. I don't want her back in my life, and I don't want her money. I paid off my mortgage when Rich died, and I like my job, so I'm set too. I don't need any of this.'

'*You* may not want her money, but come on, are you going to deny your kids a nice healthy trust fund?'

Rose sighed and looked at Bethany.

'We need to make a decision,' said Jess. 'If we decide to do it, one year isn't actually that long. It won't be easy, but it will be worth it. We'd give Mum her last dying wish, and we'd get our inheritance.'

'Then let's vote,' said Isla. Jess was right. They needed to make a decision; she didn't have time to sit here going round in circles – and neither did they, if they were going to achieve these terms.

Jess raised her hand. 'I'm in.'

Isla knew it would be a financially sound investment if they could pull it off. She just wasn't sure how she was going to achieve her task. How does one find one's true self? Still, she was sure she'd figure something out.

'I want to, but I can't run,' said Mel.

'Don't be such a quitter,' said Isla.

'You could at least give it a try,' said Jess in a softer tone. 'You do want to pay off your debts, stop renting with Perfectionist Penny and get your own place, don't you?' Mel's housemate was a nurse who worked night shifts and helped cut Mel's rent in half, but she also drove Mel crazy with her obsessive need to keep the house clean.

Mel scowled at Jess, but didn't deny it.

'If we're going to do this, we need to help each other. They have those parkrun get-togethers on a Saturday morning, Mel. You could start with that. Build up to running slowly.'

'I'll do it if you come with me.'

'Sure,' said Jess. 'And Rose, remember all those short stories you wrote just after Harrison was born? I could look over them with you, get the creative juices flowing.'

'I never said I'd—'

'Hey Mel, you could help me find a hot guy,' said Jess, ignoring Rose's protests.

Isla scoffed. 'Are you delusional? How is *Mel* going to help you? You're stunning, and she's—'

Mel grabbed a slice of pizza and stuffed the whole thing into her mouth in one go. 'Disgusting?' she asked with an open mouth, and a piece of pepperoni dropped onto the table.

'Eww!' Isla scrunched up her napkin and threw it at Mel. 'Why do you always do things like that? It's gross.'

Isla caught Rose smiling. 'So, what about it?' Isla asked her. 'Are you in?'

'I really don't want to.'

'You're not going to abandon us in our time of need are you?' said Isla, hoping to hit a nerve.

Rose sighed. 'You're ruthless. Fine, but just so we're clear, I'm not doing it for our mother, I'm doing it for the three of you.'

Jess clapped and then stopped, scared she'd wake Bethany. 'I'm not sure how you're supposed to find yourself, Isla. Maybe you could find some activities you enjoy, something that has nothing to do with work?'

'Don't worry about me, just focus on your own task,' said Isla. 'So, we're all in agreement? We're really going to do this?'

Jess beamed. 'If we stick together, if we work as a team and commit to helping each other, then I know we can do this.'

Mel nodded, and a smile crept across her face. 'I can't wait to meet the *real* Isla Turner.'

'Hell,' Isla quipped, 'I just want to see *you* run a marathon.' She wrinkled her nose. 'I'm sorry, Rose, but you need to open some windows. The smell of dirty nappies is making me feel unwell.'

Rose sniffed. 'I can't smell anything.'

'That's because you're used to it,' said Isla.

Mel and Jess sniffed the air too, and shook their heads. 'I can't smell anything either,' said Mel.

Isla stood and turned to open the sliding door.

'Wait, you've got something on your pants,' said Mel. As Isla twisted around to look, Mel reached over to where she'd been sitting. She pegged her nose with one hand and howled with laughter as she held up a soiled nappy. 'You've been sitting in shit all night, Isla.'

Mel

4

Mel

Sitting in the gym foyer, Mel bounced her knee and checked her phone: 6.55 pm. It'd been nearly two weeks since Jacki had told them she was dying. In that time Mel had fluctuated between extreme sadness, raging anger and sheer disbelief. There'd been no space in her head to even think about the marathon. Then two days ago, she'd had a call from Helen asking if she'd made a start on her task. She could still hear Helen's words ringing in her ears: *There are no shortcuts when it comes to training for a marathon. You must put in the work. Every week of training counts, there's no time to waste.*

So here she was, in the last place she wanted to be, tugging her oversized *Friends* T-shirt as low as she could and pretending to scroll through her phone as a couple of women half her age and half her size, wearing pastel-coloured shrink-wrapped gym attire, made for the exit. She couldn't understand why people would come here voluntarily. Perhaps they were being blackmailed too.

6.56 pm. *Where are you, Corey?*

Corey was a thirty-nine-year-old art teacher with cerebral palsy who had spent the last decade teaching kids with disabilities. Eighteen months earlier, Mel had attended an art workshop with Lilly, the girl she helped care for, and Corey was the teacher. He'd made Mel laugh so much that when it was over, her cheeks had ached. They became fast friends, and now not a day went by when they didn't text or see each other. Lilly's mum, Catherine, was always asking Mel if they were dating yet – she thought their meeting had been cute and romantic, and was certain Corey would ask Mel out on a date soon. But Mel couldn't think like that. She couldn't risk losing him, because he was, quite simply, the best. As in *the best friend you could ever hope for.* But he was also eleven minutes late, and Mel's nerves were starting to get the better of her. She was like a fish out of water here. She wasn't trim and toned like all these gym goers who waltzed confidently from one machine to the next.

When she'd told Corey about the terms of inheritance, he'd convinced Mel to come to his gym for an induction session. He'd set up a meeting with his personal trainer, Joe. For Corey, having a tailor-made exercise plan was a key component of living with cerebral palsy.

'Mel?' A guy holding an iPad grinned at her. His blond curled locks were scraped into a man-bun. 'I'm Joe.'

'Hi, I'm just waiting for Corey.'

'Oh, that's okay, we can start without him.'

'Can we?' Mel swallowed. The last time she'd set foot in a gym had been ten years ago, when she'd had an induction just like this one. She'd handed over her credit card details and spent the next eighteen months paying for a membership she never used. The only time she'd visited after that had been to cancel. 'I mean, I'd really feel more comfortable waiting for Corey.'

'No problem. I have a few questions to ask first anyway.' Joe took a seat next to her and swiped open his iPad. 'What's the main reason you're joining the gym today?'

Mel pressed her lips together as she considered her answer. She didn't think she should tell him that her dying mum was blackmailing her with a multi-million-dollar inheritance. 'Um, I want to get fit?'

'Great.' Joe ticked a box on his iPad.

When Mel had left home to do a Visual Arts degree in Brisbane, she'd had no idea of the cost of living or how to manage money. As a kid, she'd never needed to buy so much as a carton of milk or a loaf of bread. But when she'd stumbled into the *real* world at eighteen, the one where rent had to be paid on time and eating meant restocking the fridge, she'd thought she had it all figured out. When one credit card maxed out, she just applied for another one. By the time she'd finished her degree and undertaken additional training to be a disability support worker, she was a staggering hundred thousand dollars in debt. It was only when she started working full time that she realised it would be impossible to pay off. She could barely afford the minimum repayments.

She was angry at herself for having been so naïve. Who did she think was going to pay back the money? The problem was, she'd never had to think about it when she'd been living at home. She'd used her credit cards as she'd wanted and her mum had paid them off. She'd never even seen a statement. Helen had always dealt with that kind of thing.

It turned her stomach to think about how much money she'd spent in those first few years after leaving home. And now, fifteen years later, she still hadn't made a dent in paying it back. The interest was crippling. She even sympathised with the gambling addicts at the Turner Casino; those who kept betting, sure that the next win would erase all their debt. She could understand the temptation.

Mel tried not to dwell too much on it, but it was hard when her sisters were all financially stable. Even Jess could afford to have some nice things and she was eight years younger! It was embarrassing. Mel was just grateful they didn't know how much she owed. She'd always hoped that one day her mum would pay it all off, perhaps as a birthday or Christmas present. Plus, deep down, she'd always known the day would come when she would inherit and she could pay back the money herself. But now, her debt-free future was at risk, and the thought was terrifying.

'Are you looking to tone, lose weight or—'

'Corey!'

Using a forearm crutch on his left side and with a gym bag slung across his body, Corey entered the foyer. He spotted Mel and his eyes lit up. 'Hey, you!' He beamed, and Mel breathed a sigh of relief. His classic crew cut enhanced his sharp jaw-line, and his kind brown eyes and warm smile made her heart skip a beat. As she stood to greet him, a strong urge to kiss him washed over her. *We're just friends. Bloody good friends.* Trying her best to act casual, she punched him lightly on the arm.

'You haven't been waiting long?'

'Right on time,' said Joe. 'I was about to give Mel the full tour.'

'Great. I'll put my bag in a locker and come find you,' said Corey.

Mel navigated her way around the men and women using the free weights, and her stomach churned. She'd never felt more out of place. Her clothes and body shape made it abundantly clear that she hadn't worked out for well over two decades, and her make-up-free look was clearly no longer gym etiquette. She apologised as she dashed in front of a super-ripped guy trying to take a selfie in the mirror.

Corey joined them as Joe paused at a row of treadmills and cross-trainers. 'Okay. Mel, if you'd like to step on the treadmill, I can show you all the functions.'

'Oh, I'm not dressed for a workout,' she said.

Joe contemplated what Mel was wearing: trainers, cropped black leggings and a baggy T-shirt. He looked confused.

'These are my work clothes,' she cut in before he could comment. 'I thought you'd just be showing me the facilities today.' The thought of getting on the treadmill in front of a wall-length mirror was mortifying. 'Plus, no sports bra,' she said, hooking her finger under her bra strap and snapping it.

Corey laughed, catching the attention of a gorgeous blonde in her mid-twenties who was scrolling her phone while walking at a brisk pace on the treadmill. She smiled at Corey in the mirror and Mel looked down at her worn Nike trainers. *I bet she doesn't even sweat.*

'You don't have to run,' said Joe. 'You could just hop on, take a short walk, get the feel of it.'

Corey nodded encouragingly. 'I'll hold your stuff.'

Mel smiled reluctantly, thinking of the financial mess she was in. *Mum's bloody terms!* She handed Corey her bag and stepped up. Joe pressed some buttons and soon she was walking at a pace fast enough to get her heart rate up, but slow enough that she wasn't too out of breath.

She tugged her T-shirt down again. *Had* her task been set because of her weight? Jacki had said it was about striving for something more, pushing herself out of her comfort zone, but Mel wasn't sure she wanted to get out of her comfort zone. She liked it there. It made her feel safe, and surely that was a good thing.

Just because she didn't work out didn't mean she was lazy. In fact, she worked damn hard, for long hours and for little money, but she wouldn't change any of it. She'd dedicated her life to helping kids. Not wanting to climb Mount Everest or start her own business didn't mean her life was lacking. But apparently her mum thought differently.

Mel had never been one of the athletic kids at school. She didn't enjoy sport and had dreaded the annual sports and swimming carnivals. Her teachers always said exercise makes you feel good and endorphins make you happy, but sport just made Mel even more self-conscious about her body and fuelled the anxieties she already had. Then there were the bullies like Amber Ryan, who'd made her life a living hell. It had taken Mel years to move past those hateful comments, and the attack, and learn to love herself exactly as she was.

Even after two decades, there were still moments from the past that Mel struggled to stop replaying in her head.

Mel hadn't told Corey the full extent of the abuse she'd suffered at the hands of Amber Ryan, and she certainly hadn't mentioned she was drowning in credit card debt. Corey was a breath of fresh air in her life. He was funny and smart, and to her amazement, he *wanted* to spend time with her. She wasn't going to risk that by telling him all her dark secrets.

Mel tried to focus on the TV screen above the mirror. She couldn't hear what the news anchor was saying, but the subtitles confirmed that the world was going to shit. Yet, it all seemed insignificant to her right now. Her mum was dying, and her own small world had been turned upside down. But surely there was some hope? Maybe Jacki would get better, make a miraculous recovery, or perhaps some new drug would be invented before it was too late.

If Mel was honest, there had always been an unacknowledged distance between her and her mum. It had started when her dad had died – things were left unsaid, opportunities to grieve together had passed and, ever since, Mel had felt like a ghost in her mum's presence. Mel either went unseen or felt like a thorn in her mum's side.

Mel breathed heavily, and sweat dripped down her torso. According to the treadmill, she'd only been walking for four minutes! She imagined the news anchor announcing breaking news: a thirty-eight-year-old woman who hasn't run in over twenty years is attempting to pay off her credit card debt by running a marathon. She then imagined the news anchor bursting into laughter.

Mel hit the emergency stop button.

'You okay?' asked Joe.

Feeling unsteady on her feet, she stepped off the treadmill. 'I can't. Sorry.'

She walked past Corey and back towards the entrance.

'Mel?' he called, concerned. 'Wait up!'

He caught up with her, worry etched across his face. 'Hey, what happened?'

'It's embarrassing.'

'The treadmill?'

'These terms. Mum can't stand that I'm happy, that I've found a routine and a lifestyle that suits me. Why does she keep pushing me to be someone I'm not?' Jacki was always going on about Mel's 'wasted potential'.

Corey rested his hand on Mel's elbow and a warmth radiated up her arm. Corey was her safe place, but recently her feelings for him had become so strong that she struggled to be casual around him. She loved being with him, and thought about him constantly, but she couldn't risk exposing how she really felt. His friendship was one of the best things she had in her life. She needed him – especially now.

Her head was swimming.

'Wanna get some air?' he asked.

'Sure.'

Standing in the car park, Mel could breathe easier. 'Sorry, it was just too *peopley* in there. I stood out too much. I just want to fade into the background.'

'Don't do that.' Corey smiled, and she turned away.

How she wished she had the courage to kiss him, right here, right now.

'You know, most people in there are too interested in themselves to pay any attention to you.'

Mel laughed.

'It's true,' he insisted. 'Listen. These terms your mum has set are *weird*, and the news about her health … It's a lot to process. But if you don't want to join a gym, then don't.'

Mel sighed. 'I should go back in, apologise to Joe.'

'I can talk to him. You want me to grab my stuff? We could get some food?'

'No.' Mel shook her head. 'You go do your workout.'

'I can give you a lift home.'

'Really, it's fine. I'll get an Uber.' What was another ten dollars on her credit card? She'd just saved a small fortune by avoiding a gym membership, hadn't she?

'See you tomorrow night then?'

'Sure. Oh wait, no. Jess is dragging me to an all-singles Prosecco and Paint Night.'

'Oh.' Corey's face dropped and Mel's heart nearly burst.

'It's for her task. We promised we'd help each other.'

'Right.' Corey looked relieved. 'Because she's got to … What was it? Make a commitment for three months?'

'Her task is *way* more fun than mine,' Mel joked, and her face flushed.

Corey nodded, but his smile looked forced.

Is he jealous?

'I'll call you then,' he said as he made his way back inside.

'I'm sorry … about all this.'

Corey glanced back at her with gentle eyes. 'Don't be.'

As Mel ordered an Uber to take her home, she couldn't shake the dread that had sat in her gut since Jacki had told them her news. Everything was about to change, and there was nothing she could do to stop it.

5

Jess

'Do you like it? I think my blue hair really makes my eyes pop.' Jess stood back to examine her work. She loved painting, especially with acrylics, although she hadn't done much since she'd left uni. She loved to draw too, and always carried a sketch pad in her bag just in case she saw something that inspired her.

'Yeah, it's stunning. And, er, this is my number. If you want it.' A guy wearing a pale-pink Billabong singlet, boardshorts and yellow thongs handed Jess a dog-eared business card which, like his T-shirt, was stained with God-only-knows what.

Andy's Lawn Mowing – I mow, so you don't have to.

Jess shuddered. As the owner of a small graphic design business, Innovative Design, her speciality was company branding. Innovative Design was about creating an identity that attracted customers, and, right now, Andy wasn't even selling himself.

The aim of the Prosecco and Paint evening was to produce a self-portrait in the style of Picasso while drinking bottomless glasses of – you guessed it – prosecco. All the easels in the studio had been positioned in a circle, making it easy to check out the other participants while working on your own creation.

Naturally, flirtatious glances and sexual chemistry darted across the room like circular string art, and after an hour and a half of painting, thirty or so singles ditched their palettes for some full-on social mixing.

The host suggested that any participants interested in seeing one another after tonight should either hand out business cards or write their name and phone number on the squares of blank paper she handed out. That way, there was no pressure to enter someone's details into your phone. Jess liked it. It was old-school.

As Andy made his way back over to his friend, Mel returned from the bathroom. Spotting the business card, she asked, 'Isn't that the third number you've got tonight?'

'It's from the guy who looks like he's just stepped off the beach.' Jess nodded in Andy's direction.

'Hmm, not bad.'

'Here, you can have it.' Jess handed her the card.

'Ew, I don't want your cast-offs.'

'Really, I don't mind.'

'Jeez, if he's not good enough for you, then he's not good enough for me. Besides, I'm not here to partner up. I've got my own task to worry about.' Mel stared at her painting. 'I don't think I should have painted my lips green.'

Jess had been thinking the same thing. 'It looks weird, but in a good way. I like it.'

'Really?'

'Really.' Jess hoped she believed her. She'd always tried to be sensitive to Mel's feelings, but she was so hard to read. One minute she'd tear up because Jacki had given someone a compliment or admired their new boots, the next she'd be making a joke about it.

Comparisons between siblings were inevitable, but these didn't bother Jess. She figured a dash of competitiveness was healthy, in most cases. For example, Isla had always had one up on Jess when it came to her business achievements, but that just helped fuel her own work ethic. Rose was well ahead of her in the family department, but that just made Jess excited about having a family of her own one day. And on the flip side, Isla and Rose had both commented on how freeing Jess's independent lifestyle must be, and expressed their own desire for a few days where no one made any demands of them.

But when it came to Mel, things were different.

Anything to do with money was a sore spot for her sister, and Jess had learnt to avoid telling her about anything good happening in her life, like the holiday she'd booked or the new bag she'd bought, because these declarations were always met with a swift change of topic or a thin smile. If she ever offered to help her out, Mel would get irritated and insist her financial situation was under control, but it was clear the transition from Burberry to Big W had been brutal.

Jess glanced around the studio in search of a potential three-month lover. Toby, a restaurant owner from Wynnum who'd got chatting with her while she'd painted, raised an eyebrow at her over his glass of prosecco. Jess smiled. You couldn't miss Toby's electric-blue shirt.

Although this all-single event was more relaxed than the speed-dating sessions she'd been to in the past, it was still awkward and slightly nauseating. A room full of people eyeing each other up and making judgements wasn't a particularly pleasant experience.

'Let's get a refill,' she said, dragging Mel to the drinks table where there were bottles of prosecco chilling in buckets of ice and platters of spring rolls, mini pies and bowls of chips. Jess sighed at the lacklustre offering. Still, at thirty-five dollars a ticket, what had she expected?

Someone tapped Jess's shoulder and she turned to find a surprisingly handsome face. 'Sorry, are you two hooking up or ...?' he asked Mel. 'Because, before you make any decisions, I'd like to give you this.'

Mel went to take the card from him, but he wouldn't let go. Mel gave a little tug and the guy held it tight.

'Er, this is awkward ... It's actually for you,' he said, pulling it from Mel's grip and handing it to Jess.

'Of course.' Mel shook her head and waved it off. 'No worries.'

Jess took the card and, again, an uneasiness festered between her and Mel. No one had given Mel their number, and although she insisted she wasn't fussed, Jess knew that getting at least one phone number would do her confidence the world of good.

'I'm Pete Brookes,' the guy said, running his hand through his dark curly hair.

'Jess Freeman.' Jess never told anyone she was a Turner, even though her surname was double-barrelled. Jess wanted to be liked – or loved – for who she was, not who her family were.

Pete beamed, exposing a mouthful of perfectly straight white teeth. 'You should give me a call,' he said, bouncing from one foot to another. 'I like fishing. Caught me some decent-sized barra this morning. I could catch you some for breakfast if you ask nicely.' Pete winked and nudged her with his elbow. 'You fish?'

Jess swallowed and took a step back. 'No.'

'Oh. That's a shame.' Pete frowned and they stood in silence.

'Excuse us for one moment.' Jess grabbed Mel's arm and walked her back towards their easels. 'Let's just go,' she whispered. 'I'm not going to meet anyone here.' After Pete's exchange, all she wanted was a long hot shower. 'I hate these kinds of set-ups. They're not natural.'

'Let's take a minute to assess. Show me all the numbers you've been given tonight.'

'Why?' Jess was confused.

'Just do it.'

Jess pulled a handful of business cards out of her pocket.

'*Shit!* When did you get all of these?' Mel held up one card at a time. 'What about this guy, Craig?'

Jess looked about her and lowered her voice. 'Too old.'

'Andy?'

'Beachwear, at an *evening* function?'

'Harsh, but okay.' Mel held up another. 'Pete?'

'Seriously?' Jess glanced back at him. He was still bouncing on his toes and staring at her with an unnerving smile.

Mel held up more cards.

'*He* was way too drunk. *He* wore too much cheap cologne. And Toby? He was friendly enough, but there was no physical attraction.'

'Is he the guy in the bright blue shirt?'

Jess nodded and Mel pocketed his number for herself.

'Stop it!' Jess laughed, and Mel continued with the cards.

'*He* eyed up other women while talking to me. Can't remember who that one was, and I've no idea whose card that is either.'

'Jess!'

'Well, there's too many of them to remember.'

Mel folded her arms. 'So, the struggle is real?'

'Hey, if I can't remember them, I think that tells me everything I need to know.'

'And did you give your number to anyone?'

Jess winced and rubbed the back of her neck.

'So, now what?' asked Mel.

'We do the only thing we can. We take our Picasso masterpieces and get Chinese take-away on the way home.'

6

Rose

The librarian in charge of organising the Saturday morning workshop, 'An Introduction to Writing Children's Picture Books', sat at the back of Room 1 on the library's second floor. Every now and then, she appeared beside Rose and fussed over baby Bethany, who cooed and dribbled as her wide eyes flitted between the fluorescent lighting overhead and the brightly coloured Lamaze cube that hung from the hood of the stroller.

Rose had found the workshop in the resources folder Helen had given her, and although she had a hundred and one other jobs that needed attending to at home, she'd booked herself a spot. The idea was to get her task completed as quickly as possible.

Rose's plan that morning had been to leave Bethany at home, but Tom had been having some technical difficulties uploading his latest video, and his subscribers were eagerly awaiting the new review. The workshop only ran for two hours, so Rose said she'd take Bethany with her and crossed her fingers they'd be welcome; if not, she'd treat herself and go for a stroll along the beaches at Raby Bay to try and clear her head. Her sleeping had got worse since she'd found out Jacki was dying and Rose's baby brain had now become a dense fog that made the simplest of tasks feel impossible.

After Richard had died, Rose had eventually got used to being a single mum. She'd fallen into a simple routine with Harrison and Taylor, which had been comforting after having their world turned upside down. Other than seeing other parents at the kids' sporting activities, Rose had done everything she could to make her world as small as possible. The fewer encounters she had with other people, the easier it was to cope with daily life.

But a year ago one of the mums from school had persuaded Rose to go out for dinner in the city with some of the others. She'd told Rose it would do her good, and had promised there'd only be four of them going. But when Rose had arrived at the bar in Fortitude Valley, nearly every mum in Harrison's year was there, and so Rose's quiet dinner in the city had turned into a pub crawl with no food in sight.

It was at the second bar that Rose met Tom. He was tall and cute, and his carefree attitude and optimism were a breath of fresh air. He clearly had no idea how cruel the world could be, and Rose had enjoyed forgetting about her responsibilities for one night. She'd felt like she was twenty again, without a care in the world, and after one too many margaritas, they went back to his apartment. She'd had a great night, but when he'd called the next day to ask if he could see her again, she'd explained she wasn't ready to start dating.

Eight weeks later, Rose held a positive pregnancy test in her hand.

After the initial shock, both she and Tom had grown excited about having a child together. While dating Tom during her pregnancy, she had tried to take things slow, but instead, it had turned into a whirlwind romance, and Rose had found herself falling hard. Four and a half months ago, a month before her due date, Rose had bitten the bullet, deciding to listen to her heart instead of her head for once.

One evening, she'd sat Harrison and Taylor down and asked them whether they'd like Tom to live with them. To her surprise, they'd looked at each other and grinned. She'd then spent the next hour answering their questions and discussing logistics. When she finally plucked up the courage to ask Tom, he was both surprised and delighted.

Harrison and Taylor loved him. They thought it was cool that their mum was dating a famous YouTuber, and Rose had been surprised to learn he had millions of subscribers and big-name sponsors. She'd been even more taken aback when Tom was recognised by loads of kids, *and their parents*, at Harrison's birthday party.

In the library, Emily Grant tugged at Bethany's tiny feet. 'Aw, you don't even know she's here.' The beloved Australian author, who had written several best-selling children's picture books, was teaching today's workshop.

'Who's a good girl, eh?' said Emily. Bethany kicked her arms and legs and blew small bubbles of spit. 'Who has a good mummy?'

Rose forced a smile in an attempt to conceal her exhaustion and frayed nerves. She was relieved Bethany had been content for the last hour. It was nothing short of a miracle, given that she'd spent the previous forty-eight hours wanting to be continuously held. Every time Rose had placed her in her car seat, crib or rocker, Bethany had cried and refused to settle. It was as if she'd picked up on Rose's shock and anger at Jacki's prognosis.

Hearing Emily say she was a good mummy, even though they'd only met an hour ago, made Rose feel seen amid the chaos that was her life. Here in Room 1, surrounded by peers who shared her dream of writing for children, she could breathe. Shifting her focus onto herself for the first time in months was liberating.

On the short drive to the library, Rose had cursed her mother. Her dreams were being forced upon her, and now they were tainted by Jacki's need for control.

It was true that Rose loved to write. She'd even won a few short story competitions before Harrison was born, and had one story published in an anthology. And Rose had always wanted to write a children's picture book. But so what if she'd put her dreams on hold when Harrison came along? What her mother should have known – *would* have known, if she'd played an active role in raising her own kids – was that having children changed everything. Everything revolved around them and *their* needs. This was something Jacki would never understand. Jacki didn't know *how* to be a mum.

When Rose was a kid, her mother would suddenly return after being away for weeks at a time and would barely even acknowledge her. When Jacki did speak to her, she only ever asked Rose yes/no questions, and even then she didn't seem particularly interested in her reply. Rose never got to have long conversations with her.

After giving birth to Taylor, Rose had revived her dream of writing. She had files and files of Word documents filled with short-story ideas and rough first drafts. But then Richard got sick. And amid hospital appointments, looking after the kids and caring for her dying husband, Rose's dreams had seemed like a ridiculous indulgence. Her family came first, always.

A couple of nights ago, she'd told Harrison and Taylor their grandma was sick. The news had been met with an eerie silence. Rose had flashbacks to Richard in his final days and could only imagine what memories Harrison and Taylor were thinking of. But although they seemed sad at this news, the fact that they hadn't seen Jacki in the last three years seemed to have softened the blow a little. When Rose had finished answering their questions as honestly as she could, she declared a movie night in the living room. This always involved snuggling down under doonas dragged in from their bedrooms, sipping hot chocolate with extra marshmallows, and eating popcorn drenched in butter. Rose just wanted all of them to be together, just in case they needed her ... or in case she needed them.

Standing at the front of the class, Emily Grant adjusted her red-framed glasses, which perfectly matched her red and white polka-dot dress and bright red lipstick. 'Okay, everyone, we'll spend five minutes brainstorming. I want ideas for characters, setting, and inciting incidents. Let's get those creative juices flowing.'

Bethany cooed in the stroller next to Rose and her eyelids grew heavy. Rose breathed a sigh of relief. If Bethany napped, she'd be able to finish the workshop uninterrupted.

Rose began scribbling notes in one of Harrison's unused schoolbooks, and to her surprise, ideas came thick and fast. It was like the floodgates of her mind had been opened at last.

Content that her students were on task, Emily approached the stroller and grinned widely at Bethany, baring her whiter than normal teeth. Rose could see a smudge of red lipstick on her bottom veneers.

Rose stopped writing and pulled her cheeks into a strained smile. 'It's her nap time.'

Emily ignored her and covered her face with her hands. 'Peepo,' she said, uncovering her face.

Bethany's eyes welled and her bottom lip quivered.

'Oops,' said Emily. 'Who's a grumpy bumpy?' She covered her face again and repeated the childish game. 'Peepo!'

Rose glared at Emily. 'Really, she's due a nap.'

'Oh, I can hold her if you like?'

'No, that's okay. She'll fall asleep in a minute.'

Emily unbuckled Bethany and pulled her out of her stroller. *What the fiddlesticks?!*

'She just wants to see what's going on, don't you?'

What was wrong with this woman? Rose stood up. 'I said no!'

The room went silent. Everyone stopped writing and all eyes locked on Rose.

Emily swallowed, then smiled. 'Come on now, give yourself a break … *Rose*,' she said, reading the handwritten name tag stuck to Rose's blouse. 'You deserve it. I've had two children myself, although they have their own kids now.'

A loud noise erupted from Bethany's nappy and Emily chuckled. 'I heard that botty burp, little miss. Better out than in.'

'Here,' said Rose. 'I'll take her just in case she—'

Bethany's nappy roared, and a grey-haired gentleman on the other side of the room groaned in disgust.

'Give her to me,' said Rose through her teeth.

'Don't worry, it's only a dirty—' Vomit spewed out of Bethany like a raging river, covering Emily. Milk-coloured sick dripped down her chin and ran down the front of her dress.

Rose gasped, along with the rest of the class.

Another burp erupted from Bethany's nappy, releasing a stench stronger than rotting sewage. Emily held her at arm's length as a mustard-coloured liquid seeped through the back of her yellow onesie.

The librarian who sat at the back of the room gagged at the smell.

Rose grabbed hold of her daughter, glaring at Emily. 'I told you not to pick her up!'

The librarian handed Rose a key, one hand pinching her nose. 'Follow the corridor to the far end. The bathroom's on your right.'

A raging heat rushed through Rose, and she wished the ground would swallow her whole. She grabbed her nappy bag and hurried to the bathroom, leaving the librarian trying to wipe the vomit off Emily with a tissue.

Rose pulled down the change table in the women's toilets. She didn't know where to start. Bethany was saturated. Rose peeled off the onesie and her head jolted back. *Michelin mayhem!* She held her breath and tried to focus on the task at hand. *Is there a back way out of this place?*

Bethany whimpered.

'Shh, it's okay.' *Bloody technical difficulties! Bloody cancer! Bloody authors who think they know best!*

Fifteen minutes later, Rose emerged from the bathroom holding a clean, gargling Bethany, who was now naked and nappyless except for a muslin wrap tied around her lower half, and Rose's cardigan draped over her. With all the stress of the last couple of weeks, Rose had forgotten to restock the change bag with nappies and spare clothes. *Mother of the flippin' year!*

She paused outside Room 1, gathering her courage, but when she went back in, the room was empty save for the overpowering stench that still permeated the room. She kissed Bethany's warm cheek as she placed her in her stroller and couldn't help but smile as her daughter gurgled contentedly, oblivious to the trouble she'd caused.

As Rose packed away her notebook and pen, a fellow writer opened the door. The sticky label on her T-shirt read 'Sarah'. 'We're out here,' she said, clearly trying to hold her breath.

The workshop participants were now sitting on chairs in the library's non-fiction section. Some of the other aspiring writers smiled sympathetically at Rose, but there was no sign of Emily or the librarian.

The grey-haired gentleman's eyes widened at the sight of Bethany and then scowled at Rose. 'Emily had to go home. The poor woman was soaked through and the smell was making her feel unwell.'

'I told her not to pick Bethany up,' said Rose, annoyed that she had to defend herself.

The old man scoffed. 'Maybe next time you should get a babysitter, hmm?'

Rose bit her tongue and glanced down at Bethany, who was now sleeping soundly.

'Ignore him,' said Sarah, and the old man tutted and carried on writing. 'The librarian is making copies of Emily's notes so she can finish the workshop, so it's all good.' She gave Rose a reassuring smile.

Rose was sure she heard the grey-haired guy grunt.

'You heard me tell Emily not to pick her up, right?' asked Rose, trying not to cry.

'I did. We *all* did.' Sarah glared at the miserable old man.

Rose tried to smile, but she was too exhausted and humiliated to put on a brave face. 'You know what, I think I might just head home.'

Sarah gave her a sympathetic look. 'Are you sure?'

Rose nodded.

As Sarah walked back to her seat, the old man grumbled, 'Perhaps that's for the best.'

Rose stepped towards the elevator, then stopped and turned back to the old man. 'If you can't deal with the reality of kids, maybe a career in children's picture book writing isn't for you.'

The old man gasped, and Rose's face burned, but when she glanced over to Sarah, she grinned and winked at her.

7

Jacki

Jacki lay in her darkened bedroom and tried to sleep, but nausea, brought on by her last round of chemo, made it impossible. Finally, admitting defeat, she sat up and took a sip of the cooled ginger tea Helen had made for her. But instead of easing her sickness, it made her feel worse. Jacki had come to associate the spiced root with her condition, and she was sure she'd never be able to stomach anything with ginger in it again.

There was a light knock on her bedroom door and a small voice called from the hallway, 'Mum?'

Shit! Jacki squinted at the clock on her bedside table. It had just turned noon. She hadn't been expecting a visitor. 'Just a minute.'

Jacki combed her hands through her limp hair and was grateful that her blinds were still drawn. The dim light would at least partially hide her pale face. She shuffled over to her walk-in wardrobe and pulled a gold sequined dress off its hanger. Next, she grabbed a pair of black Jimmy Choos and threw both of them onto the floor next to her bed.

The door opened slightly. 'Mum?'

Please don't let it be Rose ... or Mel ... or Isla.

'It's me, Jess. Can I come in?'

Relief rushed through Jacki as she climbed back into bed. She was too sick to argue with Rose, or listen to Mel moaning, or give business advice to Isla.

'Come in,' said Jacki.

Jess tiptoed into the room and sat on the edge of the bed. 'Are you okay?'

'What time is it?'

'Ten past twelve.'

Jacki sat up as though just waking. 'I didn't get in till the early hours. I think I may have had a little too much to drink.'

'Helen said you went to a dinner party. Shouldn't you be resting?'

'I've never let anything stop me from having a good time before. I don't see why I should let dying slow me down.' Jacki pressed her lips together and fought the urge to throw up. 'What are you doing here?'

Jess scanned the room and spotted the gold dress lying on the handmade Persian rug. 'I'm worried about you. I came to see if you're okay, if there's anything I can do.'

'There's no need to fuss over me. I'm fine.' Jess was the most caring of her four daughters, and sometimes Jacki wished she could have been more nurturing towards her, but motherhood had only suited Jacki from afar. She'd loved showering her girls with gifts when they were younger, and she loved passing her business knowledge onto Isla. But Jacki had hated the baby stage, toddler stage, adolescent stage and, even now, she struggled to understand the choices her daughters made as adults. They always seemed to have something to complain about but never any plan to help themselves. It was only Isla who was focused and driven enough to pursue the finer things in life. Isla wanted to build a legacy, but even Jacki could see she had no idea who she was without her expensive possessions and the Turner name.

There was no denying that Jacki struggled to connect with her daughters, and perhaps after Peter died she should have made more of an effort to be with her kids. She had regrets about not spending enough time with them, but she'd been grieving too, and the only way she could deal with the loss of her husband was to throw everything into achieving his dreams for the Turner empire. At work, Jacki was confident and capable, but at home she found the role of being a mother confronting. She could do nothing right. Plus, it wasn't as if she'd left her daughters to fend for themselves. They had Helen, who was always so much better at the emotional stuff than she was.

'I didn't expect to find you hungover after partying all night,' said Jess.

'It was a spontaneous get-together, all very last minute.'

Jess tucked her hands into the sleeves of her oversized jumper. 'Do your friends know you're sick?'

'I have no intention of discussing my health with any of them. I'm no different from anyone else, we're all on borrowed time. I just have a better idea of when mine will be up.'

Jess's lip quivered.

'Come on now.' Jacki shut her eyes in a bid to stop the room from spinning. Trying to deal with her failing body was bad enough without having to be an emotional support for others. Jacki patted Jess's knee. 'There's no need for tears.'

Jess sniffed. 'Crying is a normal reaction to finding out your mum is dying.'

'You're just like your father. *He's* a sensitive man.'

'I take it you haven't told him either?'

'We haven't spoken in months.' Jacki sat up and took another sip of ginger tea. 'Now that you're a grown woman, I don't speak to him as often as—'

'As often as you'd like to?'

Jacki could hear the hope in Jess's voice. Even after all this time, she knew Jess secretly wished her parents would get together permanently.

Jacki shook her head. 'I don't speak to him as often as I *used to*.'

Jess bounced her knee. 'He asks after you every time I call him. He cares about you, Mum. A lot.'

Jacki leaned back against the headboard and the nausea subsided for a moment. 'We were only together for three months, and that was thirty years ago.'

It was a business trip to Cairns that had led to her chance encounter with Darryl. She'd been in meetings all day with project managers, discussing the design of her new hotel and casino. Later that evening, she'd been sitting at a bar in her designer pantsuit and Darryl had made some comment about her not being a local. He'd just finished a day's hard labour, and his dark hair had still been wet from his shower. He'd smelt of soap and cheap cologne. His khaki shorts and white T-shirt weren't designer, or even stylish, but they were clean and pressed, and as Darryl had paid for his beer she'd noticed his rough, calloused hands. The chemistry between them had been instant.

She'd have sworn Darryl wasn't her type, but by the time her glass was empty, his endearing smile and charm had won her over. He was tall and robust, and his strong physique and broad shoulders had been chiselled out of hard manual labour instead of the local gym. In contrast, Jacki was a successful businesswoman from the city, and a widow with three daughters. But their chance meeting had taught Jacki that the phrase 'opposites attract' had an element of truth to it. And so, Jacki's three-night stay had turned into a three-month winter fling that resulted in Jessica.

For the last three decades, her relationship with Darryl had consisted of constant bickering, raging rows and a series of highly passionate, short-lived affairs. Deep down, she knew he adored her, but they were just too different to make it work. Although he was successful in business, he despised suits, boardrooms and air-conditioning. Darryl was happiest with his hands in the dirt and a sky full of stars above him, while Jacki lived for the thrill of luxury under neon city lights. Though their paths crossed every now and then, they were always heading in different directions.

'Why can't you both just admit how you feel about each other?' asked Jess.

'Your dad is determined to stay up there, and I need the freedom to go wherever I'm needed. We'll never change, and that's all there is to it.'

Jess sighed.

When Jess was born, Darryl had moved to the Gold Coast to be with them, but he'd quickly become bored and irritated by the people Jacki surrounded herself with. He didn't care for what he called their shallow, materialistic views, and the longer he stayed, the more he itched to be back on the land. When he'd decided to go back, it had been clear that Jess should stay with Jacki, where she could grow up with her sisters under Helen's care.

'I need to freshen up.' Jacki pulled back the bedsheets and groaned as she made her way through the grand walk-in robe and into her bathroom. She closed the door and turned on the shower. Steam filled the bathroom, and the hot water on her skin made her feel a little better. When she got out, she found Jess standing at her dresser, reading the labels on her prescription bottles.

'There are so many,' said Jess. 'I don't think you should be drinking at all if you're taking these, Mum.'

'Is there any pain relief there?' asked Jacki, pulling on a fluffy white bathrobe.

'Do you have to take *all* of these?'

Jacki towel-dried her hair then ran a brush through it, checking to see if any came out. It was clear. She was lucky. So far, she'd had no hair loss. 'I should rattle with all the pills I have to take.'

'Is there really nothing anyone can do?'

Jacki stared at the bottles with their long unpronounceable names and neatly printed directions. 'They've done everything they can. They found spots of cancer all over the place.'

Jess broke down. 'But what will I do without you?'

Jacki raised her chin as her eyes prickled, and she patted Jess's arm. 'There's nothing to be sad about. I've lived a great life; I've got things most people only ever dream of having.' Jacki admired the designer clothes, bags and shoes in her wardrobe. 'I've worked hard, and look what I've accomplished.'

Jess stared at her. 'Why are you speaking like this? There's still so much for you to do. So much time to spend with us, and with your grandkids.'

'Don't worry, I'm not just going to lie down and die. There's some fight left in this old bird yet.' Jacki smiled, but every cell in her body told her it was game over. She was tired, more tired than she'd ever been. 'Speaking of grandchildren,' said Jacki, 'do you think Rose will ever forgive me? I'd love to see those kids. I still haven't met Bethany.'

'I think there's a chance she'll always be mad at you. She's come around to completing the terms though. She's just got a lot on, you know?'

'Don't we all?'

'Things would be much better if you put an end to these terms, Mum. No one likes them.'

'I didn't set them because I thought they'd be fun. I want you girls to earn your inheritance. I want you to know what it feels like to succeed.'

'I don't need a boyfriend to be successful.'

'*I* know that. The objective is to force you to break down this wall you've built around yourself. You say you want a relationship, but you're clearly afraid to commit. I'm just giving you the push you need. You'll thank me for it later. Believe me, I want you girls to have my money. I want you to succeed, and nothing screams success louder than being in control of your own destiny. To build something from scratch, from pure grit and determination, and then to see it to fruition, *that's* success.' Jacki walked back into the bedroom, tucked her damp hair behind her ears and opened her remote-controlled blinds. Daylight burst into the room, and she squinted down to the pool area and out to the helipad. 'Take a good look around. I have everything I could ever want, need or desire. It's the best feeling in the world.' She tried to smile, but the nausea was back. She sat on the edge of her bed and Jess took a seat next to her. 'I got my work ethic from my parents. My dad worked at the bank and my mum ran our house like a well-oiled machine. They may not have had a lot of money, but they were proud of what they did have and worked their fingers to the bone. When I was a little girl, I didn't know what I wanted to be when I grew up. All I knew was that I wanted to be in charge. It took years in this business for me to be taken seriously because I was a woman, but eventually I turned heads when I walked into a room, not because I was attractive, but because I was a take-no-shit ball-breaker who demanded the goddamn respect I deserved.'

'Go, Mum. You showed them.'

Jacki smiled at Jess and patted her on the leg. 'I took a lot of shit and pissed off a lot of people to get where I am today. It was pretty brutal at times, but I'd like to think I've paved the way for other women in this industry.' Jacki took another sip of tea. 'To be honest, when you girls left home and went out into the real world, I assumed you'd all be hungry for what I had. I thought you'd be begging for positions within the business, but only Isla showed any real interest. So, I let you all go about your lives and make your own way, but deep down, I still expected you to come knocking.'

'Why didn't you say anything?'

'Because I wanted you to want it like I did. I assumed that by the time my days were done, you'd all be working for me.'

Jacki and Peter had started their business by buying one hotel on the Gold Coast with the money Peter's dad had left him when he'd died. They made all the rookie mistakes and ironed out all the kinks in those first few years. They learned where you could and couldn't cut corners, figured out their guests' needs and wants, and always tried to go above and beyond. They paid their employees well, but they expected more, too. Jacki learned the importance of good communication with her staff, regular incentives, and recognition for those who went the extra mile. Nowadays, hospitality professionals all wanted to work at Turner Hotels and Casinos. If they were lucky enough to become a Turner employee, they showed their loyalty by staying for many years, and Jacki made sure they were rewarded for that too.

It quickly became apparent to Jacki and Peter that people with money were willing to spend it on high-end luxury stays. It was as if their money was burning a hole in their pocket. They were hungry for the best, so that's what Jacki and Peter gave them, and, over time, word got around that the Turner Hotel on the Gold Coast was *the* place to stay. That's when they began building the Turner empire. It was hard work, but Jacki loved it, and when Peter died she vowed to continue building their legacy. Now, guests flew from around the globe just to stay in their hotels.

Jacki had come to regret not giving her daughters positions within the business. With time quickly running out, there were now only two options for her to take. If she was to leave her vast fortune to her daughters, she had to know, without a doubt, that between them they had the skills needed to thrive. She didn't want them to become like her wealthy friends' adult children: entitled brats who hadn't worked a day in their lives. At the very least, each of her girls had been motivated enough to go to university and, over the years, had done far more than an honest day's work. Kicking them out of home might have seemed harsh in the beginning, but now they understood the value of money, and Jacki was certain they'd never take expensive luxuries for granted again.

The terms of inheritance were Jacki's way of seeing if her daughters' weaknesses could be turned into strengths. For Rose, the experience of seeking publication would teach her to accept that not everyone saw things the way she did. Some of her story ideas would get picked up, and others wouldn't, and when rejection struck she'd have to learn to dust herself off and try again. In life, as in business, you had to keep moving forward.

Choosing the marathon for Mel's task was a no-brainer. If she stuck up for herself the way she stuck up for those kids she cared for, Mel would be a force to be reckoned with. But building self-esteem meant taking a chance on yourself when it felt impossible. It happened in business all the time. Being willing to take risks meant you'd be able to position yourself ahead of the competition.

And it was clear Jess had a good work ethic, but she was picking and choosing who she wanted to work with based on the certainty that the outcome would be positive. It was the only way she would commit to a client. But with millions of dollars on the line, strong leaders had to be able to push through the turmoil that came with the unknown. Even when business relationships were rocky, both parties had to try and make it work for the sake of the overall benefits. That's what it meant to commit. No relationship was perfect, but that didn't mean it couldn't work. This was a lesson Jess needed to learn.

And while Isla's experience and enthusiasm would take her far, her lack of compassion was problematic. She needed to be reminded that people have feelings, particularly her sisters. She couldn't afford to lose them. And while profit in business was obviously a priority, that went hand in hand with being a good employer and providing good customer service. That was what the Turner empire prided itself on.

If Jacki's daughters successfully completed the terms, then she'd know, for sure, that they had what it took to ensure that the Turner name had a bright future.

If, on the other hand, they failed, then Jacki would use her fortune to help those who had no voice, or choice, in their living conditions. Aussie Animal Rescue was a deserving cause that Peter had made considerable anonymous donations to when he was alive. It was what Peter would have wanted.

Either way, Jacki and Peter's legacy would make a difference.

From the day they'd first met at a bowling alley with friends, they'd been on the same team and, in business and marriage, they'd been partners. Jacki was the one who came up with the ideas for how to improve and grow their business, while Peter made sure they were executed.

He'd been so handsome, and Mel was the spitting image of him. She was such a beauty, although Jacki had never told her that. Beauty had its advantages, but it faded with time, so couldn't be relied on. Jacki believed true beauty came from authenticity and confidence. You could look like a donkey's backside, but if you owned your gifts and talents, and backed yourself, that would make you the most attractive person in the room.

Peter had also been a kind man. He'd get fired up if he could see that someone wasn't doing their job properly, but he also gave people the benefit of the doubt, something Jacki had always struggled to do. He was generous with his time and was a mentor to the employees he thought needed a little extra guidance. This, he said, was his duty, his way to pay it forward.

Oh, how she missed his kind face. She couldn't recall how many times she'd longed for one more hug or one more kiss from him. She'd give up everything she owned to experience that again.

'Did you enjoy my grand entrance the other night?' Jacki asked Jess, shaking herself out of her reverie. 'Remember, life is about making as many dramatic entrances as possible.'

Jess smirked. 'You did look like a rock star stepping out of the helicopter. And that pilot … I'll be needing his number.'

Jacki laughed.

'But don't you think …' Jess trailed off.

'Don't I think what?' Jacki fixed her with her gaze.

'Isn't owning a helicopter bad for the environment? You really should be thinking about your carbon footprint.'

Jacki leaned against Jess. 'I suppose you're right. If you earn your inheritance, you should definitely sell it. Now come on, I need to get dressed. I've got work to do. I've slept in long enough as it is, and time is money. On your way out, can you ask Helen if she can bring me some pain relief? Oh, and ask her about the tickets I got for you and your sisters. You can thank me next time.'

Jess kissed Jacki's cheek. 'Promise you'll call me if you need anything?'

'I promise.' Jacki walked back into her wardrobe and pulled out a green silk blouse and pencil skirt.

Jess watched as she began to dress. 'Well, if you're sure.'

'I'm sure.'

Jacki carried on dressing until she heard Jess go downstairs, then she took off her clothes and climbed back into bed. Everything ached.

A few minutes later, Helen appeared at her side with tablets and a glass of water.

'Has she gone?' asked Jacki.

'Just left. I gave her the festival tickets.'

'Good.' Exhausted, Jacki swallowed the tablets then rested her head on her pillow. 'You told Jess I went out for dinner. Thank you. I know you abhor lying.'

Helen closed the blinds then tucked the bedsheets around Jacki. 'I can hardly deny a dying woman's wishes now, can I?'

'No, I suppose you can't.'

'Are you sure setting these terms of inheritance is the right call?'

'Not you too. What did Jess say?'

'That none of them are very happy.'

'Hmm. Well, like I told you, I need to see if they've got what it takes.'

'It's not all about the money though, is it?'

'They need the distraction. It's best that they don't dwell. If they're kept busy, then …'

'Then what?'

'You remember how devastated they were when Peter died. I know they were only young, but … I'll never forget that. He was the soul of the family and there was nothing I could do to protect them from that pain. Maybe this time I can.'

'You're their mum and you're dying. That will hurt, and there's nothing you can do to change that.'

'Maybe not, but if I can make it hurt a little less …'

'You're a complicated woman, Jacki Turner, but you've got a big heart.' Helen squeezed Jacki's hand as Jacki sighed heavily with fatigue and closed her eyes.

8

Jess

Jess stuck small gold glitter stars above her eyebrows at a vanity station in one of the VIP marquees at the Bay Bliss Music Festival, and silently gave thanks to her mother for the tickets. Deep, throbbing bass from one of the stages nearby pulsed with a steady thrum, reverberating between partygoers hell-bent on having a good time. The annual festival brought thousands of young travellers to Byron Bay each year. They came from afar to watch their favourite headliners perform, drink from dawn till dusk, and upload filtered photos to Instagram.

Isla scowled as she watched two women in their early twenties, dressed in high-waisted short shorts, attempt the perfect selfie. 'Those two have spent the last ten minutes trying to stick their butts and lips out as far as they can,' she said.

'Stop being mean. They're just having a good time.'

Isla flinched at the sight of a portly guy wearing nothing but boxers and a cowboy hat. 'Tell me again, what makes you think you're going to meet *Mr Right* here?'

'Let me worry about that. Just try to have a good time, okay?' Jess was determined to have some fun with her sisters, and bumping into Mr Right would be a much-needed bonus. The sooner she got on with her task the better. She didn't want to be trying to focus on a new relationship when her mum was nearing the end of her life. The sooner she could get her task over and done with, the better.

Rose returned from the ladies' room and shook water from her hands. Catching sight of her reflection in the mirror, she flattened her loose hair with her palm and glared at a young twenty-something who wore a black transparent dress over minimal underwear. 'They're all so young … and naked. Don't they know it's winter? They'll catch their death.' Rose shivered and buttoned up her denim jacket, keeping her laminated VIP pass in easy view.

'Relax,' Jess said to Rose. 'You sound like their mother.'

'Well, we're at least twenty years too old for this.' Isla frowned.

'Speak for yourself.' Jess wiped bright red lipstick from the corner of her mouth and adjusted her butterfly-sleeve crop top. 'I know loads of people who'd kill for these passes.'

Rose rubbed her breast with the palm of her hand. 'Why is it when you're rich, you get stuff for free, and when you're not, you have to pay for everything? It's all backwards.'

'Do you need to express?' Isla asked Rose.

'I'm good for a bit. I hope Tom's okay with Bethany. I've left him with plenty of breast milk. Maybe I should text him again.'

'He was fine an hour ago when you spoke to him. I'm sure he's still okay,' said Jess. 'Let's go find Mel. She texted to say she's in the Cloud Nine Craft Tent.'

'Craft tent?' said Isla. 'This place is like a kindergarten nightmare. Next thing you know, they'll have dress-ups.'

'Pretty close.' Jess nudged Isla and nodded towards the bar, where three women with long turquoise wigs wore matching unicorn headbands.

Outside the marquee, the sky was clear and a gentle breeze chilled the air. The smell of burgers and hot chips wafted across a field filled with food vendors, making Jess hungry.

They found Mel standing at a table filled with card, glitter and glue. 'Hey, girls,' said Mel. 'Look what I made for you.' She held out four badges. Written on each of them in metallic ink were the words *Mum's Rules Suck*. 'I personalised them,' she said. 'See, I've got stick people running on mine, and that's my medal for finishing the marathon. I drew a book for Rose, and I wrote *bestseller* because it will be. Jess, you need to find a man so—'

'You drew stick men with giant—'

'Dicks!' Mel's voice boomed and a group of guys turned to look, but Mel didn't notice. 'And at the top, I wrote, *Commitment Makers Only!* We know you can get a man; our mission is to find one you can stick with.'

Jess laughed.

'And for you, Isla—'

'Really, I don't need one.'

Mel handed the badge to her sister. 'Yours has lots of question marks, and I wrote, *Who Am I?*' Mel beamed with pride. 'I added glitter too.'

Isla smiled thinly.

'We've all got to wear them,' said Jess as she pinned her badge to her crop top.

'I'm wearing a nine-hundred-dollar camisole,' said Isla. 'I'm not going to put a hole in it.'

Jess rolled her eyes. 'Pin it on the loop of your jeans then. We're all in this together, so we should all wear them.'

Isla glared at Jess. 'Fine.'

'Have you made a start on *your* task?' asked Mel.

'Actually, Steve and I went to a pottery class last night.'

'Pottery?' said Jess.

'I'm trying to expand my interests, but the evening didn't play out as I imagined. It turned out the pottery teacher was useless and Steve and I left early.'

'Oh no, what happened?'

'It was such a waste of time. She just didn't know how to run a class, and life's too short for incompetent people.'

Rose yawned. 'What time is it?'

Mel pulled out her phone. 'Six o'clock.'

Isla groaned. 'How long do we have to stay?'

'Please don't moan. This is going to be so much fun.' Jess was convinced her sisters would have a great time if they just chilled out a little. It had been years since they'd all been out on the town together.

'Do you really need me here?' said Rose. 'Can't I just go back to the hotel? It's so peaceful there, and I can have the whole bed to myself all night.' She gazed dreamily into the air with a soft smile on her lips.

'No way!' said Isla. 'You're here so Jess can learn from the best. You picked up Tom in a bar, so now you can share your wisdom with her. Just think of the money.'

'I'm not a pimp,' said Rose, her reverie broken. 'I just want uninterrupted sleep. Is that too much to ask?'

'You can get plenty of sleep later,' said Mel. 'The night's still young.'

'The night hasn't even started!' Jess linked her arms through Isla's. 'Come on, let's go explore Wonderland.'

'Of course,' said Isla. 'If there's a Cloud Nine Craft Tent, it only makes sense there's a *Wonderland*.'

'It'll be fun, you'll see,' said Jess.

Isla huffed. 'Just point me in the direction of the bar.'

* * *

The energy in Wonderland was electric. A young female DJ with dreadlocks – apparently the hottest thing from LA – blasted music from the centre stage to a crowd of thousands and, all around, trees glowed fluorescent greens, blues and pinks, and giant pyramids showcased moving art and laser displays.

'This. Is. So. Awesome!' Isla shouted to Jess, who was jumping to the beat of the music. 'I have no idea what this music is, but I love it!' She screamed in delight and raised her hands.

Jess laughed. Her sister was drunk.

'Let's get another drink,' said Isla.

'Sure.' Jess loved drunk Isla. It was the only time she ever saw her sister relax and have fun. Plus, drunk Isla wasn't as much of a bitch as sober Isla. Jess pitied the poor pottery teacher who had apparently wasted Isla's precious time. That said, drunk Isla was still a judgemental snob who was quite capable of causing trouble, so Jess always kept her wits about her. 'Where did Rose and Mel get to?' asked Jess.

'I have no idea,' shouted Isla over the music.

Pushing their way through the masses of people, they stumbled across uneven ground and past the warmth of a raging bonfire. Making their way past fire-eaters, jugglers on stilts and acrobats covered in neon body paint, they headed to the VIP bar.

Jess ran her finger over her eyebrow. A couple of her stick-on stars had fallen off. 'How do I look?'

An unsteady Isla peered closely at Jess's face. The rims of Isla's eyes were red and her mascara was smudged. 'Stunning.' She lost her footing for a moment and cider splashed out of her plastic cup and over her wrist. She didn't seem to notice. 'Thanks for … forcing me to come to this,' she slurred. 'I'm having a blast.'

'That's what sisters are for,' said Jess. 'I know you all came to help me find someone I can *commit* to, but maybe you'll find the *real Isla* here too.'

Jess thought back to her teen years, when Isla would randomly drop by and take her out for dinner. She'd talk for hours about the importance of having plans for the future, how the wrong boys at her age could be a distraction, and how if she wanted something bad enough she should stop at nothing to get it. Jess thought she sounded a lot like Jacki, which probably meant it was her way of showing how much she loved her. At least, that's what her dad had said.

'I know I've found a renewed love for cider.' Isla threw her arm around Jess, then scanned the crowd. 'Have you seen anyone … you're interested in? There's got to be someone here for you.'

'I don't want to *look* like I'm looking.'

'Don't be silly. If you want someone … you've gotta go get 'em.' Isla stopped, staring at a guy with dirty blond hair that flopped in his eyes. 'I know him.'

'Who?'

'That guy, there.' Jess studied the guy Isla was pointing at. He looked to be in his early forties, and wore a pale blue Hawaiian shirt and khaki pants. 'He's got a restaurant here in Byron, and his brother was in that big movie, you know the one. They've also got another brother. He's a real sweetheart, he shops in our store sometimes.' Isla swayed and waved her hand. 'You should go introduce yourself.'

'No … He's too old for me.'

'Jess, he's only my age.'

'Exactly. You're forty-three, Isla. There's thirteen years between us.'

'Shhh.' Isla pressed her index finger to Jess's lips and nearly fell over. 'Don't tell everyone.'

Jess laughed. 'So, how do you know him?'

'I told you, his brother is a client of ours.'

'So you *don't* know him?'

'I do. Plus, I follow his famous brother on Instagram.' Isla took a sip of her cider. 'Come on, Jess. You can't waste this opportunity. If he and his brothers are rich, you know he won't just want you for your money.'

Jess shook her head. 'I'm not interested. He's not my type.'

'Rubbish. I'll introduce you.' Isla stumbled towards him.

'Wait. Isla!' Jess chased after her. 'Don't—'

But it was too late. Isla was already in front of him. He looked startled, and immediately took a step back.

'Hi.' Isla was standing way too close to him. 'I'm sorry, I don't remember your name, but my sister is on the lookout for hot, rich guys, and I said I'd introduce you.'

Jess covered her face with her hands. The poor guy looked as horrified as she felt.

'Oh, you don't have to worry.' Isla laughed. 'She doesn't want *your* money. She's going to be very rich soon.'

Jess positioned herself between them. 'I'm so sorry,' she said. 'She's had way too much to drink.'

The guy grinned. 'No worries. We've all been there.'

'Please …' said Isla, moving closer to him. 'My sister is young and beautiful. You'd be lucky to have her.'

Jess's face flushed as she gently pushed Isla out of the guy's personal space.

'I'm sure I would be,' he said, and held up his left hand. 'But I'm married.'

'See?' said Jess. 'Let's just leave him in peace, shall we?'

Isla's face paled and her shoulders hunched.

'Oh, God. No, don't—'

Isla vomited and Jess lurched out of the way, stepping on the toes of Married Guy in her three-inch heeled boots. Married Guy wobbled, then lost his balance and fell, taking Jess with him.

Jess landed heavily between the married guy's spread legs, and struggled to pull herself up. Trying to keep her boots away from the pool of vomit, she flipped over so she could kneel, but somehow found herself lying face to face on top of Married Guy, who was now trapped beneath her.

Out of nowhere, Rose and Mel appeared and pulled Jess up.

'I'm so sorry!' said Isla, the colour draining from her face. 'I can't drink cider like I used to.'

Jess was mortified. She held out her hand to help the poor guy up. 'Here.'

'No thanks.' Married Guy wasn't happy. 'I can do it myself.' Red-faced and breathing heavily, he hauled himself up and dusted off his pants. Partygoers stood around them, holding up their phones. 'Son of a—'

'I'm *so* sorry.' Jess pressed her hands to her cheeks. 'Can I do anything to help?'

Married Guy shook his head and glared at Isla. 'I think you've both done enough.'

Jess bit her lip and watched as he limped out of sight.

'Christ, Isla! You're supposed to be the one looking out for Jess,' said Mel.

Isla groaned. 'I don't know what happened. One minute I felt great, the next—'

'That was so embarrassing!' Jess tried her best not to cry.

'You're going to need some sawdust down here,' Rose told the bartender.

'*And* I've got vomit on my boots.' Jess inspected her hands and wiped them on her jeans, leaving dirty streaks. 'Where *were* you guys?'

'Rose had to express,' said Mel as she linked her arm under Isla's. 'Lean on me. Let's get you back to the hotel.'

'I feel better now,' said Isla, who was struggling to stay upright.

'That's usually the way,' muttered Mel.

'I need a shower,' said Jess. 'What time is it?'

Rose pulled her phone out of her back pocket. 'Nine-thirty.'

9

Jacki

Jacki sat in the padded grey-blue recliner in the chemotherapy unit and stared at the IV drip administering her anti-cancer drugs. Every time she moved her arm, she could feel the cannula tugging. More than once, she'd considered ripping it out.

Jacki had another thirty minutes before she could go home. The long ward-like room housed a total of ten chairs and four beds where cancer patients came to either fight for or extend their lives. Even though Jacki knew chemo would give her the best chance of a few extra months, the hospital felt like a prison. She was a busy woman, she had things to do. She hated being in that room with its drab beige colouring and plastic wipeable furnishings. As if having cancer wasn't bad enough! The décor in the ward alone was enough to push anyone over the edge.

Then there were the other patients. The sight of them made her chest tighten. For some reason, seeing them made her own sickness seem more real. *Am I staring down the barrel of my own fate?* Jacki was relieved she hadn't lost too much hair, and she hoped that would continue. Losing her hair meant people would guess she was unwell, which seemed almost worse to Jacki than being sick. She found the thought of losing her thick golden hair terrifying. She hated the idea of people staring at her, wondering if she was going to die, but worst of all, she hated the idea of them eyeing her with pity. Jacki only ever wanted to be seen as someone who was in charge of her own destiny.

'Hey, honey.' The woman in the chair next to her beamed. 'I'm Marjorie.' Dressed in blue jeans and a shapeless green printed top with a pink scarf wrapped around her head, Marjorie looked at Jacki as if she was there to make new friends.

Jacki pulled her mouth into a brief, polite smile then stared at her iPad, hoping that would be the end of Marjorie's cheerful socialising.

'Reading anything good?' asked Marjorie.

This was another reason Jacki hated her chemo sessions. Why did some people feel the need to talk or share their cancer stories? Jacki thought about drawing the curtain between them, but the mint green divider with its bold geometric shapes made her both nauseous and claustrophobic.

'I'm reading work emails,' said Jacki in a discouraging tone.

'No rest for the wicked, eh?' Marjorie opened a small toiletry bag and pulled out a bag of toffee eclairs. 'Want one?'

Jacki smiled thinly and shook her head.

'I love these,' said Marjorie, unwrapping one and popping it in her mouth. 'You can't just have one, though, can you? I'll probably finish the bag by the time I leave, but I figure you've got to give yourself some kind of reward for being in here.'

Marjorie rustled the toffee wrapper between the fingers of her drip-free hand, and Jacki winced. She stared at an email, but she couldn't focus. 'You know what?' said Jacki. 'You're right. Life's too short to not treat yourself every now and then.'

Marjorie's eyes sparkled and she leaned over and threw two toffee eclairs into Jacki's lap.

Jacki lowered her voice. 'I'm just buying myself some time. Chemo won't save me.'

'Sorry to hear that. I'm in the same boat.'

How was it that Marjorie seemed so full of joy when she knew she was going to die? When Jacki had first been told there was nothing more the doctors could do, rage had threatened to engulf her. The realisation that she couldn't buy her way out of her illness made her furious. She was used to getting whatever she wanted. So she did the only thing she could think of. She asked Helen to bring all the fine porcelain dinnerware into the back garden and smashed plate after plate. Jacki had heard about rage rooms, but she couldn't wait to book herself into one. She needed to express herself right away. By the time she'd obliterated every last piece, she'd felt a little better, but it didn't change anything. She was still dying.

Jacki watched Marjorie as she chewed her toffee. How had she dealt with the news?

Marjorie looked at her phone and laughed. 'It's my daughter,' she said, holding it up. 'She keeps sending me these funny little videos. She's always trying to cheer me up. She says we've got two options: we can spend my last few months sad and crying, or we can make the most of the time we have by cramming in as much joy as possible.'

Jacki checked her phone. There were no messages or missed calls from her daughters. She hadn't discussed her treatment program with any of them. Jess had grilled Helen about it, but Helen was under strict instructions not to tell her anything. The last thing Jacki needed was medical advice from her daughters. Of course, Rose might have some suggestions after what she went through with Richard, but Jacki only wanted expert medical opinions. She'd paid for the best specialists and had followed their treatment plans, but now there was no more to be done. The only choice she had to make was whether to suffer through more chemo in the hope of buying herself some time. That decision had been clear-cut. She was a fighter, and would be until she took her last breath.

'Do you have children?' asked Marjorie.

'Four daughters.'

'How wonderful. I only have the one, Bethany.'

'My granddaughter's name is Bethany.' Jacki chewed the toffee. Its chocolate centre was satisfyingly delicious.

'Oh, what a coincidence. How old is she?'

'Four months – no, nearly five months old.'

'Just a baby …' Marjorie sighed. 'Don't you just love that age? A real bundle of joy.'

Jacki smiled, but her heart sank. She hadn't even met her third grandchild yet. After Richard's death, Rose had refused to take her calls or attend any family get-togethers where Jacki would be present. She had told herself Rose would come around eventually, but time ticked on, and she was always too busy to go chasing after her.

'The truth is,' said Marjorie, 'Bethany and I didn't always get on. We had an argument and lost contact when she was in her early twenties. We're both so alike, you see, and so stubborn. Neither of us wanted to make the first move, but when I found out I had cancer, I put my pride aside and called her. It was the best decision I ever made.'

'How long ago was that?'

'Too long. I've been fighting this disease on and off for nearly a decade. But it looks like it's going to have its wicked way with me after all.' Marjorie unwrapped another toffee.

'I haven't even met my Bethany yet.' Jacki didn't know why she'd said that. Marjorie was a stranger, and Jacki didn't even confide in her own family, let alone people she'd only just met.

'Do they not live close by?'

'They're only an hour away. My daughter, Rose, she's angry with me. We haven't been in contact for the last few years. I suppose, looking back, I can understand why she's mad. It's just ...'

Marjorie sucked her toffee and watched Jacki attentively. 'Go on.'

'It's just ... Her husband, Richard, died of cancer three years ago.'

'How terrible.'

'I made sure he got the best treatment from the best doctors, but I ... I couldn't bring myself to visit him. I didn't see him again after his diagnosis.'

'Why not?'

'I think I was scared of seeing him sick, especially towards the end. My husband, Peter, had died of a heart attack years before, but I hadn't spent much time, if any, thinking about mortality before his death. Seeing him in the hospital morgue gave me a sharp wake-up call. I realised then that our time is limited, and I was determined to achieve the business goals we'd set together. So ... I did what I thought was best. I threw myself into my work and ploughed all the money Peter left me into building my business. I suppose I didn't want to see Richard because I didn't want to be reminded of our impermanence. Time was marching on, and I was afraid.' She had never talked to anyone about this. Not even Helen.

'Your daughter couldn't forgive you for not visiting Richard?'

'She thought I didn't visit because I didn't care, but that wasn't true. To be honest, I just thought Richard would get better. He was only young, and Rose had always been mad at me about something, so her behaviour towards me was, if anything, normal. But then Richard died. Despite everything, Rose still wanted me at his funeral. I was all dressed and ready to go …' Jacki sniffed. 'But I just couldn't do it. I couldn't get in the car. It's like I was frozen with fear. I couldn't face seeing all those people, crying and giving their condolences. I remembered it all too well from Peter's funeral. It was one of the worst days of my life. And who was I to rock up at the last hour when it was too late? What could I offer Rose and her kids then?'

'So you didn't go?'

'I made up a work excuse and got on the next flight to Sydney. It was awful. I was too ashamed to go to his funeral, but I was so ashamed that I missed it, too. These days, I try not to think about it.'

'Have you tried telling her how you felt?'

'I don't share how I really feel with anyone, except you, Marjorie, right now, and I can't fathom why.'

Marjorie glared at her. 'It must be the truth-telling toffees.' Jacki looked at the toffee wrapper in her hand, and Marjorie laughed. 'Your face! I'm joking. They're normal toffees, I promise.'

Jacki sighed. 'Right.'

'I'm glad you feel you can talk to me,' said Marjorie. 'I think facing our own mortality forces us to deal with things that we're usually able to push aside. It seems to me you need to talk things out with Rose. You said you're reading work emails. You could always call her instead.'

'My work is important too. I own Turner Hotels and Casinos.'

'You're Jacki *Turner*?' Marjorie shook her head in disbelief. 'What on earth are you doing here? Couldn't you pay to have chemo in some nice private room or at home?'

'My specialist is based in this hospital, and it calms my nerves knowing he's not too far away. Silly, I know. Also, Helen, my personal manager, said it was important to meet others going through the same thing. It was either this or attend one of those cancer groups. I figured this was the better option.'

'Helen sounds more like a good friend than a manager.'

'She's ... *extremely* good at her job.' Jacki swallowed as she realised Helen *was* her friend, her *best* friend. None of Jacki's other friends had looked out for her like Helen had. No one knew Jacki like Helen did. Their friendship had spanned well over thirty years. 'She's a hard woman,' said Jacki. 'But I've found her counsel to be invaluable. In hindsight, when I take her advice, it usually does work out well for me. Perhaps I should have listened to her a bit more over the years.' Jacki couldn't count how many times Helen had told her to make more of an effort with the girls. How different would things have been if she'd taken her advice?

'Having good friends and family around you is important. Do you have any siblings? Nieces? Nephews?'

'My parents passed away years ago, and I'm an only child. My husband, Peter, he had a sister, and she has three children. They're all grown up now, of course.'

'All I know is,' said Marjorie, 'it's your family and friends who will be at your bedside in your final days, not your job or your belongings. That's the same for all of us.'

'Are you saying my business isn't important?' Jacki raised her brows. 'Do you know how many people I employ? How many families my business supports? Plus, you know, it's not a bad thing to want the finer things in life.'

'I'm not diminishing what you've created. I think it's incredible. I had high tea with Bethany at your hotel in

Melbourne once. It was a Mother's Day gift. It was all so flash and upmarket.'

'Ah, you should have seen the casinos back in the day, the glitz and the glamour; people couldn't get enough. A weekend at the Gold Coast; sun, sea and the seduction of the slot machines. It was exciting – it still is, but it was different back then. Now, of course, I plough millions into the education and treatment of gambling addicts.'

Marjorie raised her eyebrows.

'I know, I know. Changes still need to be made, but at least I'm *trying* to counteract the harm being done. My husband always said how important it is to give back, and I do. I've set up mentoring programs in Peter's name, and then there are the charities and the donations.'

'Well, you've certainly left your mark on the world, but it's through your loved ones that you'll best be remembered. You just have to ask yourself how you want them to remember you. How would you feel if you never worked things out with Rose?'

Jacki's chest hurt. She couldn't think about that now. It was complicated. Plus, Marjorie didn't understand the responsibility of owning and overseeing a hotel chain. Still, Jacki was humbled by her honesty. She opened her second toffee and placed it on her tongue. It was good to have someone else to talk to, and even though the chances of her seeing Marjorie again were slim, she was grateful their paths had crossed.

'Thank you, by the way,' said Jacki, holding up her toffee wrapper. 'You know, I think I might get Helen to buy a bag of these on the way home.'

10

Mel

The cool August wind sent a chill through Mel. It was 6.40 am, and the recently mowed lawn at Henry Ziegenfusz Park in Cleveland was covered in sparkling dew.

Mel rolled her shoulders and swung her arms to keep warm as runners made their way to the parkrun meeting point, compression tights on, earphones in, water bottles at the ready. Car keys were thrown into a bowl on the table next to the bike rack while toddlers drank from sippy cups in their strollers and dogs tugged at their leads, desperate to be released.

Mel pulled out her phone and texted Corey. *What am I doing here?* She hit send and marched on the spot while waiting for his reply.

Corey: *Getting rich baby $$$.*

Mel: *I'm going to die.*

She stretched her arms over her head and arched her back.

Corey: *Yes, you are.*

'Perfect,' said Mel.

Corey: *But not today. Today you're going to run.*

Mel's phone buzzed again. Corey had sent a GIF of Forrest Gump running.

Mel: *Thanks for that! Call me later, enjoy your sleep in.*

Mel sighed as she struggled to put her phone back into the arm strap, which was already cutting off her circulation.

She'd read online that parkrun was for all ages and all abilities. Participants could walk if they wanted to. Knowing she was under no pressure to run the whole five kilometres made her feel a little better. A woman who must have been in her late sixties grinned at Mel, and as more runners arrived at the meeting point, they all greeted each other with friendly smiles.

An elderly gentleman nodded at Mel. 'G'day.'

'It's my first time,' she said nervously.

'Good on ya, mate.'

'Well done, you,' said another runner.

Mel beamed, relieved to discover parkrunners were super friendly, as well as super excited to run. It was all so strange. Maybe this wasn't going to be as bad as she'd imagined. She pulled a small water bottle out of the running belt clipped around her waist, and took a sip.

'What the bloody hell are you wearing?' Isla's voice boomed over the crowd that had gathered, and people turned and stared.

Mel lowered her head. Although the parkrun Facebook page encouraged runners to dress in bright colours or crazy costumes, Mel just wanted to blend in. But after a couple of recent sweaty-crotch-camel-toe disasters, she'd opted to wear her usual oversized black T-shirt and black leggings with a pair of men's blue boardshorts over the top.

Isla tugged at Mel's shorts. 'What are these?'

'Hey! These are an essential piece of kit.'

'Are Jess and Rose here yet?' Isla searched the growing sea of faces. Her red hair was neatly braided, and her Lorna Jane running gear clung to her toned frame in all the right places.

'Rose texted to say Bethany was sick, and Jess didn't drive up last night because she's got to work this morning.'

'I thought we were all going to help you with this. Do you know what time I had to get up to drive here?' Isla placed her hands on her hips. 'But don't concern yourself. Just take note that *I'm* here for you. I'll get you through this.'

'I can hardly wait.'

'You know you should have signed up for this seven weeks ago, as soon as we got the terms.'

'I've been walking, building up to it.'

'Your task is to run a marathon, not complete a walkathon.'

'And what have you been doing for your task? Have *you* even started?'

'Don't worry about me. I have a few ideas up my sleeve.'

'Like what?'

'I figure if I can try some new activities and find something I can commit to for the next year, that will count as evidence that I've opened myself up to new experiences, and that I'm willing to define myself in different ways. At the end of the day, assessing my task will be subjective. As long as I can prove my case to the lawyer, I'll have nothing to worry about.'

In other words, Isla hadn't started. Mel chewed the inside of her lip. She wouldn't dare point this out to her, though. You could never give Isla advice. She'd bite your head off in a second. Mel had learned the hard way that giving Isla some home truths wasn't worth the backlash.

A high-spirited volunteer in a fluorescent orange vest called over the newcomers, and a small crowd gathered. She ran through the rules of parkrun, and Mel's chest tightened a little.

She tried to shift the twisting in her gut by wriggling her hips and performing mini lunges. 'I can do this,' she muttered to herself.

At three minutes to seven, over a hundred people made their way to the start line.

Isla put in her Air Pods and cued up her music. 'If I lose you, I'll meet you at the finish line.'

'Wait! I thought you were going to do this with me?'

'I am, but I'm bound to run ahead.'

'You're not a runner.'

'No, but I do weights at the gym three times a week. When was the last time you worked out properly?'

'I went for a walk on Thursday, and I walked here.'

'You live there.' Isla pointed across the road to the seventies low-set brick house Mel rented with Perfectionist Penny.

Mel frowned. 'Fine, but don't go too far ahead.'

Dead on seven o'clock, a parkrun volunteer called out, 'Ready, set, go!'

Bodies lurched forward like shoppers vying to get into David Jones on Boxing Day. Mel kept her eyes down, trying not to step on the heels of those in front of her. Pushed along by the flow of runners, she had no choice but to keep moving. Her breathing quickly became shallow and her chest jolted with each stride. As the sun appeared from behind a cloud, she squinted and cursed herself for leaving her sunnies at home.

Runners overtook her. Some were plugged in and others were chatting, and all of them seemed to be breathing with no problems at all. But at least she was keeping up with Isla. *For now.*

'How are. They. Doing that?' Mel asked her sister.

'What?'

'Breathing. How. Are. They. Breathing?' Cool air filled her lungs and dried the inside of her mouth. She looked over her shoulder and saw the start line still in clear view. 'Oh, God!'

She stumbled, then lurched forward and somehow managed to stay upright. *I can't stop, not yet.* She hobbled forward.

As they reached the timber boardwalk that cut across the creek, she stuck to the edges and tried not to fall into the swampy bog.

'Wait!' she cried to Isla, who was moving ahead. 'I need to walk.'

'You can't, not yet. We're only four hundred metres in. Come on!'

Mel slowed. 'You go ahead. I'll catch up.'

'Try not to walk all of it then.' Isla overtook a couple of runners and disappeared out of sight.

Mel walked as fast as she could, and the elderly woman she'd seen earlier sprinted past. The sun's rays flickered between the branches of the tall trees and her eyes streamed. She took a sip from her water bottle and forced herself to run again. Her breathing became unsteady and her calves burned. Thirty seconds running, thirty seconds walking. That's what she'd do. Each thirty seconds of running felt like the longest half a minute of her life, but knowing she could walk soon kept her putting one foot in front of the other.

Why the hell do people choose to do this? I could be in bed, warm and snug!

Further along the trail, a young girl in an orange vest, pigtails and a green tutu took photos of passing runners. Mel forced a smile, started to sprint and flicked the peace sign at the camera lens. As soon as she passed the photographer, she stopped running and leant over with her hands on her hips. 'I'm going to die.'

'You're doing a great job!' said the photographer. 'You've only got four kilometres to go.'

Mel spotted the one-kilometre signpost at the edge of the path and tried not to cry.

'You can do it. Don't stop now!' The photographer gave a broad smile and pumped her fist in the air.

Mel blinked back tears. Her body was screaming at her to stop, and an image of Amber Ryan laughing at her stabbed at her chest. 'You're right,' said Mel, wiping her eyes. 'I can do this. I've got to do this!'

Mel broke into a steady jog, determined to get into a rhythm. Concentrating on her breathing, she sucked in air and blew it out in sync with her steps. Runners sprinted past her from the opposite direction, headed for the finish line, but she tried not to think about them. Instead, she focused only on the pattern of her breathing. Before long, she was out from under the trees. The sun was warm, and sweat trickled down her lower back. Looking ahead, she shaded her eyes with her hand.

'You've got to be kidding.'

Ahead was a winding hill. A gargling sensation burned at the back of her throat, and for a moment she thought she was going to throw up.

She took the hill slowly and tried her best to stick to her walk, run, walk routine, but she quickly had to abandon it to manage the steep incline. Her breathing was harsh, and her head spun a little. No amount of colourful clothing would ever make this fun! Further up, a few people were gathered around a runner who was sitting on the grass, her head slumped between her legs.

I knew you could die doing this!

As Mel got closer, she recognised Isla's braided hair. 'Hey, sis. You okay?'

Isla looked up. Her face was pale and clammy. 'I'm fine,' she said. 'My life flashed before my eyes, that's all. Help me up.'

A grey-haired gentleman in black compression tights took her hand and pulled her to her feet. 'You sure you're okay?'

'Yes, thanks for your help.'

'No worries.'

Isla screwed up her face and inspected the hill. 'On the internet, they called this part a playful incline.'

'Mountain of death more like.'

Isla laughed. 'I'm really okay. I just thought I'd wait up here for you. I felt bad for running off.'

'Yeah, whatever. You ready to carry on? I've come up with a plan to pace myself. Wanna try it? It involves walking.'

'Walking? Hell yeah, count me in.'

At the halfway point, they fist-bumped the volunteer on patrol and started to run again. Mel grabbed hold of her boobs, one in each hand, and winced. 'I don't think I can make it.'

'We have no choice. We've come too far to stop now.'

'I need to invest in a proper sports bra.' Mel stopped running and walked again. 'My boobs haven't seen this much action since I dated Kevin Walker two years ago.'

'Eww.' Isla jogged alongside her. 'Come on, I'll take you shopping this afternoon to buy one. But right now we just need to get this over with. Thirty seconds of running, yeah? You are strong, you are powerful, you can—'

'Stop talking to me like you're my personal trainer. You're just as bad at this as I am.'

'Hey, I go to the gym three times a week.'

'So why haven't you finished yet?'

'I'm used to lifting weights, not cardio. I'm fit in a different way. Now come on. I've got dinner plans.'

Mel picked up the pace and groaned.

'One good thing about the first parkrun,' said Isla, 'is no matter how long it takes, it's gonna be our personal best.'

'Good point. Maybe we should slow down, so we've got a chance of beating it next week.'

Isla laughed. 'Come on, I'll race ya.'

11

Rose

Rose glanced up from her laptop after reading the latest draft of her picture book to Harrison and Taylor. After spending the last week writing, rewriting and editing her manuscript, she was keen to hear their thoughts. Getting her writing to a standard she was satisfied with had taken hours. It had been like having a full-time job. In her regular day job, she worked as a part-time accountant for a small office supply company, but she was currently five months into a year's maternity leave. Part of her wished she was still working, as it would have been a welcome distraction from her mother's end-of-life crisis, but another part of her was pleased that she didn't have to juggle work on top of everything else. Even on the best of days, it was too much to manage.

'Well?' said Rose. 'What do you think?'

Harrison dropped his shoulders and rolled his eyes in boredom. With his slim face and bright blue eyes, he was the spitting image of his dad, and every now and then he would say or do something that made Rose's heart lunge. In those brief few seconds, it was almost as if Richard were checking in on them. Taylor sniffed as she sat crossed-legged on the sofa next to her. She had the start of a cold, and Rose had given her the day off school, knowing she'd probably end up being home for the rest of the week. Rose leant over and kissed her forehead.

'So in the end,' said Taylor, 'the little girl's mum doesn't love her?'

Rose handed her a tissue and rubbed her knee. 'Not so much doesn't love her,' she said. 'Her mum just never puts herself in her daughter's shoes. She doesn't think about how she might feel, and doesn't even *try* to understand things from her daughter's perspective.'

Taylor scrunched her eyes and tilted her head. 'And the little girl is okay with that?'

'Well, at first, she finds it heartbreaking. I mean, we all want our parents to be compassionate and loving, but by the end of the story, she's accepted her mum will never change, and that's what made the girl become a strong, fearless warrior.'

Taylor stood. Rose couldn't tell if she was upset by the story or if her eyes were watering because she was sick. 'Her mum is mean. Sorry Mum, but I don't really like it.' Taylor's iPad pinged from upstairs. 'That'll be Lauren. Can I go?' Taylor sneezed into her tissue and Rose nodded.

Rushing out of the living room, she nearly crashed into Tom, who was carrying two mugs of hot tea.

'Hey, slow down, speedy,' he said, raising his elbows so he wouldn't spill the drinks. 'Hang on! How are you feeling? Would you like a hot drink?'

Rose's heart welled at how much Tom loved her kids.

Taylor sniffed. 'Maybe later. Can I speak to Lauren first? She's got to go to dance soon.'

'Sure.'

Taylor spun around and darted upstairs while Tom sat next to Rose, placing her mug of tea on the coffee table. 'What did you think of your mum's story?' he asked Harrison, who was now sprawled on the ottoman, staring at the ceiling.

'I don't know. Can I go back on the Xbox now?'

'Just help me out first.' Rose leaned forward. 'Tell me, if you could sum up my story in one word, what would it be?'

Harrison sat up with his head slumped. 'Sad. Can I go now?'

A deflated Rose sank back into the sofa. 'Sure, but only half an hour on the Xbox, okay? Set your timer.'

Harrison darted out of the room and Rose stared at her laptop. The kids' reactions stung. She'd spent hours reluctantly writing and rewriting this book in a bid to give her dying mother what she wanted, and Rose resented the time it was taking. This was time she could have spent with her kids, or cleaning the house, or getting on top of the washing, or sleeping – oh, how she wished for long, deep, uninterrupted sleep. What made it worse was that her mother had constantly harped on about how precious *her* time was. The woman had only ever made time for Rose if it had been according to her terms and her schedule.

How much of Rose's childhood had she spent waiting to see her mother? She'd always felt like she and her sisters had slotted into her mother's day as an afterthought, just one more item on the agenda. On the occasions Rose had tried to spontaneously see her, she was always informed that *Mrs Turner* was in a meeting or wouldn't have time that day, and perhaps she could try again tomorrow.

Rose was determined to be there for her kids, and not just on special occasions. Some of her favourite moments with them happened while doing nothing in particular, like the conversations they had while driving home from school or while she was stroking Taylor's hair as they curled up on the sofa watching a movie, or while sitting out the front of the house watching Harrison trying to perfect a trick on his BMX. Rose soaked up these precious moments, ones that she'd never got to experience with her own mother.

Rose had hoped she could write a picture book in a couple of hours and be done with it, but she was coming to realise that it would be harder than she thought. 'What do you think of my book?' she asked Tom.

Tom chewed his bottom lip as he reread her manuscript. 'This is for a picture book, for preschool kids?'

Rose nodded.

Tom paused and stared at Rose's laptop like he was afraid to make eye contact. 'Your writing is great – it's edgy and expressive – but the topic is a bit heavy. I mean, I know what your message is, but you probably want to make kids that age feel secure first, by teaching them about unconditional love.'

'I want kids to know they can be powerful even if their parents aren't so great.' Rose closed her laptop. 'I give up.'

'Hey, this is your first try. If it was easy, everyone would do it.' Tom smiled in an attempt to soften the blow, and the dimple on his left cheek appeared. It was this beautiful smile that she had spotted from across the bar on the night they met. 'We can brainstorm some new ideas if you want?'

'Not now,' she said, resting her head on his shoulder. 'I've spent all day on this, and my head hurts.' She picked at a loose fibre on the sleeve of her grey knitted jumper. It had been windy all day, which was typical for August, but the cooler temperature had made her cold to the bone, and she had struggled to get her hands and feet warm. For a couple of hours that morning, she'd wheeled out the portable heater and turned it on full blast.

Tom rubbed her thigh. 'Have you considered talking to your mum about all of this?'

'All of what?'

'You just wrote a story about a daughter's damaged and toxic relationship with her mother.'

Rose usually loved Tom's honesty, but this time his comments got under her skin. He didn't know what her mother was capable of. He'd never even met her. If Rose was going to be forced to write a picture book, she was going to do it on her terms, and if she wanted to use the opportunity to call out her mother's lack of parenting skills, then she would. 'Tom, my mother is so caught up in her own life, she didn't even remember your name when I saw her.' Rose's cheeks burned. *Damn it!* I don't want to have to deal with any of this right now.'

'What do you mean?'

'My mother is a master manipulator. This is what the great and powerful Jacki Turner does. She bulldozes her way into your life, demanding to play both the victim and the heroine, and with one wave of her magic wand, she turns everything to shit.'

Taylor appeared in the doorway and gasped. 'Mum, you said a swear word!' Taylor took Richard's old swear jar from the bookshelf. 'You need to put two dollars in here.'

Rose smiled at the sight of the swear jar. She'd always told Richard that if she could manage to avoid swearing, *he* had to support her by putting two dollars in it every time he said a curse word. Richard would laugh as he dug deep into his pockets for loose change.

'I forgot all about that,' said Rose. 'I don't think I've got any cash on me, but I'll have a look in a minute.'

'Don't forget,' said Taylor. She disappeared back upstairs, and Rose turned to Tom. 'You see? My mother's already making me curse.'

'So, tell her. Tell her how you feel. You need to get it off your chest. You never know; maybe you can repair the damage before it's too late.'

'I can promise you, nothing good would come of it. Speaking to her would just make everything worse.'

'But at least you'd have tried.'

'I don't see why *I* should be the one to reach out when she's the one making us jump through hoops like this. She makes me so mad!' Rose scowled into her mug of cooling tea. 'And then there's her *I'll leave my fortune to all the poor animals*, like she's some kind of saviour. She made her fortune exploiting gambling addicts, for goodness' sake. Taking money from one vulnerable group and giving it to another isn't a good deed!'

'Regardless,' said Tom, 'your mum earned her fortune because she spent her life working hard, and yes, that came at a cost, but maybe she wants you and your sisters to *earn* your share of her wealth. Only a privileged few will ever get the opportunity to come into this kind of money.'

Rose closed her eyes. Tom was right. Rose was privileged. Even though she'd made her own way for the last twenty-two years, she'd spent the first eighteen surrounded by the best of everything money could buy. Even when Richard had got sick, Rose hadn't had to worry about paying the medical bills because Jacki had transferred enough money to pay for his treatment and care twenty times over.

'I'm just saying,' said Tom, 'if you don't talk to her and then something happens, you might be left with regrets.'

'I can assure you I won't be. My mother never made time for me, so if our relationship is non-existent, that's on her. She made her bed, now she has to lie in it.'

12

Jess

Jess wandered up and down the aisles at Coles with a shopping basket in hand, searching for dinner inspiration. She swore one of the most laborious parts of adulting was trying to figure out what to have for dinner every night, and being single made this task even more of a chore. There was no one to bounce ideas off and no one to ever cook for her. Plus, making a delicious, healthy meal from scratch always seemed to involve a ridiculous amount of effort for just one person, not to mention an expensive amount of herbs and an awful lot of washing up. This was why Jess considered the local sushi bar owner a close friend.

Jess examined the contents of her basket. She had four half-price chocolate bars, a tube of sour cream Pringles and three punnets of strawberries that were on special. As she strolled towards the magazines, an elderly woman spotted her and did a double-take. The woman's mouth dropped open, and then she tutted loudly, shook her head, and walked off in the opposite direction.

That was weird.

The woman kept turning back to look at Jess until she finally disappeared down the next aisle.

Some people are just downright rude.

Jess assessed her basket and sighed. 'Looks like it's sushi again.' As she looked up, she caught sight of the magazine rack beside her and the earth shifted beneath her feet. 'No. Fucking. Way!' The words exploded from her lips, and several shoppers turned to see who was using such foul language.

'What the—' Jess's head spun, and the blood drained from her face as she scanned the covers of the celebrity gossip magazines. Each one featured a photograph of her mounting Married Guy at Bay Bliss Music Festival. Apparently he was Nathan Campbell, the brother of A-list movie star Jason Campbell.

There were photos from every angle. One was a full-on shot of Jess's butt stuck high in the air as she'd tried to stand up. Another looked as if Jess was grinding up against Nathan while he was lying on the ground, and in a disturbingly blurred snap, they both appeared to be drunk and having a really great time.

Jess turned her back to the magazine rack and spread her arms wide, like Rose and Jack in *Titanic*, but it was useless. She couldn't hide the entire magazine display.

A grey-haired shopper hobbled past Jess with her trolley, and Jess shimmied along with her so she couldn't see the shocking images. The woman took no notice of her, and when she disappeared out of sight, Jess pulled out her phone and called Isla. It went straight to voicemail. 'Damn you, Isla Turner!' Jess hung up and called Rose.

'Hi, one sec,' said Rose. Jess could hear her sister talking to someone. 'Okay, I'm here.'

'Where are you?' Jess's voice shook.

'I'm leaving the library. Apparently, I need—'

'Rose!'

'To do more research on children's picture books.'

'Rose! I need you to go to Woolies and Coles and anywhere that sells magazines.'

'Why?'

Jess turned to the shelf behind her and grabbed as many copies as she could. '*Damn it!* I'm gonna need a trolley.'

'What's wrong?'

Jess darted to the front of the store. 'There are photos of me on the covers of all the gossip magazines. I'm sprawled all over that Married Guy at Bay Bliss, who, it turns out, is Nathan *bloody* Campbell – Jason Campbell's brother!'

'No! *That* was Nathan Campbell? Wow!'

Jess tried not to lose it. 'I need you to focus, Rose!' She threw her basket into a trolley and rushed back to the magazine aisle. 'Are you close to a Coles?' she asked as she wrestled with the trolley, which kept lurching to the left.

'Wait, there's a newsagent next door,' said Rose.

'How could this happen? I look like some trashy homewrecker!' Jess skidded to a halt at the magazines, scanning the headlines: *Bad Boy at Bay Bliss*, *Caught in the Act*, *Nathan's Bay Bliss Betrayal*!

'What?!'

'They can't do this, can they? It's defamation! It can't be legal.'

Another shopper parked her trolley alongside Jess and reached for a magazine proclaiming *Campbell Busted at Bay Bliss*. Jess seized it, then proceeded to grab all the other copies.

'Excuse me!' said the woman in a gruff tone, reaching across for another magazine. Jess grabbed that one too.

'Sorry, craft project.' She dropped all the magazines into her trolley, but two slipped onto the floor. The woman lurched at them, picked one up and hurried off with her nose in the air.

'I'm here,' said Rose. 'I'm at the magazines. Oh, Jess!'

'What? What?'

'I'm looking at a wall of you doing downward dog with Nathan Campbell beneath you!'

'I was *trying* to get off him!'

'*I* know that. It's just that from the angle of the camera—'

'Buy them all, every copy you can get your hands on.'

'It'll cost a fortune.'

'Just do it! I'll pay you back. Call me when you're done.' Jess hung up and called Mel, but it went to voicemail.

Confident she'd got all the magazines in that store, Jess headed to the self-serve check-out. She wouldn't have enough money in her everyday account for all the magazines, and there was no way she was going to dip into her holiday account. She'd have to put it on her credit card. Jess bit her bottom lip as she waited in line.

'You can go to check-out five,' said the attendant.

Jess hung her head, pretending not to hear. She just wanted to scan the magazines herself. But the *helpful* woman insisted, and Jess reluctantly wheeled her trolley to the empty checkout.

Her heart pounded and her face burned as she loaded her few groceries and the stacks of magazines onto the conveyor belt. *This is all Isla's fault!*

The cheery girl scanned Jess's strawberries, Pringles and chocolates, then all the magazines. 'Someone likes to read.'

Jess watched a deep frown appear across the girl's forehead. 'You know, she looks just like—'

'It's not how it looks,' said Jess, her bottom lip quivering.

The check-out girl smiled, then winked at Jess. 'It never is. That'll be three hundred and fifty-two dollars.'

A small whimper erupted from Jess as she took out her credit card. *Isla is going to pay for this! And for the bloody magazines!*

13

Mel

That same afternoon, Isla lay in a crumpled heap on the floor, howling in pain. The aerial yoga class had been a disaster. Mel should have known that trying to do yoga while swinging from a silk hammock suspended from the ceiling was a bad idea.

She was mortified. Her sister's lack of respect throughout the beginners' class had been astounding, and despite Isla's injured shoulder, Mel was struggling to find any sympathy for her. The class had come to an abrupt end after Isla had lost her grip and fallen to the floor while practising a simple transition. Her injury could have been avoided if she'd followed the teacher's instructions instead of rushing ahead, thinking she knew better. Isla had landed at an awkward angle and she was making sure everyone knew just how much pain she was in.

The poor yoga teacher was distraught. 'I'll call an ambulance?'

'No ambulance!' snapped Isla. 'Mel, take me to the hospital.'

'Hey sis, don't you think it would be better—'

'Don't argue with me. You can drive.' Isla wailed as she tried to sit up. Two other students helped her to her feet and out to the car while Mel gathered their things and searched through Isla's bag for her keys.

She stepped outside the studio and unlocked the car. The teacher followed, on the verge of tears, and Mel tried to reassure her. 'This wasn't your fault, honestly. It's my sister, she's—'

'Mel!' Isla barked from the car.

Mel hurried to the driver's side. 'Again, I'm so sorry.' The students from the class stood next to the distressed teacher and watched as Mel tried to reverse out of the tight parking spot. Mel was used to driving Lilly's family car at work, but driving a brand-new BMW that cost more than her entire credit card debt made her sweat. With Isla cursing and crying in pain next to her, it took several attempts to get out of the parking spot.

Mel wished she hadn't answered Isla's call that morning. Of all her sisters, Isla was the one she was the least close to. But when Isla asked if she'd attend a beginner's yoga class with her that afternoon, she'd been elated.

Isla never asked her to go anywhere. They were like chalk and cheese. They'd always bickered as kids over who had the most up-to-date designer brands or who owned the most shoes, and as adults they'd lived very different lives.

Mel was nothing like Isla's friends, who were all wealthy and carried a confidence that came from having a bottomless pit of money. Plus, they were stunning to look at – they were all either tall and lean, like Isla, or dainty and petite. Mel, by comparison, was a short, bigger-boned thirty-eight-year-old who bought her clothes from Big W, wore two-dollar lip gloss, lived pay cheque to pay cheque, and couldn't resist a good Groupon saving.

One of Isla's store managers had picked Mel up after work at three o'clock and driven her to Isla's house so they could go to the yoga class. Mel had never done yoga before, but she was learning to step out of her comfort zone. How difficult could stretching on a mat be? That was when Isla told her it was *aerial* yoga.

Trying to stay calm, Mel drove through the Gold Coast with the caution of a sloth, taking corners with extreme care and keeping an eye on the speed limit. Isla clutched her upper arm and screamed at Mel to drive faster.

'I'm trying to avoid the bumps.' Mel glanced at the deformed lump on Isla's shoulder and flinched.

'Just put your foot down!' Streams of black eye make-up ran down Isla's cheeks like rivers. 'I'll sue that studio. *Safe and fun* my arse.'

Mel was shocked. 'You can't sue. You blatantly disregarded everything the instructor said.' She took a sharp right and Isla groaned. 'Anyway, you signed the waiver before the class.'

'Where are you going? The hospital's back that way,' said Isla.

'The hospital is at the end of this road.'

'I'm not going *there*. It's not private.' Isla winced.

This was typical Isla. 'Who cares? Let's just get your shoulder seen to. I'm not driving anywhere else. You need a doctor *now*.'

'Stop the car.'

Rage bubbled inside Mel. She knew her sister was high maintenance, but she didn't realise she behaved like this with other people. Mel pulled the car over and turned off the engine. 'Now I know why Mum set you your task.'

'What?!'

'I didn't see it before. I just thought you were mean because I was your little sister, and that's how sisters are with each other, but wow, Isla, you're really not a nice person. Is this how you treated the poor pottery teacher? I bet you didn't even leave early, I bet she kicked you out!'

'Don't insult me, I'm injured! Now turn the car around and go where I tell you to.'

'I'm not your driver.'

'No, you're my sister, so turn the car around.'

Reluctantly, Mel did a U-turn, seething. 'Mum can see what kind of person you are. Making demands, being rude, using your money as an excuse to act out. You're a bully.' Isla whimpered in pain, but Mel didn't care. She'd put up with Isla's acid tongue for years because she was her sister, but it turned out Isla was no better than Amber Ryan. She'd had enough. 'Mum must be hoping you'll wake up and see what kind of person your money has turned you into.'

'Stop being a bitch. I'm no different from Mum.'

That was the thing: Isla was right. She was *exactly* like their mum. Perhaps, deep down, Jacki knew it too and wanted to see if it was possible for Isla to live differently, more humbly and compassionately perhaps, despite having money and power.

Twenty minutes of silence later, Mel pulled into the car park of the private hospital and squeezed Isla's BMW into a spot. Trying to leave room on Isla's side so she could get out easily, she reversed and then drove forward again, but she accelerated too hard. There was a horrible crunching noise.

'No!' screamed Isla. 'My car!'

Mel had hit a light post. '*Shit!*' She reversed and winced at the sound of broken glass and twisted metal. 'I think the post is okay,' she joked nervously.

'Never mind the post! Get out and see what you've done to my car.'

Isla was pale, and her smudged dark eyes made her look more goth than gym-goer. *What is it with wearing make-up to work out?*

Mel put the car in park and got out to inspect the damage. The headlight was broken, and the front bumper was dented. Mel sighed. Of course it had to be Isla's car that she'd damaged. If it had been Rose's or Jess's, at least they would have understood it was an accident. Isla would never let Mel hear the end of this.

14

Isla

The smell of disinfectant only added to Isla's nausea. Sweat soaked the back of her Lululemon tank top as she lay as still as she could on the hospital bed and inhaled pain relief through the gas mask. An X-ray had confirmed that her shoulder was dislocated. Now she was waiting for a doctor to see if they could put it back in place. She was thankful she hadn't landed on her right shoulder, otherwise she wouldn't have been able to text Steve, who was in Adelaide for work. He'd promised he'd be on the next flight home. Isla lowered her right arm carefully. The slightest movement sent excruciating pain jolting through her left shoulder.

Mel paced the cubicle. 'You need to stop texting and rest. You can send photos to your friends once you're better.'

Isla scowled. 'Where the hell is the doctor?'

'You're not the only patient here, and you're not dying. Just wait your turn.'

Mel was clearly pissed off, but Isla had no idea why. *She* was the one with a dislocated shoulder. *She* was the one who had to get her car repaired.

Mel's phone buzzed. 'Oh, thank God. Rose and Jess are here.' Mel peeled back the blue curtain surrounding the bed and stuck her head out into the ward. Isla shut her eyes and tried not to think of the pain, but it was impossible. It was all there was.

Jess stormed into the cubicle with a face like thunder.

'So this is what karma looks like,' said Jess, brandishing a gossip magazine. 'I brought you some light reading. Oh, and you owe me three hundred and fifty-two dollars.'

Isla's head hurt. 'What? Why?'

'Did you not see my missed calls? I'm on the cover of every trashy magazine in Australia, thanks to you.' Jess prodded the cover, and sure enough, there was a photo of Jess draped on top of the married guy from Bay Bliss. Isla squinted as she read the headline. 'Right, Nathan Campbell, that's his name.'

Nathan owned a restaurant in Byron Bay and had been a guest judge on *MasterChef* a few times. 'His brother, the movie star one, is Jason, and then the other brother has bought jewellery from the store. What's his name? *Wait!* The magazines didn't name you, did they? If the media link you to the Turner name, it could be bad for business.' That was the last thing she needed. They say there's no such thing as bad publicity, but that all depends on your brand. Wanting fame for fame's sake was a hell of a lot different from spending years building a solid reputation. At the end of the day, bad publicity was just that – *bad*.

Rose glanced around the cubicle, looking uncomfortable. 'The media reported everything except what really happened.'

'But they didn't use the Turner name, did they?'

Jess glared at Isla. '*Really?* Is that what you're concerned about? *Your* reputation? What about my reputation? *Look* at this!'

Rose placed her finger to her lips. 'Keep your voices down. People in here are sick.'

Jess crossed her arms in protest.

'Look, what's done is done,' said Rose. 'We know it was an accident. Isla had too much to drink, and we've all done that before. But Jess *is* right about one thing: you owe her three hundred and fifty-two dollars, and you owe me two hundred and eighty.'

'For *what*?'

'We had to buy as many of the magazines as we could, to stop people reading them. Now, tell me,' said Rose, taking a seat in the chair next to Isla's bed, 'what on earth made you think dangling from a piece of silk would help you uncover the *real* Isla Turner?'

Jess lifted the ice pack off Isla's shoulder and screwed up her face in disgust. 'Ouch, that's got to hurt. See, this is exactly why I didn't want to go to that class with you.'

Mel's shoulders dropped. 'You asked Jess to go to yoga? When?'

'She texted me last night.' Jess gently put the ice pack back in position.

Isla ignored Mel. When Jess had declined her invitation, Isla's next thought had been to ask Rose, but she knew Rose would just whine about breastfeeding, about how tired she was and how she'd have to fit it in around the kids' activities. The conversation alone would be draining. But there was no way Isla was going by herself, so she'd decided to ask Mel, even though they weren't exactly close.

It was uncanny how much Mel was like their dad: funny, carefree and more concerned about doing what she loved than about how much money she earned. Isla, on the other hand, was just like their mum: she knew what she wanted and would stop at nothing to get it. A lump formed in Isla's throat. Her dad had always been fun. He used to love chasing Mel around the back garden and playing board games with her. He'd always spent more time with them than Jacki, choosing to work from home so he could pick them up from school. It felt like a lifetime ago, and it was, in a way. Isla cleared her throat.

The other reason she'd asked Mel to join her was that Mel needed all the exercise she could get if she was ever going to run a marathon. Someone had to help her.

Rose stroked Isla's hair, the way a loving mother would look after their injured child. It felt good to have someone sympathetic to her cause, but the stroking was too much. Isla raised her good arm to stop Rose from fussing and winced as a sharp pain shot down her left arm. She sucked on the gas and closed her eyes against the bright fluorescent light overhead.

'What were you thinking?' asked Rose. 'Isn't aerial yoga for twenty-year-olds?'

Isla concentrated on her breathing. Aerial yoga had seemed so graceful and tranquil on the video she'd watched.

'She got competitive with the yoga teacher – in a beginners' class,' said Mel, rolling her eyes.

'Not everything's a competition, Isla,' said Jess. 'That attitude just takes the fun out of it.'

A stabbing pain radiated across Isla's chest and she inhaled. 'Well, *Mel* crashed my car!'

Rose gasped. 'Not the Lexus?'

'The BMW.' Mel scowled at Isla. 'That thing is impossible to park! It's just a small dent, and a broken headlight.' Mel's face flushed. 'It's easily fixable; Isla's just being a drama queen.'

'Looks like none of us are having a great day,' said Jess.

'I'm sorry about the magazines. Really, I am,' said Isla. Pain coursed through her left side. 'Could one of you go and find a doctor? *Please?*'

Jess threw the magazine in the bin. 'Sure.'

'Wait, I'm coming with you,' said Mel.

'You'll be okay,' said Rose to Isla. 'The girls will find a doctor who will fix you up, and then we can get the hell out of here.'

Isla knew how much Rose hated hospitals. 'Do *you* think I'm too competitive?'

Rose laughed. 'You're second in line to our mother.'

Isla frowned. Maybe it *had* been her fault. Her competitive nature had shown up in small ways in recent months. Like the time she'd broken her toe during the Boxing Day sales at David Jones. Jess had convinced Isla to come with her, and she'd got overexcited rushing to the perfume department. She'd just got caught up in the moment, she told herself. A month or so later, she'd spent a small fortune at an antique auction, on a glass vase that she didn't even like. Isla had just wanted to outbid the six-foot Parisian model who clearly thought she was better than everyone. Then there had been the incident at the pottery workshop she'd attended with Steve. It had been one of her first attempts to complete her mum's task, but the teacher had been completely hopeless, so Isla had schooled her on how a proper class should be run. Okay, she may have gone a bit far, but in her defence, she *had* just found out her mum was dying.

But why she'd had to prove she was better at aerial yoga than the instructor, she didn't know. Perhaps getting hurt was the universe's way of telling her to calm down. But she liked to win – at everything. Besides, she was good at it.

A few minutes later, Jess flew into the cubicle. Her entire demeanour had changed; she was rosy-cheeked and beaming. 'You'll never guess what!' Jess waved her phone in the air.

'Did you find a doctor?' asked Rose.

'I did, and you should have *seen* him. He was wearing a white coat with a stethoscope and everything. He was so hot!' Jess bounced on her toes. 'His name is *Dr Cavendish*, and we exchanged numbers!'

'That's great,' said Rose. 'But did you find a doctor for Isla?'

Jess's face dropped. '*Oh crap.* I'll be right back.'

Jess scooted off again, and Isla shut her eyes. This did not feel like winning.

15

Jess

Two days later, Jess sat cross-legged on the shaggy rug in her living room and leaned back against the sofa. She stared at the website she was designing, but she couldn't focus. The press had now discovered who the *mysterious brunette* was, and they were having a field day.

She opened Twitter for what must have been the hundredth time that day. Trending at number nine was #NaughtyNathan. Jess scrolled through memes and photos of her straddling Nathan Campbell. She'd spent hours flicking between Facebook, Instagram and Twitter, deleting the hate-fuelled comments left by trolls, and had been forced to change her settings from public to private.

Jess teared up as she scrolled through the comments on Twitter. Even though it had all just been an unfortunate accident, her anxiety had peaked after reading the vulgar remarks. Her heart beat so hard in her chest she went dizzy. She felt trapped inside her body. But she'd done nothing wrong! What must Nathan's wife have thought?

The comments and memes were like a slow-spreading toxin

that made her feel more unwell by the minute. She wished she could erase every trace of the incident in the media and online – she just wanted to disappear. Jess read comment after comment until her head hurt and her chin trembled. Social media platforms had a lot to answer for.

She'd spent years trying to avoid the media after an incident with Jacki at a high-profile Mother's Day brunch. Jacki had brought all her girls with her as a special treat, and Jess had only been a tyke at five years old. She remembered how excited she was to be there. But while they were in the restaurant, the number of paparazzi outside had grown to a rabble and when they'd come out, Jacki had tried to pick Jess up to keep her out of harm's way. Instead she'd lost her footing and tumbled, taking them both to the footpath. While her sisters had been lagging behind with Helen, the paparazzi had swarmed over them, desperate for a good photo. Jess and Jacki were trampled on, but still they didn't back up. Jess had screamed in terror, but they didn't care. She could still remember the deafening shouts as she looked up to a thunderous sky of cameras.

Jess threw her phone onto the sofa behind her and opened a travel website on her laptop. She typed in *Fiji* and a selection of Fijian hotels appeared. Clicking on the first one, she found the perfect getaway. It had all-inclusive beachfront bures with private heated plunge pools, a nightly flower-petal turndown service, and a host of activities, including rainforest and waterfall hikes. There was also a spa with aromatherapy pools and waterfall massages. She rolled her aching shoulders. What she wouldn't give for a full-body massage.

Jess had loved to travel as a kid. By the time she'd gone to university, she'd been to more countries than most people her age. After her sisters had left home, her mum often arranged for Jess and Helen to meet her for a few days if she was away from home for long periods. Jess loved the adventure of it all, but she also knew the free travel would end when she left home and went to university.

That's why, when Jess's best friend from high school begged her to go to California with her for three months and even said she'd pay for her plane tickets – or at least, her parents would – Jess jumped at the chance.

She hadn't planned on a summer fling with Todd, a surfer from Santa Monica, and it certainly hadn't been on her itinerary to marry him after four weeks. She'd just fallen in love, or so she'd thought. It had been great until she'd found him in bed with another woman on their one-month wedding anniversary. On the long flight home, Jess's heartbreak reminded her of the never-ending cycle of hope and grief she'd experienced every time she thought her parents might finally get together. Their love had never been enough for them to overcome their differences. Was it even possible to love someone without experiencing heartbreak? She'd heard plenty of stories and seen plenty of movies with happily ever afters, but maybe that was something she couldn't have.

Jess decided she'd never let her heart get broken again and promised herself she'd put all her energy into getting her business off the ground. She could rely on herself. She didn't need anyone else.

The Californian disaster hadn't put Jess off travel, though. The challenge now was taking time off. If she didn't work, she didn't earn. But her focus and discipline over the years had paid off, and she was proud of what she'd accomplished on her own. Innovative Design was thriving.

Still, by thirty, she'd thought she might have found someone she could stay with for more than just a few weeks. She'd dated plenty of guys over the years, but Jacki was right: none of her relationships had lasted longer than three months. By around the eight-week mark, when things would start getting more serious, Jess would find herself pulling away. She couldn't explain it, it was just the way things worked out, and there was no way she would keep dating someone when it didn't feel right.

Is Mum lonely? Her parents' relationship may have never developed into something enduring, but it was still the most serious relationship Jacki had been in for the last three decades. Did she regret not trying to make it work with Darryl?

Although Jess was single, lived alone and worked from home, she wasn't lonely. On the contrary, she liked her own company. She liked that she could go anywhere and do anything without explaining herself. There was a freedom that came with not having to please or answer to anyone else.

Perhaps her mum's terms of inheritance *were* too hard. What did it matter if Jess never made a long-term commitment to anyone? It's not like she didn't want a relationship, but you couldn't persuade the heart to feel anything it didn't really feel.

She stared at the luxurious infinity pool on her laptop. Surrounded by lush green palms, it looked out onto a turquoise ocean. Jess closed her eyes and imagined the sound of breaking waves and the warm breeze on her skin.

She jumped as her intercom buzzed. Reluctantly, she got up and pressed the speaker. 'Hello?'

'Jessica Freeman-Turner? This is Alison Silvers from the *Courier Mail*. Could I ask you some questions?'

Jess breathed hard. Her whole body went numb, and the room began to spin.

'It won't take a minute,' said Alison. 'We just want to hear your side of the Nathan Campbell story.'

Jess stepped away from the intercom. They'd tracked her down. She was trapped. Rushing into her living room, she opened the sliding door to her balcony, stepped out, and looked down three storeys to the front entrance of her building. A couple of photographers with long lens cameras stood on the pavement. Jess darted inside, closed her door and then her blinds. '*Shit!*'

Glancing down at photos of the Fijian paradise, she grabbed her phone, then paused as she considered the best course of action. She was still angry at Isla, and she didn't want to make Mel uncomfortable, so she called Rose.

Jess paced the living room while it rang. 'Pick up, pick up.'

'Hey,' Rose answered.

'Do you have a passport for Bethany?'

'What? Why?'

Jess stared at her laptop and took a deep breath. 'Because I'm about to make your day.'

16

Rose

'What did you expect?' Rose slurped her bright pink mocktail while breastfeeding Bethany. 'You booked us into a hotel with mostly couples and newlyweds. There won't be any single guys here.'

Sitting in the comfort of the sun loungers on the deck of the Fijian bure, Rose watched the ocean sparkle in the September sun as Jess finished a sketch she'd drawn of Bethany. For Rose, the last three days had been a whirlwind of packing, shopping and planning, but now she was sitting in paradise with her daughter and her younger sister. The warm sun and ocean breeze felt good for the soul. It was the most relaxed she'd felt in months. She couldn't believe it when Jess had asked her to go to Fiji with her. It couldn't have come at a better time.

'I thought there'd be other hotels close by. I didn't think we'd be in the middle of nowhere.'

Jess had sold Rose on the idea of an all-expenses-paid week in Fiji, claiming she needed help with her task, and that a holiday romance could be the answer. Rose knew it was an excuse to get out of the country until the media frenzy died down, but who could blame her? Rose happily played along.

Ever since the incident with the paparazzi when she'd been little, Jess had hated any kind of media attention, and she'd even somehow managed to avoid any Turner family publicity photo shoots or events. When Rose, Isla and Mel had been growing up, they had been unceremoniously thrust into the limelight and paraded around like props at their mother's beck and call. Luckily, Jacki and Isla were the only Turners the media were interested in now. The other sisters had managed to keep a low profile since leaving home – at least, until the Bay Bliss Music Festival disaster.

'Well, I enjoyed our couples' massage,' said Rose. 'Thank you. And Bethany did so well to sleep through it, didn't you, gorgeous girl?' Rose bopped Bethany on the nose, then reached out and squeezed Jess's arm. 'I mean it. Thanks for this holiday. It's just what I needed.' Rose was still deflated after Tom and the kids' feedback about her manuscript and, after spending the last week trying to salvage her story, she'd decided to ditch it and write something new. The only problem was, she had no new ideas. It was like her brain had shut down, and in the part where her imagination should have been, there was nothing but a vast void.

Jess's phone pinged. '*Shit!*'

'What is it?'

'A text from that bloody journalist. *This is Alison Silvers. If you want to tell your side of the Nathan Campbell story, you have my number. Enjoy Fiji.* How the hell does she know I'm here?'

'Block her number.'

'Done.' Jess stared at her phone. 'I hate this. My nerves are shot to pieces.'

'Well, I think you're handling the whole fiasco really well.' Rose switched Bethany to her other breast. 'I know how much you hate being in the spotlight.' Rose knew Jess often knocked 'Turner' off her surname, choosing anonymity over recognition.

'At least by the time we get back, the media should have a new story.' Jess closed her sketch pad and adjusted her wide-brimmed sunhat. 'All this stuff with Mum though, it's got me thinking. I've been saving all this money for the trip of a lifetime, but I have no one to go with, and I'm so busy with work I don't feel I'll ever be able to take enough time off. Meanwhile, life is passing me by, so … What the hell. Here's to enjoying life right now.' Jess picked up her fluorescent blue cocktail, raised her glass and took a sip.

'I'll drink to that,' said Rose, taking a swig of her drink.

Jess nodded towards the notepad and pen on the table. 'How's your writing going?'

'I have nothing. I'm starting to think my baby brain is permanent.'

Jess pulled a hotel towel over her legs. 'Mum's terms are impossible.'

'Mel said you collected quite a few numbers at that singles paint night.'

'It was awful. Those events are always so forced.'

'And what happened to the doctor at the hospital?'

'I called him and it went to voicemail.'

'So try again.' Rose sighed as she finished breastfeeding and burped Bethany. 'Well, let's take the pressure off. Forget about meeting someone this week. Maybe we could be proactive for you in a different way.'

'What do you mean?'

'We could try to figure out why you've never been with anyone longer than three months.'

'It's not from lack of trying.'

'You know, you shouldn't let what happened between you and Todd put you off having a relationship.'

Jess ran her fingers across her towel. Rose could see the hurt on her face. 'We were only together for eight weeks, but I was convinced I was in love with him. And it hurt, at the end – it hurt so bad. I was such an idiot.'

'Stop it. Don't talk about yourself like that!'

Jess grinned. 'Sorry, *Mum*.'

'I mean it. So it didn't work out, and yes, I imagine it hurt like hell, but at least you tried. You put yourself out there.'

'It was embarrassing, and now I have to explain to potential partners that I'm divorced, when I was only married for four weeks, which makes it sound even worse. It was such a colossal mistake.'

'Mistakes build character. They make you interesting.'

'If you're saying mistakes are a good thing, then why can't you forgive Mum?'

'You have to *learn* from them, and besides, she's never admitted to making any. Jacki Turner only makes informed choices. Now, come on, let's stay focused on you. What happened between you and that lifesaver you were seeing last year? He seemed like a pretty nice guy.'

'Blake? I told you, he made this noise when he chewed his food. I couldn't stand it.'

'And what about … Derek? That guy who worked for that printing firm.'

'He kept stroking his facial hair like it was a pet.'

'And that guy from the gym?'

'Evan. He was too tall. I had to have six months of chiro after dating him.'

Rose tilted her head to one side. 'They sound a lot like excuses to me.'

'Well, maybe I want to be on my own. There's nothing wrong with being single.'

'Then tell Mum you don't want to do your task.' Rose wiped sick off Bethany's chin with her bib. 'Tell her how damaging it is.'

'Her heart's in the right place.'

'What heart?'

'Stop it, Rose. I hate it when you do that.'

'Do what?'

'You and Mum have more in common than either of you will ever acknowledge. You both experienced the loss of a husband and became instant single parents. I just don't understand why you can't find any common ground. Sometimes, it's like you want us to pick sides, and we can't do that. We love you, and we love Mum too.'

Jess's words stung, but mostly because Rose knew she was right. Rose *did* have those things in common with her mother, but their differences lay in how they'd reacted. Plus, she was desperate for some sisterly solidarity. Jacki never showed up for them, and these terms of inheritance were completely unreasonable. Rose wanted her sisters to be as mad as she was. At least then she wouldn't always be the bad guy.

'But then I suppose we are all our mother's daughters,' said Jess, taking off her wide-brimmed hat. 'Mum couldn't even make it work with my dad, and those two are clearly in love. If they can't make it happen, what hope have I got?'

'Is that what you're scared of? Of finding the one and still not being able to live happily ever after?'

'I don't know. I've learned to accept that they don't want to be together. It is what it is.' Jess pushed up her sunglasses. 'But I know they love each other, and I keep thinking about how lonely Mum must be now without anyone to look after her.'

'She's got Helen.'

'That's not the same.'

'Does your dad know about Mum's cancer?'

'She made me promise not to tell him. She doesn't want anyone knowing, not even her friends. It's eating me up inside. But then I think about what you and Richard went through, and … I don't know how you did that.'

'Life didn't turn out how we planned, and when he died it was … it was awful … but I can't ever imagine not having been with him. He was my best friend, and if I could have those few years we had together over again, I would, even if it played out the same way. I've got no regrets.' Rose recalled the first time she and Richard had kissed. They'd been swimming at Surfer's Paradise with her uni friends, and after a week of flirting with each other, he'd kissed her as they were coming out of the water. His lips were salty and warm, and it was the best kiss she'd ever had.

Rose smiled at Bethany and bounced her on her knee. 'And now I have Tom and I've been given another chance at love. He's been a blessing for me and the kids. What I've learned is that loving someone comes with a certain amount of risk, but it's a risk worth taking.'

'Maybe you're right.' Jess twirled a piece of loose hair between her fingers. 'But Blake still wasn't right for me. Eating a meal with him nearly sent me over the edge.'

Rose laughed. 'Don't fret about your task. You'll either find someone, or you won't. Just promise me you won't force anything.'

'But what about the inheritance? We could all use the money.'

'True, but so could all the animals in those shelters. Either way, some good will come out of these terms. I mean, look at me. I'm sitting in Fiji sipping mocktails with my favourite sister.'

Jess smirked. 'Favourite?'

'Any sister who whisks me away on an all-expenses-paid holiday is my favourite.'

Jess laughed and lay back on the sun lounger. 'You know, I'd forgotten all about the Aussie Animal Rescue. Maybe they do deserve the money more than us.'

'I know you don't want to hear this, but the truth is, Mum is out of control. If she's not careful, she's going to lose all of us.'

'Don't say that.'

'I'm sorry, but she needs to learn that she can't always get what she wants. We're adults. She has no control over us.'

Jess frowned. 'What are you going to do?'

'Don't worry, I won't come between the two of you. This is between me and her.' Rose stood and Bethany rubbed her eye with her fist. It was nearly time for her nap.

'You say that, but your relationship with Mum affects us all. And so do the terms.'

Now Rose felt shitty. As she stared out towards a small group of snorkellers exploring the calm green ocean, she made a mental note to tone down the anti-mum outbursts. After all, she was here to support Jess.

Jess sighed, put down her drink and picked up her phone. 'Fine, you win.'

'How's that?'

'Well, there's only one way I can find out if love really is worth the risk. I mean, how hard can it be to date a hot doctor for three months?'

17

Isla

From the balcony of her Q1 presidential penthouse, Isla watched beachgoers scurry to and from the surf like tiny ants. The sky-high penthouse had been an expensive purchase, but the views and heated indoor pool had been impossible to resist.

On speakerphone, Isla chatted to Steve, who was in Sydney on business. At one point, they'd moved the Turner Jewellers headquarters there, but Isla was a Queensland girl at heart, and she'd missed the long surf beaches she'd grown up swimming at.

As a kid, she'd spent most of her spare time in the pool or the ocean. Helen had always joked that she was surprised Isla hadn't grown fins and a tail. Isla had fond memories of doing Nippers on the weekends. She used to love doing squads before and after school and participating in the swimming carnivals. She swam so much that as a teen, she'd cut off her long red hair, opting for a pixie-cut instead. That way, she didn't have to worry about the chlorine and the salt damage. Besides, the style had looked super cute on her.

Isla had always thrived on the highs that came with competing and winning in the pool, but her enthusiasm for swimming waned when she left school and did a master's degree in business. Her razor-sharp focus in the water always left her feeling like she could take on the world, and over two decades later, she got the same rush from working hard and making her business thrive. As much as Isla loved being in the water, a swimming career wouldn't give her the lavish lifestyle she wanted.

Isla's drive to push harder than her competitors meant she could now afford to swim in the sky. It was just a shame she had only swum in her pool once since buying the penthouse four years earlier.

'I've been looking at the numbers coming out of the Adelaide store,' said Steve. 'I want to go through them with you when I get back tomorrow. We may have to reconsider keeping it open.'

'Don't be such a drama queen,' said Isla. 'All stores—'

'Need a little time, I know, but it's had a year, and it's still not bringing in the profit we need. We can't afford to have a store that's only just ticking over.'

'We're not closing the store. We can take a look at some new marketing strategies, but I'll be damned if we're going to shut it. We're meant to be *growing* the business.'

'If it's not working down there, we should just cut our losses.'

'Cut our losses!' Isla Turner never lost money. She didn't lose at anything. 'I'm not closing it, so we need to make it work.'

'How's your shoulder?'

Isla smiled. 'Don't change the subject. You need to come up with a plan.'

'I miss you.'

Isla pressed her lips together and tried not to laugh. Her relationship with Steve was built around their business, and working and living together was trying at times. But there was no one else who could make her smile like him. He knew how she functioned on every level. He knew what she needed and when. She could be drowning in work and he would know how to help. She'd lost count of the times she'd had to work through till the early hours and, every time, Steve had rolled up his sleeves and sat in the trenches with her. Steve, like Isla, wasn't afraid of hard work and that was one of the many things she loved about him.

He was even onboard when Isla told him she was going to keep her name when they got married. Growing up, Isla had been acutely aware of how the Turner name was associated with wealth and prestige. At its merest mention, people would treat her with a respect and generosity that she hadn't in any way earned. It had been like waving a magic wand, which had allowed her to get almost anything she wanted. So when they founded their first jewellery store, there was only one name it would have.

'What time did you say Helen was coming round?' asked Steve.

'Anytime now. Why?'

'No reason. Look, I've got to go. See you tomorrow when I get back.'

'Okay, see you then.' As she ended the call, her phone buzzed with a text from Helen.

I'm on my way up.

Isla stepped back inside and made her way to the kitchen to get some ibuprofen. Her shoulder ached. It had been a week since the yoga accident, and Isla was still restless and irritated by the whole debacle. Last night, when the pain in her shoulder kept her awake, she'd tried to sift through the events of that day. She was furious the teacher had allowed her to get into a dangerous situation. She was annoyed at Mel's lack of sympathy and her inability to park a car, and shocked that Mel had been the one to go off at *her*. Her sister had never spoken to her like that in her life. Isla was also upset that Jess had been so quick to blame her for the whole Nathan Campbell incident. She hadn't even wanted to go to the festival in the first place. Plus, Jess was the one who'd got her drunk on that nasty cheap cider.

With all the drama of the last few weeks and the constant discomfort of her shoulder, it was no wonder she was out of sorts. She just had to try and stay focused on work. She needed a break from trying to find out *who* she really was.

It was such a stupid task. In fact, it was virtually impossible. How was she supposed to know if she was on the right track? You couldn't measure something so airy-fairy and subjective. It was like she was desperately trying to get somewhere but didn't know the name of the destination, or where it was. She was lost.

The private elevator doors opened, and Helen bustled into the kitchen. She had a folder under one arm and held a container of what smelt like freshly made chicken soup.

'Good, you kept your sling on,' said Helen, putting her things on the kitchen counter and giving Isla a careful hug.

'Have you had lunch yet? I made us soup,' said Helen.

'No, I'm starving.'

Watching Helen make herself at home reminded Isla that Helen was a person with her own life and family away from the Turner residence. She had a son in his late forties who still hadn't flown the nest, and she'd been married to Mick for over four decades. And yet Helen played such a pivotal role in the Turner family. Isla couldn't think of her as one of her mum's employees. Helen was family.

Isla was used to Helen's motherly fussing, although she couldn't stand it from anyone else. Over the years, she'd learnt it was easier to let Helen get on with it rather than trying to suppress her good intentions. Most of the time, Isla could tolerate Helen's insistent need to help, guide and support her family, but once or twice she'd lost her temper, and the backlash had been enough to cool her jets. Helen managed the Turner family with a firm hand, but she had a heart of gold and a clear head. She brought calm to the Turners' craziness, and kept them connected and communicating. With so many strong personalities in the mix, that in itself was a tremendous accomplishment.

Helen gazed out of the floor-to-ceiling windows, across the Gold Coast city skyline and down towards the beach. 'That view makes me dizzy. There's something not right about being this high up.'

'You get used to it.' Isla poured herself a small glass of water and swallowed two ibuprofen while Helen dug out a saucepan and heated the soup on the stove. 'How's Mum?'

'She's having a good day so far. She's asked Eddie to step up on the business side of things.'

Eddie had been Jacki's second in command for over ten years, and Isla knew she trusted him with her life.

Helen stirred the soup. 'Mel called and told me what happened at the yoga studio.'

'And?' Isla took a seat at the kitchen island.

'And … I also had a phone call from Jess, and then last night I spoke to Steve.'

'Steve? I just spoke to him. He didn't mention anything.'

'He told me about a pottery class you went to. Said you were pretty rude to the teacher there. Sounds like it's been an interesting few weeks.'

'Don't start. None of that was my fault. The pottery teacher clearly couldn't teach. Everyone was struggling to make a bowl, not just me. Anyway, they say bad things happen in threes, and they were my three … or four. So now I'm good for a while.'

'Not your fault? That's not what I heard.' Helen got out two soup bowls and a couple of spoons. 'You're saying you weren't rude to the yoga teacher, or to Mel when she was driving you to the hospital?'

'I was injured, in pain, and you know what my sisters are like. They're all overly sensitive.'

'And I suppose you were in pain when you showed more concern for the Turner reputation than for poor Jess when her photo was splashed over every magazine in Australia?'

'I *was* in pain, and I have every right to worry about the Turner brand too. It's my livelihood.'

'And Jess is your sister. From what I was told, you didn't show an ounce of compassion.'

'Hang on, I was the one in the hospital bed.' Isla didn't know why she had to defend herself. And wasn't Helen supposed to be making her feel better? She'd brought her chicken soup, for heaven's sake.

'Do you know why they all called me?'

'Because they have nothing better to do?'

'Because the Isla Turner they know doesn't listen. And if they dare say something to you that you don't like, you bite down hard.'

Isla stood. 'Now wait a minute—'

'Sit down, dear,' Helen said, her voice firm. 'You need to hear this.'

Isla sat, staring at Helen in disbelief.

'You're surrounded by people who are too terrified to tell you the truth and call you out on your behaviour. It has to stop. You're hurting those you love, and one day that will catch up to you. Even your mum can see it. Why do you think she set you your task?'

Isla's throat tightened. 'So, what, this is some kind of intervention?'

'There's no excuse for your behaviour, Isla. It's time to wake up and take a look at the damage you're doing before it's too late.'

'Too late?'

'Everyone has their limits. Don't risk losing those you love.'

Helen's words struck like a knife to the heart, and Isla's bottom lip quivered as she fought back tears.

Helen stirred the soup. 'Tell me,' she said, her tone softening. 'How are you going with your task?'

Isla sniffed and straightened her back. 'I've been thinking about it, and I decided that what you see is what you get.' Isla lifted her chin. '*This* is the *real* me. You're looking at the one and only, truly authentic Isla Turner.' But even as she said it, she didn't buy it. *Never apologise for being you,* Jacki had always told her. When her mum walked into a room, her presence screamed, *Take me as you find me or get out!* So why was she giving her this task? Did she have regrets? Or did she think Isla had gone too far and wanted to know if there was a kinder, more humble Isla hidden somewhere deep within?

Helen sighed.

'Well, I don't know what Mum wants from me! Everyone else's task is clear, but mine is a joke. I'm not going to change who I am. I get things done. I get results. Mum should understand that – she taught me everything I know. Look around you, Helen. I'm a success.' Isla cradled her sore arm in its sling. She was a winner, and winners were fearless and fierce. Being indifferent got you nowhere.

Helen poured the soup into bowls and handed one to Isla. 'I can see what you've achieved, and your mum isn't questioning your work ethic. What she wants to know is who you'd be without all of this stuff, without the Turner reputation, without the *yes* people you surround yourself with.' She blew on a spoonful of soup.

'Well, that's easy. I'd be sad. Very, *very* sad. And, I'll have you know, they're not *yes* people. I can't help it if I'm always right.'

'Have you read the information in the folder I put together for you?'

Isla knew this was coming. 'I misplaced it.' In truth, she'd binned it the moment she got home. She didn't need help.

'I thought you might have, so I brought you another copy.' Helen slid the folder across the kitchen counter.

'I'm trying all sorts of new activities.'

'And how has that gone for you so far?'

Isla could have cried. 'What's your point?'

'Your task isn't about fitting in more activities on top of everything else you do. It's about stripping back, peeling away the layers.'

'What does that even mean? You sound like some hippy from the sixties.'

'It means you have to work out who you'd be without your wealth, without the Turner name to fall back on, without Steve smoothing over relationships behind your back.'

That last remark hurt. 'He doesn't do that.' Then she remembered him apologising to the pottery teacher after she'd stormed out of the class. How many times had he apologised for her behaviour without her knowing? 'I can't change my name, and I'm not about to throw my money away in some deranged social experiment.'

'No one is asking you to. But I want you to imagine your life without those things. Go on, close your eyes right now and picture yourself in that pottery or yoga class.'

'This is ridiculous.'

'Close your eyes.'

Isla sighed but did as she was told. She pictured herself sitting at the potting wheel in the ceramics studio. 'This is stupid.'

'Now, I want you to recall the events of that session and pretend you're one of the other students in the class. I want you to look at Isla Turner. Do you like who you see? Would you want to be friends with her?'

'I wasn't there to make new friends. I have friends.'

'You didn't answer the question.'

Isla watched herself in her mind as she accused the over-enthusiastic pottery teacher of having poor teaching skills. 'Mum had just told us she was dying. I was under a lot of stress.'

'You still haven't answered the question.'

Isla fumed. Did Helen want her to hate herself? 'Fine. No, I wouldn't like her. I wouldn't want to be her friend.'

'Now, imagine you're taking the class, but you're not a Turner, and you're a woman juggling full-time work and kids and you're there for a bit of well-earned down-time. Would you have behaved differently?'

Isla sighed. 'Maybe … okay, probably.'

'Excellent. That is what it means to strip everything back, to remove the ego. The more you can practise exercises like this, the more you'll be able to see who you really are. Then it's up to you to do something about it. Keep what you love about yourself and tweak what you don't.'

Isla opened her eyes and stared at her soup. She wasn't hungry anymore. 'Well, now I feel like shit. My shoulder's hurting *and* I don't feel great about the pottery workshop.'

Helen smiled. 'But you've taken the first step. Have a look at the first few pages of the folder. There are some good ideas in there.'

Isla flipped open the folder. At the front was a list of spiritual retreats in Queensland. 'You want me to get all woo woo?'

'These retreats are for everyone. They're about going on an inner journey of self-discovery.'

'How can some stranger show me who I am?'

'Isla, it's an *inner* journey. You do the work. But it takes time and practice. You'll have to be patient.'

Isla closed the folder and pushed it away. 'I doubt my schedule will allow me to take a weekend off. I'm a busy woman. People rely on me.'

'Then think of your mum and your sisters. You're doing this for them too, remember? Jess and Rose have gone to Fiji to get away from it all. It could do you good to stop for a few days too, give you a chance to take stock of everything.'

Isla stirred her soup and the dull ache from her shoulder radiated down her arm. Perhaps a retreat would be a good idea. She could do with a holiday. In fact, maybe she *deserved* a few days away from it all. Reading novels, drinking cocktails, taking time to reflect. She could book herself in for some spa treatments too.

'You know what? Maybe you're right.' Isla took a mouthful of her soup. 'A retreat could be just what I need.'

18

Mel

Mel's eyes teared and her thighs burned. As she crossed the 100-metre mark, she slowed to a walk, sucked in as much oxygen as her lungs would allow, then bent over and tried not to vomit. Interval training was the worst. All the runners' magazines claimed that sprinting intervals were the way to go if you wanted to run faster and keep a good pace over long distances. Mel had run four 100-metre sprints and had two more to complete.

Sitting on a bench at the sidelines, Corey checked the stopwatch on his phone and pulled a face. 'That wasn't terrible ... but it wasn't great either. The definition of sprinting is to run fast, so maybe try that next time.'

Mel wanted to respond with some witty comeback, but she still couldn't breathe, so instead she raised her middle finger. Corey laughed a deep roar, and his bright eyes widened in delight. She loved his contagious smile, and she found herself grinning back, even though she was in a world of pain.

Walking back to the start line, her breathing steadied. Although she was tired, she knew she could power through the next two sprints if she dug deep. In the last four weeks, she'd had more energy, even though her muscles ached and on most days she was as stiff as a board. But she was following the advice from the folder Helen had given her to a tee, and although it was still early days, she was beginning to see results.

She could now run two kilometres without stopping, albeit slowly. In celebration, Corey was treating her to a movie at the cinema tonight. He had become her biggest supporter, and had helped her put together a training program. She kept Saturday mornings for her long runs, while mid-week, she ran shorter distances and tried to run faster. On Wednesdays she did weights at home, following a program Joe had created for her to build muscle.

Training for a marathon was time-consuming, but she had to be fully committed if she wanted to finish the Gold Coast Marathon. There were no shortcuts and no easy ways out. She just had to do the work.

'Ready?' Corey hit his phone. 'Go!'

Springing off from the white line, Mel kept her focus on the finish line dead ahead. She pushed forward with all her might and could feel the power in her thighs and arms. At the finish, her eyes teared again as she breathed hard.

'That was better,' said Corey. 'Just one more to go.'

She couldn't speak, but raised her hand to tell him she'd heard him as she turned to walk back to the start. She wished she had a different task. She'd love to write a kid's book; she was sure she'd be good at it. She'd also like to go on a self-discovery journey like Isla; meditating and grounding didn't sound that hard. She'd especially have liked Jess's task. Mel had been single for the last two years, ever since her ex, Kevin, had told her in a drunken outburst that he was bored by her inability to be spontaneous. She'd been crushed that their six-month relationship had ended. That was until she'd met Corey. Corey, who was turning up for her day after day, keeping her focused and encouraging her every step of the way.

'Five seconds left to rest,' he said.

Mel positioned her feet at the start line, ready for her final sprint.

'Go!'

Mel ran as fast as she could, using every ounce of energy she had left. Sweat poured from her forehead and ran into her eyes, but she didn't stop. As she approached the finish line, she caught sight of something long and brown out of the corner of her eye. Distracted, she stumbled and fell. 'Ow!'

Corey stood, picked up his crutch and made his way over to her. 'You okay?'

Mel sobbed as she recalled Amber Ryan taunting her after tripping her up when she was a kid. 'No. I'm not okay! This is too hard!' She rubbed her ankle and nodded towards a long brown stick on the ground. 'I thought it was a bloody snake.'

Corey laughed and sat down next to her.

'Don't make me re-run the sprint.' Mel glared at the finish line and her chest tightened. She had begun to feel like the old Mel, the one who was teased and picked on, who was weak and didn't love herself. She hated that Mel, just like she hated those kids at school who had been mean and cruel.

The self-hatred had almost been worse than the relentless bullying that had caused it. The constant ridicule at the hands of Amber Ryan had worn her down over the two years she'd attended Mel's school, but it had all come to a head in Year Ten when Amber had given her a black eye and a broken rib for daring to look at her. Although she'd been expelled, Helen had suggested Jacki move Mel to another school for a fresh start. As a result, the last two years of high school had been bearable, but the damage had already been done. Since then, Mel hadn't been comfortable putting herself out there. She always felt like someone was waiting to laugh at her, to take her down a peg or two.

Mel sniffed. The toxic voice in her head telling her she was worthless had gnawed its way back in the last few weeks. She'd thought she'd moved past all that. *Surely I'm stronger than I was twenty years ago.*

'I hate running.'

Corey placed his hand on top of hers. 'Hey, I won't make you do anything you don't want to.'

'I wish Mum would say that. I don't mind doing a task; I just don't want to do this one.'

'You're improving, Mel. That would have been your fastest 100 metres if you hadn't fallen.'

'I know I'm getting better, and I should be pleased, but it's not the same when you're forced to do something. I just feel resentful all the time.'

'Your sisters probably feel the same.'

'Jess and Rose have been living it up in Fiji. A marathon is much harder than either of their tasks. Even fit people don't run marathons. They know how tough it is.'

'But at the end of this you could be a multi-millionaire. I know a lot of people who'd run a marathon for that. But, if you don't want to do it, don't. You still have a choice.'

'Do I? I just can't believe Jess has got every guy under the sun throwing his details at her, and she still can't pick one to hang out with for three months.' Mel had always harboured a jealous streak towards her younger sister. One minute Mel had been the baby of the family and daddy's little girl, the next her dad was dead and she had a new sister who got all the attention. Jess even had a dad who belonged just to her. And she was winning in adulthood too. She was eight years younger than Mel but had somehow managed to fly ahead of her both financially and career-wise. And now, Jess had chosen to take Rose to Fiji instead of her. That hurt.

Corey smiled and shook his head.

'What's so funny?'

'I think deep down you know you have what it takes. You know you can run a marathon, but if you see it through that'll mean your mum was right. If you pull this off, you'll have to admit you've got all this hidden potential just waiting to be put to good use and, if that's true, you'll no longer be satisfied living a safe life and avoiding any risks or challenges. You'll have to really give this living gig a good shot, and I think that scares the crap out of you.'

It was like Corey had ripped off her invisibility cloak and he could see the real her. Mel's heart hurt and she wanted to throw up. This was exactly why Kevin had left her, and now here was Corey implying the same thing. 'Why would you say that? Why would you be so unkind?'

'Hey, I'm not trying to hurt you, I meant it as a compliment. I can see the potential you have, even if you can't. Plus, I know how hard it can be.' Corey raised his crutch. 'I do it every day.'

'Well, now I feel like an ungrateful whinger.'

Corey grinned. 'Tell me, what would you do if money was no object?'

'Buy a car.'

'Come on.'

'I don't know. I'd still want to be around kids. I'd like to do what you do, maybe open an art therapy studio. Put my degree to some use.'

'You really don't see it, do you?'

'What?'

'All of that is within your reach right now. You don't need money, you just need the confidence to go and get it.'

Maybe Corey was right. But the fact that Mel was being forced to do a task because of Amber Ryan was too triggering. It was like she was reliving the trauma. Memories that had faded to black had resurfaced and she was struggling mentally.

Mel took a breath. She was a grown woman now, who could have a strong voice if she was brave enough. All she had to do was make her mum listen.

19

Isla

Isla flipped down the visor in the passenger seat of her Lexus to keep the setting sun from blinding her, and adjusted the slats of the aircon to blow towards her armpits so she wouldn't get sweat marks on her khaki satin blouse. The unexpected late September heatwave was sticky and uncomfortable.

'I could have driven myself,' she said to Steve, who'd insisted on taking her to the silent retreat. 'It's only for three nights. Now you've got a two-and-a-half-hour drive home, and then you've got to come and pick me up. That's two whole days wasted.'

Steve watched the narrow winding road flanked by dense bush and dragged his hand over his shaven head. He'd started to lose his hair in his early twenties, and finally, five years ago, he'd taken the plunge and shaved it all off. Isla loved it. He looked more mature and wise. 'I don't mind, it's like a mini road trip. Plus, I've got an audiobook for the journey home.' Steve reached for her hand.

Isla slid open the visor mirror, took off her Gucci sunglasses and inspected a crease on her chin that was becoming a permanent wrinkle. 'You reckon this retreat will convince Mum I'm serious about searching for *the real me*?'

'Can't hurt, right?'

'Oh, bugger!'

Steve glanced at her. 'What?'

'I left my gold Jimmy Choos at home.' She could see them sitting pretty on the far right of the floor-to-ceiling shoe rack in her walk-in robe. They went great with the noir pantsuit she'd packed.

'I don't think you'll be needing them.'

Isla pulled at the faint crow's-feet that she'd had frozen with Botox six months earlier. 'You know, I don't think I've ever not spoken for two days.'

Steve laughed.

'It's not funny. This will be impossible.'

'Well, at least try. We need that money.'

'What are you talking about?' She slammed the visor shut.

'The Adelaide store.'

'We're working on a marketing plan. Once it gets some media coverage, it'll do just as well as the other stores.'

Lines deepened on Steve's forehead. 'Hmm.'

'*You* said we should open in Adelaide. *You* agreed it was the right move.'

Steve said nothing, and she shook her head and folded her arms. He knew she would never close a store once it opened. It would look bad. He was just being dramatic.

Steve slowed and pulled into a private road where a weathered wooden sign, perched under an early-flowering jacaranda, read *Sunshine Coast Silent Retreat*. 'We're here.' He drove up a dirt track and a confetti of purple flowers rained down on them. The road cut through towering gums and, in the branches above, Isla caught glimpses of the orange sky filled with bulbous grey and white clouds. To her right, a wallaby foraged in the tall grass.

Steve drove up a steep incline and the Lexus flew over the potholes with ease. Isla was glad they hadn't driven the BMW. 'I thought you said this was five-star accommodation.'

'I said the people who have stayed here *rated* it five stars.'

At the top of the hill, a clearing allowed space for a few cars to park, and an old wooden building sat against a backdrop of lush green mountains.

'Where's the hotel lobby?' Isla's heart quickened. 'Why is there no porter? This can't be the entrance.'

Steve parked and unfastened his seatbelt.

'Why are you stopping the car?'

'This is it.'

'No, Steve, this is a shack on a hill. You promised me a retreat. Resort-style, you know, with room service, day spas, pool, sauna. This isn't what I signed up for.'

'It's supposed to be one of the best places. They have a crazy waiting list.'

'I don't give a shit! You know what I'm like about cleanliness. This doesn't look *clean*!'

'I packed your sheets and your own pillow like always. You'll be fine.'

Steve got out of the Lexus and lifted her oversized suitcase out of the boot. She didn't move. There was no way she was spending three nights out here in the wilderness.

Steve opened her door.

'You know I don't camp.'

'This isn't camping. It's one of the best silent retreats in Australia.'

'Where are you getting this information?'

'It's on their website. You said you'd looked at it. You read the brochure, didn't you? I printed it out.'

'I didn't have time. I *trusted* you with this. You know what I like and what I don't, and I do *not* like this.' Getting out of the Lexus, she stumbled on the uneven ground and nearly rolled her ankle in her nude four-inch Fendi court shoes. 'Why would you do this to me? I can't spend three nights here!'

Steve chewed his lower lip and wrinkled his nose.

'What?' He only ever pulled that ridiculous face when he knew she wouldn't be happy. 'What aren't you telling me?'

'It's not a three-night retreat. I booked you in for ten nights.'

Isla laughed and shook her head. 'Now I know you're kidding. This whole stopping in the middle of nowhere in front of a shack was a joke. Good one!' She opened the door to the Lexus, ready to climb back in. 'You got me. Getting the suitcase out of the car, that was good. *Jeez*, I thought you were serious.' Steve remained frozen, almost as if he was too scared to move. 'You *are* kidding, aren't you?'

'That's why I drove you. I knew you wouldn't stay otherwise.'

Isla stood stock still, dumbfounded. 'No, Steve. You're lying. You have to be, because I've only packed for a three-night stay.'

Steve held up a recyclable Woolworths bag.

'What's that?'

'Some sweats and extra undies. They said it's all you'll need.'

Heat rushed through her. 'No ... I don't own *sweats*.'

'I bought you some.'

Isla stormed over and looked him dead in the eye. He was sweating profusely and blinking rapidly. He wasn't lying. 'Tell me you're fucking with me.'

Steve shook his head and rubbed his brow.

'I can't stay here for ten days, in a hut in the middle of nowhere! Not without my things! And who will run the business?'

'I will.' He held up his hands in defence. 'Don't get mad. It's all organised. You need to see this for what it is.'

'And what's that?'

'A once in a lifetime experience.'

'I can't not talk for ten days!'

'Isla, the waitlist for this place is months long. I had to bribe one of the staff members to send me a list of all the guests booked in this week, then I had to find a guest who was willing to give up their spot, which wasn't cheap, and then I had to bribe the staff member again so they'd delete the guest I paid off and replace them with you.'

'Wow! That's a lot of effort you went to, just to get rid of me.' She glared at him. 'What are you hiding?'

Steve took a step back and swallowed. 'The figures at the Brisbane store aren't so great either.'

'You said it was doing okay.'

'I didn't want to worry you, but the truth is it's the Sydney and Melbourne stores that are keeping the others open.'

'This is *our* business, not *yours*! You should have told me this as soon as you knew.' Spit flew out of Isla's mouth as she spoke, and then it hit her. '*Shit!* You *knew* how mad I'd get, so you thought you'd tell me just before you dumped me here for ten days!' Isla's voice shook. 'You brought me here so you wouldn't cop an ear-bashing from me?'

'That's not true! The next availability for this retreat isn't until the end of next year, and I didn't want you to miss out.'

Isla shook her head. 'No. That's not what's happening here. You were afraid to tell me about the business, so you decided to tell me five minutes before you took off and left me in this hell-hole.'

'You're wrong.'

Isla scowled. 'We've been in the car for the last two-and-a-half hours!'

'You're wrong ... because ...' He winced. 'I wasn't planning on telling you at all.'

Isla fumed. 'You were going to carry on lying?'

'I'm sorry you're upset.'

'Upset? I've got a weekend bag packed for a ten-night stay, and I left my favourite Jimmy Choos at home. You're telling me our business is falling apart, and you bought me sweats from—' She grabbed the Woolies bag out of his hand and searched for the tag on the pair of folded grey sweatpants. 'Anko?'

'It's Kmart's own-brand.'

Isla dropped the bag and sucked in air deeply. The bush around her began to spin. 'I'm not *upset*! I'm *livid*!'

Steve grimaced. 'You can burn the sweats when you're finished, and you don't need your Jimmy Choos here.'

Isla gritted her teeth. '*That's* the problem.'

'Don't go in there hating me. It's only a few days, then you'll be home.'

'If you're lucky,' she scoffed.

'We need the money. Do this for the business. Think of it as an investment.'

'You're talking about the terms of inheritance, about my dying mother, as an *investment*? I don't want her money – I want *her*.' Isla's throat seized and the wooden building in front of her blurred into a dark brown blob. 'This whole thing is a farce.'

Steve approached her warily and wiped a tear from her cheek. 'I'm sorry. I am, but your mum's inheritance would mean we could keep *all* the stores open.'

Isla swatted him away like a relentless mozzie. 'Don't.' How could he say that? How could he be so insensitive? She turned away from him and began to pace. Ten days! Ten days of no talking! Isla stamped her feet, curled her hands into fists and screamed. 'I have a good mind to drive home and leave *you* here.'

Steve pressed his lips together and put his hands on his hips.

Isla knew her mum's money could save her stores if it came to that, and she wanted her sisters to get their inheritance too. *Damn it!* None of this was in her five-year plan. She turned back to the Lexus and pulled out her Stella McCartney tote bag. 'I am *not* happy about this.'

'You're going to stay?'

'By the time you pick me up, you'd better have new marketing strategies for the Adelaide and Brisbane stores, or so help you I'll ...'

Isla trotted over to her suitcase, pulled up its handle and headed for the main entrance.

'You'll need these,' Steve said, holding out the Woolies bag.

Isla turned, snatched the bag out of his hand and stumbled across the gravel.

'I'll pick you up a week on Monday,' he called.

She didn't look back.

* * *

To Isla's horror, the entrance comprised of a sliding glass patio and a screen door that jammed halfway. Stuck to the dirty glass with Blu Tack was a sun-faded piece of A4 paper that read *Silence is Golden.*

She clambered inside, dragging her suitcase, and wrestled with the screen door as she tried to close it behind her. Looking around, she was convinced she'd travelled back to the 1970s. The foyer walls were decorated with vertical wooden panels, the flooring was covered with double herringbone hardwood, and exposed wooden beams drew her eye to the high ceiling, where a dark timber fan stirred the warm air ineffectually. She should have turned around there and then, got back in the Lexus and driven home. She should have left Steve here instead, given him time to think about his lies, but she hadn't. And now she was stuck here for the next ten nights in rundown lodgings that had, at most, a two-star accommodation rating and would almost certainly be home to huntsmen the size of dinner plates.

There were no signs of life in the foyer. The reception area was unattended, and there was no one to help Isla with her bags. Sweat trickled down her torso, and she cursed under her breath, spotting damp patches seeping through her satin blouse. *Why was there no air conditioning?*

The reception desk panelling was covered in dark brown tufted leather. A couple of the buttons were missing, and patches of the worn leather had cracked and faded with age. A brass clock in the shape of a sun hung on the back wall, and below it was a calendar that read *Breathe. Great tip,* thought Isla as she tried to peer through the door behind the desk, which was slightly ajar. 'Hello?' There was no reply. On top of the desk was a sign-in book with a pen attached to it by a worn piece of string. Next to that sat a small silver bell. She rang it in irritation. *Where the hell is everyone? No guest would receive such abysmal service at a Turner hotel.*

Isla flinched. Above her hung an oval pendant light, and she swore something spider-like moved inside the ribbed glass shade.

At the far end of the foyer, quiet voices conversed behind two large double doors. Opposite was another sliding glass door that led into a garden. Isla glared back at the calendar and rang the bell again. 'Hello?'

'Afternoon, or should I say evening?' A stout, muscular woman with two full sleeves of tattoos, wearing a white singlet and black jeans, stepped out of the back office. Her jet-black buzz-cut hair exposed the side of her neck, which showcased a large tattoo of a snake wrapped around a dagger. 'I'm Erin,' she said in a gruff but cheery voice. 'I'm one of your hosts, I'll be guiding you through your silent stay.'

Isla stared. Where were the enlightened hippies with long braided hair, flowing kaftans and lean bodies that could bend gracefully into every yoga pose imaginable?

Erin laughed. 'Not what you were expecting?'

Isla forced herself to look into Erin's eyes and not at the image of Marilyn Monroe on her bicep. 'No. Yes. I mean … to be honest, I'm not sure I should be here at all.'

Erin picked up a clipboard. 'Isla Turner?'

She nodded. 'That's right. *Turner.*'

'You're on the list, so that means you're in the right place. Just sign in here.' Erin tapped the sign-in book.

Isla leaned forward over the desk. 'To be honest, this *isn't* what I was expecting. How should I put this? I was under the impression this was a five-star retreat.'

'Oh, you won't be disappointed. It's one of the best retreats. You'll leave a different person.'

Isla bit her lip and noticed there was no computer for Erin to check her booking. 'My husband booked me in. Could you check to make sure I'm in the best room you have? I'll pay whatever it costs to upgrade.'

Erin spied Isla's Louis Vuitton suitcase and grinned. 'You don't pay for this retreat. It's free. This place is run on donations made by previous guests. Everyone who works here is a volunteer. We've all done the ten-day course before. I did it six years ago.'

Isla's stomach knotted. 'So … this place is like … a hostel?'

'You get your own room with a bathroom, and linen is supplied, but on the last day we ask you to wash the sheets and clean your bedroom and bathroom ready for the next guest.'

'Sorry. You want *me* to clean the room?'

'That's right.'

What the—

'All the guests will meet in the dining hall behind you after they've checked into their room. That's where you'll have your daily meals and where you can get refreshments. Dinner will be at seven tonight, and you'll be free to converse until nine, after which time all speaking will stop until 6 am on day eleven.'

Isla's heart raced. What kind of wretched place was this? If it was free to attend, that meant *anyone* could stay here. Like … *anyone*. She caught sight of the calendar again, *Breathe*, and she fiercely sucked in some air.

'Can I please have any devices you've brought with you? They'll be kept safe under lock and key until your last day.'

A nervous shrill left Isla's lips. 'No! No, you can't.'

'This is a ten-day digital detox. You did read the email with the terms and conditions?'

Isla scoffed. 'Of course I did.' She hadn't. 'Does that mean I can't keep my phone or laptop?'

'That's correct.'

'But how will I read my emails?'

'There'll be no need to consult your inbox while you're here.'

Isla stood a little taller in defiance. 'You can't expect me to just hand it over. What if I want to check the weather or the stock market?'

'Again, there'll be no need for that here.' Erin smiled, and Isla couldn't help but think she was getting a kick out of this.

'Because you read the terms and conditions, you'll know that Kindles and iPads are also forbidden.'

'You want my Kindle? What am I supposed to do for ten days? This is absurd!'

'We have a full schedule starting at 4.30 am each day. There'll be meditation sessions with times for rest and gentle exercise, but, again, you know that because you read the itinerary.'

Shit! Isla nodded. *Steve is going to pay for this.* She pulled her phone out of her bag, turned it off and handed it to Erin. Erin went to take it from her, but Isla refused to let go. Erin pulled with gentle force, and Isla reluctantly released it.

Erin placed a hand on Isla's arm. 'It's normal to feel like this, but soon you'll be reaping the benefits.'

Deep lines on Erin's face revealed a life well lived, a hard life, but there was also a lightness in her manner, a contagious quietude. Isla pulled out her laptop, Kindle and iPad, swallowing hard as she handed them over to Erin. Erin tapped her wrist, and Isla stared at her Apple watch. She'd been hoping Erin hadn't noticed it. She pressed her lips together as she relinquished it.

'Lovely, now if you could just sign in.' Erin waited while Isla filled out her details, then handed her a key with a green strip of ribbon attached to it. 'You're in Room 6. Head out the sliding doors and into the gardens. Follow the path out to the right, and you'll see the guests' rooms straight ahead. Feel free to unpack, and we'll meet you in the dining hall when you're ready.'

Isla grabbed the handle of her suitcase and watched Erin take her laptop, iPad, Kindle, phone and Apple watch into the back office. Isla tried not to panic. Instead, she focused on finding her room. *This could be good for me.* She tried to flip the whole ghastly experience on its head and be more positive. It probably wasn't healthy for her to be so upset because her devices had been confiscated. Tottering down a small gravel path that led to an open area, she came across a line of small wooden cabins.

No. This was going to be a good experience, transformative. In ten days, Isla would be a new woman, a better woman. When she got back home, she'd show her mum the best version of herself. She'd then be free to spend the next few months helping her sisters fulfil their tasks. This was going to be great. This was going to be … she pushed open the door to her room.

'Oh, hell, no!'

20

Rose

Rose cradled Bethany as the front door of The Castle swung open.

'You brought her to see me.' Jacki's eyes welled as she caught sight of her granddaughter for the first time. She reached out and stroked Bethany's fine head of hair.

Any stranger watching would have thought Rose's mother was your typical doting grandparent, but Rose knew the truth. Her mother hadn't spoken to Harrison or Taylor once since Richard had died. She'd sent them birthday and Christmas cards with cash stuffed inside, but she'd shown no interest in having a relationship with them. Rose had been heartbroken, but not surprised. Her mother had always been cold and absent; she would never change.

Rose adjusted the nappy bag on her shoulder, and Jacki beamed as she stepped aside to let them in. Mel followed behind her, limping.

'What happened to you?' asked Jacki.

'I rolled my ankle while I was running,' said Mel. 'Your terms of inheritance are dangerous. That's why we're here.'

Rose placed a quilted blanket on the floor in the corner of the dining area and lay Bethany on it.

'Oh, she's beautiful,' swooned Jacki, looking down at her granddaughter.

Rose noticed how tired and pale her mother looked without her make-up and false eyelashes. Even her hair was flat and uncombed. Perhaps that was how her mother always looked in private; Rose couldn't be sure. She'd only ever seen her in full polished regalia, even as a kid.

Jacki retied the turquoise kimono robe she was wearing, and a sickness stirred in the pit of Rose's stomach as she realised her mother really was ill – just like Richard had been. She tried to shake off her fear and the dread and focus on the task at hand. She needed to be strong, so she could tell her mother exactly what she'd come here to say.

'We're not doing the terms,' Mel announced as she struggled onto a kitchen stool. 'I've rolled my ankle, Rose is adamant she's not going to be bossed around, Jess has been publicly humiliated, and Isla is camping in the middle of God knows where and has been gagged for ten nights! This is hurting us, Mum, and it needs to stop.'

Rose was impressed. She'd come here thinking she'd have to do all the talking, but it seemed Mel had a lot to get off her chest too.

Jacki's expression didn't change. 'I knew this would happen. I just assumed it would be another month or so before we had this conversation.'

Rose tried to keep calm. 'You can't force us to do these tasks just because—'

'What?' Jacki looked Rose dead in the eye. 'Because I'm dying? Go on, you can say it.'

Rose sucked in a breath as she recalled the moment the doctors had told Richard he was dying. She'd cried the whole drive home, while Richard had comforted her. Tears pricked her eyes. 'I was going to say … because your ego needs stroking.'

Jacki took three hand-painted teacups out of the cupboard. 'Oh, this isn't about me.'

'This is *all* about you. It's all about what *you* want.' Rose's face felt flushed. 'Well, I want out. Cut me out of your will for good, I don't want anything to do with the games you're playing. I know you can change the terms whenever you want.'

Jacki dumped a heaped spoonful of loose-leaf tea into a delicately painted orange teapot. 'No one is forcing you girls to do anything. If the terms aren't met, my money will benefit Aussie Animal Rescue enormously.'

'What about *changing* my task?' asked Mel. 'I mean, how am I supposed to run if I keep getting injuries? I could do Isla's task and find out who I am. I reckon I'd be pretty good at meditating.'

'Definitely not. A rolled ankle is just another obstacle to overcome. You've got nine months until the marathon.'

'But—'

'No buts,' Jacki snapped. 'I understand your frustrations. I don't suppose it would be easy transforming into the best version of yourself. But it's not supposed to be.'

'Drop the terms. If we fail, and there's a high chance we will, I'll be stuck paying off my debts for the rest of my life,' said Mel.

Jacki raised her palms. 'Welcome to adulthood! My lawyers have set the terms, and I have *no* intention of changing them.'

'Cut me out!' said Rose. 'Do it, right now. Call your lawyers!' Rose clenched her fists to stop them from trembling.

Jacki filled the teapot with hot water. 'No,' she said quietly. 'I want you to be pushed out of your comfort zone. I want you to question what it is you really care about. I want you to ask yourselves: who are you right now, and who is it you want to be? These grievances you have are all part of the journey. Rose, you're forty; Mel, you're not much younger. You need to question everything you're doing so you can make changes now, before it's too late. I don't want you to get to the end of your life and have regrets.'

'I don't have regrets,' said Rose, shaking with fury. 'How dare you put *your* guilt onto us.' Jacki *never* considered her feelings, and she *never* listened.

'Cutting yourself out of my will isn't an option, Rose. Whether you like it or not, you are part of this family.'

'Family? What about *my* family? You hurt us, you've never apologised, you don't even know Tom or Bethany, and when was the last time you called Harrison and Taylor?'

'Whatever you think of me, I will always be your mother. There's no escape clause for that, no matter how badly you might want one.'

'Hey!' Mel shouted. 'Why does everything revolve around how much you two hate each other? It's been three bloody years! We get it!'

Silence fell across the kitchen. Rose had never seen her sister this angry.

'I'm here too, you know!' said Mel. 'I'm hurting as well. And I want—'

'I'm not interested in what you girls *want*,' hissed Jacki.

'And don't we know it,' said Mel. 'You've *never* asked us what *we* want. If you had, you'd have known that when I was a kid, I wanted my dad back, not another sister!'

Jacki gasped.

'Dad died and *you* disappeared!' Mel glared at Jacki. 'You never spoke about him. Everyone was so sad, but *no one* talked about what had happened. For years, I … I thought it was my fault he died. It was *my* birthday party, he was giving piggyback rides to *my* friends, and …'

Rose went cold. She'd never heard Mel speak like this before.

'You never once comforted me. You just … went to work.' Mel blinked away tears.

Rose knew how her mum must have felt. Losing the love of your life and having to raise your children without them was terrifying.

'And then,' said Mel, 'when Jess was born, I became invisible.'

Jacki cupped her face in her hands, but didn't speak.

Rose stepped towards her sister. 'Mel, what happened to Dad wasn't your fault. How could you think that?'

'I know that *now*, of course I do, but I was six, and Dad was my best friend, and then he was just … gone.'

Jacki stared at the teapot, her eyes welling. 'You looked like him. You still do.'

Rose pictured Harrison and Taylor and how, every now and then, Richard would appear when she looked at them. It was the most beautiful sight, but also the hardest to face.

'No.' Mel shook her head. 'That's not good enough. I was a kid … I blamed myself, and I thought you did too!'

'I'm …' Jacki started, then stopped.

Mel stared at her, clearly waiting for an apology that Rose knew wouldn't come.

A chill ran through Rose as she picked Bethany up off her blanket. How could no one have noticed that Mel had blamed herself? How screwed up was this family? Rose kissed Bethany's cheek. She wanted to scream at her mother for not noticing

Mel's grief and guilt, but then she realised she hadn't noticed either. She bit the inside of her cheek hard.

The doorbell rang, but no one moved. Helen would answer it.

'You've got a visitor,' said Helen, walking into the kitchen.

Behind her followed a tall, broad-shouldered man holding a small carry bag. He was dressed in blue jeans, a white polo shirt and a beige blazer, and his chin-length salt and pepper hair was tucked behind his ears. He stopped, and as his eyes landed on Jacki, they gleamed with delight.

'Darryl?' Jacki grabbed hold of the kitchen counter to steady herself.

'Hey, Boss,' he said in a deep, husky tone. 'I've come to see if the rumours are true.'

21

Jacki

Jacki sat on the outdoor lounge in the back garden with a pale yellow blanket draped over her lap, a glass of watered-down pinot grigio in one hand, and her phone in the other.

'You need to make this happen by close of business tomorrow,' she told Eddie, her second in command. 'Call me when it's done.' Jacki hung up and placed her phone on the table.

Darryl shook his head and took a sip of his beer. She knew what he was thinking – that she shouldn't be working, she should be resting – but what he clearly hadn't learnt, even after all these years, was that working gave Jacki life. It was what motivated her to get out of bed each morning, it was what kept her up until the early hours. It was what made her feel alive.

Jacki tried to ignore the dull pain in her stomach as they watched the setting sun dance on the water. Huge white cumulus clouds drifted across the pink sky like giant mountains, and she was reminded of the vast sky at Darryl's banana farm in Cairns.

Jacki combed the back of her hair with her fingers and wished she'd had a chance to put on some make-up and fix her hair before Rose and Mel had shown up, but the medication she was on had made her nauseous and left her with no energy at all. She had stayed in bed all morning, and even that had been hard work.

Mel's unexpected outburst earlier had knocked her for six. It had never once occurred to Jacki that Mel might have blamed herself for Peter's death. What a terrible burden she must have carried, and at such a young age. But how could Jacki have known? She hadn't been there to pick up on the clues, she hadn't even asked her daughters how they were coping with the loss of their dad. Jacki had just ramped up the hours she worked and the amount of gifts she brought home for them, which they always seemed to like. Now she couldn't help but wonder how many other things about her daughters she'd failed to notice.

The sky turned from pink to purple and was being consumed by a distant deep navy. 'I wish I'd watched more sunsets,' said Jacki.

'Sunrise and sunset are the best times of the day.' Darryl leaned back and took another swig of beer. 'If you'd stayed up north, you'd have seen them all.'

'Is that why you came all this way? To remind me what I missed out on before I croak it?'

Darryl laughed heartily and she couldn't help but smile.

'Jess told me there's nothing more the doctors can do.'

His dark eyes fixed on her and a pang of sadness washed through her. 'I have all the money in the world, but doctors and specialists can only do so much, no matter how much I pay them.'

Darryl sighed like his worst fears had been confirmed. 'How are the girls taking it?'

'They're mad at me. Did Jess tell you about the terms I set for their inheritance?'

He laughed again and nodded. 'So that's true too?'

'It gives them something else to focus on. They'll thank me when I'm gone. It's my last chance to help guide them towards having the best life they can.'

Darryl shook his head. 'I can't believe it's going to end like this.'

'Hey, I'm not done and dusted just yet. You know you didn't have to come all this way. You could have just called.'

'If I'd phoned to ask how you were, you would've given me some crap about how you were fine, and you would have told me not to come. I needed to see for myself.'

'So you thought you'd rock up with no warning?'

Darryl grinned. 'That's right, gorgeous.'

Jacki flushed and sipped her wine. 'Well, you should have saved yourself a journey. I *am* fine. You wasted your money on that flight.'

'Oh, I got my money's worth an hour ago when I set eyes on you.'

Jacki stared into her glass. 'Don't do that.'

'What?'

'You do this every time you're here. I can't do it again, not this time.'

'What do I do?'

'You sweet talk me like we're teenagers, but then you leave and … and I have to pick up the pieces.' It had been years since they'd been together. Over the last decade, Darryl's visits had been less frequent, and Jacki made sure her scheduled visits to Cairns were short enough that there was no time to see him. Deep down, she was afraid that if she went back to his farm after all these years, she'd never want to leave. She never let on, of course, and she did so love the hustle and bustle of the city, but every now and then she would think back to those months spent with him and the girls nearly three decades ago, and let herself imagine the life she could have had if she'd chosen differently. If she'd chosen love over money.

Darryl put his beer on the coffee table and fixed her with his gaze. 'Pick up the pieces? I didn't know that's how you felt.'

'What difference would it have made?' She smiled thinly and tried not to remember what it felt like to have him hold her.

'You should have told me.'

'And then what? You would have pestered me to come and live with you up on the farm. That was never going to happen.'

Darryl reached over, took the wine glass out of her hand and placed it on the table. Her heart raced as he took her hands in his.

'You're right, I would have pestered you, and you would have rejected me, but no matter the outcome, it would have been worth it because at least I'd know I tried everything I could to win you over.' Darryl's eyes shone. 'It's always been you, Jacki Turner.'

She lifted her chin. 'Are you trying to get a slice of the inheritance?'

He roared with laughter, but then his smile faded and his deep brown eyes fixed on hers. 'I'm not here for your money.' Darryl stroked her cheek with his thumb and stared at her lips. 'I'm here for *you*.'

Jacki resisted the urge to kiss him, even though it was all she wanted. She had to be realistic: she was too sick, and it was too late. They'd had so many chances to be together, but the truth was neither of them had been willing to make the sacrifices needed to make it work.

Darryl dropped his hand from Jacki's face and smiled. 'Last night, after Jess told me you were sick, I packed my suitcases and—'

'Suitcases? Plural?'

'I left Jake in charge of the business. I'm here to look after you – permanently.'

'I don't need looking after. I'm not an invalid. Besides, if I need help, I've got the girls and Helen.'

'You're keeping the girls busy earning their inheritance.'

'Helen has been taking me to appointments and sorting my medication. It's all under control.'

'She has enough to do running this place, plus she has her own life with her own family.' Darryl raised his eyebrows. 'But if you really want me to leave, I will.'

'You know you won't.'

Darryl smiled. 'You're right. I have no intention of leaving. So, it looks like you're stuck with me.'

Tears pooled in her eyes, and she resisted the urge to run her hand through his hair. 'You hate the city.'

'I do.'

'And you hate being away from home.'

'That's true too, but I won't let you check out of this life alone.' Darryl squeezed her hands gently. 'Let me stay. Let me help you.'

'You'll get bored. You'll realise I'm quite capable of looking after myself, then you'll regret leaving the farm.' Jacki wasn't sure who she was trying to convince. She half-hoped that saying she didn't need to be cared for would make it true, but in reality, she relied on Helen more than she wanted to admit. She held her breath, hoping she hadn't talked Darryl out of staying. When he'd walked into the kitchen earlier that evening, she could have cried. She was so happy to see him.

'I promise I'll only help if you want me to.'

'Fine.' Jacki sighed, and hoped he couldn't sense her relief. 'But just so we're clear, our relationship is *strictly* platonic.'

Darryl nodded. 'You got it, Boss. Right then,' he said, and turned towards the house, 'I'd best go unpack. Now, are you sure you don't want me to put my things in your room?'

Jacki laughed. 'Don't push it.'

22

Isla

On the third morning of the retreat, Isla sat cross-legged on a large flat green cushion and stifled a yawn. She had no idea how long she'd been sitting with her eyes closed. All she knew was that at four-thirty that morning she'd shuffled into the community meditation room half asleep, dressed in, horror of horrors, the Kmart sweats Steve had bought her. It turned out they were the only clothes she had that were suitable for sitting on the floor for ten hours a day.

The meditation room had the same seventies vibe as the foyer, with wooden floors and panelled walls. Large windows, which ran along three sides of the spacious room, gave lush panoramic views of the surrounding rainforest, with one side overlooking the green rolling hills of the hinterland. It was a million-dollar view.

Through her partially closed eyes, she'd counted nineteen people meditating, not including their teacher, Stan, a bald guy in his late seventies who sat cross-legged at the front of the room wearing a white linen shirt and pants.

How they were able to shut out the world and keep so damn

still was beyond her. They'd all looked so calm and peaceful as they'd followed Stan's instruction to focus only on their breath. This had irritated Isla, whose mind had been running a hundred kilometres an hour during all the meditation sessions she'd done so far.

But now, sitting as still as she could with her eyes shut, she could feel the breath in her body. All the windows in the room had been opened, allowing the rainforest to come alive around them. With her eyes closed, she became aware of the fragrance from the eucalyptus trees and the damp forest floor, and the steady thrum of cicadas that pulsed through the room like a heartbeat. Every now and then, a breeze swept across the room and danced around Isla, wrapping itself around her like a drunk friend who had abandoned the concept of personal space.

A dull ache burned in her lower back, and she discreetly leaned to her left and then to her right, trying to ease the sensation.

At the start of the session, Stan had suggested that those struggling to quieten their mind should consciously ask themselves what their recurring thoughts were trying to tell them. Were they fears or worries that needed examining, or were they thoughts that needed to be let go? Isla's mind fizzled and boiled, and she clenched her jaw. Her mum was dying, two of her stores were struggling, she and her sisters had to jump through hoops to secure their inheritance, and what was Isla doing? Sitting on the floor for ten hours a day, trying not to think about any of it.

Meditation bells clanged, signalling the end of the session. Isla opened her eyes and winced as she massaged her lower back with her fist. The other guests around her slowly began to stir. A young twenty-something to her right, who wore a bright tie-dyed T-shirt and black harem pants, glowed and smiled, like she'd just had a full body massage followed by a facial. *What is it with these people?*

Isla's joints cracked, and a stiffness overwhelmed every limb as she attempted to stand as gracefully as she could. Following the other guests, she walked down the gravel path that led to the dining hall where breakfast was being served, but at six-thirty in the morning it was still too early for her to eat, and the smell of scrambled eggs turned her stomach. Guests formed an orderly line at the servery, but Isla bypassed the food and headed to a table of refreshments.

Another downside, or perhaps utter failure of the retreat, was the absence of coffee. On her first morning, she'd almost wept when she'd realised she couldn't have her shot of espresso or mid-morning double-shot soy latte. The only refreshments on offer were iced water, cordial (*What am I, ten?*), orange juice and decaffeinated tea. On the fold-out table in front of her there were two hot water urns along with a stack of paper cups, small packets of white sugar, brown lollipop sticks for stirring and a small jug of full cream milk. Isla wanted to scream. *This isn't an Alcoholics Anonymous meeting!* It was supposed to be a retreat! How was she expected to get through the day without caffeine? She was sure it was on Maslow's hierarchy of needs, right there at the bottom of the triangle, next to breathing, food, water, shelter, clothing and sleep.

After breakfast on the first morning, Isla had gone straight to her room to read the welcome pack and the retreat's terms and conditions. She found a simple sentence in standard text, stating there would be no caffeine at the retreat. It wasn't highlighted, written in bold, capitals or italics. It was merely *mentioned*, as though it was inconsequential. And so she had no choice but to make a strong black decaffeinated tea in a paper cup.

After forty-eight hours of listening only to her internal chatter, Isla was getting on her own nerves. She needed to talk to someone. She needed to read the news, check her emails, get updates from her store managers. She was desperate to vent to Steve, to vent to her sisters *about* Steve, and to drink coffee! There was no way she could do this for another eight days.

Discreetly, Isla slipped out the dining hall and found herself in the large foyer. The reception desk was unattended, and the office door was ajar. Isla stopped in her tracks and looked back towards the hall. No one had followed her, and all the volunteers were busy serving breakfast. She calculated it was at most twenty steps between her and her phone. If she was quick, she could find it and get out without being spotted.

In the office, Isla closed the door behind her and made a beeline for the desk. She opened the large bottom drawer and saw at least ten phones, three kindles, two iPads, Isla's Apple watch and her laptop.

What the—

It was unlocked!

Isla grabbed her phone and slid it into her sleeve. She closed the drawer, hurried back to the office door and, when she was confident it was all clear, dashed out.

In the safety of her sparsely decorated room, she pulled out her phone and jumped up and down in wild, triumphant delight. The thrill made her hands shake and her heart soar – *she was alive!* She turned on her phone and unlocked it, but froze when she saw she had ninety-three unread emails, forty-three missed calls and seven voicemails. Her heart pounded.

Focus, she told herself. *Call someone.*

She closed the blinds and listened for any movement outside. It was all clear.

She automatically went to call Steve but then stopped herself. He knew she wasn't meant to have her phone, which meant they'd spend the whole call discussing the importance of sticking to the rules.

Isla called Rose, but it went to voicemail, and she wasn't sure Jess had fully forgiven her yet. *Damn it!* She hesitated, then huffed and called Mel.

As it rang, Isla peeked through the blinds to keep watch.

'Hi.'

'Mel? Is that you? Where are you?' Isla whispered.

'I'm. Running. And. The answer's. No.'

'What?'

'I'm not. Helping you. With your. Task.'

'Don't start. I haven't spoken—' Isla coughed. 'I haven't spoken for over forty-eight hours!'

'Wow.'

'I'm losing it in here. I can't have my phone, Kindle or laptop, and there's no coffee! No fucking coffee!'

'How are you. Calling me. If you can't have. Your phone?'

'*No coffee!* Can you believe it?'

'I ran six kilometres. Last week. I can believe. Anything. Now.'

Isla paced the room. 'Listen carefully. You need to tell Rose to come and get me.'

Mel breathed heavily on the other end of the phone. 'Steve and Helen said you might do this.'

'Do what?'

'Try to escape. Sorry, but we've been given strict instructions not to help you.'

Isla sat on the edge of her bed. 'I can't do this. I can't be here. I'll go insane. You've got to talk to Mum. Get her to put an end to these terms.'

'I tried, but – *Shit! Ah! No! Help!*'

'What? What is it?'

'I'm being attacked! *Aaargh!*'

'Mel! Mel! Talk to me!' At the end of the line, there were muffled sounds, then grunts and screams. '*Mel!*' Tears flooded Isla's eyes. Someone knocked loudly on the door of her room, but she ignored them. 'Mel, talk to me! What's happening?'

'I'm running. I won't let the bastard get me!'

'*Who?* Mel, where are you? I'll call the police!'

'I'm bleeding!'

Mel's breathing was deep and fast, and the knocking on the door got louder. Isla burst into tears. Her sister was being assaulted, and there was nothing she could do.

'It's okay, I'm safe. I think he's gone. *Shit!* I thought I was a goner for sure.'

'Call the police!'

'For a magpie?'

'A *magpie*? *Shit!* I thought you were being attacked by some psycho!'

'I was, I'm cut up like a scratching post. I tell you what, this running gig is seriously dangerous.'

Keys jangled outside Isla's room and the door was flung open. Erin, dressed in a black singlet and skinny jeans, calmly held out her hand.

Isla's shoulders sagged. 'Hey Mel, I've got to go. I suppose I'll see you next week then, yeah?'

'Okay, good lu—'

Isla ended the call, took a long, defeated deep breath and handed her phone to Erin.

* * *

On the last night of the silent retreat, Isla sat in complete stillness in the meditation room. She rested the backs of her hands on her knees and took long, steady breaths. Beads of sweat trickled down the inside of her T-shirt and a mosquito buzzed around her head, but she paid no attention. She was calm. In this restful state, her body seemed to hum, like she existed on a different frequency.

Over the last few days, she had learnt how to bring her awareness fully into her body and release any tension she was holding by consciously relaxing each limb one section at a time. She'd also figured out how to quieten her mind, and now, instead of reacting to every thought, she was able to meet them in the moment, acknowledge them for what they were and then let them go. For the first time in her life, she understood that her thoughts weren't *who* she was.

On the evening of day five, in an open grassy area outside, Isla had leaned back in her chair and looked up to find the universe staring back. As Stan had spoken, a calm had come over her. His melodic words had washed over the group, and his soothing, unhurried tone had hovered in the air like a welcome cool breeze.

'Who are you?' Stan had asked.

Who are you? This was the question Isla needed to answer!

'Look around you. At the trees, the stars, the chairs, the buildings.' Stan had paused for a moment, allowing the guests time to do as he asked. 'Now, I want you to look again. But this time, don't name what you see. Look at those things without labelling them. Just *be* in their miraculous presence.'

'Now,' said Stan after giving them a moment, 'I want you to think about yourself and answer the question, who am I?'

That was easy. She was Isla Turner! Jacki Turner's daughter. Owner of Turner Jewellers, Steve's wife, sister to Rose, Mel and Jess, boss to her employees. She was rich, stylish, a role model, an influencer—

'If you made a list in your head,' Stan said, 'I want you to now consider that you are none of the names and labels you just gave yourself.'

Although Isla's eyes were closed, she had to stop herself from rolling them back into her head. Who was she if she *wasn't* those things?

'For the sake of quick and easy understanding between humans, we label everything. If we had to describe the things around us to get our meaning across, it would take too long. But the things we label are far more complicated than the simple names we give them. So, I ask again, who are you, if you are not the names, roles or labels we give ourselves and each other?'

Isla's head started to hurt, but then she got it.

I'm the voice in my head, the bloody voice in my head.

'As most of you have discovered by now, you are not your thoughts,' Stan said.

What?

'You are the space *between* your thoughts. The pause between inhale and exhale. You are *the observer*.'

Isla opened her eyes. *You've got to be kidding me!*

It was all getting a bit woo-woo, but over the following days, Isla caught glimpses of what he'd meant. During walks around the grounds, she watched the large blue and black butterflies and consciously let go of their name, allowing herself to simply *be* in their presence. In those moments, she witnessed the butterflies with a state of wonder and awe that she hadn't experienced before. She marvelled at the symmetry and colours of their wings, and their agility as they flew through the rainforest. It was strange how she'd never really stopped to look at them in detail before.

During meditation over the following days, there were moments when she used her breath and the mantra *I am* to explore her inner state. In that space, where there were no expectations, no one to impress and no views that needed expressing, she slipped into a state of Zen, and discovered absolute contentment.

Now, on the last evening of the retreat, the meditation bells chimed, and she gently moved her head from side to side. She didn't want to leave the dreamlike state she was in. She wanted to stay just a little longer.

After making her way outside to where a drinks station had been set up, she poured herself a glass of water. Then she went and sat in one of the camping chairs, ready for Stan's final talk. The night sky was cloudless, and bright stars looked down on them.

'Tonight,' said Stan as the last person took their seat, 'you have one task. The universe asks only one thing of us, and that is to bear witness to its miraculous existence. We don't have to *be* or *do* anything other than observe the gift we have been given. We are spectators to it all: the beauty, the brutality, the realities and the illusions. You, *we*, are the beholder of miracles, and that will always be enough.'

Stan fell silent, and Isla rested her head on the back of her chair and stared up at the universe.

She'd learnt so much from Stan, but one of the greatest gifts from the last ten days was realising she didn't have to *always* speak. All she'd had to do during the retreat was listen, to the volunteers' gentle instructions, to the sounds of the rainforest, to Stan's words of wisdom, to her own breath. And, after the first few days of resistance, she now found it to be blissful.

Isla had always been excellent at communicating her needs. Ever since she could talk, she'd been overly keen to express her views and wants. She'd always assumed that made her a good communicator. Yet, throughout the retreat, she'd realised that although she was very comfortable talking, she didn't actually spend much time listening. She recalled all sorts of encounters during her life – business meetings, parties, family get-togethers, discussions with Steve – and contemplated how often she had let others voice *their* views. How often had she let them speak without interrupting them?

As Isla thought of her relationships, a sinking feeling stirred. She relived past conversations and recalled the way most people reacted when she was talking – defeated, irritated, defensive. Isla thought about her sisters and the glances they often gave each other when they thought she wasn't looking. Why hadn't she just stopped and listened to what they had to say? Why did her opinion matter more than anyone else's? Did she *always* have to be right?

Maybe it was something she could work on.

23

Jess

As Jess walked across the floor of the Gold Coast Turner Casino, lights flashed and chimes rang out from the maze of gaming machines. She made her way towards the blackjack tables and her phone buzzed with a text from Brett, the hot doctor. She had arranged to meet him twice for coffee since she'd texted him five weeks ago from Fiji, but each time he'd stood her up because of a work emergency. Now he was cancelling their catch-up this afternoon. Jess sighed. *No worries,* she replied. She could take a hint.

'Jess!'

She glanced up to find her dad, wearing jeans and a short-sleeved navy polo shirt, watching a game of blackjack with a glass of beer in his hand. He looked smart, with his clean-shaven face and newly cut hair. She knew he'd made an effort for Jacki. Back on the banana farm, he always let his hair grow long and wild.

Jess kissed her dad's cheek. 'You've started early, it's not even midday. Don't let the lighting and tinted windows in here fool you.'

'I'm only having one,' said Darryl. 'I just need something to take the edge off after dropping your mum off for surgery.'

Jess rubbed his arm. Her mum was having surgery for a blocked bowel, and she could see her dad was worried. 'I wish she'd let me take care of her more. She refuses my help. I have to get daily updates from Helen to know what's going on with her.'

'Thank goodness for Helen, right?'

'She's the best. Did the hospital say when Mum would be out of surgery?'

'They said they'd call to let me know how it went.'

'How was she when you dropped her off?'

He rubbed his brow. 'Quiet.'

Jess tapped her fingers on her thigh and turned to watch a group cheering at a nearby roulette table. Her mum was never *quiet*. 'So what's with meeting me here? You wanna play a game?'

'Nah. I've seen what gambling can do to a man. I've lost good friends to places like this.'

'So why meet me here?'

'I … I just wanted to feel close to your mum while she's …' Darryl cleared his throat. 'She loves the thrill of a casino, you know.'

The lines on her dad's face had deepened, and fear clutched Jess's chest at the realisation that he too was getting older. She'd noticed he walked with a slight limp now, and would press his knuckles into his lower back when he thought no one was looking. He was too proud to admit he was in any pain. *It's just what happens after a lifetime of hard work,* he'd said to Jess when she'd asked him about it.

Up until recently, Jess had only ever thought of her parents as robust and resilient. There was nothing they couldn't overcome – they were untouchable. But now, with her mum in hospital and seeing her dad with his aging body, she was forced to face the fact that her parents were mere mortals, just as vulnerable as the next person. The idea scared her.

Jess linked her arm through her dad's. 'Let's get some fresh air,' she said. They made their way over to the foyer, where they were greeted by a concierge named Ray, who led them out to the pool area.

'Would you like a private poolside bungalow or cabana?' asked Ray.

'No, thank you,' said Jess. 'We're going to have coffee at the bar.'

'Very well,' said Ray, bowing slightly. 'Please don't hesitate to ask if you need anything else.'

They sat at the poolside bar and ordered coffees.

'Even after all these years, I still can't get used to the VIP treatment when I come here,' said Darryl.

Jess put on her sunglasses and inched her chair out of the hot sun. Her phone buzzed; Brett had replied to her text. *Forgive me! Raincheck?*

'Who's that?' asked Darryl.

'Just the doctor friend I was telling you about. He cancelled, again.'

'Doesn't sound like he's good enough for my daughter.'

'I told you, we're not dating. We've chatted on the phone a couple of times, that's all. He seems like a nice guy.'

'Nice?'

'He saves lives and he's busy. He works nights.'

'Are you putting up with him because of the terms your mum set?'

'Well, there's no one else I'm interested in, so I may as well play this out and see what happens.' Staying in contact and arranging coffees with Brett had meant she'd been able to keep her sisters off her back. As far as they were concerned, she was trying to hook up with Brett, but matters of the heart couldn't be rushed.

Darryl leant back in his chair and crossed his arms. 'The world tells us you have to find someone in order to be happy, but that's just bullshit. You can be alone and be perfectly content. Look at me.'

'You had Mum whenever you came down here to visit.'

'A weekend here and there maybe.'

'There's always been something between you two. Perhaps the possibility that there could be something more made you feel less alone.'

The bartender placed their coffees in front of them, and Darryl ripped open two sachets of white sugar and poured them into his cappuccino.

'You know she loves you, don't you?' said Jess, and her throat ached. 'I haven't seen her with anyone else for over a decade. I mean, I've seen her flirting, that's just who Mum is, but it's you she really loves.'

Darryl stared into his coffee. 'That may be so, but we had our time, and it wasn't meant to be. I'm here now, though, and that's all that matters.'

Jess smiled and tried to ignore the ache in her heart. If only her parents had wanted the same things, they might have spent their lives together.

'What's most important now is that you don't get caught up with all this *terms of inheritance* nonsense.'

'I just want to make Mum happy.'

Darryl laughed and squeezed her hand. 'Jacki's the only one who can do that, just as only you are in charge of your happiness. But, if you insist on completing the task you've been set, promise me you'll do it on your own terms. Got it?'

Jess nodded, but she had no idea what he meant. All she knew was that they were already a week into October, and if she had to be in a relationship for longer than three months by the time July rolled around, she needed to get a move on.

* * *

Jess took a sip from her third glass of merlot, even though her neck and chest were flushed and, much to her dismay, she couldn't fit in another mouthful of the delicious mushroom risotto. Brett had booked a table at the cosy Italian restaurant in Main Beach, after she'd agreed to meet up with him. Five weeks after her mum's surgery, and complete radio silence from Brett, she'd received a text from him out of the blue.

I'm finally off night shifts. If you're still interested, I'd love to catch up.

She'd decided to give him the benefit of the doubt, even after all the cancellations. At least now she could tell her sisters she was going on a date. Jess had been on two dates since the terms had been set. One with a neighbour in her apartment building and another with a guy she'd gone to uni with who had sent her a DM. The only reason she'd agreed to go was to keep her sisters off her back. Neither date had worked out.

She should have known better than to date a neighbour. Aaron was nice enough, but his five cats put her off. *Five!* In a one-bedroom apartment! After letting him down gently when he'd asked her on another date, she prayed she wouldn't bump into him in her building.

Date number two was with her old uni friend Matt, but the evening hadn't panned out as she'd thought it would. It turned out her date hadn't been a date at all. Matt had forgotten to mention that he'd also invited a few of their other old uni friends too. Jess did have fun, but the majority of her friends were married with small children, which meant that at ten o'clock half of them left to relieve their babysitters, while the other half, whose kids were sleeping over at grandparents' or friends' houses, partied extra hard. At 2 am, Jess had left them to it.

After that, Jess hadn't tried as hard as she should have to meet someone, preferring to stay curled up in front of the TV with a camomile tea.

But now, tipsy from the wine and surprisingly good company, Jess was glad she'd made the effort tonight. Brett had made the evening easy, from booking the table to making menu suggestions and keeping her entertained with his stories. He'd been telling her all through dinner about his fascinating life as a doctor in the Emergency Department. The stories he told were both disgusting and horrifying, but hearing how Brett dealt with all the drama in such a composed way was impressive. Jess could never do what he did. She didn't handle emergencies well. When Rose's waters broke when she was pregnant with Harrison, they'd been shopping in Myer. Jess had totally freaked out and had started screaming at people to 'Do something'.

For Jess, it had been a relief to not have to do all the talking. The way Brett told his stories was so compelling that at one point two of the waiters had stood transfixed at their table listening to Brett talk about how he'd once given CPR to a woman on a flight from Brisbane to Sydney. He'd saved her life at 35,000 feet. The waiters had given them free drinks after hearing that.

'Why did you text me after all this time?' she asked Brett as the waiter cleared their plates. 'You said you're working day shifts now, but you would have had days off before. Why didn't you want to meet up earlier?'

Brett held up his palms. 'Truthfully, I didn't know if I was ready to date. Work can be intense, and about six months ago the relationship I'd been in ended. I think I just needed a little more time to heal before I moved on.'

'So when you cancelled our dates before … '

'I wasn't making excuses, they were genuine reasons, I promise.'

'Well, I appreciate your honesty.'

The waiter returned and placed the bill on the table, but when Jess reached for her purse, Brett touched her arm.

'Tonight's on me,' he said, handing the waiter his credit card. 'It's the least I can do after cancelling so many times. I'm glad I didn't put you off completely. I've really enjoyed tonight.'

'Me too.' And she meant it.

Brett smiled and held her gaze a touch longer than necessary. Jess couldn't help but smile back.

The waiter handed Brett his credit card and wished them both a good night as they left. Outside, under the glow of the street lamps, Jess breathed deeply. The warm mid-November air reminded her that summer was just around the corner. She much preferred the warmer months – summer dresses, iced tea, and barbecues with family and friends.

Rose and Richard had hosted the best family barbecues. Jacki only ever showed up once, but Helen and Mick always made an appearance. Rich and Steve would take charge of cooking the meat, which they always incinerated, but nobody seemed to mind. Harrison and Taylor were only little then and they always begged Jess to go on the trampoline with them. Rose was so content in those days. It was sad to think about how it all turned out, but at least she had Tom now, and Bethany. They were making her smile again, after all the grief and heartbreak.

'Thanks for that,' said Jess.

'My pleasure.'

'Where's home for you? I'm in Southport.'

'I'm just a short walk away.'

Jess ordered an Uber.

'Can I see you again?' asked Brett, his eyes shining.

Although he'd told Jess he'd had a great time, and there was no doubt there was some chemistry between them, Jess was surprised he wanted to see her again. After all, he didn't really know much more about her than he had before this evening – he'd done all the talking. Jess hadn't told him she was a Turner, and she certainly hadn't told him about the terms of inheritance. He didn't know she loved to draw in her spare time because he'd hardly asked her anything about her life. All he knew about her was that she had her own business and that she loved risotto and drinking merlot. 'Sure. I'd love to go on another date.'

'Can I kiss you?'

Jess blushed and nodded. His lips were warm and tasted of whisky.

'I'll text you then,' he said.

'Great.' Jess's Uber pulled up, and just as she was about to get in the car she paused and turned back to him. 'Hey, Brett,' she said. 'Is there any chance we can get a selfie together?'

'Of course,' he said, looking pleased with himself. He squeezed up close beside her and as Jess took the photo he kissed her cheek.

Jess laughed, but guilt churned in her stomach. He probably thought it was cute she wanted to capture the moment. If they became a couple, they could look back on this night with fond memories. And Jess did want to remember this evening, but for a different reason. If things got serious between them, she'd need evidence to prove when they'd started dating.

How romantic.

24

Rose

Rose fidgeted in the leather armchair. She couldn't get comfortable. 'Why don't you have one of those chairs you can lie on? You've got plenty of room.'

Rose's therapist, Grace, sat opposite her, pen and notebook in hand. Her thick-rimmed glasses and abundant curly red hair drowned her delicate face. As in all their previous sessions – when Rose had sobbed non-stop, or when she'd paced the office like a robot, or even when Rose had announced, a little over a year ago, that she didn't think she needed to see her anymore – Grace was calm and kind.

'Do you feel like you need to lie down, Rose?'

Rose had spent the last twenty-five minutes going into detail about her mother's cancer, the terms of inheritance, and all the mishaps that had occurred since they'd been set.

'Can I stand?' asked Rose, chewing her nails. 'I think that might be better.' Without waiting for approval, she took up her usual pacing track in front of the large bookcase. 'Look, I just have a question about boundaries and then I'll be on my way.

There's no need for this to become a permanent thing again. I just need some advice, that's all.'

Grace scribbled in her notebook. 'I'm all ears.'

'How the hell do I keep my mother out of my life without letting my sisters down? I mean, I can't, can I? There's just no way around this. I'm being forced, against my will, to write a children's picture book. It's ridiculous! I'm forty years old. I shouldn't have to do anything I don't want to, and yet here I am, being forced to do what my mother tells me.'

Rose glanced at Grace. She wanted confirmation that her mother had gone too far this time, but, as always, Grace revealed nothing.

'It's hard when we take things personally.' Grace's words were soft. 'But your sisters were given tasks too.'

'And they don't want to do them either. They might have agreed to, but they really don't want to.'

'Perhaps this is less about you and your sisters and more about your mother, and what she's going through right now.'

'Exactly. She's *always* been manipulative. She doesn't care about what we want or need. She only cares about herself.' Rose pressed her hands to her stomach and stopped pacing.

'Why do you think your mother gave you the task of writing a picture book?'

'Because she hates me.' Slipping back into the leather armchair, Rose took a sip from her glass of water. She was exhausted. 'I used to write all the time when I was a kid. I'd make up fun little stories and draw pictures to go with them, then I'd give them to my friends at school. I wrote to escape. I'd go and find a spot in the house that overlooked the water, and I'd watch the yachts sail out to the ocean. I'd make up stories about who was on them, where they were going and who they were running from. They were good stories, too.

There was one book that Mel found hilarious. It was about a pirate, I think. I must have read it to Mel a hundred times. Honestly, she'd lie on the floor crying with laughter. But when Dad ...'

The room blurred and her throat ached.

'I miss him,' she sobbed. 'I'm finding it harder and harder to hold onto the memories of him.'

'Your dad?'

Rose nodded. 'I can't remember what his laugh sounded like or how his hugs felt. He'd give us these super-sized hugs where he'd squeeze us extra hard for as long as he could. It was the best.'

Grace made more notes.

'When people talk about grief, they never talk about how your memories fade over time. It's getting harder to see them both in my head, and I don't want them to go.'

'Them?'

'Dad and Richard. I've got to keep their memories alive, especially all the ones I have of Richard, for Harrison and Taylor. I don't want him to disappear. I don't want him to fade away like Dad.' Tears flooded her cheeks, and Grace handed her a box of tissues.

'Tom and Bethany are my world now, but I still love Richard too. He should be here, hugging and kissing our kids. He should be tucking them in at night, watching them play soccer, and cooking them pancakes for breakfast on the weekends. I loved him so much, and now my mother is dying too ... I'm not sure my heart is strong enough to carry the weight of it all.'

'Your heart *is* strong enough. It's strong enough to hold your love for all the people you've loved and all the people you will love in this lifetime. And yes, the memories may fade, but that's okay. Everyone you love leaves an imprint on you that can never be erased. It's permanent. So perhaps, instead of always trying to remember your love for them, just open up your heart, and receive the love they had for you. It's there, I promise.'

Rose took a breath and closed her eyes. As she exhaled, she imagined her dad and Richard's love flooding her. Instantly, the tension in her body disappeared, her anger eased and she felt lighter.

Grace checked her watch and smiled. Their time was up.

Rose pulled a couple of extra tissues from the box and stood. 'Same time next week then?'

Grace stood and placed a reassuring hand on her shoulder. 'I've already booked you in.'

* * *

There were two weeks left of the school year, and Rose's calendar, which hung on the back of the pantry door, was jam packed. Harrison's Year Six farewell assembly was the following week and there were two class pool parties, an end of year ceremony and a Christmas disco. Rose's list of things to do was as long as her arm. She needed to get some cash out for the kids so they could buy presents from the Christmas stall at school, and she also had to buy Christmas cards and candy canes for them to give to their friends, as well as gifts for their teachers and Christmas T-shirts for free dress day. Rose was in Christmas overload and it was only November.

After the Sunday roast had been devoured, Rose and Mel stood next to each other, washing and drying the remaining pots and pans that wouldn't fit in the dishwasher. Tom was upstairs giving Bethany a bath while Harrison and Taylor had retreated to their bedrooms after loading the dishwasher.

Every Sunday, since Rose and Mel had been to confront their mother about their terms of inheritance, Rose had invited Mel over for Sunday dinner.

'Thanks for dinner, Rose. I love coming over to hang out with you all,' said Mel, as she scrubbed the bottom of a pot with a scourer.

'You're welcome any time, you know that.'

'But, you know you don't have to invite me every week. I wouldn't be offended if you didn't ask me.'

'Don't be silly, we want you here.' Rose frowned at the tea towel in her hands, which was now too wet to dry anything.

'I know you're inviting me because you feel guilty about how I felt after Dad died.'

Rose put down the saturated tea towel. 'I'm not, but ... I should have realised. Blaming yourself like that ... I'm so sorry, Mel.'

'You don't have to apologise. It wasn't your fault.'

'But, you're my little sister and I wasn't there for you.'

'That's not true. Plus, you were eight years old, and you'd just lost Dad too.'

'The thought of you at six, having that burden. It makes me so ...'

'Sad?'

'Angry. You should never have been made to feel that way, and if our mother had been around, she would have realised something was up. She could have protected you from all that pain.'

Mel rested her head on Rose's shoulder. 'It means a lot to hear that you've got my back, but Mum was grieving too.'

'I just don't understand her. When Rich died, all I wanted to do was scoop Harrison and Taylor into my arms and hide away from the world. The three of us slept in the same bedroom for a year. We needed to be close to each other.'

'There's no doubting Mum is a strong woman, and we both know she's never been the maternal type, but maybe the pain was too much for her to bear when Dad died, and that's why she threw herself into her work the way she did.'

Rose looked at Mel. 'Who have you been talking to?'

'Corey. He suggested I try to look at it from Mum's point of view.'

Ever since Jess had pointed out what Rose and Jacki had in common, Rose had been thinking about how different their reactions had been to losing their husbands. Richard's death had brought Rose closer to her children, whereas when her dad had died Rose had lost her mother completely to the Turner empire.

'What else did Corey say?'

'That being a single mum would have been hard for her, and that she was probably trying to do the best she could.'

Rose chewed at her bottom lip. She knew all too well what it was like to navigate parenthood alone. For the first twelve months after Richard's death, Rose had moved through life on autopilot. She'd watched Harrison play soccer, paid the bills, done the grocery shopping, but emotionally she'd been in shock. The world no longer made sense.

Mel put the last pot on the draining board, and pulled out the plug.

'Come with me,' said Rose, heading into the living room. She dragged a large storage box over towards the sofa.

Mel took a seat. 'What's in there?'

'This is a blast from my past. It has all my old English books from school, and notebooks full of stories I wrote when I was a kid. I thought looking back might help me come up with some ideas for a children's picture book, but it turns out I was a pretty deep kid.'

Mel pulled out a notebook, which had a picture of a daisy on the front, and opened the first page. '*"Musings by Rose Turner. Thought of the day: To live fully means to feel it all."* *Shit!* How old were you when you wrote that?'

'I must have been at high school.' Kneeling, Rose dug deep into the bottom of the box and pulled out two small trophies labelled *Rose Turner: Best Original Story* and *Rose Turner: Gold Coast Story Search Winner*. 'I won these when I was in high school too, remember?' She handed the trophies to Mel and recalled the thrill of the wins. She'd spent hours working on those short stories, and knowing her hard work had paid off made Rose feel seen. For the first time in her life, she'd felt like she was good at something. 'Sometimes, when I'm writing, it feels like *I'm* not doing the work, it's more like something is working through me. Crazy, hey?'

'Isn't that what it means to be in the zone? I get that sometimes when I'm running; it's like my body isn't struggling anymore, it's just going with the flow. It doesn't last very long though.'

'Even if we hadn't been set the terms of inheritance, I still would have written again. Writing is such a big part of who I am. It's just … life got in the way, that's all.'

'You've got a real talent, Rose.' Mel picked up another notebook and flicked through it.

Rich had always said the same thing. Before they'd got married, when she'd found out her short story was going to be published in an anthology, Rose had come home from work to find the living room filled with helium balloons. Rich had bought her a bottle of bubbly and made her a cake. On top he'd written in wobbly icing, *Rose Turner: author extraordinaire*. He'd misspelt extraordinaire.

'Hey, listen to this,' said Mel. 'It's another "Musings by Rose Turner". *"Every encounter, no matter how brief, enables us to see who we are in this moment. Our action, or inaction, is an invitation to move closer or further away from who we aspire to be."* Crikey. I wish I could write like you.'

Mel handed her sister the worn grey A5 notebook. Rose's words were decorated in blue ink with tiny hand-drawn swirls and small flowers. She turned the page and there, in the centre, in her handwriting, were the words *Whatever you do, don't end up like Mum!*

25

Jacki

Jacki's mornings, which had once been filled with Pilates at dawn, coffee, reading the news, and ten o'clock daily briefings, were now consumed with the battle of trying to swallow a large number of pills, forcing down what little breakfast she could stomach, and sleeping late.

It was two weeks before Christmas and it had just gone two in the afternoon. Staring at her reflection in her bathroom mirror, Jacki ran her fingers over the scars on her stomach and over her protruding collarbone. After the surgery a couple of months ago, the weight had dropped off her. She scoffed. It was ironic that after a lifetime of wishing to be naturally skinny, she'd come to find that the gaunt look didn't suit her. What a lot of wasted energy she'd spent over the years trying one diet or another, only to find she'd been perfect the way she was.

Jacki sighed and pressed her hands against the cool marble sink. How she wished she could go back in time and ask Helen to make an appointment with her doctor when she'd first started getting the pains in her abdomen. If only she'd slowed down long enough to listen to what her body had been trying to tell her – that something was wrong.

She was so tired. It was like waking up every day with a hangover, but without the fun of the night before. Late afternoon was usually her best time of day. After resting in the morning and managing a few mouthfuls of food, she found she had a little more energy. Every afternoon for the last week or so, she'd sat in the shade in one of the Adirondack chairs next to Darryl and watched the yachts sail past her house while they sipped iced tea and reminisced.

But now, after only managing a couple of mouthfuls of scrambled egg at lunch, she ached all over. She knew she had to eat to keep up her strength, but everything had a strange taste. The doctor had recommended meal supplement shakes, but Jacki had put off trying them, sure her appetite would pick up again soon.

'Knock, knock,' called Darryl from the doorway of her bedroom.

Jacki pulled back her shoulders, lifted her chin and closed her robe across her chest. 'Come in.'

In the two and a half months since Darryl's arrival, the three of them had fallen into a comfortable routine. Helen cared for Jacki until lunch, and then she'd spend the rest of the day managing the house while Darryl took over the caring duties. Jacki hated the idea of having carers, and when they swapped 'shifts', she shooed them out of her room, unable to stand the way they talked about her meds and condition like she was their patient.

Darryl walked through Jacki's walk-in robe and rapped his knuckles on the bathroom door frame. His damp hair was combed back out of his face, making him look ten years younger.

'Enjoy your swim?' Jacki forced a thin smile.

'Came to see if you're okay. You're usually downstairs by now.'

'Just tired, that's all.'

Darryl studied Jacki. 'You look pale, and Helen said you haven't eaten.'

'I had a couple of mouthfuls of scrambled egg.'

'Like she said, you haven't eaten. She bought you some of those shakes.'

'Don't you start.' Jacki's bottom lip trembled. Her bones ached, and her joints were sore and tender. 'I hurt, all over.' Unable to hold in her emotions anymore, she let the tears fall.

Darryl moved into the room and wrapped her in his arms, squeezing her gently. She pressed her cheek to his chest, and tears dripped onto his shirt. She couldn't remember the last time she'd cried. She'd always viewed tears as a show of weakness, and Jacki Turner didn't do weakness. Yet now, in Darryl's embrace, she didn't feel weak; she felt relieved.

Darryl stroked her head. 'What can I do?'

'A bath? A hot bath helps with the pain. And maybe … one of those shakes? I could give one a try, I suppose. I just don't want to feel like this anymore.'

Darryl led her into her walk-in robe and guided her to the large white leather ottoman.

'Have a seat here. I'll run the bath and go fix up one of those shakes. I might give one a try too.' He turned on the bath taps and disappeared downstairs.

Jacki loved how hard he was trying to make her feel comfortable. He'd never usually drink a meal replacement shake, but he'd do it for her in a show of solidarity.

Sitting alone, Jacki examined the expensive contents of her wardrobe. It was like sitting in a time capsule. Some people would look through old photos to recall moments from the past, but each garment and accessory in Jacki's extravagant wardrobe told its own story. The black silk taffeta Chanel dress she'd worn the night she'd attended the ARIA awards. Her gold Alexander McQueen clutch was a favourite for glamming up her Carla Zampatti dress, and Jacki recalled using the to-die-for bag a couple of years before, when she'd had dinner with friends in Paris. The restaurant had a stunning view of the Eiffel Tower, which had looked glorious all lit up. For that one week, Jacki had let herself imagine what it would be like to be Parisian, swapping g'days for bonjours and Aussie dollars for Euros.

Hanging in the far corner, she spotted her Aje Concept dress, which she'd worn to last year's HM Awards for hotel and accommodation excellence. Once again, Turner Hotels and Casinos had won every award they had been nominated for. To know her hotels were winning, year after year, was exhilarating. The competition was fierce, and the standards were high.

Jacki loved being a valued and respected member of the hotel community. She'd worked hard to build what she had today, and she'd done it alone, with only Peter's words from years gone by to steer her in the right direction. If she was ever unsure, she'd always ask herself, *What would Peter do?*

Jacki wished Peter was here to see all she'd achieved. She'd had so many wonderful experiences, and had met so many remarkable people. She'd been to places and seen things others only dreamt of. But now, sitting on her own among her things, a sadness came over her. What had been the true cost of her success? Although she loved telling stories about her extravagant adventures, it wasn't the same as recalling them with someone who had been there too.

There had been the odd man who'd wined and dined her, but Jacki hadn't had a constant companion on these adventures. The thought left a deep ache in her chest. Could there have been room in her heart for a travelling companion? Jacki knew she couldn't have forced Darryl to come back to the Gold Coast, but maybe she could have delegated her work a little more, leaving more time to spend with her family, more time for her to love and be loved. *Goddamn it!* Jacki didn't want to reach the end of her life with regrets, but here she was, surrounded by *stuff* – stuff that didn't care for her or remember the good old times.

'Here we go.' Darryl placed the chilled drinks on the dresser. 'Helen's gone home, she said to say goodbye. Did you know it's her hubby's birthday today?'

'Damn it, I totally forgot.' Jacki turned her hands into fists. 'I'll have to call Mick later.'

Darryl turned off the bath tap, then handed her a vanilla shake. 'Right, beautiful. Let's try these together. Ready? On two.' Darryl grabbed his drink and held it up. 'Two.'

They each took a sip and then looked at each other.

'Not bad, eh?' Darryl took a large gulp. 'What d'you reckon?'

Jacki licked her lips. It was a little sweet, but the icy texture eased her nausea. 'Not bad.' Jacki nodded. 'I think I'll drink the rest in the bath.'

'Righto, I'll leave you to it then.' Darryl turned to leave.

'Wait, I can't … I need your help getting in. It's pathetic, but I'm just too weak. I don't think …'

'Oh, sure thing.' Darryl put down his glass and took her hand. He helped her over to the claw-foot bathtub, then took her glass and placed it by the sink. 'Okay?'

'This is where I really need you. Warning, I've changed a bit since the last time you saw me naked.' Jacki undid her robe and let it drop. Usually Helen helped her bathe by putting a chair in the shower. That way, she could conserve her energy. But right now, Jacki needed the warmth of the bathwater to ease her aching body.

Darryl smiled reassuringly, and there was no mistaking the warmth in his eyes.

She took his hand and stepped into the tub, but as she put her weight on one leg, she lost her balance. She wrapped both arms around his shoulders to steady herself, and he anchored his feet as she lowered herself in.

'Well, that was a little less graceful than I was hoping.' The soothing water cradled her body. 'Oh, that's good.'

Darryl, who was still stooped over, grabbed his lower back then dropped onto his knee. 'Ah, bugger!'

'Oh, no!' Jacki reached out to him. 'Have I hurt you?'

'My bloody back's gone. I can't move.'

'Oh! What can I do?'

He screwed up his face in pain. 'There's … nothing you can do.'

'I'll call Helen.'

'She's not here, remember?'

'I'll call her at home then.'

'With what?'

'Your phone. Let me get your phone.' She leant over the side of the bath and reached for his back pocket.

'It's downstairs.'

'Mine is by my bed, but I can't get out of the bath without your help. *Shit!* We're stuck.'

Darryl winced. His face was ashen.

'What are we going to do?'

'I don't know.' A smirk spread across his face.

'Why are you smiling?'

'Well, there are worse places to be right now.'

She looked down at her naked body then splashed water at him. 'Eyes up.'

He laughed, then choked in pain at the movement.

Jacki grinned at the dripping wet giant of a man kneeling before her and started laughing too.

'We could be here for a while.' Darryl grinned.

Tears of laughter streamed down Jacki's cheeks. 'What are we going to do?'

'I've got an idea,' he said, and tilted his head towards her. 'Hey Google, play a love song.'

'Okay. Here's the love music station from YouTube music.'

The song 'Drive' by The Cars lilted through the bathroom, and Darryl slowly shifted himself upright.

'What are you doing?' she asked.

'I'm doing what any man who gets on one knee in front of you should do.' He reached for her hand and took it in his. She could feel him trembling. 'Jacki Turner.' He looked her dead in the eyes, even though he was clearly in a lot of pain. 'You're the bloody love of my life. The moment I saw you I knew I was in trouble. Everyone knows you're the smartest person in the room, but not everyone got to know you like I do, and for that I'll always be grateful.'

Jacki stared into his beautiful brown eyes and held her breath.

'Jacki Turner, will you marry me?'

Pressing her wet palms on either side of his face, she kissed him hard. When she pulled back, she grinned so widely her cheeks hurt.

'Is that a yes?'

'You old romantic,' she laughed. 'Yes. Hell, yes!'

26

Jess

For the last three days, Jess had been on a high. After a lifetime of wishing her parents would get married, it was finally happening, and she was elated.

They'd decided to tie the knot on Christmas Day, which was less than two weeks away. Jacki had insisted the wedding would be a small affair, with only immediate family invited. She'd asked Helen, Jess and her sisters to make all the arrangements. She said it could be their wedding gift to her.

Jess had been working till midnight for the last few days trying to finish her clients' projects early so she could focus on planning her mum's dream wedding. There was so much to do. *Is it even possible to plan a wedding in two weeks?*

Sitting in the wedding cake shop, Jess took a bite of lemon sponge. Gemma, the owner, had brought out a selection of cakes for her and Brett to sample.

Jess still wasn't entirely sure how she felt about Brett, but she was trying to stay positive. The first couple of weeks had been fun, and she'd genuinely enjoyed his company, but things had taken an overly enthusiastic turn when he realised she was

Jessica Freeman-*Turner*. Once he made the Turner connection and then learnt about her run-in with Nathan Campbell, he'd stepped up his game, showering her with gifts and romantic gestures. Jess had a feeling he got a kick out of dating a 'cover girl', but when she'd questioned him about it, he'd denied any such thing.

Brett held up his phone, checked his hair was perfect, then took a selfie of them. 'I have to post this.'

'You can't!' Her mum had been adamant that the wedding be kept a secret.

'I won't put anything on there about your mum.'

'There's a shelf of wedding cakes behind us. People will think *we're* getting married.'

'Would that be so bad?' Brett made puppy dog eyes at her.

'You're getting way ahead of yourself. No posting photos. We've talked about this.' She'd refused to let Brett post any photos of her on social media. She didn't want any follow-up articles about her finding a new guy.

'You're *my* girl. I just want to show you off to the world. Is that so bad?' Brett kissed her forehead and rested his hand on her thigh.

'I'm not *yours* or anybody's.' The words came out sharper than she'd intended.

Brett raised his brows, and an unease sat between them, but Jess didn't have it in her to soothe his ego.

'Well, I can't decide which cake I like best. I need to call Rose.' She left a sulky Brett stabbing a fork into a slice of white chocolate mud cake and stepped outside to call her sister.

If Jess had been as into Brett as he was into her, then she might have found it sweet that he called her *his* girl. But she couldn't think about that right now; she had a wedding to plan.

'Rose?'

'Hey, I'm about to go through the check-out at Target. What's up?'

'I'm wedding cake testing with Brett. Which do you think Mum would like best? Red velvet with cream cheese frosting or lemon with raspberry buttercream? I'm thinking lemon. Mum likes anything citrusy, right?'

'Honestly? I've got to get a trolley full of presents home and in the house without the kids seeing, I've got to take Bethany to her swimming lesson and drop Taylor off at her friend's for a sleepover, I've got no idea what we're having for dinner and we're supposed to be putting the Christmas tree up today. Can't you decide?'

'Fine, red velvet it is. Everyone likes red velvet.' Jess looked back into the shop, where Brett was wiping the corners of his mouth with a napkin and chatting to the owner. *Was it bad that she didn't want to go back in?* 'How's your writing going?'

'My writing? I don't even have time to answer that question, let alone actually write anything. Hey, Isla said Brett's been invited to the wedding. Is that true?'

Jess sighed. 'Mum wants him at the dinner.' Jess thought it was too soon for Brett to meet her family, but Jacki had insisted.

'Doesn't he have his own family to spend Christmas with?'

'Brett told his parents he'd been invited to *Jacki Turner's*. He's so excited.'

'I'm guessing our mother's insistence is her way of keeping track of your task.'

'Rose, give it a rest.' Jess wished she'd give her mum a break for once.

'Look, I've gotta go.'

'Fine. See ya.'

'Wait … hang on. Get the lemon cake … she *loves* lemon.'

'Then lemon it is.' Jess hung up and stepped back inside the shop, where she was immediately assailed by the freezing air con.

'Jess, I was just telling Gemma here about last Friday's crazy shift at the hospital.' Brett's eyes sparkled and the dimple on his cheek deepened as he smiled.

'He's a real-life hero,' swooned Gemma.

Jess softened her demeanour. 'Yeah, he's the real deal.' Maybe she was being too hard on Brett. Perhaps the pressure of trying to make their relationship last longer than three months was clouding her judgement. He was charming, and passionate, even if he was a little self-obsessed. She only had to date him for another eight weeks. Surely, she could stick with him for that long.

Couldn't she?

27

Mel

Running, especially in the heat of summer, was something Mel never thought she would, could or should do, but here she was on Christmas Eve, on track to completing another ten kilometres. It was traditional for Christmas to be as hot as hell in Queensland, and this year was no exception. The forecast promised high temperatures and high humidity for the coming week, which meant running either early in the morning or as late as possible, when it was cooler.

After finishing work at three, Mel had popped to the shops for some last-minute Christmas gifts before fitting in one last run before the festivities began.

Mel was excited because Rose had agreed, if a little reluctantly, to join the Turner family at Mum's house, not only for the traditional Christmas celebrations but also for the wedding. It would probably be their last Christmas together as a family. There had been so many split celebrations over the last few years, and it wasn't the same without Rose.

The last two weeks had been a crazy mixture of work, bridesmaid's dress fittings, Christmas shopping and getting up extra early to fit in her runs. She'd also been down to her mum's twice to help Jess and Helen with the wedding arrangements.

Rose, Tom and the kids were picking Mel up from her house; she had just received a text saying they'd be there soon. She had everything packed, but she'd need to have a quick shower.

She'd picked up the Christmas present she'd ordered for Corey and left it with his neighbour. Mel had timed it purposefully so he wouldn't be home. She didn't want to be there when he opened it, as she knew her face would burn like hot coals. She'd also bought a pavlova from Woolworths, because Mum still wanted to have the traditional 'bring a plate' Christmas lunch, even though she was bringing in caterers for her wedding reception.

This had irritated Rose. *Our mother,* she'd whinged on the phone to Mel the day before, *can afford the best chefs in the world, but on the busiest day of the year, when everyone is already exhausted, she expects us to bring a bloody plate.* Rose was right. It would have been nice just once to have had a full traditional turkey and all the trimmings, but bring-a-plate was Jacki's tradition. If they didn't do it, it wouldn't feel like Christmas.

Mel ran through Henry Ziegenfusz Park and checked the running watch Isla had bought her. She was forty-eight minutes in and had run eight kilometres. She was doing well, but she'd left her house late and the sun was setting fast. She'd be running the last two kilometres in the dark if she didn't get a move on.

With her music paused and her breath steady, she ran along the paved footpath and down the mountain of death where Isla had nearly passed out on their first parkrun. At the bottom, the already fading light darkened further under the canopy of trees, and she squinted to try and see clearly.

A loud ringing made her jump, and her arms struck out in fear. It was her phone. *Shit!* She answered and kept running.

'Hello?'

'I called to thank you for my gift.' It was Corey.

'You're not supposed. To open it. Until tomorrow.'

'Are you running?'

'I'm always. Running. Or didn't. You notice?'

'What distance are you doing?'

'Ten kilometres.'

'That's the third time this week, isn't it? That's awesome, *you're* awesome!'

Mel grinned. If she wasn't already hot, sweaty and red-faced, she would have blushed.

'I mean ...' Corey stumbled over his words. 'How far you've run is awesome. Consistently running ten kilometres is amazing.'

And it was. Six months ago, she couldn't run two hundred metres without feeling like she was going to die. She'd gone from doing no exercise at all to running a well-paced ten kilometres. The last four months of training had been brutal, but each kilometre she ran without stopping was a milestone to be celebrated. Last week she'd run thirteen kilometres for the first time. Maybe running a marathon was possible after all.

She had Corey to thank for helping her get this far. He'd slipped into the role of her personal trainer, scheduling sprint sessions and calling her at the crack of dawn to make sure she was out of bed and moving. He would even meet her with coffee after her early morning runs. His optimism provided her with the motivation and encouragement she needed.

For Christmas, she had bought him a cap she'd had embroidered with the words 'Mel's Personal Trainer'. 'I wanted to make your job title official, and say thanks for helping me.'

Corey laughed. 'I love it. It's great.'

'I couldn't do this on my own.'

'Sure you could.'

'Are you kidding? There's no way!'

'You could.' There was a pause. 'But I've really enjoyed hanging out with you more. It's been fun.'

Mel beamed as she ran through a densely wooded area, and the path darkened again. Hanging with Corey was always so easy. He was funny, he always cheered her on, and his positive outlook on life made her feel good – *really* good. Incredible even. God, how she just wanted to kiss his beautiful lips and run her fingers through his hair.

'I've enjoyed it too. Like … a lot,' she stammered. 'So, will you help me see this through to the end? This is all about to get so much harder and—'

'I'm in. You can count on me to be there.'

Mel did a little jump as she ran. *Shit! She was falling hard for him.*

'Oh, and thanks for *your* Christmas present. I ate some rocky road this morning.' Corey had bought her a small hamper of her favourite chocolate from a store on the Sunshine Coast. She'd mentioned it in passing a few weeks ago and he'd remembered.

'What happened to not opening presents until Christmas Day?'

'It was a matter of life or death. I was starving.'

He chuckled. 'Then I'm glad I could help. Well, have fun at the wedding tomorrow. Send me photos.'

'Will do.'

'Merry Christmas, Mel.'

Her heart tightened as he spoke her name. 'Merry Christmas.'

Hanging up, she widened her stride and pushed forward like she'd never done before. Sweat soaked through her top, and her sports bra rubbed on the underside of her breasts, but she didn't stop. She couldn't. The only way home was back the way she'd come, under the canopy of the surrounding trees, across the creek, and through the park.

She looked all around her to make sure she was alone. Surely no one would want to attack her on Christmas Eve. Even psychos would have plans, wouldn't they? She was thankful the moon was bright, as all trace of daylight disappeared. She pulled out her personal alarm, then turned on the torch on her phone, trying to control her jumpiness.

There's no one behind me! There's no one behind me!

She was breathing hard and her heartbeat thudded in her ears. There was a rustling in the trees, but she told herself it was just a brush turkey or a lizard, and pushed on.

Please Santa! Just get me home for Christmas!

Before she knew it, the path opened up onto a grassy area. She could have cried with relief. *Nearly there!* But just as she caught sight of her house in the distance, another piercing ring cut through the silence. She jolted in fright and, caught off balance, fell. As she put out her hand to save herself, a screaming siren sliced through the humid air. She dropped her phone and alarm, covered her ears and looked around for her attacker, but there was none. With her heart in her throat and her hands still over her ears, she struggled to get to her feet.

'Shit!'

The ringing was coming from her phone, and the relentless siren was her personal alarm. With trembling fingers, she turned off the alarm and answered her phone, blinding herself with its light.

It was Rose. '*Damn it*, Rose.'

'That's not a very festive way to greet your sister. Where are you? We're at your place right now, but you're not home.'

Mel hobbled across the open field opposite her house. She could see Rose at her front door. 'I'm behind you, in the park.'

Rose turned, and Mel waved her phone, the torch still on.

'What are you doing? Only psychos hang out in the park at night.'

Mel jogged with a limp. 'Really?' Her palms stung where she'd scraped them, and her breathing was ragged. Reaching her front door, she bent over and clamped her eyes shut, trying to compose herself.

'Are you okay?' asked Rose.

Mel's watch beeped, and she checked her distance and pace. 'Holy holly bells!' She stood upright and grabbed Rose's arm. 'I just ran a new personal best!'

28

Rose

Rose watched her kids unwrap their presents in her mother's living room and tried to smile. Jacki had spoiled her grandkids with eye-wateringly expensive presents. She had bought Harrison a new PlayStation, an eight-hundred-dollar BMX and a new fancy gaming chair. Taylor had been given a new iPad, laptop and a cruiser bike, while Bethany had received a whole heap of Fisher-Price toys and a three-storey doll's house. It was ridiculous and embarrassing, and Rose had no idea how they would get it all home.

Of course, the kids were in heaven and would probably remember this morning for the rest of their lives. Harrison had declared it the best Christmas ever. It had hurt, but Rose had to keep smiling. She didn't want to spoil Christmas Day *and* her mother's wedding day. Her sisters' patience regarding her relationship with Jacki was wearing thin, so she had resolved to grin and bear it, but it was only breakfast, and she was already struggling.

'They can't keep those gifts,' she told Tom mid-morning as she paced up and down the pontoon in the backyard, her long flowing floral dress lifting slightly in the hot breeze. Tom, dressed in his usual khaki shorts and a Minecraft T-shirt, listened attentively. She loved that about him – he always let her vent. Up at the house, Mel was watching Bethany while Harrison and Taylor rode their new bikes around the gated forecourt.

'She thinks she can just buy love like it's a Gucci bag, but it doesn't work that way.' Rose folded her arms. 'And now, if I say anything, I'll be the bad guy.'

Tom winced. 'I get it, I do, but maybe she just wants to treat them while she can.'

'Don't do that. Don't take her side. She spent thousands of dollars on those presents. It's embarrassing. Plus, I don't want my kids growing up thinking this is normal!'

'I agree, but try not to let it get to you. Don't let it ruin our Christmas.'

'*Our* Christmas? This isn't *our* Christmas. It's hers. It's *her* Christmas and *her* wedding day. *God!*' She clenched her hands. 'I know I sound like a bitch, and I wish I could just let her have it all and not care. I wish I could be happy that my kids are having the greatest Christmas of their lives, but …'

Tom gave her a hug. 'I know.'

She pulled back and took a breath. 'I just need to let it go.'

Up in the garden, Jess was arranging chairs for the sunset wedding. A cheery Helen helped, and they both sang Christmas carols at the top of their voices. They'd decided on a boho-themed wedding. Jess had called on some of Isla's connections to secure bridesmaids' dresses at the last minute, and had picked the flowers and organised the decorations. Her attention to detail made Rose's head spin. Jess was in her element.

Rose was proud of her youngest sister, and she was glad she was finally getting to witness the happily ever after she'd always wished for. Jess had spent her life hoping they'd one day get married and today her dream was coming true.

'I'm happy for Jess,' said Rose. 'I'm glad she gets to have this moment.'

Tom put an arm around her and kissed the top of her head as they made their way back up to the house. Walking past her dad's hidden memorial garden, she spotted her mother sitting on the small bench.

'I'll catch up with you in a bit,' she said to Tom.

'What are you going to say?'

'I haven't decided yet.'

Rose headed for the towering bamboo, not entirely sure why. She was angry with her mother, but the opportunity to talk to her alone was rare, so she followed her gut. 'Got room for one more?'

Sitting in a white cotton robe, Jacki looked up in surprise and smiled. 'Rose, of course.' She slid along the bench. Rose sat down beside her and stared at the white cross and the small gold plaque with her dad's name etched into it. Water trickled from the marble fountain and for a minute they both sat in silence.

'I come in here every day when I'm home. I still miss him.' Jacki pushed her hands into the pockets of her robe and sat up straight.

'I miss him too.' Rose would give anything to have one more hug or one more conversation with her dad. She closed her eyes and tried hard to remember the sound of his laughter.

'I think your dad and Richard would—'

'Stop.'

'I was going to say they'd be proud of—'

'They're not here!' Rose forced herself to stop speaking. Her words had come out harsher than she'd intended, but she couldn't listen to her mother talk about her dad and Richard like she was the perfect widow and mother-in-law, keeping their memory alive.

'Richard was—' started Jacki.

'I said stop!'

'What?' Jacki shook her head, looking perplexed. 'I'm just—'

'Don't sit there and talk to me about my husband like you knew him.'

'I was only going to say—'

'What? Are you going to tell me what Richard would think if he could see us now, or that he was a great dad and husband, or what an unbelievably kind man he was? I already know that. *I* was there, and you weren't. You have no clue about anything in my life, so just – *don't*. I don't want to ever hear you talk about Richard.' Rose clasped her fingers over the edge of the bench and squeezed it tight.

Jacki pressed her lips together as she stared at the white pavers under her pedicured feet, then nodded. 'You're right. I wasn't there,' said Jacki. 'And … I hurt you. I'm sorry.'

Rose bit her bottom lip. Would they be having this conversation if her mother wasn't dying? Wanting to make amends in the final hour was just too convenient, and try as she might, she couldn't move past it. Her mother had disappeared when she'd needed her most, and it just hurt too much.

'I got … scared … when Richard got sick,' said Jacki. 'And remembering the loss of your dad all those years before … I froze. I just couldn't do it again.'

'*You* couldn't do it again.' Rose placed her hands on her cheeks in dismay. 'Oh, my God! You think everything is about you. Well, newsflash: it's not. When Richard died, it was about him, and me, and the kids. You left us the names of specialists and a bottomless pit of cash, but *you* were what we needed, and *you* were nowhere to be found. You didn't even go to his funeral.' Tears fell down Rose's cheeks and she balled her trembling hands into fists. 'You don't get to talk about Richard, do you hear me? Because you weren't there when we needed you the most, and that is unforgivable.'

Rose stood. 'And your Christmas gifts are embarrassing. You can't buy your way into my family, not if you had all the money in the world.'

Jacki burst into tears.

As Rose headed out of the memorial area a wave of regret flooded her, but it was too late. She'd finally told her mother how she really felt. After all these years, it should have felt good, it should have felt like a weight off her shoulders, but it didn't. As Rose dashed into the house, tears soaking her cheeks, all she could think was how spiteful her words had been.

* * *

Lanterns lit the way as Jacki walked up the aisle towards Darryl, who waited with tears in his eyes. As she reached the large golden arch, decorated with lush pale greenery, pampas grass and flowing white macrame, Jacki handed her bouquet to Jess, and Darryl took her hands in his. Rose had to admit her mother looked stunning in her lace mermaid wedding dress, with pretty cap sleeves and a small train, and Darryl was very handsome, dressed casually in tan pants and a white shirt.

As Jacki and Darryl exchanged vows, Rose couldn't help replaying the conversation she'd had with her mother. For the rest of the day, she'd experienced a mixture of relief and guilt. Surrounded by the building excitement of Christmas and the wedding, she'd tried to contain her growing sense of detachment. She'd watched an elated Jess busy herself with last-minute details, and looked on as her kids had the time of their lives playing with all their gifts, but while Rose did her best to appear upbeat, she couldn't shift her lingering resentment.

Forcing herself to focus on the present moment, she chewed the inside of her cheek as Darryl struggled to say his vows without crying. Across the aisle, Jess and Mel bawled. They wore the same dress as Rose and Isla, a pale pink pleated v-neck dress with a chiffon skirt, and a delicate flower crown. Even Isla shed a tear. Rose exhaled. She envied her sisters' relationship with her mother, but couldn't understand how they could so easily forgive her absence over the years.

Perhaps Rose struggled because, after twelve years of being a mum herself, she knew what she'd missed out on. Growing up, she'd tried to tell herself that her mother's absence was typical, but her instinct had told her otherwise. For years she'd wondered if she was just being sensitive, but she knew now that the ache in her heart had been real, and justified. The realisation had hit home the day Harrison had been born.

Rose's love for her children seeped from every pore and flooded into every aspect of her life. There was no way to stop it, and no way she'd ever want to.

But being a parent wasn't all rainbows and sun showers. It was bloody hard. From day one, she was forced to question her values and beliefs. Her patience was continuously tested, and she had to enforce ever-shifting boundaries, all the while wanting to shield her kids from hurt and pain. She had to allow her kids space to navigate their own way through a world that made no promises, other than that change was around every corner.

Being a parent was like having a mirror held up to you twenty-four hours a day and constantly being asked if you liked what you saw. But Rose did it. She faced it all head-on, even after Richard died, when she'd lost her bearings and no longer knew which way was north. She kept showing up for her kids, over and over, day after day, because she loved them more than anything in the world. No matter how hard things got, she'd be there, because that was what it meant to love unconditionally, and that was what it meant to be a good mum.

A tear ran down her cheek, and Jess caught her eye and smiled. But these weren't tears of happiness; Rose was crying for what she would never have – a mum who loved her exactly as she was, and who *wanted* to spend time with her.

She was genuinely happy that her sisters' experiences with Jacki had been better than hers. But she couldn't help wishing things had been different.

Jacki and Darryl kissed as the sun began to set, and Jess and Helen threw confetti over the newlyweds as they walked back down the aisle. As the photographer gathered the guests into various groups, Rose took in the garden. Jess had done an incredible job, giving the space a luxe boho feel. She'd hired a large lace teepee for the kids to chill out in, and created relaxed adult spaces using vintage wicker seating covered with lush turquoise, coral and terracotta textiles. Large vases were filled with pampas grass, and there was an abundance of festoon lighting, dream catchers and gorgeous macrame to give a truly bohemian vibe.

After the photographs had been taken, Jess found Rose, kissed her cheek and linked her arm in hers. 'Wasn't it beautiful?' she said. 'It was like something out of a fairytale.'

Jess's eyes sparkled in the dim light, and Rose smiled at her sister. 'You've done such a fantastic job. I can't believe you organised all of this in two weeks.'

'Let's just say I knew exactly what I wanted. I mean, what *Mum* wanted. Having an unlimited budget was useful too.'

'Well, it was one hell of a wedding gift you gave her, pulling this off. There's no way the rest of us could have done this.'

'I just can't believe Mum and Dad finally got their happily ever after.'

Rose was distracted by a good-looking guy walking with unwavering confidence into the garden. He was clean-shaven, wearing navy suit pants and an expensive-looking white shirt.

'Who is *that*?' asked Rose, admiring his model looks. He grinned and waved at Jess. 'Oh wow, is that …'

'Brett.' Jess half-smiled.

'You don't look too pleased to see him.'

'No. I mean, I am. Who wouldn't be pleased to *see* him?' The twinkle in Jess's eyes returned, then faded. 'It's just, well—'

'Hey, gorgeous.' Brett strolled up to Jess, took her by the waist and kissed her. 'You look stunning.'

'Thanks.' Jess flushed. 'Brett, this is my sister, Rose. Rose, this is—'

'Doctor Brett Cavendish, but you can call me Brett. I work at the Gold Coast Private Hospital in the Emergency Department.'

Rose nodded. 'Yes, I—'

'I just came from there, actually.' Brett raised his chiselled chin and scouted the garden to see if anyone else was within earshot. 'I put my hand up to work Christmas Day. A lot of my colleagues have families, so I thought I'd do the right thing. Let *them* have the day with their kids.' Brett stared expectantly at Rose, waiting for her response.

She grimaced. She'd met his type plenty of times before, and she wasn't about to give him the satisfaction of—

'Oh, *shit*! You're the hot doctor!' said Mel, making her way over to them.

Brett turned to Mel and gave her a smile so utterly charming, it didn't look real. Rose suspected he'd practised it so many times in the mirror that he was almost smiling at himself. Clearly, he knew how good he looked.

'Jess has told us *nothing* about you,' said Mel. 'She must have thought we'd all get jealous.'

Jess cleared her throat. 'Brett, this is Mel.'

'Are you the one running the marathon?' he asked with a knowing look. 'I think what you're doing is *remarkable*. After I ran my third marathon two years ago, I said, "No more, I have to give my time to my patients." Marathon training is so time-consuming, don't you find?'

Mel gazed at Brett with a look of awe and relief that someone finally understood her pain. 'It is *so* time-sucking. No one gets it. *No one* understands.'

Standing under the palm trees, Helen, wearing a blush pink maxi dress, held up her champagne flute and tapped it with a fork to announce dinner. 'If everyone could take their seats.'

Mel linked her arm in Brett's. 'Tell me everything you know about how to prevent nipple chafing.' Rose nearly choked on her champagne as they walked towards the long table, which was adorned with hanging wicker lanterns.

Jess winced and glanced at Rose. 'Mum said three *months*, right?'

'How long has it been?'

'Nearly six weeks, but it's started to feel like six years.'

They burst out laughing.

Rose took her seat opposite Mel and next to Tom, who was clipping Bethany into a highchair. Darryl and Jacki sat at the end of the long, wide table against a backdrop of pampas grass swaying in the hot breeze. Gold charger plates, cutlery and crystal glassware sat on dusty-pink table runners, which complemented the pale palette of pink and green florals that ran down the centre. On each plate lay a white napkin in a gold napkin ring inscribed with the letters J&D.

After a five-course dinner and lots of champagne, Darryl stood and tapped his champagne flute. Everyone went quiet. 'I just wanted to thank you all for being here with us today. It means the world that we could all be together.'

Rose bounced her knee under the table.

'The road that led me to this point has been a long one; long and winding.' Darryl laughed. 'But as of this afternoon I can finally say I'm honoured to call myself Jacki Turner's husband.' Jess whooped with delight and Steve drummed his hands on the table. 'The only thing I'm worried about is what my wife will make me do to earn my inheritance.' Everyone laughed, and Rose tried not to cry.

'Jokes aside,' he said, 'although I've lived in Cairns all these years, I still feel like I've been part of the Turner family. Jess, girls, I love you all. Plus, you all look beautiful tonight. And finally, to Jacki, my wife ... my love ...' He paused and tried not to cry. 'I will love you forever.' Darryl took Jacki's hand and kissed it. 'That's it, that's all I wanted to say.'

Everyone clapped and cheered and when he sat back down, Jacki declared that she too had something she wanted to say. Rose took another sip of champagne, feeling light-headed. She wasn't sure how much she'd had to drink because every time she took a sip, her glass was full. The waiting staff were too good at their jobs.

'Jess. Girls,' said Jacki, looking to her daughters. 'You managed to pull off the dream wedding. Today has, quite simply, been a dream come true. I don't know how many more Christmases or family get-togethers we'll have, but I'm thankful we had today. This day has been a wonderful gift.' Jacki held onto the table in front of her, and Rose could see that beyond her mother's perfect hair and make-up, and her stunning wedding gown, she was frail and more vulnerable than she'd ever seen her before.

Rose rolled the gold napkin ring between her fingers and rubbed her thumb across the letter J. Had she spoken out of turn earlier? Could she have kept her feelings to herself, at least on her mother's wedding day? Had she ruined what would otherwise have been a perfect twenty-four hours for her mother?

For Rose, guilt often went hand in hand with family get-togethers. She always struggled to keep her feelings to herself. Growing up, she'd often let a snide comment slip about her mother's behaviour. Her sisters always told her to keep her thoughts to herself, even though she knew they were thinking the same thing. And now here she was again, doubting herself.

Jacki looked at Darryl beside her and placed her hand on his shoulder. 'There are some people who aren't physically here today but are with us in spirit.'

A startled Rose glared at her mother, and her heart pounded.

'I know I would have Peter's blessing today,' said Jacki. 'In fact, I'm pretty sure he'd be shocked it took me this long to remarry.' Darryl smiled, and reached up to hold Jacki's hand. 'And there is someone else who isn't here, someone else we miss dearly.'

No, no, no! Rose's face burned as her mother stared directly at her.

'I'm pretty sure,' said Jacki. 'No, I'm *certain*, that Richard is looking down on us all today, at his beautiful children, and wishing he could be here. He was a proud father who loved Harrison and Taylor, and he loved Rose deeply. I know he is watching us, and I know he is proud to be part of this family.'

Under the table, Tom squeezed Rose's knee, and her lip quivered. *How could she?* How could her mother do this when only a few hours earlier, she'd explicitly told her not to talk about Richard?

Rose could feel all eyes on her, and she knew they'd see her tears and think Jacki had made a lovely gesture, but she knew the truth. Her mother was cold and manipulative, even if no one else could see it. *How can she be so insensitive?*

Jacki smiled as she raised her glass. 'To Richard and Peter, who are forever in our hearts.'

Champagne flutes were held up. 'To Richard and Peter.'

Rose took a sip from her glass and stared down at the napkin ring.

'Are you okay?' asked Tom, leaning towards her.

She nodded, but at that moment she felt dizzy with rage and hurt. Just when Rose thought she'd seen all of her mother's tricks, she'd wounded her more than she'd thought possible. As the guests chatted among themselves, a feeling of clarity washed over her, making her desperately sad. Jacki would never be the mum she wanted her to be. In this final hour, as she inched closer to death, Jacki Turner had revealed her true colours once and for all.

29

Isla

Isla sat at the long table and watched the guests dance under the festoon lighting. Jess's wedding day playlist had them all up and moving, and Isla laughed as she watched Mel perform ghastly robot dance moves.

'Want to dance?' asked Steve, handing her a glass of merlot.

'Maybe later.'

'That's not like you.' Steve sat next to her. 'You're usually dragging me onto the dance floor. Everything okay?'

'Do you think this will be Mum's last Christmas?'

Steve took a sip of his white wine. 'It might be.'

'This could be the last time we're all together like this. It just makes me so sad, you know?'

Steve rubbed Isla's back. 'It's okay to be sad, but make sure you enjoy this time too. Don't mourn the moment while it's happening.'

At the other end of the table, Rose rocked Bethany in her stroller and, behind her, Tom and Harrison played a giant version of four in a row.

Isla sipped her merlot then gathered her courage. 'There is something else,' she said. 'I wasn't going to say anything today, but if I don't get it out, I'll burst.'

'What?'

'Not here.' Isla stood. 'Follow me.' She led Steve through the house and out to the front driveway, out of earshot of everyone else. She began to pace the grand entrance. 'You have to promise not to freak out.'

'Okay.' Steve's eyes narrowed as he watched her intently. 'What's going on?'

'You know how much I love you, right?'

'Of course.'

'Well. I've been thinking, for a while now, ever since the retreat: I want to move into Mum's apartment in Brisbane.'

'But we live in the best penthouse money can buy.'

'You're not hearing me. *I* want to move into Mum's apartment in Brisbane – alone.'

'What?' Steve stepped back in shock. 'You're leaving me?'

'No, no, it's not like that.'

'Then tell me. What's it like?'

Isla pressed her palms together. 'I've never lived alone. We married so young, and during the retreat I realised I've never just hung out with myself. I've always been with you.'

'Why is that suddenly a problem? You've done the retreat. You've completed your terms of inheritance. I thought we were just waiting for your sisters to catch up?'

'I've been thinking a lot on my early morning walks. I've been trying to dig deep to find out who I am under all these roles I've created for myself, and I've begun to see things much more clearly. I feel different somehow, like something's shifted in me. I'm more patient, and I've been listening more. You said that yourself.'

'And you have, but—'

'But there's so much more I don't know about myself. I feel like I need to find out who I am on my own. I need space to just be.'

'You've done what your mum asked. There's no need to take things further.'

'Mum said I can stay at the apartment for six months.'

'You've already spoken to her about this?' Steve ran his hand over his chin. 'What about us? I mean, *six months*!'

'We'll still see each other. Nothing really changes. It's just a bit of breathing space. You can come to the city and take me out for dinner, like we're going on a date.'

'I don't want to date you. You're my wife!' He shook his head. 'Did your mum suggest this ridiculous idea? I thought she liked me? I thought you *loved* me!'

'I do love you, don't doubt that. I'm not leaving you, I just need—'

'*Space*. You keep saying that, as if I'm suffocating you.' He dragged his fingers over his head.

Isla rolled her eyes and took a deep breath. 'Stop being so dramatic! I told you, I love you.' She sighed, irritated by his overreaction, but forced herself to try and see things from his perspective. 'Look,' she touched his arm, 'I don't want to go my whole life never having been alone. It's always been you and me, and it always will be, but I want to find out if I'm the same person without you.'

'Does your mum think you can do better? Is that it?'

'This has nothing to do with Mum, but I'm finally starting to see why she wanted me to go on this journey. I'm learning so much about myself, the good and the bad. It's like I'm seeing everything for the first time. I've spent years putting all my energy into us and the business, but now I need to focus on me.'

'But you do. You're always out shopping, getting your nails done, having some kind of massage or spa treatment. That's all about you.'

'That's exactly what I'm talking about. That's all superficial – temporary. The clothes, the hair, the nails, the eyelashes, that's not who I really am. I enjoy those things, and I want to look good, but what's more important is who I am once all that's stripped away.'

'Just because you want to look good doesn't make you superficial.'

'I didn't say that. I'm saying, if I don't do the work on the inside, then everything on the exterior becomes a mask, another layer that's hiding who I really am.' She stepped closer to him and stroked his cheek. 'I'm sick of the façade and the boxes I've spent my life trying to fit into.' In the last couple of months she'd tried to see herself through others' eyes, and she hadn't liked what she'd seen. 'I just want to be … *me*.'

'I have no idea what that means.' Steve paced, shaking his head, then paused to look at her. '*Damn it!*'

Isla smiled.

'You promise you still love me?'

She stepped towards him. 'I promise.'

'I don't like any of this.'

She nodded. 'I know.'

Steve sighed and put his hands on his hips. 'And it has to be six months? You can't do three?'

'Six months takes me up to the marathon.' Isla bit her lip and waited for him to come round.

'I want you to know, this *isn't* what I want. I think it's ridiculous.'

'Noted.'

'Well then … it looks like I've got no choice.' Isla wrapped her arms around Steve, and he hugged her back. 'I suppose I'd better brush up on my dating skills.'

30

Jess

Jess had arranged to meet Brett at a tapas bar in Broadbeach at seven. At a quarter past seven, her phone buzzed.

Sorry, finished work late. Just grabbed a quick shower. Five mins away.

Spanish guitar music played in the restaurant, and Jess ordered a glass of sangria and people-watched while she waited.

On her way to the bar, Jess had called Rose to see how her writing was going. Apparently, her sister had lots of ideas for characters and a setting, but she couldn't think of a story. Every time she thought of an idea a quick Google search told her someone had already done it. Jess told her to keep trying. She was sure she'd come up with a great idea.

The real reason Jess wanted to speak to Rose was that she needed her own cheer squad. Jess had been dating Brett for nearly eight weeks. If she could last another month, she'd meet her terms of inheritance, but she was struggling.

'Four and a half weeks isn't *too* bad,' Rose had assured her. 'Just tell him you're busy at work, then you'll only have to see him a couple of times. As soon as you hit three months, you can get out of there.'

Jess sighed. 'I don't know if I can do that. Isn't it cruel to keep a relationship going if I'm not interested?'

'Of course it is, but in this case it's a hell of a lot crueller for you. I bet you ten dollars when you meet him tonight he'll tell the waiter he's a doctor within the first ten minutes.'

'I bet you twenty it's within the first five.'

'You're on. But seriously, just end it with him tonight if you don't want to see him anymore. It's not worth it.'

'Mum's inheritance isn't just a few thousand dollars. That money would change our lives.'

'It's not worth selling your soul for.'

Rose was right. It was one thing to run a marathon or write a book to meet the terms of inheritance, but it was another to mislead others and play with their feelings.

'I'll give him one last chance,' said Jess. 'I know deep down there's a less self-centred Brett. Maybe he's only been *temporarily* consumed by his ego.'

Jess took a sip of the sweet sangria and checked her phone for the time. Seven twenty-five. She drummed her fingers and surveyed the other couples around her, eating tapas and sipping cool Spanish beer in the summer heat. *Was she being too hard on Brett?* After all, he may have boasted that he was saving lives daily, but he was also telling the truth. She thought how handy it would be to live permanently with a doctor. If she ever choked on her food, or got bitten by a venomous spider, he'd know what to do.

But as impressive as his CV was, and as gorgeous as he was to look at, he wasn't the right fit for her. When they went out for dinner, he was often rude to the staff, talking down to them. He was always the one to decide where they ate, dismissing

Jess's suggestions, and while they had fun in the bedroom, Brett wasn't particularly concerned about her enjoyment. *Not consulting Jess* had been trending in their relationship for a while.

Looking at her phone again, she opened the stopwatch and made a deal with herself. If Brett could hold off from telling their waiter he was a doctor for longer than five minutes, she'd stick with him a little longer. If he couldn't, she was out of there, and she'd be back to square one as far as her task was concerned.

'Sorry I'm late.' Brett appeared behind Jess and kissed her cheek. He smelt of soap and expensive cologne; his hair was damp and brushed back.

She hit start on the stopwatch then slid her phone under a napkin. Brett seemed genuinely pleased to see her, and a pang of guilt washed through her as he took a seat opposite her.

'Is that sangria?' he asked, looking at her glass. 'I might join you.' He held up his hand and caught the attention of a waiter. 'You want another one?' he asked her.

'Sure, why not.'

Brett read the waiter's name tag. 'Finn, could we have two more sangrias? I just finished a shift in the Emergency Room at the GC *Private* Hospital. I'm a doctor.'

Jess winced, pulled out her phone and hit stop. Thirty-seven seconds – it was possibly a new record.

The waiter made a note on his pad, then disappeared.

'You know what?' said Brett. 'I might get a shot too. It's been a *long* day. I'll be right back.' Brett stood and made his way towards the bar.

Jess stared at the paused timer, then texted Rose.

You owe me twenty dollars.

31

Rose

Sitting at a high table at a wine bar in Raby Bay Harbour, Rose took a sip of her lemon, lime and bitters and gazed out at the fiery sunset. Its reflection on the water set the marina alight.

Isla took a sip of her white wine. 'When are you going to quit breastfeeding? Surely ten months is long enough?'

'She doesn't have as many feeds now. Oh, that reminds me.' Rose pulled out her phone and showed Isla a video of Bethany crawling across the living room floor and pulling herself up on the ottoman. For the last few weeks, Bethany had been getting more active and Tom had been on a mission to babyproof the house. Rose loved how protective he was of his little girl, and how excited he got about her hitting all her milestones. When she'd babbled the word *dada* for the first time, he'd cried.

Isla strained a smile. Rose knew she wasn't one for cooing over babies, even if Bethany was her niece. She'd been the same with Harrison and Taylor.

'So why are we here?' asked Rose. Isla had called her earlier saying she desperately needed to meet tonight, but Rose questioned her sister's sense of urgency. Since moving into the Brisbane apartment a few weeks ago, Isla clearly had more time on her hands and, as a result, Rose had seen a lot more of her sister than usual.

'This is an intervention,' said Isla.

'For?'

'For you. I spoke to a publisher friend of mine today and called in a favour. She's willing to take a look at your picture book manuscript.'

'But I don't have anything for her to read.' Since the start of her task, Rose had only written one story, which Tom and the kids hadn't liked. In the months leading up to Christmas, she'd been struck with a bout of writer's block, which was probably brought on by her constant tiredness and the rising tensions between her and her mother. Then since Christmas and the wedding, she'd been too angry to write. Plus, the kids were still on school holidays, and that made it impossible to find the time. She'd only just started drafting a new story.

'She's closed for submissions right now, but she said you could email it to her along with a query letter and she'd take a look. She's going on long service leave in the middle of February, so you need to act fast.'

'But that's only three weeks away. I've only got pieces of a first draft.'

'It's a picture book. They're only short.'

'Exactly, every word counts.' Rose shook her head. 'You just don't understand the skill it takes to write a picture book.'

'What I understand is that you need to grab this opportunity with both hands. What's your story called?'

'I don't know, I haven't got that far.'

'Then what's it about?'

'A heartless mother.'

'You're kidding, right? I know nothing about kids, but even I know that won't sell. *Damn it!* I should have intervened earlier.'

'This is my task. You don't have to concern yourself.'

'When we signed up for this, we said we'd help each other. Plus, I'm beginning to think part of my task is to think less about myself and more about others, so here I am, showing up for you, just like you've always wanted. You should be proud of me.'

'I'll admit this version is an improvement on the Isla who told me I needed a complete makeover if I was ever to find another man after Rich died.'

'Yes, well, I was only trying to help.'

'But, ever since the retreat, I've gotta say, I can see a difference, and I like it.'

Isla beamed, then checked her ego. 'Look Rose, and I say this with the kindest of intentions, you need to ditch the I-hate-my-mummy themes and think about the type of book you'd like to read to Bethany. It should be entertaining.'

'I'm writing from my heart. That's what writing is. You have to bleed on the page.'

'Maybe if you're writing some tragic literary novel, but not a picture book for kids. You have to let this toxic feud with Mum go. It's getting old.'

'You don't get it.' Rose sighed and glanced up at the couples and families strolling from one restaurant to the next, pondering over the menus displayed out front. Rose was done trying to justify her anger. Her sisters would just have to deal with it.

'I *do* get it.' Isla tucked a strand of her red hair behind her ear. 'But Mum's not the first person in the world to disappear when things get hard. Sickness and death are just too terrifying for some people to deal with.'

A bat flew across the darkening sky, and Rose tapped her finger on her ice-cold glass. There was a truth to what Isla said, but Rose just couldn't understand the choices her mother had made.

'When Dad died,' said Isla, 'we all had our own way of coping. Mel blamed herself, I pretty much didn't leave my room for a year, Mum threw herself into the business, and you were riddled with separation anxiety.'

Rose looked to her sister. 'I was?'

'You were eight, but you screamed every time Mum had to leave the house. You were convinced she was going to die.'

'I don't remember that.'

'You wouldn't let her out of your sight. It went on for months. But what was she supposed to do? She couldn't just stop working. Besides, everyone thought you'd get over it eventually.'

'And did I?'

'Well, you hated Mum when she left, and because of that you hated her when she was at home too. She couldn't win.'

'I remember wanting her and she was never there.'

'We were safe, we were loved. Maybe Mum didn't show her love in the way you wanted, but she did try. Plus, we had everything we could ever want as kids; we went to the best schools, we never went without. We had an amazing childhood.'

'We had all that because some poor bugger had one too many drinks at the casino and gambled away their rent money.'

'And that's unfortunate, but department stores are full of shopaholics and pubs are full of alcoholics. Everyone's addicted to something. You need to stop making Mum the bad guy.' Isla smiled and leaned forward. 'Do you remember that pirate ship in the backyard?'

'That was embarrassing.'

'It was all for Mel, remember? She went through that phase of drawing treasure maps, and she was always wearing that bloody eye patch. Okay, the pirate ship was a bit over the top, but I think Mum felt guilty because her birthday party had been so horrific. She *was* a good mum, Rose.'

Rose forced back tears and fixed her gaze on her drink. 'We might have lived under the same roof, but our childhoods were clearly not the same. She never showed up for me. She wasn't a good mum. *I'm* a good mum.'

'You're a *great* mum. It's just that you both approach motherhood differently, that's all. Mum has never been the affectionate type, whereas you shower your kids with kisses and cuddles, and you're always there for them. You're so patient and kind. There's no way I could do it. Your kids are lucky to have you.'

'I know you're trying to help,' said Rose, 'but you just have to accept that my experiences are different from yours. I can't, and won't, just sweep it all under the rug.'

'Fine. But you're still up for the task, right?' Isla glared at her. 'Just promise me you'll write something and send it to this publisher soon. And make it something kid-friendly, okay?'

Rose sighed. Her mother had managed to turn her dream of writing a book into a nightmare. 'All right, I promise.'

'Great!' Isla finished her wine and looked to Rose's half-empty glass. 'Drink up, it's your round.'

32

Mel

Two weeks later, on Brisbane's north side, Mel took a swig from her water bottle and wiped the sweat from her brow. It was twenty minutes until the half marathon, which started at 6 pm, and Mel was grateful for the slight breeze after the stifling hot February day. Running in the heat was something Mel had got used to over the last few months. If she was going to complete a full marathon at the beginning of July, she had to train consistently – there was no putting it on hold. Her hard work was paying off. Last week she'd managed her longest run yet: eighteen kilometres. This was the distance the running magazines said you needed to run when training to complete a half marathon, which was twenty-one-point-one kilometres.

Mel knew she could do it. She'd trained hard, steadily upping her long-distance runs since Christmas, and now she was ready to hit a new milestone.

'Have you got everything?' asked Corey. 'Running belt, earphones, phone, water? And you're wearing insect repellent?'

Mel nodded and rolled her shoulders.

'Where's Isla?' Corey scanned the pop-up market stalls, which sold all different types of running gear.

Isla had driven Mel and Corey to the event. Now that she was living in Brisbane, they'd seen more of each other and, in an unexpected turn of events, Isla had become one of Mel's biggest supporters. She'd bought Mel some expensive running trainers, and she was also paying for some personal training sessions with Joe at home. She'd even made 'Run, Mel, Run!' T-shirts, especially for today.

'She was on the phone to Steve.' Mel took a seat on a nearby wall. 'I think they were arguing, something to do with one of the stores. She walked off towards the market.'

Corey took a seat next to Mel, rested his crutch on his lap, and smiled.

A fierce heat rushed through her. Her feelings for him had intensified over the last few weeks, almost to the point where she couldn't function normally around him. She would say ridiculous things and was getting clumsier with each encounter. Simple tasks like drinking coffee without spilling it or opening her front door without dropping her keys were near impossible.

'Why are you smiling?'

'After tonight, you'll be halfway to reaching your goal.'

She closed her eyes and tilted her head back. She hoped Corey was right. Was she being ridiculous thinking she could do this?

Corey placed his hand on hers and she was suddenly aware of how much she was sweating. 'Don't start doubting yourself. You've got this.'

She turned to face him. 'Are you a mind reader?'

He laughed. 'I just know you.'

She stared at him, her heart racing, and for a moment she got lost in his gaze. He was beautiful. Breathing deeper, she could feel the rise and fall of her chest. She wanted to kiss him so badly. She'd wanted to kiss him during training sessions, when he'd turned up at her house with a new breathable running cap for her, when he'd called to check how her long runs had gone, when he laughed, and always, always when he looked at her like this. How had she ended up here, sitting next to this incredible person who knew her so well, yet still kept showing up?

He raised his hand and stroked her cheek. Mel closed her eyes and leant forward to kiss him.

'No. Fucking. Way!'

They turned to see a runner standing next to them with her hands on her hips and a huge open-mouthed grin on her face.

'Melanie Turner! It *is* you!'

Mel squinted as she tried to figure out who had just interrupted what she was sure would have been a magical first kiss.

'Don't tell me you've forgotten. It's *me*. From school. Amber Ryan.'

Mel's heart dropped into her stomach. *Amber Ryan*. It couldn't be. Not *the* Amber Ryan who'd bullied her at school, who was responsible for her being here right now. She leant towards Corey and whispered, 'Did she just say Amber Ryan?'

He nodded.

No, no, no! 'You've got to be kidding me.'

'Right?' Amber smirked. 'Melanie *bloody* Turner! It's been a minute or twenty.'

Mel stood, and an athletic-looking Amber, dressed head to toe in Jaggad running gear, threw her arms around her with such a force Mel stumbled backwards.

'How are you?' said Amber, stepping back. 'You look ...' Her eyes scanned Mel's body. 'Just like you used to. You haven't changed one bit, in what? It must be twenty years since I last saw you.'

Mel pressed her lips together. She was shaking. 'Mm-hmm.' The last time she'd seen Amber Ryan was when she'd given her a black eye and a kick in the ribs in Year Ten.

'Who are you here to support?'

Corey stood and pointed to the running number clearly pinned to Mel's top. 'As you can see, Mel's running.'

Amber's mouth dropped open. 'No. Way! That is … astonishing. Have you run a half marathon before?'

Mel forced a smile and looked to the ground. 'No. First time.'

Amber raised her heavily drawn-on eyebrows and laughed nervously. 'Well, good on you for giving it a go. This is my eleventh half-marathon, and I can tell you that the last five kilometres are a bitch.' Amber looked about her. 'You know …' She stopped smiling and lowered her voice. 'I just wanted to say—'

Another woman, caught in the crowd that was heading towards the start line, called out, 'Come on, Amber!'

'Oh,' she said, looking embarrassed and annoyed that she'd been interrupted. 'I'd best go get my spot. Good luck. Hopefully I'll see you at the finish line. If not, you'll find me on all the socials.' Amber pushed her way back through the crowd, and a stunned Mel turned to Corey. 'Someone is playing a sick joke on me right now.'

'Don't let her get under your skin,' he said.

'Did you *see* her? She looked like a running goddess. Who the hell runs eleven half-marathons? That's not normal, is it?'

'Just focus on you. It doesn't matter what anyone else is doing.'

'I'm not supposed to be here.' Mel scanned the crowd of runners. 'Look at me, I'm a joke! They're all toned and fit and—'

Corey placed a hand on her arm. 'Stop it! Don't cut yourself down like this after all your hard work. *I* couldn't do what you're doing, and neither could any of these people who've come to watch.'

Mel lowered her head.

'Look at me. Come on.'

She looked up at him and sighed.

'You're amazing. Now say it.'

Mel smiled. '*You're* amazing.'

'Okay, clever clogs,' he laughed. 'Now say, *I'm amazing*.'

Mel shrugged. 'I'm amazing.'

'What's this?' he said, imitating her shrug. 'Stop that. I want you to shout, *I can do this!*'

A nearby runner who'd overheard nodded encouragingly at Mel.

She laughed. 'I can do this!'

'And I'm gonna run rings around that bitch!' yelled Corey.

'Shhh!'

He shook his head. 'Say it.'

Mel regarded the runner again.

'You don't need my permission,' he said.

Mel took a deep breath and shouted at the top of her voice, 'I'm gonna run rings around that bitch!'

A silence fell as people turned and stared at them. Then Mel, Corey and the other runner burst out laughing.

'What's with all the shouting?' Isla appeared with a handful of gel sachets. 'Here, they were selling these at one of the market stalls. They're energy gels. The seller is a professional runner. He said all serious athletes use them. If you take them after thirty minutes, it'll give you the boost you'll need to finish.'

'You bought them for me?'

'I'm here to help you, remember?'

Mel tucked them into her running belt. 'I've read about these. Thanks.'

Corey checked the time on his phone. 'This is it.'

Mel winced. 'Wish me luck?'

'Good luck,' Corey and Isla said in unison.

Mel blew the air out of her lungs and made her way towards the start line. She tried to clear her head and focus on the task ahead, but her hands trembled and her heart raced. The image of Amber Ryan kicking her all those years ago flashed in her mind and Mel's eyes prickled.

'I can do this!' she muttered under her breath. If she ever wanted to be debt-free, she *had* to do it, but the truth was, she didn't know if she could.

* * *

The thought that Amber Ryan was among the runners and had probably been hitting PBs without breaking a sweat for years made Mel nauseous. It was going to be hard enough running half a marathon as it was.

But now, running past the five-kilometre sign, her legs and pace were strong. She'd found her rhythm. The last light of the setting sun threw streaks of orange against the sky, and moths fluttered in the glow of the streetlamps. She passed a water station where volunteers dressed in crazy costumes cheered on the runners, danced to music and shouted words of motivation. Mel grabbed a cup off the long table and drank some water, but didn't stop.

After running for forty minutes, she reached into her running belt and pulled out an energy gel. She'd read about the need for these when you ran long distances. It had something to do with sugar levels and carbs. It was all very scientific. She'd never used them before but now seemed like the perfect time. Maybe this was her chance to show Amber Ryan what she was really made of.

Mel ripped open one of the sachets and sucked out all the gel. The sweet berry flavour tasted so good. She pulled out another gel and devoured that one too. She took a sip from her water bottle but was careful not to drink too much. She still had a long way to run.

At the eight-kilometre sign, she checked her watch. She was on track, maybe even a little ahead. One of the best things about running with other people was that they seemed to somehow push you along a little quicker, and you certainly never felt like you could walk for a while, which she'd done a couple of times during training. Now she pushed forward with a renewed confidence and took out another gel, determined to get a new personal best. It was the hit she needed, like a surge of energy being transfused straight into her bloodstream. She was flying.

Smiling to herself, she recalled her first parkrun with Isla, when she'd thought she was going to die. She'd run eighteen kilometres twice in the last couple of weeks and was about to smash out a cool twenty-one-point-one kilometres. Mel realised it didn't matter that Amber Ryan was here tonight. She was exactly where she was supposed to be. She was kicking ass, and if Amber Ryan was here to see her do it, so much the better. The universe had set up this moment perfectly. It was the closure she hadn't known she needed.

As she ran past the eleven-kilometre sign, she gave a thumbs-up to some volunteers dressed in yellow tutus and golden glittery top hats, who were cheering the runners on. Suddenly she felt a stabbing twinge in her stomach. She grabbed her tummy and the sensation faded, but as she flipped up the lid of her water bottle, her gut twisted and spasmed again.

'Oh, no!'

Mel carried on running, determined not to lose time over a stitch. She tried to massage the pain away, but it just got worse. She was going to vomit. Up ahead, she could see the next water station and behind it, some public toilets.

She didn't have a choice. She had to stop. *Damn it!*

If she was quick, she wouldn't lose too much time. She was already ahead of where she'd expected to be at this stage. She could still run a good time.

Inside the bathroom, all three cubicles were occupied. Mel marched on the spot, but then her stomach tightened so much she bent forward in pain. *This wasn't a stitch!* She banged on one of the cubicle doors. 'Hey, I'm bursting here. Any chance of speeding it up?'

A door opened and another runner came out. 'All yours.'

Mel rushed inside and, just as she managed to pull down her undies and running shorts, a pain radiated through her torso and abdomen with such intensity that she couldn't help but cry out.

Outside her cubicle, a woman shouted, 'Watch out, dose of runner's trots in the middle cubicle.' A fist banged on her door and the same voice called, 'Bad luck, doll. Maybe you'll get to finish the next one!'

Mortified, Mel cradled her stomach as it knotted again, and sobbed.

An hour and a half later, she sat on the kerb under a flickering streetlamp and waited for Isla and Corey to pick her up. She took small sips of water but was careful not to drink too much. She didn't want to trigger any more bowel movements. Sweating and dehydrated, her insides felt raw, and she was zapped of energy. Public toilets were awful at the best of times, but they were horrendous if you suffered a major bout of diarrhoea. Nothing less than a three-ply toilet roll should ever be on offer in any bathroom – public or not.

Mel felt like an idiot for letting Amber Ryan get to her. If Amber hadn't shown up, she wouldn't have eaten the bloody energy gels – at least, not three of them in twenty minutes. How stupid was she? Who was she kidding, thinking she'd be able to finish a half marathon, let alone a full one? She was delusional.

Isla's Lexus pulled up on the side of the road, and Isla and Corey got out.

Isla rushed over and helped her to her feet. 'Oh, Mel. Are you okay?'

She shook her head. 'I just want to go home. I need a shower.'

Corey gave her a sympathetic smile. 'Don't let this get you down. You can still run the distance another day. You don't need a medal.'

Mel couldn't look at him. 'No, I'm done. I quit. I was an idiot for thinking I could do this.' All this time, she'd been kidding herself that maybe she *was* capable of being more than she'd allowed herself to be. She'd taken risks and now look what had happened. She'd come face to face with the demons from her past *and* been humiliated in front of the guy she'd been falling in love with.

'Hey, you're being too hard on yourself.' Corey went to hug her.

'Please,' cried Mel. 'Don't come near me.' Her clammy skin and sore tummy made her nauseous and, after spending the last hour and a half in a public bathroom, she felt like she'd just crawled through a sewage pipe. 'I'm gross and disgusting, and I'm not who you think I am.' Mel couldn't stand the thought of Corey, beautiful Corey, seeing her in such a repulsive state.

'What does that mean?' he asked.

'I'm not amazing! I can't run and I'm in debt up to my eyeballs. Amber was right all those years ago, I am a loser!'

'Mel, stop talking like this!'

'I'm in a shitload of debt. That's the only reason I was playing along with these stupid terms. Without this inheritance, I'll be in debt forever!' She sniffed. 'And then, on top of it all, there's you. You keep saying I can do this when I can't. You built up my hopes, and now I look like a fool. Well, I don't want your help anymore.'

Corey stood, dumbfounded.

'*Mel,*' said Isla.

'No! I'm sick of all this. Mum can stick her terms.' She sobbed and looked at Corey. 'Why are you even here? I'm an embarrassment.'

He stepped forward again. 'You're just—'

'Done! That's what I am! *I'm* done, and *we're* done! It's game over.'

33

Jess

Sitting at a beachfront bar at Burleigh Heads, Jess knocked back a shot of tequila, hoping it would calm her nerves. She hadn't been on any dates since ending her relationship with Brett that night in the tapas bar. He'd been caught off guard and, within the space of about ten minutes, he'd gone through all five stages of grief: denial, anger, bargaining, depression (he'd declared quite loudly that he couldn't live without her), until finally he'd hit acceptance. It had been a strange thing to watch. Jess had been sad that he was sad, but knew it was the kindest thing to do. It wasn't fair to lead him on.

She turned away from the bar and looked out towards the beach. The crashing waves were luminous in the moonlight. Her ex-husband, Todd, had loved to surf at night and, although it had always scared Jess to death, she'd admired how he'd pushed the boundaries, felt the fear and done it anyway. Jess needed some of that courage now.

Isla had set her up on a blind date, claiming that in doing so she was hitting two birds with one stone. Helping others was now a key component of her own task, she'd decided, and as

Jess was still single and it was already March, Isla had decided it was time to intervene. It was true that time was ticking, but Jess wasn't sure an Isla intervention was a good thing. It hadn't turned out so well for poor Mel, after all.

As the liquor sent warmth flooding through Jess, she tried to relax. All Isla had told her about the guy she was meeting was that his name was Adam. That was it. Isla had insisted Jess didn't need to know anything else about him, claiming she didn't want her going in with any preconceived ideas. This date was pretty much as blind as you could get, but Jess trusted Isla. After all, it was in her best interests to find a good match. They all had a lot to lose.

'Jess?' She glanced up to see a broad-shouldered guy with a cheeky smile and slicked-back dirty blond hair standing beside her.

'Adam?' Jess clumsily tried to stand as she held her hand out to greet him.

'Hey. Please don't get up,' he said, pulling out the barstool next to her.

Isla had done well. The rolled-up sleeves of his white shirt enhanced his muscular arms, and his dark jeans and brown casual shoes were stylish, but relaxed. He was gorgeous. Glancing behind him, Jess noticed he'd also caught the eye of a group of women at a nearby table celebrating a hen's night.

Adam looked at her empty shot glass. 'I hope you haven't been waiting too long?'

'I was early. Thought I'd settle my nerves before you arrived.'

'Yeah, the dreaded blind date. It's all a bit weird, isn't it?'

'Weird's the word.' Jess cringed. *Weird's the word? Who says that?*

The women at the hen's night still hadn't taken their eyes off Adam. Jess had to admit he was easy on the eye.

Ignoring them, she focused on the painful task of getting to know her date. 'How do you know Isla?'

'I've been a customer of hers for years. She lined me up with some great pieces of jewellery for my exes.'

'Oh. Great.'

Adam winced. '*Sorry*, that was bad. I've known you less than twenty seconds and I've already brought up my ex-girlfriends.'

Jess laughed. 'Really, it's okay. We've both got a past, right? I was once married for a month, and he broke my heart when he cheated on me. There. Now we're even.' *Shit! Where did that come from?*

Adam's eyes softened and Jess played with her empty shot glass. 'Can I buy you another drink?' he asked.

'Sure. I'll have a dirty martini.'

'Great choice, I'll have the same.' Adam caught the attention of the bartender and ordered the drinks. Jess pressed her lips together, trying not to grin. She couldn't get overly excited. Most of the guys she'd dated were beautiful, but they hadn't led to anything long term yet.

A shrill of excitement erupted behind them, and then the bride-to-be was being pushed towards Adam. *What the hell?*

'You know,' said Adam as he passed Jess her drink, 'I wasn't sure you'd show tonight after all the drama with my brother.'

Jess frowned. 'Your brother?'

'Nathan Campbell.'

The blood drained from her face. 'What?!'

Adam winced once more. 'By your look of horror, I'm assuming Isla didn't tell you?'

'Nathan Campbell's brother is Jason.'

'That's right. I'm his *other* brother, Adam.'

'You've got to be kidding me.'

'Excuse me.' The bride-to-be edged towards Adam, phone in hand. 'Is there any chance I could get a photo with you?'

Adam looked to Jess, unsure of what to do.

'It'll only take a sec.' And with that, the bride-to-be sidled up next to him and took a selfie.

Jess glanced around the bar and noticed that other people were staring. The rest of the hen's party swooned as they made their way over, some taking photos and others videoing.

'I've got to get out of here.' Jess hopped off her stool, shading her face with her hands, and made for the exit. She couldn't believe this was happening.

'Wait! Where are you going?' Adam called after her, but his words were lost in the sea of liquored-up women who now surrounded him.

Outside, Jess didn't slow. She had to get away from Adam. If anyone posted photos of them on social media, the press would have a field day. She could see the headlines now: *Keeping It in the Family! Campbells Share the Love!*

Jess pulled off her heels and cursed as she sprinted to her car. *Damn you, Isla Turner!* She opened her car door, threw in her shoes and pulled her phone from her bag.

As soon as Isla answered, Jess let fly.

'What the hell were you thinking?'

'Don't be mad. I told you I knew Nathan's brother, the one who bought jewellery from us. Anyway, I realised you two would make a great couple.'

'This is a disaster.'

'You should be thanking me. You're on borrowed time with your task, and he's as dreamy as they get. You can't deny that.'

'No, but—'

'Then, you're welcome.' And with that, Isla hung up.

'*Bitch!*'

'Hey, Jess! Wait up!' On the other side of the car park, Adam waved and ran over to her. Jess folded her arms and pursed her lips.

'I'm sorry. That was a nightmare.'

'You can say that again. You know I was splashed across all the trashy magazine covers straddling Nathan?'

'I know. After a bit, he saw the funny side.'

'I'm not sure his wife would be quite so amused.'

'She was there. She saw what happened.'

Jess fumed. 'Why would you arrange to meet me here with so many people around? You must have known you'd be recognised.'

'Honestly? That never happens. People have no idea who I am. They must have been die-hard fans of Jason's, or follow Nathan or something.' Adam dragged his hand through his hair and stepped back. 'I'm sorry.'

Jess sighed. 'Don't be. It's not all on you.' She dropped her arms to her sides.

'Can we try again?' Adam held up his hands. 'I don't mean go back in there, but maybe we could go for a walk on the beach? No one will know who we are. And your sister was convinced we'd be a good match.'

'Yeah, well, Isla is going through a phase of trying to *help* her sisters, and let's just say it's not going well.' Adam grinned and she couldn't help but smile back. 'One walk, that's it.'

'That's good enough for me.'

Jess locked her car and walked barefoot towards the beach. 'So,' she said, trying to regroup. *First dates are the worst.* 'What do you do for a living?'

34

Rose

Sitting at the kitchen table, Rose opened her laptop and bounced a distraught Bethany on her knee. She opened her inbox and nervously hovered the cursor over an unopened email from a small publishing house. She had noticed it earlier, scrolling through her phone while waiting for Harrison to finish soccer, which ended up running over by forty minutes. *Forty minutes!* Rose had been too nervous to read the email in the car. She'd wanted to nurture the hope that her manuscript would be picked up for just a little longer.

While Rose waited for Harrison, she'd done some online research into getting a book published the traditional way. She was horrified to discover that it was a *slow* process. One article cheerfully informed her that once an author signed a publishing contract, it would be at least a year or two before their book was released. Rage had simmered through her – Jacki had set her up to fail! There was no way she could get published in time, even if her story was good enough. There had been no mention of this in Helen's resources folder, only information about writing workshops, books on the craft of writing, and articles about self-publishing. But Rose couldn't self-publish. A picture book needed pictures.

Now, Bethany cried uncontrollably in Rose's lap, refusing to be put down. She had skipped her afternoon nap and was now an inconsolable, over-tired, hungry mess. Meanwhile, Tom had spent the day at a Lego exhibition and had texted Rose over an hour ago to say he was stuck in traffic.

In the kitchen, Harrison pulled off his soccer socks, left them where they fell, then walked to the fridge and peered inside. 'What's for dinner?'

Rose squinted, trying to relieve the tension in her pounding head, and shushed Bethany while rubbing her back.

'Mum, what's for dinner?' Harrison called again over Bethany's cries.

'I don't know! Let me sort Bethany out first. Go and have a shower. And put your socks in the laundry!'

'But I'm starving!' Harrison kicked one of his socks aside and ran upstairs.

'Hey, socks in the—' But he was gone.

Bethany wailed louder and Rose winced. She stood up and grabbed a packet of wipes from the nappy bag to clean the baby's streaming face. Rose had planned to make lasagne for dinner, and had even defrosted the mince, but right now cooking a family meal seemed an impossible task.

Taylor, who had showered in what seemed like record time, bounced into the kitchen and swung open the fridge. 'How long till dinner?' She wore her llama pyjamas, and her loose wet hair was forming a large damp patch on the back of her top.

'You need to towel-dry the ends of your hair. Your back's soaking,' said Rose.

'It's fine. When's dinner?'

'*Please*, out of the fridge. I'll make lasagne after I've fed your sister.' Rose attempted to put Bethany in her highchair, but she was having none of it.

'But that'll take forever. I'll die of starvation,' said Taylor.

'Out of the fridge! I'll call you when it's done.'

'Can I have some crackers?'

'No.'

'A banana? That's healthy.'

'Wait for your dinner.'

Taylor let out a deep groan then shot upstairs.

Rose pulled a fruit pouch out of the cupboard and waved it in front of Bethany. 'Are you hungry?' Bethany hid her face against Rose's shoulder. She would usually try to give Bethany something more substantial for dinner, but right now she just needed her to settle.

After a small battle, Rose got her to sit in the highchair and managed to spoon some puree into her mouth.

Rose's phone pinged. It was Isla. *Have you heard back from any publishers yet? You need to keep writing more stories just in case. XXX*

Pain radiated across Rose's forehead. Isla had been texting her ideas and writing tips constantly over the last few weeks. She'd been tempted to block her number.

Sitting on one of the dining chairs, she turned her laptop to face her. She took a deep breath and opened the email from the publishing house. After Isla's intervention, she had written a new story about a little girl whose mother leaves her at a department store. Feeling more confident, she'd also written a query letter, which had been even harder than writing the story itself, and had sent it not only to Isla's publishing friend but to some other agents and publishers too.

When she'd sent off her manuscript, she'd imagined agents and editors picking up her story from the slush pile, reading it and declaring that this was exactly the type of story they'd been waiting for. Finally, a story for people whose mothers suck. *How refreshing!* But as the rejections started coming back, it was pointed out, on more than one occasion, that because it was parents and grandparents who usually purchased picture books, a story about a neglectful mum wouldn't sell very well. This small publisher was the last one Rose had been waiting to hear back from.

Dear Rose,

After reading through your manuscript, we regret to inform you ...

Disappointment seared through her. It didn't matter that her mother had set her an impossible deadline; her writing wasn't good enough anyway. She had failed.

Bethany started to cry again. 'No, no, no,' said Rose. 'Here, more pear?' Bethany flicked the spoon away in protest. Her cheeks were bright red, and Rose pressed the back of her hand to her forehead. She was burning up. '*Damn it.*'

Rose's phone rang. It was Tom.

'Thank God,' said Rose. 'Bethany's got a fever, my head's about to explode and the kids are starving. Where are you?'

'Someone just rear-ended me at the lights.'

'*What!* Are you okay?'

'I'm fine. My neck's a little stiff, but the paramedic just gave me the all-clear.'

'*Shit!*'

'My car's a write-off, though. The police are talking to the other driver, and I'm just waiting for the tow truck.'

'But *you're* okay?' Rose was shaking. 'I love you. I *can't* lose you too.'

'I'm all good, I promise. The car's—'

'I don't care about the car. Just come home, *come home.*'

'I'll be home soon, but don't worry, everything's okay. I'll call you back in a bit.'

Rose trembled as she hung up. Bethany cried out, and Rose stood and wiped her damp cheeks. Panadol, she needed Children's Panadol. Pulling out the tub of medicines from the small first-aid cupboard above the fridge, she found what she needed and lifted the bottle from its cardboard packaging. It was empty. *Are you kidding me? Who the hell puts back an empty bottle?*

'Mum!' Taylor called from upstairs. 'Mum, I'm starving!'

Bethany's cries climbed another decibel, and Rose's phone rang again. She threw the empty bottle in the bin, then leapt towards the kitchen table and answered it. 'Tom?'

'No, it's your *mother.*'

Rose looked at her phone. *Could she hang up?*

'I'm calling because—'

'I don't have time for this,' Rose cut in. 'I don't know why you're calling, but this phone call … it's too little too late.' Rose shook her head in disbelief. 'I haven't heard from you since the wedding, and now what? You're calling me like we have some kind of relationship?'

'I wanted to—'

Rose paced the kitchen. 'What? Apologise for the speech you made? Or do you just want an update on this sick little game you're making us play? Whatever it is, I'm not interested. I'm busy, and I don't have time for you.' Rose exhaled sharply, and hot tears spilled down her cheeks. 'How does it feel to get a taste of your own medicine?'

'I'm sorry, you're upset,' said Jacki.

Bethany screamed.

'You're un-fucking-believable,' said Rose. 'I'm not interested in anything you have to say and, frankly, it's embarrassing that you think a phone call out of the blue could undo what a crap job you've done of being my mum.'

'I only called—'

'It's too late! I'm *done*. I'm *done* with this conversation. I'm *done* with the terms of inheritance, and I'm *done* with you!'

Rose hung up, lifted Bethany out of the highchair and grabbed the car keys. 'Harrison! Taylor! Get in the car! We're going to the chemist, and then we're getting pizza!'

35

Jess

Jess followed Rose through the Aussie Animal Rescue stalls, past dogs who were patiently waiting for someone to give them a new home.

'What are we doing here?' Rose asked Jess.

'I thought we'd come to see where all Mum's money will go if we don't manage our tasks. Mum did say we should check them out.' Jess peered into a kennel. 'Oh my. Look at this cutie.' An Australian cattle dog barked at them then sat with his tail wagging and tongue hanging out. Jess read the details. He was four years old and his name was Rusty. 'He's gorgeous.'

'How's it going with Adam?' asked Rose.

'Are you asking because you care or because there are only four months left to complete these stupid tasks?'

'Because I care. You know that.'

'Sorry, I can't think straight. Adam seems pretty amazing, and he keeps texting, but dating him would come with all sorts of problems.'

'If you like him then you should give him a chance.'

'I need time to think. It's only been a week, but Isla keeps texting me, and I swear to God I'm going to block her for good if she doesn't butt out of my personal life. She's suffocating.'

'Jessica?' A red-haired lady in her fifties wearing blue jeans and an Aussie Animal Rescue polo shirt smiled warmly as she walked up to them. 'I'm Anna. Thanks for taking the time to come and visit us. I've been told you'd like to know a little more about what we do here?'

'Yes,' said Jess.

'Well, our mission is to rescue and care for all types of animals in need, and we also find loving homes for pets who have no owners. We never give up on any animal. They can stay with us for as long as it takes to heal and find a safe home.

'Rusty here was in a terrible state of neglect when he first came to us, but now he's ready for a new home, aren't you, sweetheart? This year alone, we've already rehomed well over a thousand animals.'

Jess frowned. 'But it's only the beginning of March.'

'There are a lot of animals that need our help. Would you like me to introduce you to an extra special doggy friend of mine?'

Jess clapped her hands. 'Yes, please.'

Anna pointed to a door leading to a play area outside. 'If you go through that door, I'll bring her out.'

Jess and Rose sat on a bench in the shade. Today's temperature was expected to reach thirty-two degrees, and Jess could feel the sweat running down her torso.

Rose crossed her legs and tapped her foot. 'Our mother called last night.'

'What did she want?'

'I don't know. Bethany was screaming, the kids were starving and Tom had called literally thirty seconds before to tell me about the car accident. I was a mess, and I was furious.'

Jess could tell there was more to the story. 'What did you say to Mum?'

'We argued. Well, *I* went off at her and then hung up.'

'*Rose.*' Jess felt sick. 'Couldn't you have just listened to what she had to say? You know she's not been feeling so good.' Darryl had called Jess the day before and told her Jacki hadn't been out of bed for the last two days. 'You don't know how long she has left, Rose. Do you really want her to die without resolving things between you?'

Rose chewed at her fingernail. 'Perhaps I should have told her to call back later, but I'm so done with her and her games. She caught me at a crappy time, and …' Rose's voice broke. 'I got my final rejection letter for my manuscript last night, and I found out it takes years to get a book published the traditional way. She set me up to fail; there's pretty much no way I'll complete my task.'

'Well, I doubt you'll be the only one. Poor Mel has lost all confidence after the half-marathon disaster, and I'm pretty much forced to date Adam if I stand any chance of completing my task.'

'I bet she never wanted us to succeed. I mean, look at this place. Can you imagine the press coverage she'd get for leaving her fortune to these centres?'

'That's not why she's doing it.'

'Isn't it? I can just see the headlines now: *Selfless Multi-millionaire Leaves Legacy of Kindness.*'

Anna opened the gate, and behind her a small white dog with beautiful brown eyes walked into the play area with a set of wheels harnessed to her.

Jess's heart burst. She had never seen such a cute, brave pupper in her life. 'Oh, my word.'

'This is Maxine,' said Anna. 'She's a nine-year-old Maltese mix who has hind leg paralysis from a musculoskeletal condition. Her last owner was a woman in her late seventies who died in her sleep.'

'Oh no! How long has Maxine been here?'

'About six months,' said Anna, who was now kneeling and rubbing Maxine's ears. 'A lot of families want the younger animals, and although they love Maxine, they soon come to realise how much care and support she needs.'

Rose's phone rang. 'Sorry,' she said, pulling it out of her bag. 'It's Isla.'

Jess rolled her eyes and Rose walked away to take the call.

'Would you like to give Maxine a treat?' Anna asked Jess.

Jess dropped to her knees and rubbed Maxine's head. She was so soft. She just wanted to pick her up and hug her. 'I'd love to.'

Anna took a dog treat out of the pouch she wore around her waist and handed it to her. Jess held out the doggy snack and Maxine gently took it out of her hand. 'She's so friendly.'

Anna grinned. 'She's a good girl, aren't you, Maxine?'

'I'm sorry, Jess, we have to go,' said Rose, rejoining them.

'But we've only just got here, haven't we, gorgeous?' Jess rubbed Maxine's neck and she licked Jess's arm. 'Oh, look, she likes me too.'

'Jess.'

Jess looked up at her sister, whose face had turned ashen. Something was very wrong. 'Sorry, Anna,' she said. 'We're going to have to go.' She kissed the top of Maxine's head. 'I'll come back and see you soon, okay gorgeous? I promise.'

As they left the centre, Jess turned to Rose. 'What is it?' She grabbed Rose's arm. 'What's happened? *Tell me!*'

'It's Mum.' Rose's eyes welled. 'She died twenty minutes ago.'

36

Rose

After the funeral service, Rose and her sisters were chauffeur-driven to Jacki's house. Jacki had arranged a Chrysler super stretch black limo for them to travel in, stating that she wanted only her daughters to ride in it, even though it could easily fit thirteen people. People stared as they passed, and Rose was relieved that no one could see through the tinted glass.

In her final months, Jacki had planned every last detail of her funeral. There had been no decisions to make and nothing to organise. Helen had been left in charge of notifying family and friends of Jacki's death, while her lawyer took care of informing the board of directors.

Rose pulled at a loose thread on the hem of her dress and stared out the window. People were going about their daily routine, looking as if they didn't have a care in the world. But who knew what was really going on in their lives. She was struck by how strange it was that a non-eventful day for one person could be life-changing for someone else. Since her mother's death two weeks earlier, Rose had felt like she'd been living in a time-lapse, with the world around her travelling at hyper speed while she was stuck, stationary, in a numb void.

The funeral service had been packed. There were so many people that some had been forced to stand outside in the blazing sun. Meanwhile, those who sweltered indoors used their service programs, featuring a picture of Jacki dressed head to toe in Gucci, as a fan to cool themselves. Everyone had worn brightly coloured clothes – a request her mother had made before her death. Darryl said Jacki hadn't wanted the day to be gloomy or depressing. She wanted her funeral and wake to be a celebration of her life. Rose wore a yellow floral dress with small purple flowers.

The service had been carried out by Pastor James, whom Jacki had known for over twenty years. He lived in Sydney, but Jacki would fly him up to attend her social gatherings whenever she needed to add some funk to an event. Not only was he devilishly good-looking, he was also funny. He had a dry wit that would make you laugh so hard your cheeks ached, and at the heart of all his stories was a lesson that tended to linger for days after.

As Pastor James recounted the first time he met the famous Jacki Turner, dread had filled Rose's chest. What had Jacki called to say on the eve of her death? Rose hadn't let her get a word in. All she could recall was the fury that raged within her. When had she become so angry? Since the terms of inheritance? No. Since Richard's death? She knew it was before that. And then she'd recalled the *musings* she'd written in high school. *What a long time to spend being angry.* And now she would have to live the rest of her life haunted by the last conversation she'd had with her mother.

Halfway through the service, Bethany became unsettled and began to kick up a fuss. In the end, Tom took her outside while

Rose sat between Harrison and Taylor. She held their hands and watched them wipe away their tears, feeling something like envy. She hadn't cried yet. It was as if the moment she'd heard the news of her mother's death, her heart had built a protective covering around itself. Ever since, she'd been unable to feel anything – not sadness nor anger. Nothing.

Jacki's heart had given out before the final stages of her cancer could finish her off. It had been a shock to everyone. All week, Rose had been told, mostly by strangers, that it was probably a better way for her to go. *At least she didn't suffer.* It was strange to hear her mother being talked about in the past tense.

As everyone laughed at Pastor James's stories, Rose had caught sight of Helen seated across the aisle. Helen had winked at her and given a small knowing smile, like she understood that she wasn't ready to laugh yet. Rose didn't think she'd ever laugh about her mother. Right now, she wasn't quite sure which stage of grief she was in. Shock? Disbelief? Or perhaps Rose had been grieving the loss of her mum for years, stuck in the anger stage? Perhaps her mother's physical death had just jolted her into the next stage: depression.

For a full hour and a half, Rose had half-listened to stories and recollections that showcased her mother's work ethic, drive and ambition, her ability to host the most elaborate parties and events, and her devotion as a loving mum. Throughout the service, Rose had felt the stares of strangers crawling over her. She'd wanted nothing more than to escape that hot, sticky room and be alone, where she could breathe.

Rose dreaded the wake. The last thing she wanted to do was put on a brave face and accept everyone's condolences. Her dad's sister, Aunt Phoebe, had turned up at the service with Rose's cousins, Mia, Martha and Barnaby. Rose hadn't seen any of them for five, maybe six years. They all lived in Sydney, and the last time they had all been together was at Mia's wedding in the Blue Mountains. Catching up with Dad's side of the family was something Rose missed after he'd died. Family was something Rose's mother had less and less time for over the years.

'Your dad loved Jacki with all his heart,' Aunt Phoebe had told Rose outside the crematorium. 'He worshipped the ground she walked on. Although your mum and I lost contact over the years, I still admired the great Jacki Turner from afar.'

There were no other relatives at the funeral service; Jacki had been an only child. But there had been plenty of strangers, most of them rich, and there were a few celebrities and prominent social media influencers. And now they were all headed to the house where Rose grew up. It felt like an invasion of privacy. Why couldn't they have held the wake at the Gold Coast Turner Hotel? Surely that would have been more logical. But, like most things where her mother was concerned, Rose had no say in the matter.

In the limo, Rose and her sisters sat in silence. Mel stared at the champagne flutes that rattled in the minibar opposite her. She pressed her palms against her cheeks and her bottom lip quivered. 'God, I miss …'

'I know, I miss her too,' said Jess.

'I was going to say Corey, but I miss Mum too. Everything's gone to shit.'

'It was a nice service,' said Isla. Her red hair was scraped into a low bun that clashed with her bright pink maxi dress. *It was the brightest thing in my wardrobe,* Isla had told Rose earlier. *I know it's loud, but today is about what Mum wanted.*

It always is, thought Rose.

'Pastor James was hilarious.' Mel's bright yellow A-line dress hugged her waist and Rose noticed how toned she looked. 'At one point I thought I was going to piss my pants laughing.'

Jess dug a tissue out of her bag. Her mascara had run a little under her eyes. 'It really was lovely. Mum wanted everyone to have a good time; she wanted a service people would remember.'

Rose placed her hand on Jess's knee but said nothing.

'*Christ,* these things are killing me.' Mel kicked off her white heeled shoes, placed one foot on her knee and tugged at the nail on her big toe. 'Aarghh, it's going to come off. It's hanging by a thread.'

'You are so gross!' Isla squirmed. 'Put your foot down.'

'That's not the half of it. You should see my nipples. *No one* said anything about chafing when I signed up to do the marathon.'

'Mel, *please* stop,' said Isla.

'I just want you to appreciate how hard I've trained. I'm literally losing body parts.'

Rose looked at Isla. 'You said we're meeting the lawyer tomorrow morning?'

'Yep, Victoria. She'll be at Mum's house at nine.'

Mel placed her foot on the seat to inspect her toenails. 'Do you think we still have until the marathon to try and get our inheritance, or do you think now that Mum's … it all goes to Aussie Animal Rescue?'

'Do you know how shallow you sound?' Jess scolded. 'We're on the way to Mum's wake, and you're talking about her money.'

'I'm just asking.'

Isla pushed Mel's foot off the seat. 'Mum said legally we have until midnight on the day of the marathon to complete our tasks.'

'Then why are we meeting her lawyer tomorrow?' Rose had secretly been hoping the terms of inheritance would be called off.

'I guess we'll find out tomorrow.'

The stretch limo pulled into Jacki's driveway and Mel picked up her shoes. 'Just so you know, I'm not putting these back on. My feet need to breathe.'

Isla scoffed as they climbed out, but Rose didn't move.

Isla looked back at her. 'Are you coming?'

'I don't want to go in. Can I just stay here until it's over?'

Isla held out her hand. 'Stick with me. My aim is to get rid of everyone as fast as possible. If that fails, I've got the key to the wine cellar, so we can hide down there.'

Rose took Isla's hand. 'Fine.' She scooted along the seat and got out of the limo with little grace.

Her mother's house was already buzzing with people dressed in bold, blinding colour. The entrance hall was filled with brightly coloured balloons, and 1980s party music was being played out by the swimming pool. A temporary dance floor had been laid in the backyard, and a DJ encouraged guests to help themselves to food and drink. Catering staff dressed in matching gold sequinned tops handed out champagne to the guests, and life-size cardboard cut-outs of Jacki in different positions, wearing various designer party outfits, were scattered around the place. Jacki Turner was everywhere.

Rose looked about her in dismay. 'She *didn't*.'

Holding a bottle of beer and wearing a pink flamingo Hawaiian shirt, Darryl stood next to Rose and watched as guests made their way to the dance floor, juggling champagne flutes and canapés. 'Oh, yes, she did.' Darryl took a long drink of his beer.

'Did she really want all this?'

Darryl shrugged. 'Your mum couldn't bear the alternative. She didn't want anyone to be sad. She wanted everyone to celebrate who she was.'

Rose pressed her lips together and turned to face him. 'Did she tell you about our last phone call?'

Darryl nodded.

'You know what an awful person I am then?'

'Your mum knew how you'd all react when she set her terms of inheritance. She knew you were overwhelmed and spoke out of frustration, she *knew* you had to get it off your chest. But whatever has happened, and regardless of whether you girls complete your tasks or not, Jacki was very proud of you – *all* of you.'

'You're being very kind, Darryl, but I'm not sure I believe that.' Rose watched as the guests began to relax. Most of them looked like they were enjoying themselves! 'Did she know she was getting close to the end? Is that why she called me?'

'She'd been feeling good that day. She'd managed to sit in the garden and we drank cocktails. Perhaps she did know, deep down.'

Rose's throat ached. 'It's hard to love someone you don't particularly like, but … I *did* love her. I think that's why it hurt so much that we never saw eye to eye.'

Darryl rubbed the top of Rose's arm, and tears pooled in his eyes.

Out of nowhere, Isla appeared, holding two glasses of champagne. 'If another goddamned person asks me when we're putting the house on the market, I'm going to lose it.' Isla handed Rose a champagne flute and took a large sip from her own. 'Look at them.' Isla nodded towards a woman pointing to the kitchen wall like she was making plans to knock it down. 'Bloody vultures. Wait, isn't that guy a real estate agent?' Isla stormed towards them and Rose looked back at Darryl.

'I'm glad you got to spend time with my mother at the end. She loved my dad, but with you it was different. There was a different type of chemistry, and even though you weren't always together, I know you were the love of her life.'

Darryl held up his beer. 'I'll drink to that.'

Rose clinked her flute against his bottle and took a sip of the cold champagne. It was going to be a long afternoon.

37

Isla

Hours later, Isla headed out to the pool area to find Mel and Jess slow dancing with a cardboard cut-out of their mum. A disco ball had been strung between two palm trees, and it sent light sparkling across the sisters, dazzling in the darkness of the late evening.

Isla grabbed a beer from a silver ice bucket. 'Well, that's the last of the guests,' she said, opening the bottle. 'I thought they'd never leave.'

'You did a great job,' Mel called from the dance floor.

'No thanks to you lot.'

Rose sat on a sun lounger and sipped red wine. Mascara was smudged beneath her eyes from where she'd been drowning her sorrows. Tom had taken the kids home a couple of hours earlier. Rose was going to sleep at Jacki's house and catch a ride home with Isla and Mel tomorrow after meeting with their mother's lawyer.

'Okay, ladies,' announced the DJ. 'Here's the last song of the night.'

Isla took a seat next to Rose. 'I reckon half those guests were only here for the free food and booze. I caught one of them taking selfies with one of Mum's cut-outs. I mean, *selfies*, at a wake! The audacity! Darryl said to say goodnight. He was a little wobbly on the stairs. I think he had a bit too much to drink.'

Rose raised her glass. 'Haven't we all?'

Isla noticed that the whites of Rose's eyes were red. She'd seen Helen swap her sister's wine out for coffee earlier, but Helen and Mick had left an hour ago, and it seemed an unattended Rose had gone back to wine. 'How much have you had to drink?

'Not enough.' Rose took another swig.

'I'll take that.' Isla took the glass out of Rose's hand. 'And I'll get you some food.'

In the kitchen, Isla filled a plate with leftover canapés. She half expected her mum to waltz in, drink in hand, and demand she join her on the dance floor. Isla couldn't believe her mum was gone. She'd been her idol, role model, business adviser. Who would she turn to now when she needed advice? Isla was growing increasingly concerned about the Brisbane and Adelaide stores, but she hadn't shared her worries with her mum.

That afternoon, Steve had pulled Isla aside and told her that if they didn't get her mum's inheritance, there was no way they could keep those stores open. They'd gone over and over the figures, and they couldn't see another option. Isla hated the idea that they were losing money. Since opening their first store a decade ago, they'd only experienced success. Closing two stores was a sign of failure, and Isla Turner didn't fail.

Back outside, she handed the plate of food to Rose, along with a glass of water. The disco lights were turned off, and Mel stumbled barefoot towards Rose and curled up next to her. Isla watched Jess get the DJ's business card.

'Well, you can't say she hasn't tried,' said Isla.

'She's not interested in him, she's dating Adam. *Shoot!* I shouldn't have said that.' Rose clamped her eyes shut like she was trying to stop everything from spinning.

'Really? Well, that's great news,' said Isla. 'Why didn't she tell me?'

'Because you keep going on and on about her task! You're driving her up the wall.'

'I'm trying to keep you all focused!' As far as Isla was concerned, she was the only one who'd been committed to helping the others with their tasks.

Mel looked over to Jess. 'Who's going to tell her it's too late?'

Isla frowned. 'Too late? It's not too late.'

'I reckon the deal's off,' said Mel. 'We ran out of time. That's why the lawyer's coming tomorrow. All Mum's money will go to those cute cats and dogs and guinea pigs.'

'Mum gave us a year. That's set in stone,' said Isla.

Mel sat up. 'But wasn't the whole point of this so that Mum could *see* us achieve her terms?'

Isla put her hand on her hip. 'I didn't go through all this only to be told we ran out of time. We've still got three and a half months.'

Jess walked across the dance floor and pulled up a chair next to her sisters. 'What are you talking about?'

'The terms of inheritance,' said Rose. 'But it makes no difference. Even with over three months, there's no way I'll get a picture book published.'

'And there's no way I can find someone and be in a relationship with them for longer than three months.' Jess pulled out her hair tie and her dark curls fell across her shoulder. 'I'd have to find someone in the next two weeks.'

'She knows,' said Rose, and Jess's eyes narrowed. 'I'm sorry, it just slipped out.'

'I've seen him twice, that's all.'

'And now you've got a back-up just in case?' said Isla, nodding towards the DJ.

'Do you ever let up?' Jess held up the business card. 'I got this for a friend who needs a DJ. He's not even single – or straight – he told me he'd have to be careful not to wake his boyfriend when he gets home.'

Mel inspected her big toenail. 'Rose is right, though. Completing our tasks is impossible. I didn't even finish the *half* marathon. I messed up my friendship with Corey, my toenails are coming off, and my nipples look like I've got a fetish for sandpaper. I just want things to go back to normal.'

Rose swung her feet over the side of the lounger and pushed a goat's cheese vol-au-vent around her plate. 'We were kidding ourselves if we ever thought we could do what she wanted. Her expectations were too high. In the end, it was just another way for her to control us.'

Jess glowered. 'Mum didn't want to *control* us.'

Rose scoffed. 'Wake up. The facts are right in front of you and you still can't see them. We were her pawns, doing exactly what she wanted, when she wanted.'

Isla sighed. '*Don't*, Rose.'

'What? I'm just telling it like it is. She used her money to get us to perform like puppets, and we fell for it.' Rose stood, held out her hands to steady herself, and staggered towards the bucket of beers.

'She was trying to help us,' said Jess.

Rose laughed. 'She was trying to marry you off! I mean, really, who cares if you're single forever? What business was it of hers?' Rose pointed to Mel. 'And what was she thinking, trying to get you to run a marathon? What was she trying to tell you? That you're lazy? That she wanted you to lose a few kilos? *What?*'

Mel teared up.

'*Hey!*' said Isla. 'That's enough!'

Rose shook her head. 'Even *you* weren't good enough, and you're the big family success story. Look at the sacrifices you made. You're not even living with your husband anymore, and for what? *She* did that to you.'

Jess fumed. 'You're just mad because the last time you spoke to Mum, you were a bitch and hung up on her, and now you have to live with that!'

'What?' said Mel.

Rose took a swig of beer and stumbled. 'You're so right. I am mad. I'm mad that she died thinking I hate her. I'm mad that she wanted money and success more than she wanted to spend time with me.' Rose looked towards the helipad. 'We were *right here*, she still had time to make things good between us, but she didn't. Instead, she sent us on a wild goose chase for her own amusement. She was sick and never once asked for our help. She was so bloody stubborn.' Rose wiped her streaming nose on the back of her hand. 'But what really hurts, what I can't forgive her for, is that she always wanted us to *be* better or *do* better! Why couldn't she just love us for who we were? Why couldn't she see that we're perfectly imperfect!'

Everyone fell silent, and tears spilled down Isla's cheeks.

Jess stepped towards Rose and hugged her hard. Mel moved in and wrapped her arms around them both.

Perfectly imperfect. That's what Isla and her sisters were. That was the fundamental truth at the core of what it meant to be human.

Isla looked at her wedding ring and wished Steve was with her. Moving towards her sisters, she opened her arms wide and attempted to hug them all at once.

But even though Isla knew Rose was right, the fact still remained: they had three and a half months left to complete their tasks. Isla had no choice. If it meant she could keep her stores open, they had to see this through to the end. They had to complete the terms of inheritance.

38

Rose

Sitting at her mother's kitchen table, Rose rubbed her fingers against her forehead as she sipped coffee and nibbled at the toast Isla had made her. It had been years since she'd had a hangover like this. In fact, the last time Rose had got so drunk was the night she'd hooked up with Tom, which resulted in Bethany's conception.

Rose had slept in her old bedroom, and when she'd woken she'd found Isla curled up next to her. Her sister had watched over her all night. Rose couldn't recall the last time she had been so caring towards her. The old Isla would have let her fall asleep on the sofa in the living room without a second thought. Could it be that all the inner work she'd been doing had actually made her kinder?

Sitting opposite Rose, Mel ate a bowl of cornflakes while Jess sipped green tea. Isla leant against the kitchen counter, drinking an espresso. No one spoke a word, and an uneasy tension simmered between them.

The doorbell rang.

Isla put down her coffee. 'That'll be the lawyer.' She disappeared, and returned a minute later with the lawyer following behind.

Wearing a navy pencil skirt and a long-sleeved ivory silk blouse with an oversized bow at the neckline, Jacki's lawyer look liked she'd just stepped off the cover of *Vogue* magazine. She was younger than Rose had expected.

'Victoria, I'm not sure if you remember my sisters, Rose, Mel and Jess,' said Isla.

Victoria smiled. 'Of course, Jess. And Mel, I think I met you a couple of Christmases ago at Jacki's Boxing Day party? The one with the ice sculptures?'

'Oh yeah,' said Mel.

'But I don't think Rose and I have ever met.'

Rose forced a smile.

'I won't take too much of your time.' Victoria placed her laptop on the kitchen table. 'Jacki wanted you to watch a video she pre-recorded. She made it in case she died before the deadline for the terms of inheritance.' Victoria shot a glance at Mel as she opened her laptop. Then she turned her computer screen to face Rose, Mel and Jess while Isla stood behind them.

'Ready?' asked Victoria.

Mel placed her hand over Jess's and nodded.

Jacki's face appeared on the screen and Jess immediately burst into tears. Jacki must have made the video in the early stages of her illness, because she seemed to glow on the screen. Her hair was perfectly styled, and her face carried a little more weight than she'd had at her wedding. Wearing a bright pink designer dress and full make-up and sitting by the pool with her helicopter parked behind her, Jacki looked like her old self – a woman who always got what she wanted. Knowing now that her mother was no longer a physical being, only ash and bone, made Rose shudder. Was she really never going to see her again?

'G'day girls.' Jacki folded her hands in her lap. 'My wish and my hope is that you don't get to see this video. My plan is to hang around for as long as possible, but of course cancer is one thing I haven't been able to control. No amount of money will save me now.'

Jess sniffed, and Mel silently passed her a tissue.

'I do know, however, that if you're watching this, my funeral and wake will have already taken place.' Jacki clapped her hands in delight. 'Oh, I do wish I could have been a fly on the wall. Did you like the cardboard cut-outs? I had so much fun dressing up and having those photos taken.'

Rose was about to roll her eyes but stopped herself.

'How is Darryl?' asked Jacki, then paused like she was giving her daughters time to answer. 'Look after him, won't you girls? I do love him very much.' Jacki placed a hand on her heart. 'Anyway, enough of the chit-chat, let's get to business. You probably want to know why I'm making you watch this. And if I know you, as I do, I would guess you've been arguing about whether the terms of your inheritance still apply. Well, the answer is yes, they do.'

'No!' Mel put her head in her hands, and Isla sighed with what sounded like relief.

Jess leaned closer to the laptop. 'Shh.'

'I know how some of you feel about these terms,' said Jacki. 'And you have every right to feel *whatever* it is you're feeling. I imagine some of you are struggling, and I know I won't be everyone's favourite person right now.'

Rose flushed.

'The tasks I've asked of you aren't easy, but growing into your true self is supposed to be hard. *That's the point*. The doubts, the missteps, they're part of the journey. The times you fail are the most important, because that's when you're broken open and where you really get the chance to move beyond what you thought was possible.' Jacki smiled.

'So, what's it going to be, girls? Are you going to give up now, or are you going to see this through to the end? Each of you has a decision to make. You must let Victoria know before she leaves whether you will fully commit to the terms. As you've probably guessed, the same rules apply. You have until midnight on the day of the Gold Coast Marathon to fulfil the terms. If any of you are to get my inheritance, all of you must succeed.' Jacki took a deep breath. 'My advice? Don't give up. See it through to the end, and be there for each other.' Jacki paused and pressed her lips together. 'And so, I suppose, here's where we say goodbye – except for you, Rose, I have a bonus video for you. By the way, Rose—'

Rose shook her head.

'I hope you didn't drink more than two glasses of wine at my wake. You know you can't handle your alcohol. Remember what happened last time you had too many drinks? Okay, now I'm done.' Jacki picked up a flute of champagne off the small table beside her. 'To my daughters, good luck. Try to have fun, and know that I love you.' Jacki raised her glass to the camera. 'Until we meet again.' She took a sip of the sparkling bubbles, and the screen went black.

Victoria closed her laptop and placed some papers on the kitchen table. 'You'll need to sign these before I leave to confirm that you will, or won't, be participating in the terms of inheritance. I'll go wait in the car and give you some time to discuss this in private.'

'Is it necessary?' said Rose. 'The papers? It's all so formal.'

'If you don't commit, I'll need to begin administering the deceased's estate. If you do, then Eddie, the Chief Operating Officer, will be informed of his continuing role until the deadline,' said Victoria.

'You don't need to leave,' said Jess as she dried her eyes. 'I'm still in.'

Isla walked around the kitchen table to face her sisters. 'Me too.'

'Oh, are you less than three and a half months away from enlightenment?' asked Mel.

Isla stuck out her chin. 'We have nothing to lose by giving this everything we've got. Think of the money.'

Mel screwed up her face. 'Why are you so concerned about money all of a sudden? You have more than all three of us put together.'

Isla peered at her feet.

'Hey,' said Rose. 'Are you having money troubles?'

'Of course not.'

Rose watched Isla glance to the side. 'You're lying.'

Isla pursed her lips.

'Why didn't you say something?' said Jess.

'The Brisbane and Adelaide stores are … not doing so well. A cash injection would mean we could keep them open while we figure out a way to bring in more clients.'

Mel scowled. 'So you don't *need* the money then? The other stores are okay?'

'Yes, but Mum's inheritance would take the pressure off, just like it would for you girls.'

Jess sniffed. 'We all want the money. That's not the issue. We have to decide if we're prepared to give it our best until the deadline. We're either all in, or we're all out.'

Isla stood upright. 'Well, I'm in.'

'I'm exhausted.' Rose's shoulders sagged. 'All I've had are rejections for my book. I'm struggling.'

'Then we need to work together. Really help each other,' said Isla.

Jess frowned. 'The only way you can help me, Isla, is by backing off.'

Rose winced and Mel cleared her throat. Isla's mouth dropped open.

'What I mean is, I just need a bit more space,' explained Jess. 'I know you're motivated, and your heart's in the right place, but please, you've got to ease off.'

Looking disheartened, Isla glared at each of her sisters. 'Do you all feel that way?'

'Maybe just cool it a bit with the follow-up texts,' said Rose.

Jess stood and hugged Isla. 'You have been unbelievably supportive. You're not the Isla Turner you were nine months ago, we can all see that. But now we have to listen to each other and work as a team. As a family.'

'Fine,' said Isla. 'I can ease off if that's what you all want. But we should do this. We've got nothing to lose, right?'

Rose could see the determination in Jess's and Isla's faces. They weren't going to give up, even if they were probably going to fail. *Damn it!* This wasn't about her and her mother anymore. It was more than that. Rose had to know if she could write a picture book worthy of publication. Writing was part of who she was and, even though her manuscripts hadn't been accepted yet, she was determined to prove to herself that she could complete the task she'd been set. 'I suppose I'm not the first writer to get rejected. Maybe I could get some professional help and see what happens.'

'That's more like it,' beamed Isla. 'Living apart from Steve is torture, but I'm learning so much about myself. I'm not just doing this for Mum. I'm doing it for me too.'

Rose held her breath. Was she really going to do this after everything? 'Fine. You can count me in.'

Mel dropped her forehead to the kitchen table in defeat. Jess rubbed her back and they waited for her decision. Eventually, Mel raised her head and stuck out her bottom lip. 'I guess my toenails will grow back eventually, and there is this chafing tape that's supposed to work miracles. But *come on*, it's forty-two point two kilometres! I'm going to need you guys to help me.'

'We can do that,' said Jess.

'Then it's agreed?' Isla turned to Victoria. 'We're all in.'

Mel dropped her head back to the table and raised her fist in the air. 'Let's finish this!'

Rose winced as a stab of pain shot through her pounding head, then she raised her mug in solidarity. 'But first, coffee.'

* * *

After all the paperwork had been signed, Rose followed Victoria into her mother's study on the second floor. Floor-to-ceiling windows overlooked the driveway and showcased the tall palm trees that swayed in the breeze. The wall behind her mother's desk featured an oversized built-in bookcase. Sitting alongside a vast number of books were expensive-looking sculptures, business awards and framed photos of her mother with celebrities. There were no photos of Rose or her sisters.

'Jacki asked you to sit here to watch the video.' Standing behind Jacki's desk, Victoria pulled out the lavish swivel chair and opened her laptop.

'Can't I just sit here?' Rose pointed to the white leather three-seater sofa that faced the window.

'Sorry. Mrs Turner left specific instructions.' Victoria held up a folder.

'Of course she did.' Rose walked behind the desk, and an eerie feeling crept over her. Her mother's office had always been out of bounds when she was a kid – she'd only ever hovered on the threshold, and had certainly never been allowed behind the desk.

Victoria opened a folder on her laptop and indicated a file. 'Just press play when you're ready.' She left the room, closing the door quietly behind her.

Rose blew the air out of her lungs and took a seat at her mother's desk. It was an old-fashioned solid timber desk stained a dark walnut colour. A single drawer sat directly under the workspace, and there were deep drawers on either side. Rose ran her hands across the top. How many hours had her mother sat here, making deals, speaking to her board of directors, planning strategies to expand the business?

Rose looked around the room, and that was when she saw it. Flooding the wall and surrounding the doorway were framed photos of Rose and her sisters. There was a photograph of Rose, about seven years old, wearing togs and goggles at the beach. Jess as a baby, sitting on Isla's lap. Mel, in her sports uniform, aged about ten. There was a picture of her parents having dinner at some fancy restaurant, and a photo of Isla and Steve on their wedding day. The wall of memories blurred, and Rose had to blink away her tears to see the images clearly. Above the door frame was a large photo of her dad on the day he died. His face was painted like a clown, his grin was wide, and his eyes sparkled. Next to it hung a photo of Rose with Richard, Harrison and Taylor. It had been taken on their holiday at Stradbroke Island, their last before Richard had died.

Rose looked at the laptop in front of her. Her sweaty palms left handprints on the glossy desk as she moved the cursor and hit play. Her mother appeared in the same setting as the video she'd watched with her sisters, but this time the lines between her mother's eyebrows, which were usually hard to see because of all the Botox she'd had, were deeper and more profound.

'Rose. If you're watching this, then I'm hoping you're sitting at my desk. I have something for you. In the top drawer of my desk, you will find a key. You can open it now if you like.'

Rose pulled open the drawer and, sure enough, there was a key. How strange it was to be following her dead mother's instructions. It was almost as if she was in the room with her.

'That key will open the bottom drawer on your right. You can open that now too.'

Rose swung her chair around and opened the deep drawer. Inside was a wooden box.

'Take out the box and open it,' said Jacki.

Rose did as her mother asked. Inside, there was a gold locket on a chain.

'This necklace was given to me by my mother on my wedding day. If you open it, you'll see there's a photo of me when I was about twelve months old on one side, and on the other there's a photo of my parents on *their* wedding day.'

Rose opened the locket, etched with small delicate swirls, and found the two small black and white photos inside. In one, Jacki sat, legs outstretched, on an armchair. She looked just like Taylor when she was a baby. In the other picture, Rose's grandparents stood outside the entrance of a church. Her grandad looked smart in his dark suit, and her grandma was stunning in her floor-length wedding gown.

'Money-wise, this locket isn't worth much,' said Jacki. 'My parents weren't well off, but when it comes to sentimental value, this is one of the most valuable pieces I own. I had originally planned to give this to Isla – it seemed right, given that she owns Turner Jewellers – but the other night, when I was sitting where you are now, it became obvious that this should be yours.'

Rose glanced up at the screen and her mother smiled at her.

'This locket means so much to me because it reminds me, or *reminded* me, of where I came from and who I mattered to. What I've realised in these final months is that family is the foundation of who we are. We don't get to choose it, we might not even like it, but our family shapes who we become. I want you to have this locket because when I think of what it means to be a *good* mum, I think of you and the example you set for your children. You show up for them during the good and, most importantly, during the bad times. Your kids are fortunate to have you as their mum, Rose. I know they will be loved unconditionally and, what's more, *they* know they will always belong.'

Jacki choked back tears, and Rose closed the locket and pressed it to her heart.

'It's strange how often a tragedy or death makes us stop long enough to smell the roses, and *you*, my wild Rose, are sweet and good and always in bloom. Our relationship has always been strained, and I know it's unlikely that I left this world with us on good terms, but I want you to know that I do love you, no matter what has been said or done. We may not have agreed on most things, and our differing views, combined with that stubborn streak we both have, often made things difficult between us. But, honestly, if we got to spend another *decade* together, I believe we'd still struggle to find neutral ground.

And you know, I think that's okay. I think perhaps that's just how it is between us. And recently I have begun to accept this.'

Fat tears dripped onto Rose's blouse.

'If my time gets cut short, and things are still left up in the air, then let me just say this.' Jacki took a breath. 'If I need to apologise, then *I'm sorry*. If you need my forgiveness, then *you are forgiven*.'

Jacki pressed her palms against her cheeks. 'You are a wonderful mum, Rose. I'm only sorry I couldn't be the mum *you* needed.' Jacki smiled, then wiped away a tear and waved her hand to stop the recording. The screen went blank.

Rose sat in stunned silence for a moment, then succumbed to her grief. She cried so hard her nose streamed and her whole body shook.

After some time, Rose carefully put the locket back in its wooden box, closed the laptop and stood. Her legs were like jelly, and her hands trembled. As she made her way towards the door, she felt like she was floating, like she was somehow lighter. The burden she'd been carrying had been lifted.

Rose dried her face with her hand and stepped out of the study.

'Are you okay?' asked Victoria when she emerged.

Rose shook her head and sniffed. 'She always did have to have the last word.'

39

Jess

A few days later, after Jess had said a tearful goodbye to her dad, Rose and Jess made their way to the Aussie Animal Rescue centre. Jess had invited Rose to stay at her place for a few nights while Tom took the week off work to look after the kids. That way Rose could take some much needed time for herself; she'd been a mess after the funeral. Jess made a mental note to tell Tom the next time she saw him that he was a sweetheart.

Rose had told her sisters about the video Jacki had left for her, and Jess had been relieved she had some closure after that disastrous last phone call. Jess had to admit she was jealous of the extra video – she knew that was ridiculous, but it was just how she felt. She missed her mum.

'I'm glad you decided to hang out with me for a few days,' Jess said to Rose. Jess hadn't been getting much sleep since Jacki had died, and it had been comforting to have Rose close by.

'It's such a load off to not have to think about what the kids have got on today,' said Rose, 'and to not fret over whether I've washed Harrison's soccer kit or worry about what I'm making for dinner. For the last few weeks, I've felt like I'm about to crack at any moment.'

'I think taking some time out has helped both of us.'

Jess and Rose had spent the last couple of days sleeping in, eating brunch at local cafes and brainstorming ideas for Rose's book. They had come up with a fun, colourful story about a family of ducks.

Adam had also called and invited Jess out for a drink next weekend.

She'd hesitated before agreeing. Adam had been working in advertising, but had decided to try his hand at acting. He had recently finished filming a new TV show, which was his first real acting gig. It made Jess reluctant to see him again. Yes, he was gorgeous and, yes, he came across as very sweet, but whereas Adam was drawn to the spotlight, Jess wanted to remain in the shadows. Still, she'd promised she'd try to complete her task, so she'd decided to stick with him a little longer.

Jess pulled into the Aussie Animal Rescue car park. 'I hope I'm doing the right thing.'

'Oh, Jess, I really think you are. It'll be good for you to have some company,' said Rose. 'I've always worried about you spending so much time alone.'

Jess had decided to foster Maxine, the nine-year-old Maltese mix she'd met on the day her mum died. She hadn't been able to stop thinking about the friendly dog, and had offered to foster her until Aussie Animal Rescue could find her a permanent home.

Stepping out of her car, a cool breeze brought welcome relief from the weather, which had been unusually hot and humid for late March. Jess tucked her phone in her bag, and she and Rose made their way inside.

Anna greeted them at the entrance. 'I'm so excited for you to begin your new chapter today. I told Maxine the news last night, and she wagged her tail in approval.'

Joy bubbled inside Jess and she clapped with excitement.

'There's some paperwork I need you to fill out. Shall we do that now?'

'Sure,' said Jess.

Inside the foyer, Anna disappeared into the back office and Jess and Rose's phones buzzed simultaneously. Mel had started a group chat.

Mel: *Amber Ryan has sent me a Facebook friend request!!!!!*

Isla: *Block her!*

Mel: *Why would she want to be my friend?*

Isla: *She doesn't. She's just snooping.*

Mel: *I am totally freaking out.*

Jess: *You don't have to do anything. Just ignore her.*

Isla: *Breathe! I know it sounds woo-woo, but it works.*

Mel: *Okay. I'm ignoring and breathing.*

After filling out the paperwork, Anna took Jess and Rose to see Maxine. When she opened the kennel door, Maxine wagged her tail in delight.

'Hey, beauty.' Jess scratched Maxine's head and rubbed behind her ears.

'The fact that you work from home is great, Jess,' said Anna. 'It's important Maxine gets the proper care she needs.'

'I think you and I will be great friends.' Jess picked up her new companion and kissed the top of her head. 'What do you say? Do you want to come and keep me company?'

Maxine lifted her head and licked Jess's chin.

Anna smiled. 'I think that's a yes.'

40

Mel

Mel's pace was steady and her mind was clear. For the first ten kilometres, her legs had felt like lead weights and her tread had been heavy, but now, nineteen kilometres into her second half marathon attempt, she was in the zone. Her breath was in sync and her mind was quiet. She was doing it.

Jess rode her cruiser bike alongside her. Maxine sat in the basket on the front, wrapped in a soft blanket and surrounded by extra water bottles for Mel.

'You're doing great,' said Jess.

Mel raised her hand in acknowledgement, but kept her focus. After they had agreed to commit to the terms of inheritance, Mel had found a renewed determination to see this thing through. It would have been such a waste to have made it this far, only to stop. Three more months of training, and then she'd never have to run again.

Mel's first plan of attack was to run the half marathon. She knew deep down she could do it. Self-doubt had got the better of her on her last attempt, but Mel had promised herself she wouldn't take her eye off the prize again.

She'd asked Jess to help her, and together they'd plotted a route. Mel didn't need it to be an official race, and she didn't want a medal. She just had to run a half marathon distance. She would then spend the next few weeks increasing her long runs, slowly building to the thirty-two kilometres she needed to be able to run before the marathon at the beginning of July.

Mel ran past a dead magpie. It lay on its back in the gutter with one wing spread out, and ants crawled over its head and body.

Do birds have souls? She could tell the essence of the magpie was no longer there. It was merely a body. Mel looked up to see if there were any other magpies in nearby trees. Had the magpie been a mum or dad? Was it missed by any of its kind? Mel shook her head and sniffed. It was a *bird*, she told herself. It was silly of her to get upset.

Mel was pleased her mum had chosen to be cremated. She'd half feared Jacki would want to be buried in some large marble tomb that loomed over all the other graves in the cemetery, but instead she'd asked for her ashes to be sprinkled somewhere meaningful to her daughters.

'You want some water?' asked Jess.

Mel nodded and took the bottle from her.

'You've only got one kilometre to go!'

Mel looked at her watch and realised Jess was right. She was going to do it!

Although her legs were tiring, a surge of euphoria flooded her. She held her pace steady and remained conscious of every breath.

But now that she was close, a sinking feeling came over her. She missed Corey. They'd texted a couple of times since the half marathon, and she'd called to tell him about her mum. The next day she'd received some flowers with a note that read: *To Mel, I'm sorry about your mum. I'm here if you need me. Corey XX.*

And Mel *had* needed him. She *did* need him. She desperately wanted to kiss his lips, she wanted to know what it was like to have his body pressed against hers, and to wake each morning with him beside her. But she'd ruined it. She'd been so mean to him; she was sure things would never be the same between them again.

She couldn't believe Amber Ryan had ruined her life once more.

Mel pushed forward and her calves burned.

Amber may have forgotten what a bully she'd been, but Mel hadn't, and she never would. She cried out in frustration; she had to get Amber out of her head.

I can do this! She breathed hard. *I am amazing! I am Melanie Turner!*

At twenty-one-point-one kilometres, her watch beeped, and she stopped running.

Jess hit the brakes on her bike and squealed. 'You did it! You ran a half marathon!' In the basket, Maxine barked in delight.

Mel laughed and bent over, pressing her hands against her thighs. 'I hope you're watching this, Mum!' she shouted. 'Gold Coast Marathon, here I come!'

41

Isla

Isla and Steve held hands as they strolled through the markets one Friday night in late April. Wind chimes clanged in the breeze, and the smell of homemade soap mixed with sweet churros made Isla smile. The evening was abuzz with people as she stopped to look at a stall that sold novelty clothes for dogs.

'I wonder if Maxine would fit into this?' Isla held up a cute Ewok costume. 'I think she would. Jess would love it.' Isla paid for the outfit, and the stall owner put it in a paper bag and handed it to her.

'That's very thoughtful of you,' said Steve.

Isla pulled her cardigan around her and they continued down the long street. She liked the cooler months in South East Queensland because she finally got to wear jeans, jackets and boots. It was such a novelty after nine months of wearing her light summer wardrobe.

Steve bought a spiral potato on a stick and she purchased a bottle of kombucha, then they made their way towards the Brisbane River, cutting past the man-made beach where swimmers relaxed. Light from the city's skyscrapers sparkled on the river, and a CityCat flew at speed across the water.

'Shall we go and have a drink down by River Quay Green?' asked Steve.

'Sure.' Although the last few months had been the hardest of her life, Isla couldn't help but feel content. In the midst of her grief and her worries about the business, she had managed to find some peace. A year ago, she would have drunk herself into a numb void. Losing her mum and the thought of losing two stores would all have been too much, but after months of self-examination and taking the time to just hang out with herself, she felt like she could see clearly for the first time in her life.

Steve threw his potato stick in the bin. 'Penny for your thoughts.'

'I was just thinking about how good I feel. It's weird. I mean, I should be stressed and sad and overwhelmed, but I'm not.'

'I can see it too. In your body, and your manner.'

'What do you mean?'

'You *look* more relaxed. Also, the old you wouldn't have let me get a word in edgeways tonight, and you'd be nagging at me to eat dinner at a restaurant and not off a stick from a market stall. Plus, you haven't once mentioned the business – that's not like you at all.'

'I've just got a feeling that no matter what happens, we'll be okay. We'll get through it.'

Steve smiled. 'What have you done with my Isla?'

She stopped and turned to him. 'I'm right here.'

'Does that mean you're coming home?'

'After the marathon.'

'You haven't got used to the single life?'

'I'm not *single*. I'm married to you.' Isla nudged him with her elbow. 'Having space is still important, even though I've missed you. But I've gotta say, I have liked being alone too.'

'Thanks.'

'You're welcome.' Isla grinned and carried on walking. 'Hey, I found this great little dumpling place down the road from the apartment. They're amazing.'

'I don't like dumplings.'

'I know, that's why I'd never tried them before, but now I have, I know they're delicious.'

'What else have you discovered?'

'I don't like watching the news, I've started journalling, I like taking long walks at sunset – oh, and I've binge-watched all the *Star Wars* movies.'

'No! You said you hated *Star Wars*. You refused to watch them.'

'Well, I thought I'd give them a go, and I surprised myself. I've also started swimming again.'

'Wow. That really is great. Does this mean you're ready to let go of the Adelaide and Brisbane stores?'

She stopped again. 'No, it doesn't!'

'They're losing money.'

'We only have to wait two months. If we get Mum's inheritance, I'll use that to save them.'

'But that won't mean they'll start making a profit.'

Isla looked at Steve with amazement. 'Don't you dare change the rules on me.'

'I'm simply stating the facts. We can't keep those stores open just because you're too proud to let them go.'

Steve's words cut deep. 'How can you say that?'

'Well, it's true, isn't it? The only reason you won't see sense is because it will look like you've failed. You're still hung up on appearances, and worried about what people will say.'

'Well, aren't you? It would only take one negative news story to tarnish the reputation we've spent years building. I see the way people look at me. They think I'm entitled. They think I was handed Turner Jewellers on a gold platter, but I've … *we've* … worked too hard to let it slip away.'

'You're unbelievable.' Steve scoffed. 'You talk about wanting to find out who you are, about how important that is – so much so that we don't even sleep under the same roof anymore – and yet you're standing in front of me telling me that what other people think is more important than the truth. You can't control what other people think, Isla. You can only control you. And if you're not even being honest with yourself, your radar will always be off, and you'll never make a good choice.' Steve shook his head and stepped away from her. 'Do the meditation, discover new foods, be kinder to your sisters, I'm all for it, I love it even, but look in the mirror, Isla, because deep down you're still telling yourself the same old stories.' Steve turned and walked towards the car.

'Don't walk away from me,' said Isla. 'Where are you going?'

'I'm giving you your *space*,' said Steve, throwing his arms in the air, and he disappeared into the crowd.

42

Rose

Rose sat in a coffee shop and bounced her knee under the table. 'What do you think?' Rose had sent Patricia, her new editor, a copy of her children's picture book manuscript and had paid for her feedback and a one-on-one meeting. 'Everyone who's read this story really likes it,' said Rose.

Patricia had had several children's picture books published by one of the big five publishers. And in addition to hosting writing workshops and retreats, she took on aspiring authors as clients to guide them through the writing process. Patricia scrunched her nose and peered over her spectacles. Her grey hair was cut into a sharp bob, and her slightly crooked nose gave the appearance of a strict teacher.

'It's nice that you've had positive feedback from people you know,' said Patricia. 'But that only tells me you have friends.'

'Oh.'

'I'm sorry, Rose, but there's nothing here we can salvage. You need to put this story to bed and come up with a new idea. Start from scratch.'

'What if I change the ending? Perhaps the mother duck

could tell the ducklings that she loves them, even though she doesn't always show it.'

'You're paying me to be honest, and my honest, *professional* opinion is that this would give children nightmares.'

Rose slumped forward and pressed her hands against her cheeks. Every time she thought she had a new story it turned out that, yet again, she'd written about the same theme. It was clear she still had a lot of issues to work through, and she'd be sure to bring it up with Grace when she saw her tomorrow. 'This is impossible. I'll never get published.'

Patricia took off her glasses. 'I can see what you're trying to do,' she said. 'You want to prepare kids for the real world, and that's a good thing. I just think that, maybe, whatever happened between you and your own mum is still a bit too raw? Perhaps those themes would be better in a fictional novel, maybe even an autobiography. For now, let's brainstorm some new ideas. Focus on writing an entertaining story for kids, rather than on the lesson you want to teach them. You're a mum. What were your kids interested in when they were little?'

'Do I really have to start from scratch? I've spent hours on this manuscript.' Since going back to work part-time two weeks earlier, Rose had even less time to write. If she was to start over, she'd have to get up at the crack of dawn to carve out some quiet writing time.

'Sometimes ideas work, and sometimes they don't, but it's all valuable experience. You always learn something.'

'Like what, how *not* to write?'

'You can write. There's no denying that. It's the content we need to sort out.'

'Sorry I'm late.'

Mel appeared at their table, and pulled up a chair.

'What are you doing here?' said Rose.

'I'm here to help you. We're doing this together, remember? That was the deal. So, what did I miss?'

'We're starting from scratch,' said Patricia.

'Thank goodness for that. You know I actually had a dream that I was one of those poor ducklings and—'

'You said you liked it.'

'I didn't want to hurt your feelings, and I thought it was healthy for you to vent your frustration.'

'Seriously?'

'But now we're running out of time,' said Mel, pulling a notepad and pen from her bag. 'I've been thinking all morning, and I've got some ideas.'

Rose sighed, and Patricia frowned as Mel waded through her notes.

'Sorry, it's here somewhere,' said Mel, scanning down a long, handwritten list. 'Aha! Here we go. You could write a story about why kangaroos jump, why koalas sleep for so long, or why the kookaburra laughs, but do you want to hear my favourite idea?' Mel grinned triumphantly. 'Magpies.'

'Magpies?' said Rose.

'Can I ask what all that is?' Patricia pointed to another list on Mel's notepad.

'Oh, this? It's a list of my top fifty movies.'

'What's at number one?'

Rose sighed again and looked at the ceiling.

'Oh, that's easy. *Pitch Perfect*. Best. Movie. Ever.'

'Which one?' said Patricia.

'The first one.'

Patricia nodded. 'Origin stories are always the best.'

'Right?' agreed Mel.

Rose rubbed her forehead. 'Can we please focus on my book?'

'Of course,' said Patricia. 'So, tell me more about these magpies?'

Rose clamped her eyes shut.

Mel lifted the sleeve of her T-shirt and pointed to her arm. 'See this?'

Patricia put on her glasses and leaned forward to inspect Mel's arm.

'A magpie did that.' Mel tilted her head and pointed to a small white line on her neck. 'Cheeky bugger got me there too. I was cut up bad, wasn't I Rose?'

'What's that got to do with writing a children's book?' said Rose.

'Well, that's what I thought your book could be about.'

'About you being attacked by a magpie?'

'We really need to move away from the idea of scaring kids,' said Patricia.

'No. Your story would explain *why* they swoop. They're trying to keep their babies safe.'

Patricia beamed. 'Genius.'

'Really?' said Rose.

'Write a story about that, and you've got a book that'll sell across Australia every swooping season.'

'I can do that,' said Rose. 'At least, I think I can.'

Patricia replaced her glasses with a pair of sunnies and stood to leave. 'Email me when you've written the first draft, and I'll take a look.'

43

Jess

Jess sat on the oversized root of a giant Moreton Bay fig and stroked Maxine's head while Adam paced in front of her. The last few days had been intense, and not in a good way. The paparazzi had found out she and Adam were dating. Photographers had lurked outside her apartment and followed her to the gym and the grocery store. Adam had been cast as the star of a new and much-anticipated TV show, and they were both now getting lots of attention.

Yesterday, Jess received the news she'd been dreading. Rose texted her to say there were photos of Jess and Adam at the beach in one of the gossip magazines. Not only had Jess been snapped in her bikini, but the heading read: *Same Turner, Different Brother.* Her response had been to throw up. Her nerves were in tatters.

She was so angry at herself for not following her gut. She'd always known dating Adam was a bad idea, but Isla's persistent badgering and then her recommitment to her terms after her mum's death had stopped her from ending it.

She was just so grateful she had Maxine. Jess's heart ached

thinking of how she'd spent six months at the rehoming centre, wondering where her owner was.

Maxine had helped Jess with her own grief. When she'd cried uncontrollably, which had happened a lot in the last month, the dog had laid her head in Jess's lap, kissed her face, or licked her hand. It was like her new friend was telling her she understood what she was going through, that she was grieving too, but it would all be okay because they had each other.

After a month of getting used to Maxine's medications and learning how she needed to be cared for, they'd finally found a routine. Sometimes Jess got overwhelmed knowing her furry friend depended on her for everything. Yet, despite this, she'd fallen in love with her new roommate, and so the decision to adopt her had been a no brainer. Jess knew her relationship with Maxine wouldn't last forever – she was already nine years old – but Rose had been right: you couldn't live your life in fear of your heart being broken. Living fully meant loving as freely as you could, regardless of the outcome. And so, as of an hour earlier, Maxine was officially her fur baby.

Now, sitting in the shade of the evergreen tree, hands trembling, she was particularly grateful for Maxine. It felt like she was the only one who understood how Jess felt.

'Just ignore the paparazzi. Pretend they're not there,' pleaded Adam. 'You don't have to end it.'

Jess looked around the deserted park, scanning for photographers. 'I can't ignore them. The bloody journos keep calling, and I can't switch off my phone in case it's a client. I've had to block Alison Silvers three times because she keeps calling from different numbers. The woman is relentless. I know you don't mind all the attention – it will probably even help your career – but I can't go through this again. I've always been honest about that.'

'Give it a week and they'll lose interest.'

'They won't. And besides, those magazines have an amazingly long shelf life. Do you know how many I've stolen from hairdressers and doctors' waiting rooms? That story about me and Nathan is still haunting me.'

'This is different. We're together.'

Jess shook her head. She was so tired. The grief of losing her mum had taken its toll. There had been days when she hadn't wanted to get out of bed, nights when she'd cried herself to sleep. Some days she could have sworn she'd glimpsed her mum at the grocery store or walking down the street. She'd had to delay work with a couple of clients as her output had decreased. She'd be in the middle of designing a logo or researching colour schemes for a brand, and her mind would drift off into a memory of her mum.

And then there had been the added pressure of the terms of inheritance. She'd continued to date Adam, but her heart hadn't been in it. In the midst of grief, she couldn't think clearly, and she didn't have the strength to pretend that everything was okay. She wasn't sleeping or eating. She was numb. Last night, she'd stared at the ceiling fan above her bed for hours. She knew what she had to do. After nearly two months with Adam, she had no choice but to break up with him. She knew he would be upset, and so would her sisters. Ending it with him meant there was no way they would get their inheritance, but she was on the verge of a breakdown, and something had to give.

Adam stepped towards her and took her hand in his. 'I know it's only been two months, but I think we're great together.'

'I can't do this. I'm not in a good headspace, Adam, and this scrutiny is just too much. I'm sorry I've hurt you.'

'Don't be sorry, just change your mind. We can get through this.'

Adam's gentle tone pulled at her heartstrings, but she had to stay strong. 'Before mum died, she set terms that me and my sisters have to adhere to in order to get our inheritance.' It would be easier for him to walk away if he knew the truth. 'We each had one year to complete the task she set us.'

Adam shrugged. 'Okay.'

Jess swallowed and bowed her head. 'My task was to find a relationship I can commit to for longer than three months.'

'Wow.' Adam stepped back and ran his fingers through his hair. 'Is that why Isla set us up? You were running out of time, is that it?'

'The deadline is the beginning of July. Ending this, *us*, means my sisters and I won't get our inheritance.'

'So what you're saying is you'd rather give up your vast fortune than spend another month with me. *Shit!* You must really hate me.'

'I *don't* hate you, really I don't, but my mum just died, and I can't focus on my work, and what with the paparazzi and us still being so new, I just can't deal with it all at the same time. I'm drowning over here.'

Adam glanced at the dark canopy of leaves above them, then back at Jess with a sad smile. 'Well, I guess you still get your inheritance.'

'What? What do you mean?'

Adam looked to Maxine, who was sniffing the grass. 'What was your task again? Find a relationship you can commit to for longer than three months? You've already done it, Jess. You didn't need me.'

Jess stared at Maxine. Adam was right. By the time the deadline for the terms of inheritance came around, Jess would have been Maxine's guardian for over three months.

Adam dragged his hand across his chin. 'Looks like you'll be getting your inheritance after all.'

44

Mel

Ever since she'd completed her half marathon run with Jess, Mel had been walking on air. After months of hard work and discipline, she'd surprised herself, and now she was convinced she'd broken through some kind of confidence barrier. She'd steadily built up her long runs and had recently run thirty-two kilometres, the distance she needed to achieve if she had any chance of completing a marathon. After her mum's death, coming face to face with Amber Ryan, and the humiliating ordeal with Corey, Mel was sure her luck was changing, and she was optimistic about life again. But she also knew luck was about being ready, and with one month to go before the marathon, she wasn't leaving anything to chance. She had to deal with her childhood demons.

Two days earlier, she'd made a pact with herself to get her life in order. After booking an appointment with a financial adviser, she had accepted Amber Ryan's Facebook friend request, and yesterday she'd plucked up the courage to message her. They'd arranged to meet at Raby Bay Harbour in Cleveland. Mel, who had cycled from her house, leaned against the railings and watched a large yacht refuel while she waited for Amber to arrive. Behind her, the precinct, which overlooked the pretty marina, hummed with people, and live music blasted from one of the wine bars.

'Mel?'

Mel turned to see Amber Ryan walking towards her, dressed in light skinny jeans, an oversized mustard-coloured jumper and nude heels.

'This is so great!' Amber air-kissed Mel. 'I couldn't believe it when I got your message. Shall we go have a drink before we decide where we want to eat? Oh, this will be just like the old days.'

'I'm not staying,' said Mel. 'I have somewhere else I need to be.'

Amber looked nervous. 'But I thought—'

'I remember the *old* days a little differently from you. I remember the pain of my broken rib and my black eye, and your vicious bullying and humiliation. At the half marathon, you acted like none of that had happened, and that made me so mad.'

Amber's face paled. 'Let's go for a walk.'

'I told you, I'm not staying.'

'Okay, fine,' said Amber, speaking at a lower volume and turning beetroot red. 'You're right. Of course I remember how I treated you. When I saw you at the half marathon, I was so shocked to see you. I knew it was my chance to apologise, but I got nervous, and then the race was starting and … the truth is, it was only when my daughter started school and got picked on that I realised how despicable my own behaviour had been.' Amber choked up. 'I'm so sorry, Mel. For it all: the attack, the name-calling, the looks, the sniggers … all of it. If I could take it back, I would.'

'That's the thing, though, isn't it? You can't. The damage has already been done.' Mel and Amber stood in silence. 'Why did you behave the way you did?'

'Isn't it obvious?'

Mel shook her head.

'You were Melanie *Turner*, the girl who had everything. You even had the Prime Minister over for afternoon tea. I was jealous.'

Amber reached for Mel's arm and squeezed it gently. 'I *am* sorry. Truly.'

'Is she still being picked on?' said Mel. 'Your kid?'

'Yes.'

'Then … I'm sorry too.'

Amber winced. 'Is it too late to be friends?'

Mel reached for her helmet and put it on. 'That ship sailed long ago, but maybe we could both focus on the kind of person we want to be, instead of reliving the past.'

Amber smiled thinly. 'Sure.'

Mel walked away, then turned back. 'Out of curiosity, what was your finish time for the half marathon?'

'Oh, I didn't finish. I twisted my ankle one kilometre from the end.'

'Shame,' said Mel with a frown, but as she got on her bike and cycled away, she couldn't help but smile.

Euphoria pumped through her as she cycled full speed towards Cleveland Point, where she'd arranged to meet Corey at the lighthouse. Mel hoped she'd be able to put her memories of Amber behind her and move forward. She would never forget what had happened, but she was glad she'd been able to get some kind of closure.

As Mel coasted down the slope towards the lighthouse, she suddenly felt nervous as hell. She was going to tell Corey she loved him. He was gorgeous and funny, and her biggest fan. At least, he *had* been her biggest fan. All she could do now was hope he still was. How foolish she'd been to push him away when she needed him the most, and to not reach out properly before now. It had been four months since the half marathon, and she'd missed him deeply.

Mel cycled past the houses that backed onto the bay. The salty air filled her nostrils and she held out her hand, letting the breeze filter through her fingers. As she caught sight of the lighthouse, her heart raced.

Then there he was. Beautiful Corey, waiting for her. Her chest tightened and she pedalled harder, but as he turned and caught sight of her, he frowned and shouted her name.

Mel glanced around as a car pulled out of the parking spot to her left. She hit the brakes, but it was too late – she couldn't stop in time.

* * *

That evening, Mel lay in a bed at Redlands Hospital. Her sisters had left her with Corey to go and get some dinner. Mel was sore and bruised, but she'd been relieved to learn her injuries were only superficial. 'I'm supposed to run a marathon in four weeks,' she'd told the doctor. He'd assured her that after plenty of rest, she should be okay to run.

Corey sat in the chair next to her and held her hand. It was the first time they'd been alone since they'd got to the hospital.

'You gave me the scare of my life.' Corey stroked her hand and then her hair.

'I was just so happy to see you I lost concentration for a minute and—'

'Bam! Straight over the handlebars. I could see it all happening in slow motion. It was crazy. Then you were just there on the ground, and I thought … I thought—'

'I was dead?'

'No, I thought, when did Mel start riding a bike?'

She laughed. 'Stop it. It hurts.'

Corey smiled. 'Sorry, but seriously, I thought … a bike? With a basket? I imagined you as more of a mountain bike kind of girl.'

She laughed again. 'Stop! Please.'

'Think of it as payback for taking so long to meet up with me. *You* might be the one in hospital, but I'm the one who nearly died of a broken heart.'

'What?'

Corey brushed the hair out of her face. 'I love you. I never want to be without you. The past few months have been hell.'

Mel's chest ached, and not just because she'd hit the ground with brutal force and zero grace. 'I love you too, and I'm sorry I hurt you when all you've ever done is cheer me on. Marry me.'

Corey looked alarmed. 'What?'

Mel had no idea where that had come from, the words had just spilled from her lips. But what the hell, she figured. Life is too short to mess around when it comes to matters of the heart. Her mum had taught her that.

'But we haven't even kissed,' said Corey. 'What if I say yes, then you kiss me, and you hate it, but I've already said yes. Then you feel like you can't take it back, so we get married, and you're stuck with a crap kissing husband for the rest of your life.'

'Good point. Or *I* could be the bad kisser, and then I'd feel bad for *you*. Hang on. Let's just erase the part where I asked you to marry me for one second, no, wait, *thirty* seconds, and we'll see, shall we?' Mel grabbed Corey by his T-shirt and kissed him. His warm lips were soft and good, even pressed up against her ballooned lower lip.

'Does that hurt?' he mumbled.

She shook her head. She wanted him so badly, and after a minute it all got too much and she pushed him away.

'Well?' he asked.

'That'll work.' She smiled, even though it hurt. 'How about you?'

'An A+.'

'Really?'

'Really. So, does the offer still stand?'

'You bet,' she beamed.

'Then let's do it,' he said, grinning from ear to ear. 'Let's get married!'

45

Rose

It had taken Rose only a week to brainstorm and write a new story. This time, Patricia's feedback was far more encouraging. She'd suggested a couple of minor changes, but overall she'd loved it. *It's two thumbs-up from me.*

Relieved, Rose had called Jess. She didn't know what to do next. She knew she finally had a good story, but she wouldn't have time to get her manuscript published the traditional way, and she still had no illustrations.

That's when Jess suggested self-publishing.

'I wouldn't know where to start,' said Rose. 'Plus, I really only have half a book. A picture book needs pictures.'

'I could pull together some black and white line images,' said Jess. 'That won't be too time-consuming, and I can deal with the technical side too, but it'll cost you to get the book printed.'

Rose's head swam as she tried to make sense of it all. She couldn't do this without Jess's help.

'Leave it to me,' said Jess. 'This is going to be so much fun. I'll mock up a couple of pages, and you can tell me what you think.'

Now, on a chilly morning in the second week of June, after weeks of working with Jess to get the illustrations right and dealing with the stress of turning all their hard work into a real book, Rose met Jess outside the Aussie Animal Rescue centre. In her hand, she held a copy of her children's picture book, *The Misunderstood Magpie*. It was the first print copy she'd seen. On the cover, a magpie sat high in a tree and watched as a family went for a walk. Rose's heart raced as she ran her finger over her name at the bottom of the cover, alongside Jess's.

'It's real.' Rose squeezed the book in her hands. 'I can't believe it!'

Jess bounced on her toes with excitement. 'You did it!'

'*We* did it. This wouldn't have been possible without you and Mel.' Rose hugged her sister. 'It looks amazing.'

Jess looked towards the entrance of the Aussie Animal Rescue centre. 'Are you ready?'

'I sure am.'

Jess lifted a box full of copies of *The Misunderstood Magpie* out of the boot of her car. 'Then let's do this.'

Two weeks earlier, Jess had sent Anna a copy of the book and asked if Aussie Animal Rescue would consider selling it in their stores and on their website. Jess explained they would get to keep all profits. *It's what our mum would have wanted*, she'd told Anna. They had loved the book, and were more than happy to sell it.

Walking into the centre, they were greeted by Anna.

'Thanks for doing this,' said Rose.

'We should be thanking you. We get lots of families visiting us here and going on our website. I'm sure these will fly out the door. Some of the volunteers who work here have already said they want a copy.'

Rose couldn't believe her book was going to be for sale. It was a dream come true.

'I just want to say,' said Anna, 'I thought the dedication at the beginning of the book was lovely.'

Rose and Jess had known straight away who they wanted to dedicate their book to.

To our mum, who taught her daughters to spread their wings.

'Will you be writing any more books?' Anna smiled hopefully at Rose.

'Actually, I think I will, and I already know what the next one will be about.' Rose beamed.

Jess looked surprised. 'You do?'

Rose wrapped her arm around her sister. 'It's going to be about a brave little dog called Maxine.'

46

Jess

Jess and her sisters sat at their mum's kitchen bench as Helen poured champagne. Mel proudly showed off the Turner Jewellers engagement ring Corey had bought her.

'It's stunning,' said Rose. 'You're getting married! I still can't believe it.'

'Nor me.' Mel's face lit up. 'Corey said all I'd needed was some sense knocked into me, but I pointed out I was already on my way to see him when I had the accident, and was probably concussed when I asked him to marry me.'

Jess laughed. 'You make the sweetest couple.'

Helen handed out flutes, and Isla held up her glass. 'A toast. To Mel and her hubby-to-be Corey. We love you both.'

They clinked glasses, then sipped their champagne.

'Also, I have something I want to say.' Isla swallowed, nervously pushing her hair out of her face. 'Not only am I moving back in with Steve next week, which is very exciting, but we've decided to close the Brisbane and Adelaide stores.'

Jess's mouth fell open. Those stores meant everything to Isla. 'But why? We're so close to getting Mum's inheritance. Couldn't you hold on to them a little longer?'

'I came to realise – or more accurately, Steve pointed out – that I was only holding on to those stores so tightly because I was worried about what people would think. I wasn't making good business decisions. It turns out he was right. I was trying to protect my ego.'

Mel nearly choked on her champagne. '*Holy shit!* Who are you, and what have you done with my sister?'

'I'm impressed.' Helen raised her glass.

'I'll say this,' said Isla. 'It's been *a process.*'

Mel shook her head. 'We're really doing it. Rose got her book published. Jess made a commitment to Maxine, and Isla … *Christ,* Isla only went and transcended into a half-decent human being.'

Jess laughed.

'So that just leaves me,' Mel continued. 'I've got to complete the marathon next week.'

'We know you can do it,' said Jess. 'We've seen how hard you've trained, and we're so proud of you, but if you don't finish, it doesn't matter.' And it didn't, not to Jess anyway. Their journey hadn't been easy, but they'd also bonded like never before. 'You know I'm actually pleased Mum set us these terms. We got to spend way more time together, and I wouldn't change any of that.'

Helen raised her glass and nodded. 'Now it's my turn to make an announcement.' Helen pulled out a stool from under the kitchen island and took a seat. 'Mick and I have got two seats booked on The Ghan. We leave on Monday and won't be back until the following week.'

'What?' Isla gawped. 'But we'll need your help presenting all the documents to the lawyers. I still have to make a convincing case that I know who I am. I *need* you for that.'

Mel forced back tears. 'I can't run a marathon without you.'

Helen held up her hand. 'Girls, you've got this. You don't need me anymore, and you haven't for quite some time.'

'But why leave now, with one week left to go?' asked Rose.

'It's part of the terms.'

Jess didn't understand. 'What do you mean?'

'Your mum booked the trip for Mick and me. She knew you girls would be stressing in the last week.'

'So she got rid of our security blanket,' said Rose. 'That sounds like Mum.'

'You girls aren't *girls* anymore. You are strong women who can do anything you put your minds to. Your mum always knew that. That's why she set the terms, and that's why she wanted you to see this through to the end alone – or at least together.'

Jess hugged Helen. 'We'll miss you.'

'It's only one week.' Helen sipped her champagne. 'And I must admit, I can't wait.'

As everyone drank their champagne, Jess couldn't help but feel they were fast approaching the end of an era. The terms of inheritance would soon be over and, whatever the outcome, things were going to change. Her mum's house would be sold, and Helen wouldn't be there anymore. Rose was right: Helen was their safety blanket. She was the person they could confide in and talk to about anything. Helen was *home*.

Mel must have read Jess's mind. With tears in her eyes, she whimpered, 'Everything's changing again.'

'Oh, sweetie,' said Helen, smiling. 'That's the only constant there is.'

47

Mel

At 7.15 am in Southport, thousands of runners stretched and checked their running equipment. The sun had been up for less than an hour, and the cold winter air made Mel's nose run. Wearing new running gear, a gift from Isla, and a bright yellow tutu, Mel rolled her shoulders and tried to ignore the butterflies in her tummy.

Corey rubbed Mel's arm. 'You've got this.'

Mel nodded, but she couldn't help but think that until she crossed the finish line, she *didn't* have it. There were forty-two-point-two kilometres between where Mel now stood and completing the task her mum had set her. She was so close, but still anything could happen. Plus, she hadn't run for four weeks because she'd been too bruised and sore after the accident. She'd done some low-intensity exercise – swimming at the local pool and taking some long walks – but she was worried it wasn't enough.

Isla had booked her an appointment with Dan, a physio who ran ultra-marathons. Dan had reassured Mel that she'd done all the training needed to run a marathon, and that not running for four weeks would be okay. Her body would remember what it had done up to now. This had made her feel better, but it had been difficult trying to rest. She'd even found herself *missing* her training sessions.

'Mel!' Isla pushed her way through the crowd, with Jess and Rose close behind her. They were all dressed in brightly coloured T-shirts, tutus and headbands.

'Look,' said Jess, who wore a bright yellow T-shirt with a giant L on it. Her three sisters stood side by side, and their T-shirts spelt her name.

Mel covered her mouth with her hands. 'You're the best! Thank you. I just hope I can do this – for all of us.'

'A year ago, we couldn't even do parkrun,' said Isla, who wore a bright pink T-shirt with a letter M. 'I still couldn't, but you … you're amazing, no matter what happens.'

'One step at a time.' Rose smiled. She wore a bright green T-shirt with an E. 'Just focus on that.'

'And maybe don't overdo it on the energy gels, yeah?' Jess laughed.

'Right. One step at a time, and ease up on the gels – got it.' Mel checked her watch as runners began moving towards the start line. She spotted the pacer she was going to follow and looked back at Corey. 'This is it then?'

He kissed her. 'This is it.'

She swallowed. 'See you at the finish line?'

'Hell yeah!' said Isla.

A bustling excitement moved through the crowd as the countdown started.

10, 9, 8 …

'You've got this,' shouted Rose.

7, 6, 5 …

Jess clapped her hands. 'We love you!'

4, 3, 2 …

'Remember – gel control!' Isla stuck two thumbs up.

1!

Mel blew the air out of her cheeks. 'Mum, this is for you!'

* * *

One of the best things about the Gold Coast Marathon was that the course was one of the flattest in the world. For the first thirty-two kilometres the road ran parallel to the ocean, and for the last ten it veered out to Runaway Bay before looping back to the finish line.

At eighteen kilometres, Mel hit the zone. Her legs were light, and running was no longer an effort. Her mind had stopped chattering and was perfectly calm. These moments were bliss. She didn't experience them every time she ran, and this state didn't always last very long, but the euphoric contentment made all the hours of training and all the aches and pains worth it.

The streets were lined with supporters. Their presence lifted Mel's spirits and reminded her that she was actually doing it – she was running a bloody marathon. How ridiculous was that?

The only person missing today was her mum. Mel couldn't help wishing she was there to see it. However, she did know that if she finished her mum would have been both proud *and* shocked.

As Mel ran past the thirty-one-kilometre mark, not far from the start line, she caught sight of Corey on the sidelines chatting to her sisters. Mel shouted out, trying to get their attention, but there were too many runners, and they didn't hear her. Tears streamed down her cheeks. She didn't know if she was crying because she was happy or because she was exhausted.

Watching runners go past in the opposite direction, headed towards the finish line, was torture. The roads went on for what felt like forever. Every time she rounded a corner she was certain the turning point would be in sight, but it wasn't. At about thirty-three kilometres, she had to walk. Her hips and calves screamed at her to stop, and each step sent shock waves up her legs. This was the furthest she'd ever run, and it felt like there were lead weights attached to her ankles. Walking with her hands on her hips, she whimpered in pain – she couldn't run anymore.

At a drinks station, Mel grabbed a cup of water and carried on walking, her head bowed. Everything hurt. She still had nine kilometres to go, and was convinced she was going to fail. A fellow runner patted her on the shoulder as she ran past. 'You can do it!' she shouted. 'This is what we trained for!'

Mel looked up, but before she could work out who had spoken, the person had disappeared. She took some deep breaths. The runner was right. All those hours of training had been about getting to this point. She'd known the last ten kilometres would be the hardest, both physically and mentally, but she also knew she could do it. She'd done this so many times over the last year. Each time she'd upped her distance it had been hard, but each time, she'd surprised herself. Today was no different. She just had to push herself beyond what she thought was possible one more time.

'I am strong,' she chanted. 'I can do this!'

She picked up her pace and repeated the mantra over and over, even though she was in pain, even though she was tired, even though the end was nowhere in sight.

At the northern turning point, she cried with happiness. She had just over five kilometres left. *It's just like doing one parkrun,* she told herself, and then she cried again. It was going to be the longest five kilometres of her life.

As a runner trundled past her, she reminded herself that she wasn't in competition with anyone else. They each had their own journey to take. All she had to do was put one foot in front of the other and not let self-doubt seep into her mind.

How many years had she let Amber Ryan knock her confidence? Yet here she was, exceeding her own expectations because every time she'd set out on a run, she'd believed in herself. Some days, she'd had barely an *ounce* of self-belief, but it was that sliver, that minuscule amount of kindness and respect for herself, that had brought her to this moment. From here, anything was possible.

Mel had envisioned herself getting a second wind at the forty-one kilometre mark and sprinting over the finish line, arms held high in celebration. But of course real life wasn't like the movies. By the final leg, she could no longer hold her head up, and tears blurred her vision.

Corey and her sisters came into sight at the last bend. They all screamed and waved at her, and she waved back with an almost overwhelming joy. She had never been so happy to see them.

She pushed herself forward and, as she crossed the finish line, the timer ticked: four hours and twenty-seven minutes.

She had done it!

Mel was hit with a wall of emotion. Elation and relief that it was over, deep sadness that her mum wasn't there to witness her achievement, bursting love for Corey and her sisters, a significant craving for Helen's banana bread, and a whole lot of pride. Plus, there was pain – an all-over, knee-splitting, hip-wrenching tonne of pain.

Her sisters nearly knocked her over as they rushed to hug her all at once.

'Tell me this is real!' She had no energy left. 'Tell me it's over!'

'You're amazing!' screamed Jess, jumping up and down in excitement.

'A whole marathon! I can't believe it!' cried Rose.

Isla squeezed her so hard she was sure her limbs would fall off. 'It's real, Mel. You did it. You're a bloody powerhouse!'

Isla stepped back, making room for Corey, who was beaming. Mel fell into his embrace and sobbed. 'I didn't think I was going to make it. I nearly didn't. For a while there, I lost all faith in myself.'

'That's okay.' He kissed the top of her head. 'I didn't lose faith in you for a second.'

48

Isla

That afternoon, Isla and her sisters sat at their mum's kitchen bench after handing over their evidence for completing the terms of inheritance. Isla had presented receipts for attending the ten-day silent retreat and the pottery and aerial yoga classes. She had also written a letter explaining who she believed the real Isla Turner was. It had taken all week to write, and now she just hoped she had successfully fulfilled her task.

Mel had handed Victoria her medal for completing the marathon. Rose had given her a copy of *The Misunderstood Magpie*, and Jess had submitted the foster and adoption papers she had for Maxine. Victoria had then disappeared into Jacki's study to assess.

'Is it enough, do you think?' Isla stood up and paced the kitchen. 'Mine was such a wishy-washy task.'

'None of us could have done any more.' Jess stroked Maxine, who was sitting on her lap. 'We did all we could.'

'I'm so worried I didn't meet the brief. What if I went about my task the wrong way?'

'Read us the letter you gave to Victoria,' said Rose.

'I told you, it's personal.' Isla couldn't bring herself to ask for her sisters' help with the letter, and without Helen or her mum's advice she'd had to dig deep and trust her gut. It had been a challenging and sobering task, and one that had forced her to be truthful with herself. But she'd done it alone, without anyone else's opinions and without considering what anyone else would think. It was the most honest she'd ever been.

'We can't tell you what we think if we haven't read it,' said Mel.

'Fine.' Isla inhaled, opened the Word document on her iPad and hoped her sisters wouldn't judge too harshly. '*Who is the real Isla Turner?*' Isla cleared her throat. 'When my mum asked me to find out who I really am, I thought it was a joke. A year ago, I knew exactly who I was. I had a list of roles I associated with, and I was proud of them, but when I began to scratch the surface of who I thought I was, I discovered I was living in an egocentric bubble. At first, I was convinced that adding more roles to my list would help clarify who I am, but it turned out pottery and yoga weren't my thing.'

'No shit,' laughed Mel.

'After an intense silent retreat, six months living alone and some deep inner reflection, I thought I might have a better definition, but I don't. I'm afraid I can't tell you *who* I am.' Mel's jaw dropped. 'All I can tell you, after a year of searching, is who I *aspire to be*.' Isla clutched her iPad tighter. 'I aspire to be kind and loyal like my sister Jess, and brave and gutsy like Mel. I aspire to be open, honest and able to accept what's happening even when the shit hits the fan, just like my sister Rose. I want to be a patient listener like Helen, love unconditionally like Steve and, finally, I want to be fearless, just like my mum. The truth is, I've got a lot to learn, but when my time comes to an end, I don't just want a list of roles and achievements on my gravestone; I want a list of my best qualities too. I know this letter tells you more about who I'm *not* than who I *am*, but I know that Steve, Helen and my sisters will keep me grounded enough to have the best chance at becoming the Isla Turner I aspire to be.'

Silence filled the kitchen and Isla winced. Had she blown their chances of getting their inheritance?

'That was beautiful.' Jess choked back tears as she scooped Maxine up off her lap and hugged Isla.

'That was really good,' agreed Mel, nodding.

Rose beamed. 'Looks like we've got another writer in the family.'

Jess sat back down. 'You explained who you're not and who you want to be. That's who you are, right now, in this moment.'

Isla smiled. 'You know, Rose, once this is all over, you could write a memoir: *How the Turner Sisters Lost It All.*

'Don't! I'm nervous enough as it is.' Mel rubbed her palms on her thighs. 'We're about to find out if we're going to be multi-millionaires. This is life-changing.'

'It's weird.' Rose curled a strand of hair around her finger.

'I was thinking, whatever happens, Mum's contribution to Aussie Animal Rescue could still be her legacy,' said Isla. 'I think we need to stop and ask ourselves where this money would do the most good.'

'I've been thinking that too,' said Jess. 'It kind of feels like we're taking the money away from a good cause. I can't stop thinking about all those animals who need help.'

'Hey, *I'm* a good cause too.' Mel pressed her hand to her chest. 'I mean, I know I've got a plan to pay off my debts now, and I take ownership of that, but I really want a car.'

'It's strange getting that money when we didn't earn it,' said Rose. 'Mum obviously had her reasons for wanting her money to go to Aussie Animal Rescue. I mean, there was a really high chance that we weren't going to pull this off. There still is.'

'Why *did* she want to leave all her money to the animals?' said Mel. 'Did anyone ask her?'

'It was because of your dad,' said Jess. 'She said he always wanted to adopt a dog, but it triggered Mum's allergies, so instead he made huge donations to the charity. She wanted to do something with the money that he would have approved of.'

Mel frowned. '*Shit!* Now I feel bad.'

Isla pressed her hands together. Over the last few days, she'd been thinking about where her mum's money would best be used. 'What if we just give them all our inheritance, even if we do pass the terms Mum set?'

'What?!' Mel stood. 'That's okay for you to say. You've got a bottomless pit of money.'

'*I'll* buy you a car,' said Isla. 'A new one, and I'll pay all your running costs for a year.'

'You're not thinking clearly!' said Mel.

Isla caught Rose and Jess exchanging a glance, but she couldn't tell what they were thinking. 'I know this sounds bizarre, but maybe it's the right thing to do. We can always help each other, but those dogs and cats—'

'*And* all the wildlife they rescue,' added Jess.

'They have no one,' said Isla. 'Aussie Animal Rescue literally saves their lives. Think about it. How much money do we need? We can keep filling our pockets, but, I'm telling you, there are no limits when it comes to wanting more stuff. This is a real chance to give back. It could be Mum's legacy.'

'Okay,' said Jess, snuggling her chin into the top of Maxine's head. 'I'm in.'

Rose stared at Isla. 'Mum and I didn't get on, so taking her money would feel, I don't know ... wrong somehow.'

Mel placed her hands on her head in despair. 'Have you all lost your minds? You can't change this once the decision's made. You know that, right?'

'Think of the animals.'

'Don't pull on my heartstrings, Jess! This is *my* decision too.'

'Sorry. You're right. We all have to agree.'

Now it was Mel's turn to pace the kitchen. 'Just give me a minute.' Mel eyed Isla. 'And you'd buy me a car? For real?'

'For real.'

Mel slumped her shoulders. 'I do want a car. Is that bad?'

Isla laughed. 'Of course not.'

'None of us need the money,' said Rose. 'I mean look at us, look at how far we've come and what we've achieved over the last year. Plus, we've got each other, but those animals, without Aussie Animal Rescue, they'd have no one.'

Mel paused, breathing slowly. 'I suppose you're right. I have all of you, and Corey, and Helen, plus I know what I'm capable of now. Okay. Count me in. Let's use Mum's inheritance to do some good.'

'Then we're unanimous?' Isla looked at each of her sisters. As they nodded, Victoria walked into the kitchen with her laptop and took a seat at the head of the table. Her face gave nothing away, and Isla bit her lip.

'Before you start,' said Isla. 'There's something we need to say. My sisters and I have just been speaking, and we've decided—'

'I can't believe we're doing this,' said Mel.

Isla took a breath. 'We've decided that, regardless of the outcome, we'd like all of our inheritance to go to Aussie Animal Rescue.'

Victoria fixed Isla with a serious look. 'You do understand how much money we're talking about? You and your sisters would receive none of it.'

Isla nodded. 'That's right.'

Victoria beamed, her eyes sparkled and she smacked both her hands on the table. 'Oh, my God!'

Isla looked at her sisters, confused. 'What?'

'That was so intense!' Victoria cried with delight.

'What do you mean?' said Rose.

Victoria sat up straight and blew the air out from her cheeks. 'Congratulations, ladies, you have just inherited the majority shareholding in Turner Hotels and Casinos.'

'So, we *passed*?' said Mel.

Isla shook her head, frowning at Victoria. 'I don't think you understand. We just said that we *don't want* the money.'

Victoria opened her laptop. 'And that is how *you*, Isla Turner, just passed Jacki's terms of inheritance. Mel, Jess and Rose all clearly achieved their goals. But your mother stated that the only way she could know for sure that you had taken a deep dive into who you are was if you were forced to see yourself without all your material wealth. Your mother stated that only if you turned down your part of the inheritance would you be ready for your next challenge.'

Isla and her sisters looked at each other in disbelief.

'Which is what?'

'Here, your mum left another video for you all. I'll let her explain.' Victoria turned her laptop to face them and hit play on a video.

'Girls.' Jacki appeared on the screen in the same bright pink dress as in her previous videos. She glowed with what seemed to be excitement. 'If you're watching this, it means you've all passed the terms of inheritance, and, I've got to say, I am *very* proud of you all. As you may be starting to realise, there *was* a method to my madness.' Jacki crossed her legs and sat up a little taller. 'By succeeding in your tasks, you have proven to me that you have what it takes for your next endeavour – Turner Hotels and Casinos. There is no doubt now that you each have the skills required to run the business and keep it making a profit while at the same time looking after the loyal, hardworking staff I employ.'

'This was a test?' snapped Rose.

'Shh!' said Mel.

'The rest of my estate will be divided according to what you agreed before watching this video. This means my assets, with the exception of the majority shares I own in Turner Hotels and Casinos, will either be split into four and shared between Rose, Mel, Jess and Aussie Animal Rescue, who will receive Isla's share, or, if Isla talked you girls into donating your inheritance too, given wholly to Aussie Animal Rescue. Congratulations. You are now the legal owners of my legacy: Turner Hotels and Casinos. The future of the Turner Empire is in your hands. It's your turn to make your mark, and what you choose to do with it is up to you. My only request is that you do your best to make me and Peter proud.'

Rose sank back into her chair, and Mel whispered to Isla, 'Does that mean we get to keep the helicopter?'

'Now comes my final goodbye,' said Jacki. Jess, who had Maxine tucked under one arm, took Isla's hand in hers. 'My daughters, you are exceptional. Looking back, I now know I could have been a better mum for each of you. I didn't always get it right, and for that I'm genuinely sorry. But you are four of the strongest women I know, and I'd like to think I played a part in that somehow. I love you all. You were a gift, and I know you will go on to excel in all areas of your lives. Good luck, and remember, all that matters in life is how much and how well you love, so be sure to love one another *fiercely*.'

The screen went black, and Isla and her sisters were silent.

Victoria turned her laptop to face her. 'There's a lot of paperwork that needs signing, and I'll need to arrange a meeting for you all with the board of directors.'

Mel rubbed her forehead. 'I don't get it. What's running a marathon got to do with running a chain of hotels and casinos?'

Rose rocked back and forth in her seat. 'I should have known there was more to this.'

Jess sniffed as she sat back down and stroked Maxine. 'We don't know the first thing about running a hotel or casino, let alone a whole bunch of them.'

Isla laughed.

'What's so funny?' asked Mel.

'She knew I'd talk you into giving up the inheritance before *I* did. How is that possible?'

Rose's face flushed. 'Turns out she knew us better than we know ourselves.'

'But how?' said Mel.

Rose looked at her sisters, her eyes full of tears. 'It's just what mums do.'

49

Rose

The next day, under a bright blue cloudless sky, Rose sat on the sand at The Spit and watched Tom build a sandcastle with Bethany. Nearby, Harrison and Taylor played frisbee, and all around her dogs ran in and out of the ocean. She yawned and turned her face to the warm sun.

She'd had a sleepless night after learning that she and her sisters now owned Turner Hotels and Casinos. Naively, she'd assumed that once the terms of inheritance had been completed, everything would go back to normal. Over the last few weeks, she had found herself craving the monotony of simple everyday routines and a life without the pressure and drama of being a Turner. But clearly, that wasn't going to be. In two days, Rose and her sisters had a meeting with the board of directors, and she was sick with nerves. The weight of expectation was crushing.

'Hey, Rose!'

Rose turned to see Jess waving at her. Holding Maxine under her arm, she ploughed across the sand. Isla, Steve, Mel and Corey followed close behind.

Harrison and Taylor rushed over to Jess and Maxine, who excitedly wagged her tail.

'Do you have her wheels?' asked Taylor.

Jess handed Maxine to Harrison and pulled Maxine's wheels out of her bag. 'You'll need to take her down onto the hard sand. Come on, I'll show you.'

Rose turned to Isla. 'Do you have Mum?'

Isla held up a Gucci tote bag. 'She's right here.' Inside the bag was the urn that held their mum's ashes.

It was strange to think that her mum, the famous Jacki Turner, the woman who turned every head when she walked into a room, was now a pile of ash and bone. Rose greeted Corey and Steve, then kissed Mel's cheek. 'And how's our marathon runner?'

'A little stiff, but I'll be right. I'm still processing what happened yesterday afternoon.'

'I only got a couple of hours sleep last night thinking about it,' said Rose.

'Right then,' said Isla. 'Shall we do this now?'

Rose took a deep breath and nodded. They'd chosen this location because it was somewhere they could all come and visit again if they wanted to.

Tom stood and picked up Bethany. 'Let's go get some water,' he told her, and picked up the red bucket they had brought with them.

'Who is Jess talking to?' asked Isla as they made their way towards the water.

'Oh look,' said Mel, pointing. 'His dog has wheels too.'

Jess was talking and laughing with a guy who Rose could only describe as hot as hell and, sure enough, at his feet was a Labrador with his own set of back wheels.

'Hey,' said Jess when she spotted everyone. 'This is ...' She glanced at the guy uncertainly.

'Nick, and my buddy here is Max.' Nick patted his dog's head.

'Can you believe it?' beamed Jess. 'Max and Maxine!'

Rose laughed and shook her head.

'Well, I have to go, but it was great meeting you,' said Jess.

'Hey, can I give you my number?' Nick smiled at Maxine, who was nose to nose with Max. 'These guys look like they could be great friends. Perhaps they could get together for a playdate.'

Jess flushed as she pulled her phone from her back pocket. 'Sure. I'd love that. I mean, *Maxine* would love that.'

After exchanging numbers, Jess linked arms with Rose and they walked towards the water.

Rose smiled. 'He seemed nice.'

'Right?' Jess grinned. 'And his dog, *Max*, who has *wheels*! What are the chances?' Jess tugged at Rose's arm, and Rose laughed as her sister fought to keep her composure.

At the water's edge, Rose stood next to her sisters. Isla held the black urn, lifted the lid and pulled out the bag containing their mum's ashes. The four sisters walked out a little further and waited for a wave to come in.

'Should we say something?' said Isla.

'We love you, Mum!' shouted Mel.

Cold water rushed over their ankles, then up to their shins, and Isla emptied the bag of its contents. As the wave slid back out to the vast ocean, taking their mum with it, a peaceful calm washed over Rose.

'How the hell are we going to run a chain of hotels and casinos?' said Mel, shading her eyes from the sun.

Jess sighed and wiped a tear from her cheek.

'We are Turner women,' said Isla. 'There's nothing we can't do.'

'Isla's right.' Rose smiled. 'What could possibly go wrong?'

ACKNOWLEDGEMENTS

I'd like to acknowledge the Quandamooka people and the Quandamooka Country on which Terms of Inheritance was written.

Every year HarperCollins Australia runs The Banjo Prize. Plucking up the courage to enter was one of the best decisions I ever made. I was elated when I got the call to say I'd been shortlisted, and when I got another phone call two weeks later saying they wanted to publish my novel, I was thrilled. A huge thank you to my publisher and editor, the amazing Bert (Roberta Ivers), whose excitement and passion for the Turner women always leaves me giddy with joy. I can't thank you enough. Thank you to Vanessa Lanaway for your eagle eye and clear vision, and to Kylie Mason and Scott Forbes for your expertise and guidance. I'm blessed I got to work with you all. Thank you to Christa Moffitt for the fabulous hot-pink book cover. It screams Jacki Turner, and I love it! To the whole incredible team at HarperCollins Australia, thank you for turning my Word document into a shiny book I can hold in my hands — it turns out dreams really can come true.

Thank you to Sasha Wasley, Nicola Moriarty, Rachael Johns, Kelli Hawkins, Rae Cairns, Petronella McGovern, Meredith Jaffé, Cass Moriarty, Kim Kelly, Penelope Janu, Sara Foster, Pamela Cook, Maggie Alderson, and Tabitha Bird for your kind words and enthusiasm. It means so much to me.

To my book club girls: Melissa Strader, Belinda Comino, Julie Schomberg and Sharon Mackey. I can still remember the glint in all your eyes when I pitched you the idea for this novel. It stoked the belief that I was onto something, and because of that I decided to write the book. Thank you for your love, support, feedback and contagious excitement for *Terms of Inheritance*. Our book club rocks!

Thank you to Vanessa Fringer and Julieann Wallace for reading my first draft and for all your feedback. As any writer will tell you, giving your work to readers for the first time is scary, but I know I'm always in safe, honest and loving hands with you both.

To Anne Maclean, thank you for sending out an email all those years ago asking if I'd like to be part of a writer's group. I said yes, even though I was terrified and had major impostor syndrome because I hadn't written anything for years. It was definitely a *feel the fear and do it anyway* moment. Your email pushed me to stop thinking about wanting to write and forced me to get some words written.

Thank you to Redland City Council Libraries. In 2013 I entered the Redlitzer short story competition. To my delight, my story was chosen to be published in the Redlitzer Anthology. After this happened, my next thought was, *I wonder if I can write a novel?*

To the wonderful team at the Australian Writers' Centre, thank you for the fantastic Furious Fiction competition. Over the years, Furious Fiction pushed me out of my writing comfort zone and allowed me to experiment with different genres and writing styles. Every Furious Fiction weekend, I got the satisfaction of finishing a piece of writing and sending it out into the world. Many thanks also to the amazing Furious Fiction community, whose encouraging words always reminded me that I wasn't alone in my writing endeavours.

Thanks to all the Brissie writers, including Grant Ison, Ray See, Liv Dunford, Amanda O'Callaghan and Poppy Gee, to name just a few. These amazing people love to chat about all things writing, and support and encourage the writing community in real life and on social media. Thank you for your love and support.

Thank you to my cheerleaders, Roanna Sands, Melanie Jones and Andrea Deighton. Can you believe this is happening? Thank you for being such supportive friends through this roller-coaster writing journey.

To my dad, you always encouraged me to chase my dreams, and after you passed away you taught me to sit up and pay attention. Because of you, I'll always stop to smell the roses, dream big, then bigger again. I miss you so much!

I dedicated this book to my mom because I wouldn't be the writer I am today without her unwavering love and support. She has either read or listened to me read pretty much every draft of everything I've written over the last nine years. She has the patience of a saint and a heart of gold, and her belief in me got me through many challenges that go hand in hand with writing a novel. I love you, Mama.

Tim, I turned it on and off again, but … I'm kidding. You've supported me in every dream I've ever pursued, and I'm so grateful you're by my side – I love you. Bradley and Lucy, you are the lights of my life. It's a privilege to be your mum. You're funny, kind and creative, and I'll always want to hang out with you. I love you both more than you'll ever know.

And to my dear readers, I'll be forever grateful that you chose to read this novel. I nurtured this story, pouring everything I had into it, but it was always missing one thing – you. And so, as *Terms of Inheritance* goes to print and is shipped out to so many wonderful bookstores, my hope is that this novel will bring as much joy to your world as it has done to mine.

**Read on for an excerpt
from *Emergency Exit Only*,
Michelle Upton's new book about
second chances, available at
all good book stores**

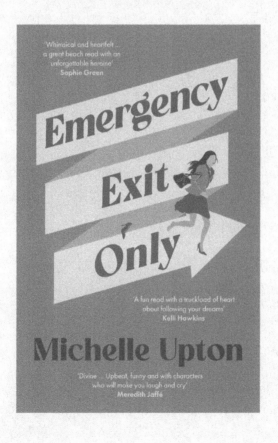

Prologue

The day after her thirty-fifth birthday, Amelia Harris nearly died.

Having consumed one too many celebratory glasses of prosecco the night before, she needed coffee. Badly. But her decision to caffeinate before work almost proved fatal.

She ordered her cappuccino then waited, the relentless February humidity compounding her nausea. A wild cackle erupted from the other side of the cafe and Amelia froze. She knew that laugh.

Amelia glanced across the busy coffee shop. Dark, deep-set eyes met hers, and as Amelia stared down at her black, flat court shoes, she cursed, knowing she'd looked away a second too late.

Keeping her head low, she eyed the exit. Should she run, or play it cool? She just didn't have the capacity to deal with this woman right now.

Sweat trickled down her torso and her gut screamed at her to run. She sighed then turned for the door. She could get her caffeine fix elsewhere.

'Amelia!' The barista called, but she was already gone.

Outside, she fumbled with Fudge's lead, while the three-year-old cavoodle licked her wrist.

'It's okay,' she said to her fur baby, but it was her own nerves she was trying to steady. She didn't need this right now. Not this early on a Wednesday morning. Especially not while she was hungover.

'Come on, Fudge. Let's go.' Amelia marched down the street, quickening her pace with each step. Oblivious to her haste, Fudge slowed at every tree and post, sniffing enthusiastically, tongue out, tail wagging.

'Amelia! Wait up!'

She flinched. That wasn't the barista calling after her.

Amelia ignored the voice and hurried forward, tugging at Fudge's lead. Her faithful friend spotted the force of nature who was hurrying after them and growled.

'Nearly there, girl,' said Amelia, out of breath, but as she stepped off the kerb, the figure behind them yelled out, 'Amelia! Stop!'

The voice was shrill and desperate, and Amelia couldn't help but look back. Seeing the warning in those heavily pencilled eyes, she turned and spotted the electric scooter hurtling towards her.

But it was too late.

1

24 hours earlier

The average person will spend approximately 90,000 hours of their life at work. Amelia Harris had discovered this fact after a quick Google search while eating lunch at her desk late yesterday afternoon, and she pondered this now as she closed her desk drawer, which contained her stationery, sorted by colour.

Going over her desk with an antibacterial wipe, Amelia sighed, satisfied that everything was in order. Knowing her workstation was clean and tidy, with each item in its proper place, brought her a sense of calm.

At the desk next to her, the shelling and chewing of pistachios had finally ceased, and had now been replaced with restrained giggling. Maureen was a voluptuous woman whose overconfidence in make-up application matched the enthusiasm of her bold A-line style dresses, which were always covered in bizarre prints. Today's was a brilliant blue with a strawberry ice cream print. Amelia smiled. It was a far cry from her own conservative office wear, but she had to admit, it was fun to look at.

Maureen covered the mouthpiece of her phone and whispered to Amelia, 'Could you be a doll and pop into the printers during lunch to collect the pull-up banner for Gary?

He's got a late meeting tonight. You can just leave it in Meeting Room 1.'

Heat crept up Amelia's neck and she tugged the collar of her blouse. She didn't want to say yes, but she already knew she would. Maureen was always doing this. For years, their desks had been positioned next to each other, even though Amelia worked in accounts and Maureen was a marketing coordinator. A few years back, Amelia's boss, Gary, had told her this was a tactic to keep Maureen on task. He'd said Amelia was one of his hardest workers, and the most focused. Putting Amelia next to her meant one less distraction for Maureen, who loved to gossip. But it had the opposite effect for Amelia. As well as being a constant source of noise, Maureen was always asking Amelia to do favours for her – favours that were part of Maureen's job description, like picking up a banner from the printers.

'Please,' begged Maureen, batting her false eyelashes. 'I'm swamped over here, and I have a lunch meeting. You'd be saving my bacon.'

Amelia chewed her lip anxiously, feeling trapped. Why couldn't Maureen save her own bacon for once? Amelia knew she was being taken advantage of, but she just didn't have the courage to refuse. Maureen was fiercely dramatic and could be overbearing, and Amelia had to admit she was a little scared of her. Maureen was unapologetically Maureen, yet everyone else in the office loved her.

'Sure, I'll pick it up,' said Amelia, hating herself for relenting. Why couldn't she just say no?

'You're a lifesaver.'

'Who are you talking to?' Amelia asked Maureen, glancing at the phone in her hand.

'Eva.'

Amelia fought to keep her expression neutral. Eva, an ex-colleague of theirs, who had never been very kind to Amelia, had moved to the Cairns office a few months back. Secretly, Amelia had been relieved when she'd heard she was leaving.

Maureen turned away to continue her conversation. She whispered something to Eva then burst into a fit of laughter. Amelia's cheeks burned and she pressed her lips together, feeling sure they were laughing at her.

Maureen was notorious for having private phone calls and hushed discussions at work. She insisted all her conversations were work-related, but Amelia doubted that was true. If she was discussing business, why was she always lowering her voice? And what about office supplies could possibly be so funny?

Although Amelia was well into adulthood, there had been moments during her work life that had made her feel like she was back at high school. There was the overconfident sales team, the gossips in HR and the tech geeks of the IT department. Working in accounting meant Amelia was an outsider to the nerds, just like she'd been at school. But, as when she was a teenager, she'd learned to make peace with this.

Amelia placed her tub of orange segments on her desk and glanced up at the fire escape door opposite her workspace.

EMERGENCY EXIT ONLY
ALARM WILL SOUND IF
DOOR IS OPENED

For nearly a decade, Amelia had sat at this desk and paid no attention to the fire escape. Recently, however, she'd found herself wondering exactly what classed as an emergency. Would having to listen to Maureen peel and crunch pistachios be considered a valid reason to use the emergency exit? What about having outdated software freeze on you for the third time in ten minutes? Surely enduring Gary's terrible jokes would count.

Amelia's was the only workstation in the office without a view of the corridor of gum trees in which, occasionally, a koala was spotted. But Amelia didn't complain. She'd rather put up with the view of the fire exit than risk upsetting any of her work colleagues. Besides, she was here to do a job, not stare out the window. If she needed a reminder of the outside world, she could wait until her five-minute hydration hiatus, which she took from her contracted one-hour lunch break. The window next to the office water cooler looked out over the park at the back of the building.

Over her ten years at Queensland Office Supplies, Amelia had settled into a productive routine, and she had found that mini brain breaks increased her work output.

Amelia grabbed her water bottle, which was almost empty, and checked the time on her computer: 9.57 am.

As she glanced at the water cooler station, she bounced her knee. Pete, the water cooler guy, who restocked the water bottles every other Tuesday at 9.45 am, was still there, chatting to Craig, who was most likely giving him a rundown of the most recent episode of *The Bachelor* or whatever reality TV show was currently airing. Their laughter echoed across the office. *Damn it!* They were going to be a while.

It wasn't that Amelia didn't want to talk to them. It was just that the fewer interactions she had, the less time she'd spend overthinking those conversations later that night. Avoiding others might seem extreme to some, but for Amelia, it was vital to keeping her stress levels on an even keel.

Amelia's phone buzzed, and she saw she had two texts from her mum, Toni.

The first message read: *Happy birthday sweetie. I hope you're having a fabulous day!*

Today, Amelia had officially made thirty-five trips around the sun, but she hoped no one at QOS would remember. She really didn't want a fuss.

The second text was typical of her mother: *Was wondering if I could borrow some money to pay the rates. They sent me an angry letter! I'll pay you back. Love you XXX*

Amelia sighed. Her mother never paid her back. Ever.

Since getting her first part-time job in high school, Amelia had been helping her mum financially. It was the reason Amelia had no savings.

Toni had always worked. When Amelia was little, her mum had been a librarian. But after Amelia's dad died when she was eight, they'd moved to Cleveland, a bayside suburb on the south side of Brisbane, and she'd had to change jobs. Since then, her mum had never stayed in a job for long, although she'd managed to keep her volunteer position at the Lifeline op shop for close to five years now.

'There are too many rules working for someone else,' Toni had once complained to Amelia after announcing she'd quit her job at Woolies. 'I'm a creative, and I refuse to have my wings clipped. I need to fly!'

You need to pay your bills is what Amelia wanted to say, but she didn't want to hurt her mum's feelings.

And so, Amelia helped her mother when she could.

Amelia texted back: *Just let me know how much and I'll sort it.*

Amelia closed her drawer and breathed deeply, then shivered. She pulled on her cardigan, glancing over at Suzie in HR, who was forever dropping the temperature of the air con. Amelia knew it was hot outside, but she didn't understand Suzie's insistence on Arctic conditions in here.

At 10.06 am, Craig finally wandered back to his desk and Amelia checked the route to the water dispenser. It was all clear. Only Pete, the water cooler guy, hovered, testing the bottle he'd just replaced. Pete was always on time with his deliveries, and Amelia liked that he was consistent. But Pete liked to chat. Amelia was sure his boss would have something to say if he knew how much time Pete spent chinwagging with the people in the office. Today, he had lingered even longer than usual, and was now overlapping with her break. Amelia took a breath and combed her long, mousy hair with her fingers. She grabbed her water bottle and marched towards the water cooler.

As she made her way through the maze of workstations, no one paid her any attention.

'Hey, how's your day going?' Pete, whose sandy-coloured hair matched his uniform, flashed her a dazzling smile.

Amelia considered telling him she'd been tempted to throw her computer out the window, thanks to the outdated software she had to use to manage all the business's accounts. Gary's insistence that QOS couldn't afford an upgrade was infuriating, especially given they'd just bought brand-new desks for the whole sales team. But Amelia didn't want to come across as a whinger. While the thought of going to work never made her jump out of bed with excitement, she was, overall, content in her job, and she knew that if she kept her head down and didn't make a fuss, the days would tick by without any unnecessary drama. That was all Amelia wanted: a drama-free life.

Amelia gave Pete a quick smile, hoping to avoid conversation.

'Cheers.' He held up his cup, took a sip, and stepped aside so Amelia could fill her water bottle. It had a cartoon drawing of a cavoodle on it that looked just like Fudge.

After she filled her bottle, Pete rested an arm on top of the water cooler. 'They reckon the temperature's going to reach thirty-five today,' he said.

'Wow!' she said, desperate to flee.

'We could do with some decent rain. My lawn is like straw.'

Amelia nodded sympathetically and glanced back at her desk. She tapped her fingers on her bottle and cleared her throat. Small talk made her nervous.

As Pete rambled on about the dry summer they were having, Amelia's breath became shallow and her palms clammy. She rolled her shoulders and checked her watch. 'Sorry, I have a Zoom call,' she lied.

'Oh, okay. Well, catch you next time,' said Pete.

Amelia turned on her heel and scurried back to her desk. After wiping down her pens, all labelled A. HARRIS, which she'd bought from the fancy stationery store Duly Noted with her own money, she lay them parallel with her keyboard, focused on her breath and waited for the recurring sense of panic to disperse, but it didn't.

What was wrong with her?

Amelia grabbed her bottle and took a sip of cold water. Her heart thudded in her chest, and for a moment she thought she was going to stop breathing altogether. She stared at the *EMERGENCY EXIT ONLY* sign longingly. Her need to get out of the office was all-consuming.

Maureen, who was finally off the phone, furiously tapped at her keyboard. Amelia closed her eyes and sucked in air. These episodes had occurred increasingly over the previous few weeks, and they were lasting longer. Amelia gripped the desk and forced herself to focus on her breathing.

After a minute, she felt a little better, but she needed to stand before the sensation came back. She needed a distraction.

It was far too early for her lunch break, but still, with trembling hands, she made for the small office kitchen without considering who'd be in there.

Amelia was out of sorts, but she didn't want to believe she was having a panic attack. Maybe she was coming down with something.

'Well, who do we have here?' Gary boomed as he slipped a pod into the coffee machine.

The kitchen was ridiculously small for the number of people who worked in the QOS office. There was just enough room for a sink that had a handy boiling water tap, a microwave so old it was practically vintage, a few cupboards packed with an assortment of crockery, and a coffee machine in which no pods ever quite fit, meaning it took a serious amount of wrestling before you could get your caffeine fix.

There was also a dishwasher, which was always either full and hadn't been turned on or full and hadn't been emptied, which meant a sink full of dirty mugs and dishes waiting to be loaded. Unable to stand the mess, Amelia took it upon herself to load and reload the dishwasher twice a day, allocating the first five minutes of her lunch break and the first five minutes of her fifteen-minute afternoon tea break.

Gary checked the time on his phone. 'It's not lunch already, is it?'

Amelia's face flushed. She'd broken her routine, and could tell she was in for some of Gary's hysterical observations.

'I just need coffee.'

'Ah! Do I need to dock this break from your pay?' Amelia stared at him in horror, and he laughed. 'I'm kidding. I'm kidding!'

Amelia stretched her lips into what she hoped looked like a smile, then pulled open the sticking cupboard door and searched for the mug she'd had made at Officeworks. It had her name printed on it in large, bold text so everyone knew it was hers.

As Amelia pulled open the dishwasher to see if it was in there, she caught sight of Luca sitting at the kitchen table, scrolling through his phone while sipping coffee from her mug. Her chest tightened.

Gary pulled up a seat next to Luca and sipped his steaming coffee.

'Amelia!' Craig stopped in his tracks and checked his phone. 'It's only just been your hydration break, lovely. What's wrong?' He tilted his head. 'Are you unwell? Do you need to go home?'

Gary glared at Craig. 'Leave her. You're fine, aren't you?'

'I just need coffee, that's all.' Amelia went to the kitchen sink and washed her hands with the antibacterial foam soap.

'Well, if you're up for breaking your routine today, a few of us are heading to Molly's Cafe for lunch,' said Craig. 'You want to join us? It's me, Gary, Suzie – not Maureen, she's got other plans. Luca's coming, aren't you, mate?'

Luca raised his hand without looking up from his phone.

'Oh, and Pete said he'd meet us there too.'

After washing all the soap off her hands, Amelia pumped some more into her palm. 'It's Tuesday, I've got a—'

'Tuna mayo sandwich with carrot sticks and a bottle of sparkling water,' cut in Craig. 'That's exactly why you should come. I've worked here for a year, and you've never come out with us, not once. Come on, Amelia! I'll sit next to you, and you can tell me all about Freddy.'

'Who?' asked Amelia.

'Her dog's name is Franky,' said Luca, eyes still down.

'Actually, it's Fudge.' Amelia dried her hands and glanced up at Craig.

'Go ahead,' he said. 'I know you have a burning desire to wash your hands for a third time.'

This was a habit of Amelia's that had become a bit of a joke in the office. She smiled. 'I need to wash my hands three times and you need three coffees before ten am. There's nothing wrong with having a routine.'

'My trips to the kitchen keep the blood pumping.' Craig raised one knee at a time. 'Deep vein thrombosis is a real concern for me. Now, come on, Amelia. Come to lunch with us,' he said making puppy dog eyes at her.

She should have been tempted. After all, it was her birthday. But the fear of saying something stupid or making a fool of herself stopped her. 'I can't,' she winced. 'I've got to run an errand at lunch today, sorry.'

Craig's shoulders slumped. 'You know you're missing out on the best grilled-chicken BLT this side of Brisbane.'

Amelia nodded, but her attention had returned to Luca's slender fingers, wrapped around her mug. She wanted to say something, but couldn't bring herself to do it. She eyed the other mugs in the cupboard, but the thought of drinking out of one of them made her queasy.

She dried her hands and made an excuse to leave. 'I just remembered I have a can of Coke at my desk, but don't worry,

Gary, I'll make sure I deduct these three minutes from my afternoon tea break.'

As Amelia made her way out of the kitchen, she heard Craig say, 'She pretends she's joking, but we all know she's being serious.'

Luca laughed. 'She's such a goody-two-shoes.'

Amelia felt as though she'd just been punched in the stomach.